RIVER OF
SECRETS

ALSO BY ROGER JOHNS

Dark River Rising

RIVER OF
SECRETS

ROGER JOHNS

Minotaur Books
New York

RIVER OF SECRETS. Copyright © 2018 by Roger Johns. All rights reserved. Printed in the United States of America. For information, address St. Martin's Press, 175 Fifth Avenue, New York, N.Y. 10010.

www.minotaurbooks.com

The Library of Congress Cataloging-in-Publication Data is available upon request.

ISBN 978-1-250-11012-1 (hardcover)
ISBN 978-1-250-11014-5 (ebook)

Our books may be purchased in bulk for promotional, educational, or business use. Please contact your local bookseller or the Macmillan Corporate and Premium Sales Department at 1-800-221-7945, extension 5442, or by email at MacmillanSpecialMarkets@macmillan.com.

First Edition: August 2018

10 9 8 7 6 5 4 3 2 1

For Nooty

Acknowledgments

Many thanks to Terra Weiss, Jill Cobb, Grace Wynter, and Kay Heath, for welcoming me into the Decatur writers' group and for teaching me so much. To George Weinstein, for his thoughts on an early version of the story. To my wife, Julie, for her vital and continuous faith and support. To Paula Munier, my agent, for her guidance at every stage. To April Osborn, at St. Martin's Press, for bringing her remarkable editing talents to bear on this book, making it so much better. To David Rotstein, at St. Martin's Press, for creating such a beautiful cover. To all at St. Martin's Press, for performing the necessary magic to bring this book into the world.

RIVER OF
SECRETS

When he heard the key slide into the lock, he reached inside his shirt and ran a finger along the smooth edge of the tough plastic loop.

Heavy footfalls on the old hardwood floors told him one person—a sizable individual—had entered the kitchen through the side door.

Expletives, followed by a muttered self-rebuke about having forgotten something, confirmed the new arrival's identity. Herbert Marioneaux was home.

The sound of a case being zippered open, along with the scuff and rustle of items shifted around on a table, pinpointed Herbert's location in the dining area of the large front room. Then the steady, rhythmic ticking of computer keys started. People could be so vulnerable when they were under the spell of some routine activity—something that put them at ease and commanded their undivided attention—but he knew that now was not the magic moment.

Herbert's booming voice broke the quiet. The call.

Ordinarily, this would have been an excellent time to shine. Pedestrians were known to step into fast-moving traffic once they became mesmerized by a call, but this was Herbert's nightly Skype session with his wife.

"You look lovely," Herbert told her. "Yes, especially without your makeup."

Using the loud conversation as cover, he rose from his hiding place inside the spare bedroom and moved toward the hallway and waited. The intimate patter continued for several minutes.

Once the conversation ended, the keystrokes resumed along with the soft sound of easy-listening music and the shuffle of papers. After several more minutes, the time felt right.

He emerged from the dark room, taking care to avoid the creaky floorboards he had discovered in the hall while he waited for the man of the hour to return from a hard day of screwing the taxpayers.

Herbert sat at the dining table, facing away, staring intently at a laptop.

As he closed the distance between them, he slid his hand inside the front of his shirt.

The floor groaned under his final step.

Herbert stiffened and turned.

He dropped the loop over Herbert's head and yanked hard on the free end.

ONE

Wallace Hartman didn't fancy herself a burglar, but when Davis McCone called with larceny in his heart she jumped at the chance—even though she was a Baton Rouge police detective and she would be stealing from her own mother.

Uncle Davis. She had called him that when she was a young girl, although he wasn't really her uncle, just a good family friend. In fact, Davis was the man her mother had dated, before electing to marry Walter Hartman instead. They had all managed to stay friends, and Davis and his eventual wife, Gail, had been uncle and aunt to the Hartman children.

"Come have dinner with us tomorrow evening," Davis said.

"Us who?"

"Me and your mother."

"She didn't mention the two of you were having dinner."

"I only managed to talk her into it a little while ago. It's a birthday shindig."

"You know she doesn't like calling attention to her birthday."

"She enjoys acting like she doesn't like it."

"Why do you want me there? I'll just be a third wheel."

"Not a wheel . . . a thief. And bring Mason."

Mason Cunningham had entered Wallace's life several months ago as a DEA analyst pursuing an investigation that intertwined with one of her own. He had remained as much more than that. Since Thursday, Mason had been in DC. He was returning this afternoon.

"Okay. We'll be there," she said. "And just so I've got this straight, you actually want me to steal something for you?"

"You'll enjoy it. I promise. And your mother will be delighted. I promise that, as well."

There wasn't much Wallace wouldn't do for Davis. When Wallace's father had been killed, along with her husband and her elder brother, by a man who had made a vocation of drinking and driving, her life had hit a wall. Wallace and her mother, Carol, and surviving brother, Lex, had all hit the wall. Carol had gone almost mute with terror, confessing to Wallace that she'd become afraid of her own shadow. That if so much could be taken so quickly, then nothing was safe.

Instead of becoming afraid, Wallace had become angry. Angry that the killer was given a slap on the wrist and put back on the street. Angry that those who killed with a bullet the size of a fingertip could be imprisoned for life, even executed, but those who killed with a bullet the size of a Buick were often dealt with as if they were the victims.

Davis and Gail had worked hard to provide a sense of stability for the remnants of Wallace's family. But it was Davis who had helped the most. He made sure friends and relatives came around to lift the burden of the day-to-day when necessary. He took time away from his law practice to make sure things that needed to be done got done.

Eventually, from somewhere deep inside, Carol found a way to cope. At first, she focused on putting one foot in front of the other, trying hard to impose some distance between herself and the devastating events. Then, one day, the dam broke and she began a period of proper grieving.

It had been painful to see, but Wallace took it as a sign that it was okay to begin the process of repairing and getting on with her own life. She considered herself to still be a work in progress, and she credited Davis and his wife with helping to make that progress possible.

Sitting on the back steps of her Garden District bungalow, a half-finished cup of coffee on the concrete step next to her, Wallace watched a pair of squirrels chase each other around the trunk and through the branches of the giant pecan tree that dominated the back of her lot. She marveled at the speed and agility of the chittering creatures as they made gravity-defying jumps through the leafy canopy.

As she reached for the book that lay next to her cup of coffee her phone buzzed again. It was Chief of Detectives Jason Burley, her boss. She felt sure he wasn't calling to invite her to a birthday dinner.

TWO

The room was a wreck. The man's bloody fingernails and the deep gouges on his neck told the story of his futile attempts to save himself. Once he realized he wouldn't be able to, he had apparently panicked, thrashing around, smashing into furniture, scattering papers and lamps in his wake. The whites of his eyes were freckled with the petechial hemorrhages so emblematic of strangulation. He was curled into a fetal position on the living room floor of the little house in Spanish Town, a trendy older part of Baton Rouge near the state capitol building.

Wallace recognized him. Anybody from Louisiana would. Herbert Marioneaux—white, late sixties, a former pastor, and until now, a state senator from one of the rural districts deep in the Florida Parishes east of Baton Rouge. Many saw him as a crass social and political opportunist—an unashamed chameleon who was periodically in the news because of his sometimes controversial views and his often overheated rhetoric.

Wallace knew his story well. During his firebrand college years, when he learned to court media attention, Marioneaux had undergone a very public conversion experience, swapping out his hostility to organized religion for a loud and endlessly proclaimed fundamentalism.

Later, when it looked as if his career in the pulpit had given him everything it had to offer, he underwent a second conversion. This time he evolved from being a committed segregationist to a lover of all humankind, and then he promptly ran for office. Most members of the media predicted his second transformation would turn out to be a bait and switch calculated to get him elected and that separate but equal remained his true religion.

Herbert's final evolution had come courtesy of the ligature around his neck—a tough plastic slip lock of the kind used to bind wiring bundles together or hold air-handling ducts to their overhanging supports. It was essentially a longer, thicker version of the zip ties police sometimes used in place of handcuffs. It had been slipped over Marioneaux's head and pulled tight. So tight he hadn't been able to get his fingers under the plastic, although he appeared to have given it his best shot. He would've had to slit his own throat to get it off. His killer had not offered him the mercy of that option.

Given Marioneaux's past, Wallace knew his list of enemies could be long and complex. He was on the wrong side of history, no matter which side he took, which meant he was bound to attract a lot of resentment. But the scene in front of her went way past resentment—it spoke of rage.

A chair had been dragged over next to where Marioneaux had fallen. A table lamp, its shade crooked and badly dented, rested on the seat, and a book-sized hand mirror was propped against one of the legs. A well-lit reflection of the dead man's face filled the glass. Arranging the corpse and the other elements of the scene to produce this grim tableau probably meant the killer wanted it known that he or she had watched and waited as the suffocating slip lock finished its work. That tended to make Wallace think this was personal between the killer and the victim.

She saw no evidence of a security system, but that didn't mean there wasn't one. Subtle, less visible systems were becoming popular as homeowners became smarter about how to thwart the growing tendency of break-in artists to identify and neutralize obvious protections.

Every window in the house was locked and none of the doors showed signs of forced entry. So far, nothing indicated whether the killer had lain in wait or had come in with Marioneaux or at Marioneaux's invitation.

An old pouch-style briefcase sat upright on one of the chairs by the table. The flap was folded back and an empty foam-lined laptop sleeve stood amidst the papers and folders. Wallace looked around the room for the computer, but it wasn't there. She didn't remember seeing it in any of the other rooms, but she would check again.

She stepped into a corner that looked as if it hadn't seen much action and surveyed the scene. Closing her eyes, she tried to imagine how the events in the room had unfolded, what sequence of events could have resulted in the chaos in front of her. Colley Greenberg, her mentor when she became a detective, had taught her how to do this. Study everything you see. Hold the scene in your mind's eye, and then try to run the tape backward. Some of their colleagues laughed it off as voodoo lessons, but it worked. More than once, it had shown that possibilities that at first seemed attractive were, in fact, remote or impossible, and vice versa.

Athletes did it all the time, Colley had told her. They visualized the path of the tennis racquet before swinging at the ball. They pictured the arc of the gun barrel before drawing a bead on the clay pigeon or imagined the perfect flight of the basketball before propelling it toward the hoop. The very best, he was convinced, could see the action forward and backward, before it actually happened.

Wallace wanted to take the scene back to the moment and the location where the killer dropped the slip lock over Marioneaux's head. Where had they been standing? Or had Marioneaux been sitting when the killer came up behind him?

She studied the room trying to deduce the order in which each object was knocked from its customary place. Knowing how the killer came to be where he or she was, at the critical moment, might say something important about the relationship between predator and prey. Just as she was on the verge of losing herself in her mental reconstruction of the scene, an angry voice broke her concentration.

"I don't care who you are. This is my father's house and I have a right to be here."

The sound came from the direction of the side door—a hall and a kitchen away.

Wallace pulled herself away from the murder scene and strode toward the sound of the voice.

"Now get out of my way."

Through the open door Wallace could see the driveway that ran along the side of the house. The afternoon sun silhouetted the officer blocking the door as well as the man outside who was trying, so far unsuccessfully, to bull his way inside.

"Sir, this is a crime scene—"

"Are you not listening to me? I just told you—"

"And my officer just told *you* this is a crime scene." Wallace gently moved her colleague aside and faced the man. Even though he was one long step below the threshold, they stood eye to eye. To her five-eight that made him close to six-and-a-half feet—a very fit, very broad-shouldered six-and-a-half feet.

"And who the hell are—"

Wallace flashed her ID placard right up in his face without waiting for him to finish his question. "Step back into the driveway." Over the man's shoulder, she saw a well-dressed woman who looked to be in her mid-sixties, standing several steps away, in the shadow of the sagging wooden fence that bordered the cracked concrete. The familial resemblance between her and the man in front of her was clear. Wallace watched as she ended a call and dropped her phone into her shoulder bag.

"Tell me your name, sir." Wallace moved toward him, her left hand raised, claiming the territory ahead of her as she maneuvered them both to the bottom of the steps. "Is the lady by the fence with you?"

"She is." The man glared down at Wallace.

"I'm waiting," Wallace said without looking at him.

"For what?"

"Your name."

"This is my son, Glenn Marioneaux." The woman at the fence stepped forward and took Glenn's arm. "And I'm Dorothy Marioneaux. What's happened here, Officer? Has there been a break-in?"

"Is this your home, ma'am?"

"My husband, Herbert Marioneaux, is a member of the state legislature," Dorothy said. "He's a senator. He rents the house as a place to stay while they're in session. I just drove in from Crofton. That's where our family home is."

"What brings you here, today, Mrs. Marioneaux?"

"We're meeting him here—Glenn and I—and then going for lunch at one of the restaurants in Catfish Town, down by the river. Herbert usually takes Saturdays to catch up on things, but he has this afternoon free. I just left him a message that we're here. He'll be walking over from the Capitol building when he's done."

"Do you know if he's expecting anyone else here, today?" Wallace asked.

"For Christ's sake, can't you just tell us what's happened here?" Dorothy's voice grew shrill. "Before you give us the third degree?"

"Sure. Walk with me." Wallace led them toward the sidewalk by the street. Just as they reached the curb, an ambulance slowed in front of the house. Its flashers were off and the crew looked to be in no particular hurry. Wallace studied Glenn and Dorothy as the vehicle stopped. Dorothy's eyes moved from the unlit light bar on top of the ambulance to the women in the front seat. Even though the windows were up, it was obvious from her lunatic expression and suggestive hand movements that the paramedic in the passenger seat was telling a crude joke. The driver was shaking her head and laughing. In the space of a single second, Dorothy's expression toggled from puzzlement to fear. She drilled Wallace with an expectant look.

Slowly, Wallace nodded. This was one of the worst parts of her job. When she most wanted to reach out, to console, to tell them she knew how this felt, she couldn't. First reactions were too valuable to ignore or to interfere with. It hadn't been her intention for Glenn and his mother to see the ambulance and then jump to conclusions, but the opportunity had presented itself and, as painful as it was to see, it was not something she could afford to waste.

"Oh no." Dorothy broke for the house.

With casual athletic grace, Glenn reached out and closed a huge hand gently around her thin upper arm. Her mouth opened, but no sound came out.

"Momma, don't." Taking hold of her other arm, he lowered his head until they were nearly nose to nose, until he was almost looking up at her. "Don't do this. You don't know what's in there."

The backup alarm sounded from the ambulance as it inched up the driveway. Wallace herded the Marioneauxs onto the grass in the front yard to let the vehicle pass.

"Let . . . me . . . go." Dorothy struggled to free herself from Glenn's grasp, her lips peeling back to expose clenched teeth. She said each word as if it were a separate sentence. Her gaze followed the retreating ambulance as it edged carefully through the officers and the crime-scene techs who milled about like stagehands prepping a set.

"You happy now?" Glenn looked over his shoulder at Wallace. His eyes were hooded. Whatever he was feeling over the death of his father was masked by an ugly smile mixed with a touching regard for his mother. "Is this what you wanted? You get off watching other people's grief?" He pressed his cheek to the top of his mother's head. After a moment, she collapsed against him and started sobbing. "Leave us be, why don't you?"

"Mr. Marioneaux, I know this is a difficult moment." Glenn opened his mouth, but with a raised finger Wallace preempted whatever challenge he was about to offer. "I *do* know. Now please, just listen. I'll need to speak with you and your mother, and it will need to be soon. You can wait for me out here, until I'm finished in the house, or we can meet at the downtown police building this afternoon."

"This is just so wonderful, just so damned thoughtful." He pressed his lips tight together and then raised his bare wrist toward his face, pretending to consult a wristwatch. "It hasn't been two minutes since we found out my father died and already we're suspects."

Wallace knew what was coming next.

"If only you people worked this fast looking for whoever did this."

"We'll meet you downtown, Detective." Dorothy looked at Wallace. Her eyes were bloodshot and she looked haggard, but her voice was strong. She patted Glenn's chest and pushed away from him. "I need to sit down." She turned and walked to the passenger side of a late-model Cadillac sedan parked at the curb.

Wallace watched as Dorothy pulled open the back door and settled into the seat.

Glenn stared at Wallace. His lip curled and his nostrils flared as if he smelled something unpleasant. After a few seconds he moved away from her and stalked off toward the Cadillac.

Wallace returned to the house. In addition to the Marioneauxs, she would need to interview Tonya Lennar, the cleaning lady who made the freaked-out call to 9-1-1 when she found the body. It was going to be a long day.

THREE

Wallace flipped through her notes, then looked up at the woman sitting across the table in the interview room. Tonya Lennar was in her late twenties, white, nicotine skinny, and she had the busy hands of someone feeling a few smokes shy of her quota.

"So, Miss Lennar. I'd like to take you back through your recollections, but this time, I'm going to stop you and ask questions along the way. Do you think you're up for a second go-around?"

Tonya nodded.

"Something to drink?"

"No, thank you."

"Fine. Let's start again from just before you entered the house."

"Well, like I said, I knew Mr. Marioneaux probably wouldn't be in, he almost never is on days where I get there in the morning, but I knocked anyway. Just in case. I didn't want to walk in on the man if he was coming out of the shower or something. I seen enough of that when I was a motel maid. You know what I'm saying?"

Wallace nodded, encouraging Tonya to continue.

"You just wouldn't be*lieve* how many men forget to put the Do Not Disturb sign on the door and then just *happen* to come parading out of the bathroom, naked as you please, right at the ex*act* moment that Housekeeping's coming in."

"Did Mr. Marioneaux ever treat *you* to a parade of that sort?"

"Oh, no ma'am. He was a real classy gentleman. Anyway, like I said, he wasn't hardly there on days when I showed up late in the morning, but he always left a nice tip on the counter for me. So, I knocked and waited. Knocked some more. Waited some more. When he didn't come to the door, I got the key from the hiding place where he always left it for me, and then I let myself in."

"Tell me again, what was the first thing you remember about the moment you stepped into the house? And please, take your time. Think back through what you saw, what you heard, smelled, anything at all."

"Well, like I said, there isn't really much to tell. I just went through my routine. I called out, letting anybody in the house know I was there, who I was, why I'm there. I sure don't want to get mistaken for a burglar and get shot or clubbed or nothing."

Tonya pursed her lips and rocked her head back and forth a few times. She didn't look anxious to tell this part of the story again. Her first time through had been rough. Retelling had a way of solidifying images in one's mind, especially the kind one might rather forget.

"So I started my walk-through. You know." Tonya hunched her shoulders and clamped her hands between her thighs. "Just to see what was what, so I could figure out where I was gonna start and all." Her brow furrowed and she scrunched her nose. "You know." She squeezed her eyes shut. "And then I found him." She breathed hard through her mouth and her eyes started leaking. "At first I didn't see him. Just all the shit busted loose in the room, like they had a wild party or something. I clean a lot in that neighborhood and some of them folks that work in the Capitol throw some crazy-ass parties."

"Had you ever seen the aftermath of any parties like that at Herbert Marioneaux's place?"

There was a knock at the door to the interview room. Wallace half stood and looked back over her shoulder, through the porthole. She pulled the door open. A message slip was thrust toward her. The Marioneauxs had arrived. "Put them in Room Four," Wallace said to the messenger. "Tell them I'll be with them in about ten minutes. And keep Room Eight open as well. I'm going to separate them and interview them individually. Sorry," Wallace said, pushing the door shut and turning back to Tonya. "Please continue."

"No, I never seen any partying or nothing." Tonya looked at her hands. "He was real particular about how things were. He was the easiest clean I had. Just dust and vacuum, empty the dishwasher, scrub the fixtures, and things like that. Super neat, you know. Clothes always hung up. Even the hangers was just so in the closet." She squinted and held her thumb and index finger a few inches apart as if she were taking a measurement. "Only time the bed was unmade was when it was time to change the sheets."

"What did you do after you walked into the room?"

"Like I said, at first I didn't see him. Just this big holy mess, and then . . . it was like looking at one a them big pictures in a museum. You know how your eyes just naturally get pulled along till, eventually, you end up seeing everything. It was like I knew there was gonna be something just awful and I didn't *want* to keep looking, but I couldn't make my eyes quit moving." Tonya pressed her lips together in an unsuccessful attempt to keep them from quivering. "Until . . . I was just looking at him." Tonya sniffled and covered her nose and mouth with her hand. Granular zombie streaks of mascara ran down her cheeks.

Wallace waited until the wave of emotion appeared to pass. "Just a moment ago, you said you knew something was going to be 'just awful.' You hadn't actually laid eyes on the body, yet, so can you recall what made you think that?"

"No. Not really." Tonya wiped her eyes with the heels of her palms. "Just . . . I don't know. Something."

"Okay. Maybe it'll come to you later. What about other people? Did you ever see anyone else in the house?"

"No. I could tell other folks had been there from time to time, but I never actually seen anybody there."

"Any indication that he might have been sharing his bed with someone?"

"Every now and again, I'd see a suitcase in the bedroom. Expensive-looking stuff. I just assumed, from the initials on it, that it belonged to his wife."

"A laptop came into the house, with Mr. Marioneaux, last night. It was not there when I went through today."

"Unh-uh. I didn't take it."

"And I'm not accusing you," Wallace said politely. "Perhaps you saw it or you know where the senator might have kept such items when he wasn't using them."

"No, ma'am." She shook her head vigorously, causing her pony-tail to slap back and forth. "Can't help you with that one. I don't touch nothing like that. Never."

Wallace wondered what life was like when every question about missing property felt like an accusation.

"One more thing. I'm sorry, I know this is tough, but please bear with me."

Tonya nodded. Her eyes were open, but Wallace was pretty sure her mind's eye was focused on whatever she had seen when she entered the crime scene.

"Every house has a smell all its own. Think back. Was there anything in the air that wasn't usually there? Cologne or perfume? Body odor? Unusual food smells?"

It was a long shot, but if Tonya was familiar with the normal smell of the house from having cleaned there so long she might notice something different—something that might prove useful.

Tonya looked to her right, allowing her eyes to wander up the wall and across the ceiling to the corner. Her mouth pulled to one side as she considered Wallace's question. "Not that I can recall." She shook her head.

"Thank you, Miss Lennar. I apologize for putting you through all this. It's possible that as the intensity of the experience fades, other details might spring to mind. Please call me, if you think of anything."

Tonya rose and scouted around the base of her chair for her belongings. She jumped when she looked over to find Wallace staring at her.

"What did you do with the key? The one you said Mr. Marioneaux hid for you."

"Oh my God. I totally forgot about it." Tonya extracted the key from the back pocket of her jeans and laid it on the table between them. "Sorry about that."

"That's perfectly okay. It's been a difficult day." With the tip of her pen, Wallace slid the key across the table and into a little evidence bag. "I'll have someone drive you back to the house so you can show them where this was kept."

"I remember something now." Tonya looked down at Wallace. "You asking for that key made me think of it."

Wallace waited, her pen poised over the page.

"The bumpy side of the key, the teeth, he always left the key with the teeth facing one way—like all the other neatnik things he did. Today, the key was facing the other way, and I remember thinking about that for just a second or two, but then it went right out of my head till you asked me for it just now."

"It's fascinating that you would notice such a tiny detail."

"Well, like I say, he kept things just so. You know—one of them place-for-everything kind of people. So when something's different it kind of sticks out."

"But not everyone would notice that. You're very observant."

Tonya looked pleased with herself. "It actually pays pretty good to kind of tune in to the way your customers live. You know what I'm saying?"

"I think I do. So, when you say 'always,' do you mean that literally? Always, always, always—no exceptions."

"As far as I can remember, yeah. Every time." She pushed out her lower lip and nodded, staring off into the middle distance.

"Did you ever tell anyone where the key was located?"

"Oh no, no, no. That's a pretty smart crowd living in that neighborhood. The minute somebody got ripped off that way, the word would go out and that'd be the end of Tonya cleaning anywhere around there."

Wallace stopped in the doorway to Interview Room Four. Dorothy Marioneaux's eyes had the hollowed-out look of a refugee. Glenn hulked nearby. His expression was sour, but his words went the opposite way.

"I'd like to offer my apologies for my earlier bad behavior, Detective Hartman."

Then offer them, Wallace thought.

"I know you were just doing your job. Mother and I are grateful for your efforts. So, please tell us how we can be of help?" He leaned back, shoulders and head resting against the wall, looking first at his mother, then at Wallace.

Wallace pushed the door closed as she entered the room. She looked down at Dorothy, who, so far, had not moved or given any indication that she was even aware that others were moving and talking around her.

Wallace wondered whether Glenn and his mother were cut from the same cloth as Herbert, politically speaking. She couldn't recall any stories about Herbert's family, but she was not a compulsive newspaper reader and she had banished television to the outer darkness after her freshman year of college.

"I'm so very sorry for the loss of Mr. Marioneaux. And I'm sorry we have to deal with this right now. But time is always of the essence, in a case like this."

"A case like what, exactly?" Dorothy snapped out of her distracted state, eyes riveted on Wallace. "I'd like to know precisely what we're dealing with. So far, my son and I have not actually been *told* a single solitary fact." Her voice rose with every sentence. "We figured out, from the ambulance and your nod and a wink, that Herbert passed away. And with your crime-scene crew everywhere we know he didn't die peacefully in his sleep. I don't appreciate being kept in the dark."

Glenn had played the difficult role at the house, but now Dorothy had taken over that part and Glenn appeared to have adopted a cooperative demeanor. Wallace smiled inwardly at the irony of two civilian interviewees running a good-cop-bad-cop routine on a real cop.

"A homicide in which the victim was well-known for having controversial views. Views that were, to say the least, very off-putting to a great many people."

"That was a long time ago," Dorothy said, sounding incensed. "But the small-minded had no intention of forgiving him or letting him forget."

Wallace looked at Glenn, then back at Dorothy. "Mrs. Marioneaux, I'll need to interview you and your son separately, so I'm going to move Glenn to a different room while you and I speak first."

"Is this really necessary?" Glenn asked.

"I'm afraid it is."

Wallace walked Glenn to Room Eight, then returned to Dorothy. It was evident she had been crying, but she gave Wallace a defiant look.

"Aren't you going to read me my rights, Detective?"

"You're not in custody, Mrs. Marioneaux. If you don't want to be here, you're absolutely free to leave. But at the moment, I have no leads on who might have killed your husband. My officers are doing a door-to-door, but so far, we're coming up empty."

"It occurs to me that you never told us how Herbert was . . ." Dorothy's eyes got shiny and full and she bit down on her lips.

"It appears he was . . . asphyxiated. Something around his neck."

She didn't mention the slip lock or the mirror. Those details needed to remain out of the public eye until their strategic value was better understood.

"But it's also possible that asphyxiation was not the cause of death, that that was done . . . afterward. The autopsy will shed some light on that."

"Good Lord. Who would do such a thing?" A hand fluttered against her chest.

Wallace studied Dorothy, wondering if the revelation would free up a useful memory.

"I couldn't begin to tell you where to look," Dorothy said. "But you're correct. He did have enemies. Herbert was something of an expert at making enemies. It was almost as if he collected them like trophies."

"How so?"

"He thought of himself as being in a constant state of growth, and he could be very dismissive of people who didn't feel like they needed to keep up."

Dorothy reached into her purse and pulled out a tissue with a lipstick blot in one corner. With a clean area, she dabbed at her eyes. Her gaze left Wallace and focused on the wall to her right and she went quiet for several seconds.

"But every time he changed," she continued, "he claimed the views he was letting go of were some sort of false consciousness that he was waking up from. When it came time for him to make good on his campaign promises, the people who had supported one version of Herbert often found out that a new version had taken over his senate seat. It confused people, and angered them. What he considered progress others thought of as disloyalty or just pandering to some new group of voters."

Dorothy carefully spread the tissue on the table and began smoothing the wrinkles.

"But weren't some of those changes good things? Didn't you say that he had parted ways with his less inclusive views?"

"He *had* moved on. But you know and I know that not everyone would consider those to be changes for the good. And for others, no matter how far in the past his original sins were, it would never be far enough. They were bound and determined to see the old Herbert as the only Herbert, probably forever."

"Can you make a list of people who might have held a strong enough grudge that they might take such extreme action?"

"Yes, of course. It may take a while, but I will certainly do that."

"Then let's focus for a minute on more concrete events. Things that might have occurred recently that point toward . . . what transpired. Can you recall if he received any overt threats? Odd calls in the middle of the night? Unexpected meetings he was called away to? Anonymous letters or funny-looking packages in the mailbox? Anything?"

"Not that I know of." Dorothy's eyes remained focused on her labors with the tissue, which she was now folding in half. "Whenever the legislature was in session, he was rarely in Crofton. He stayed in that little rental house in Spanish Town. If the kinds of things you mention happened here, he never told me about them."

"Did you speak often when he was in Baton Rouge?"

"We spoke every night, and I drove in occasionally, like today, and we would meet for dinner or something." Dorothy continued folding the tissue into ever smaller squares. "Every once in a while, if there was something interesting going on—some big political to-do, or maybe a concert or a play—I might come in for the weekend."

"Did you have your nightly call, last night?"

"We did. It was a little after eight o'clock." Dorothy absently polished a spot on the table with the folded tissue.

"When he called, was he at the house in Spanish Town? Is it possible he could have been elsewhere?"

"It was a Skype call. I could see he was in the house."

"How long did you speak?"

"Maybe ten minutes. He said he was exhausted and just wanted to finish up something he was working on and go to sleep."

"Was that the last time you talked to him?"

She nodded, unable to speak, but she never looked away from Wallace. After a few long, heaving breaths, she regained some of her composure. "We made a plan for lunch today and that was it. You never know when it'll be the last time, do you?"

"No. We don't." Wallace's mind flashed back to the moment she learned about the car crash that claimed so much of her family, and she felt herself slipping under the shadow of that long-ago heartbreak. "Did Herbert seem anxious to get off the phone?" she asked, pulling herself back into the moment.

"No. Tired, but that was all."

"Was there a worried tone in his voice?"

"No. Not that, either." She covered the tissue with one hand and dropped her other hand into her lap. Her chin came up and she nibbled on her lower lip. "In fact, even though he was tired, he seemed to be in high spirits. Having lived with him for nearly forty years, I know that that sort of manic exhaustion of his usually meant that he was on the verge of doing . . . something." She shook her head and puffed out a long breath through her mouth.

"Like what?"

"Detective Hartman, he was a complicated man, forever questioning the basic assumptions that shaped his thinking, and he wasn't afraid to make changes. In some ways, he was like a bottle of champagne with a loose cork. Something was going to pop off, but you never really knew exactly what, or when."

Dorothy's eyes drifted away from Wallace and she seemed to grow thoughtful.

"Could you tell if he was alone in the house?" Wallace asked.

"Well, I didn't see anyone else on the screen, and I didn't hear any voices in the background."

"Forgive me for putting this so bluntly, Mrs. Marioneaux, but—"

"Could this have been the work of a jealous husband? Were there other women? Is that what you're going to ask me?"

"I'm sorry, but yes."

"I'm not aware of anything like that." She ticked the fingernails of one hand against the tabletop with a faint galloping rhythm. Her gaze was steady, but her mouth looked weak. "But it might be too much to hope that something so simplistic as a vow of marital fidelity could cover all the bases for a man whose inner life was as rich as Herbert's was." Her eyes drifted to the side again. "What do you think, Detective Hartman?"

"I didn't know your husband, Mrs. Marioneaux."

"And I was not insinuating that you did," she snapped. "You may rest assured I was merely asking your opinion about strong, intelligent men. Men who . . . attract attention." Dorothy tilted her head back and looked down her nose at Wallace. "Is there something specific that makes you feel like it's okay to poke your nose into such an ugly little place?"

"I know this is unpleasant, but we can't afford to leave any possibilities unconsidered."

Dorothy pushed her lips into a tight smile.

"What about Glenn?" Wallace asked after a few seconds, surprised that she was having to suppress the urge to show a bit of irritation toward Dorothy. As a rule, she was of the opinion that the torment that came with the loss of a spouse was a license to be disagreeable.

"What *about* Glenn?" Dorothy asked.

"Might he have an insight into this part of his father's life?"

"You'll have to ask him those questions."

"Were he and his father close?"

"Why do you keep asking me questions you should be asking Glenn?"

"Did you or Mr. Marioneaux have other children?"

Dorothy hesitated. "Glenn is our only child." The corners of her mouth pulled into a prim expression and her eyes lost focus, as if she was looking back at distasteful memories or thumbing through a catalog of old suspicions.

"Mrs. Marioneaux?" Wallace waited until the woman's gaze came back in her direction. "Are there other children?"

She straightened in her chair—shoulders back, chin out. "Your guess is as good as mine, Detective." A flurry of expressions chased across Dorothy's face, finally settling into a thin, angry smile.

"Thank you for your time, Mrs. Marioneaux. You have my word that we will do everything in our power to find who did this."

A look of pain crept into Dorothy's eyes, pushing aside the anger from moments ago.

Even though it was years ago, Wallace could recall, in great detail, the turmoil her own husband's death had unleashed within her. Things had been too chaotic to even think about in any clear fashion. She never knew, from one minute to the next, which feelings would try fighting past the others, competing for her voice or commanding her silence. She had felt alarmed, even guilty, at some of the thoughts and reactions that bubbled up.

She was on the verge of offering Dorothy some words of counsel on how to deal with what was coming, but she didn't feel like she knew the proper things to say. Even after all her years as a police officer and after all the personal misfortune she had suffered, the emotional syntax of grief still felt like a foreign language.

"One more question," Wallace said. "It appears the senator brought a laptop into the house with him, but it's not in the house now."

"I have no idea where it might be. Did you ask that cleaning woman? I know he has someone come in."

"She doesn't know, either."

"Then, you might ask the folks in his office."

"I'll do that."

"Does this mean you think robbery was a motive?"

"He was wearing an expensive watch. His wedding ring and his wallet with several hundred in cash and a collection of plastic were still with him."

Dorothy shrugged and shook her head. "I'm sorry for being so difficult," she said. "Somewhere deep inside me, I always had a feeling things might come to this, given the way he led his life. Even so, it still comes as a shock. I wish I could be more help, but I just don't know anything." Her eyes brimmed and her mouth took on a scowl of self-reproach.

"I'll have someone walk you to the lobby."

After handing Dorothy off to one of the civilian employees, Wallace returned to the interview rooms, but Glenn was gone. His business card lay in the center of the table in Room Eight. Wallace turned the card over.

"Sorry. Something came up. Will call soon," was scrawled on the back.

Occasionally, interviewees snuck out, like this, but it had never happened to Wallace. Before she let herself get irritated, she called the number on the front of the card. It went to voicemail and her irritation began to assert itself. She left a message, trying to convey the urgency of the situation without sounding like there was murder in her voice.

FOUR

Wallace worked her way across the cavernous police garage to the section where impounded vehicles were examined. The smell of gasoline and exhaust, and the endless bang of metal on metal, was giving her a headache.

A crime-scene tech met her beside Herbert Marioneaux's vehicle. Together, they did a standard forensic evidence gather. Unlike most people, the late senator had not used his vehicle as a mobile storage unit for anything. The exterior paint had a high glossy sheen and the interior was meticulously maintained. There wasn't even a stray gas receipt in the console. The car looked like a dead end.

Head down, lost in thought, Wallace trudged back toward the exit.

"Hey, Wallace."

She looked up. Shirley Cappaletti, a veteran homicide detective, was standing near the doorway, scribbling something onto a form.

"Hey, Cappy. What's shaking?" She raised her voice to be heard over the thunking of a hydraulic lift.

Shirley handed the form to a man in coveralls and then turned to face Wallace.

"A banner day for homicides in River City—two within four hours of each other. You caught Marioneaux, you lucky duck, and I caught the other one—a woman named Lydia Prescott. Talk about a shitty deal."

"What's the story?" Wallace asked, hoping she sounded interested.

"Single, black, middle-aged. Just adopted a kid who was about to age out of foster care."

"Somebody pissed off about parental rights getting terminated?"

"Looks like she was just in the wrong place at the wrong time. A smash and grab, with maybe too much emphasis on the smash part. Blunt force trauma to the head. Car, purse, briefcase, basically all of her movable possessions were taken. We found the car, torched." She pointed at the blackened hulk of an automobile near the back of the garage.

"Any leads?"

"Not a one."

"Where did it happen?"

"Right outside her house. Which was also her place of business."

Wallace arched an eyebrow.

"Nope." Shirley shook her head. "Not a working girl. She ran a research firm. Focus groups, public opinion polls, market research—that sort of thing."

The killing itself was bad enough. Thinking about the newly adopted kid who'd just had hope snatched away made Wallace want to cry.

"Yeah, really," Cappy said, noticing Wallace's miserable expression, matching it with one of her own. "Look, I gotta run. Let's catch up sometime."

"Sure," Wallace mumbled, unable to shake Lydia Prescott's newly orphaned child out of her head.

Three hours after he had given her the slip, Glenn had still not returned her call. She tried again. He didn't answer again. She got his home address from the DMV database and drove by, but he wasn't there. She drove to the business address on his card, but he wasn't there, either.

Frustrated and irritated, Wallace called Dorothy to see if they were together, but Dorothy said she hadn't seen him since before her interview.

"He's gone through a second divorce," Dorothy said. "It's been a while, but it seems to have left some lasting wounds. And now, with Herbert's death . . ." Her voice trailed off. "He tends to withdraw when he's feeling troubled. That can make him difficult to get hold of."

"If you just absolutely had to get to him, where would you look?"

"My best guess is that he's climbed into a bottle, somewhere. Or maybe he's rented himself a friend for the weekend. He's got plenty of money, so it's certainly possible he's doing both. Hotel lounges and other such watering holes might be a good place to start."

"I'm sorry. That can't have been an easy thing for a mother to say about her son."

After several quiet seconds, Dorothy spoke in a strong, unemotional voice. "I'll let you know if I hear from him, Detective." Then the line went dead.

On her way back to the police building, Wallace requested a be-on-the-lookout for Glenn's automobiles. It seemed he owned several.

The boxes of items taken from Marioneaux's rental house in Spanish Town filled two shelves in the corner of the evidence room. Several boxes contained personal belongings and yellow tablets filled with handwritten notes on everything imaginable—ideas for legislation, reminders about who needed to be called and who needed to be avoided, diary-like entries about discussions with other politicians or what he thought of certain developments in the state or the country. There was no rhyme or reason to how the information was organized. It looked as if he had written things down as they occurred to him.

The last few boxes contained what appeared to be early drafts of legislation he had sponsored or co-sponsored, and books. So far, none of it suggested who or why anyone would murder the senator.

Wallace and her new partner, LeAnne Hawkins, had spent the last few hours rooting through the whole mess, with nothing to show for their efforts. LeAnne had been a detective for less than eighteen months and she was widely regarded as a difficult personality.

LeAnne's last partner had politely referred to her as training resistant when he came by to congratulate Wallace on her good fortune.

Wallace's original plan to keep LeAnne busy on matters that didn't require them to be together had fallen apart. The strategy had worked once before, when Wallace found herself partnered with someone who felt like a burr under her saddle. But LeAnne was quick to see through the ploy.

"I may not be Miss Congeniality," she had said, "but I'm not Miss Dimwit, either."

"And I never said you were."

"You didn't have to. Only a dimwit would miss this bullshit trick you're trying to pull."

"LeAnne, look—"

"No, Wallace, you look. I get it that you miss Colley. I'm sure he was a great partner. But it's clear to everyone, except maybe you, that you're angry about him having to retire. However, I didn't give Colley MS. And it's not my fault that you think he's the only person on earth worthy of riding shotgun with the likes of you."

"Whoa, whoa, whoa. Where are you getting this from?"

"Maybe you missed the part about me not being a dimwit, so if we need to go through that again, you just let me know."

Wallace had opened her mouth, ready to fire back, but in a humbling moment of clarity that snapped her head around she realized

LeAnne was right and arguing would only make her look foolish. She *was* angry.

Colley's retirement had been hard for her to accept. And without her noticing, the anger had mutated into a hostility toward even the idea of being paired with anyone new because a new partnership signaled the end of the old one.

Wallace had said the only decent thing she could. "No, LeAnne, you're exactly right. Thank you for pointing that out."

Sensing the opportunity that usually comes in the wake of a heated clearing of the air, Wallace had redoubled her efforts to make the partnership work. While their frank exchange had helped Wallace recognize and deal with her feelings about Colley's absence, so far it had had absolutely no effect on her relationship with LeAnne.

The sound of a box being slid across the floor refocused Wallace in the moment.

"This guy was such a dirtbag." LeAnne opened the next box in the stack.

"I'm not aware of any provisions in the criminal code that justify homicide because the victim is believed to be a dirtbag."

"You can be such an idealist." LeAnne laughed. "He might have been a smart dirtbag, though. Look at these." She held up two well-used volumes, biographies of Gandhi and Martin Luther King.

Wallace also spied a dog-eared copy of *The March of Folly*, Barbara Tuchman's bitter chronicle of how political inertia carried cultures over the precipice once leaders became blind to the obvious need for a change of course.

"Interesting." Wallace glanced at the titles, then returned her attention to the box she was looking through. She picked up an ancient-looking book. The front and back covers had broken away at the hinges. A rubber band held the covers and the pages together.

She slipped the rubber band off and began leafing through it. Long passages had been underlined in pencil and notes were made in the margins—references to the superiority of races and clean bloodlines. None of it looked like Marioneaux's handwriting, but many of the markings had been smudged and some were impossible to read. Wallace handed the book to Leanne.

LeAnne's eyes got big as she flipped through the table of contents. "See, I told you he was a dirtbag." She handed the book back and Wallace dropped it into the box, glad to be rid of its touch.

"I've been thinking about how to divide this investigation between the two of us."

LeAnne rolled her eyes. "Let me guess. You want me to go to Siberia to see if the Russian government was involved, while you cruise around Baton Rouge solving the case."

Wallace waved away LeAnne's comment. "I want you to put Tonya Lennar under a microscope."

"The cleaning lady?"

"She'd been working for Marioneaux for several months, so it's possible she discovered something that others might have found to be useful leverage against him. Maybe somebody was putting the screws to Marioneaux and he was refusing to play ball, or maybe he was threatening to expose their scheme."

"Did she say or do something during her interview this morning that makes you think this?" LeAnne leaned against the shelving unit, giving Wallace her full attention.

"All politicians have skeletons in their closet. They're all vulnerable, and they can all be leaned on if those skeletons fall into the wrong hands. See who Ms. Lennar is connected to. Who she's hanging around with."

"Starting . . ."

"No time like the present. Keep me in the loop on what you find." Wallace placed the cover on the last of the boxes.

"And what will you be doing?"

"I'm off to Siberia."

Wallace left the evidence room and returned to her cubicle to begin a deep dive into Herbert Marioneaux's unusual life and untimely death.

The online material about the senator seemed endless. Wallace combed through everything she could find—newspaper reports, magazine interviews, blog posts—literally thousands of mentions on the internet. If nothing else, Marioneaux had been a polarizing figure. But so far, nothing she found, not even the most venomous opinions—and there were plenty of those—seemed to hold a motive for murder.

At some point, Wallace realized she was the only person in the Homicide Division. She checked the clock in the corner of her computer screen and cursed under her breath. Once again, she had lost track of time. She and Mason had planned on an early dinner and a long walk through his neighborhood. Now it was nearly ten o'clock.

There was still a lot to look at, but fatigue was slowing her down. When she found herself, for about the tenth time, reading the same sentence without understanding a single word, she gave up.

"Remember me?" she asked when Mason answered her call. She pulled out of the parking lot and turned left.

"Long day?" Mason asked.

"Endless. Sorry about not calling and for missing dinner."

"We're fine."

Wallace could tell he was irritated. Colley's retirement and LeAnne's arrival had aggravated the yawning chasm in her professional life, but Mason had unexpectedly assumed a place in her heart that had lain vacant for longer than she cared to think about. On days like today, she felt like her priorities were backward.

"Mason, you have got to be ticked off. I know I would be."

"It's been rough in my part of the world today, too. There's just no fight left in me."

"I wouldn't consider it fighting, unless you call me dirty names."

Instead of his usual chuckle there was silence.

"Mason?"

"No, really. I'm fine, just tired, and I've still got a ton of work. Let's catch up tomorrow."

"That reminds me. I've got an invitation to pass along. For tomorrow." She turned west on Government Street.

She told him about the birthday dinner for her mother. He sounded excited. She promised to call him during the day. He promised not to wait by the phone. She laughed in spite of her exhaustion.

Just as Wallace backed into her carport, her phone buzzed. The number looked vaguely familiar, but not in a good way.

"This is Detective Hartman."

"Wallace, hey, Barry Gillis, here."

Now she remembered. A local TV reporter.

"No comment, Mr. Gillis."

He laughed. "I haven't even asked you any questions."

"Yet I've already answered them all. Wasn't that considerate of me?"

"You can call me Barry. We are old friends, you know."

Wallace had met Barry in the context of an earlier investigation, when he was just getting started in the TV reporting business. He had approached her with a proposition—he would be her go-to guy in the media if she would be his inside track with the police department. His exact words had been, "If you show me yours I'll show you mine," followed by an eyebrow waggle and an elbow nudge.

After he had mistaken her rattlesnake smile for tacit agreement, he went a step further and asked her out on a date. Wallace had resisted—just barely—the urge to empty her sidearm point-blank through his sternum. And, despite her consistent rebuffs over the years, he persisted with the dogged cheerfulness of a salesman.

"I'm not telling you anything about the Marioneaux case, Mr. Gillis."

"What do you know about the press conference he had scheduled, for Monday morning?"

She hadn't even known Marioneaux had called a press conference, but if she admitted that, Gillis would know he had information to trade with.

Her hesitation was all the encouragement the reporter needed.

"He promised me an exclusive interview beforehand—which
would've been earlier today—as long as I agreed not to air it until
after the press event."

"Have you spoken with his staff?" She was immediately sorry she
asked a question, because he always took questions as invitations to
drag out the conversation.

"Not yet. You want a peek at what I find out?" he asked.

She could picture his overactive eyebrows and his wide-eyed,
open-mouth smile. She regretted not shooting him. "I'll be doing
my own Q and A with them, but thank you. And listen, I've got to
run." She pressed the End Call icon.

FIVE

Wallace gazed at the Trombone Shorty bobblehead on the shelf in her cubicle, praying the little tchotchke would magically send her some crucial bit of inspiration. Once it became clear he was going to let her down, she returned her attention to her computer screen. What felt like the millionth article mentioning Herbert Marioneaux stared back at her. A brief wave of nausea reminded her that she had forgotten to eat lunch again.

Her entire morning been taken up with online research, requisitioning phone records for Marioneaux and those of his wife and son, and scrutinizing the early returns on the crime-scene forensics.

The only identifiable fingerprints in the house belonged to Herbert and Dorothy Marioneaux and Tonya Lennar. The house key Tonya had used had been no help. Too many people had touched it, and the techs had been unable to isolate anything legible from the tangle of prints.

The report from the officers who had canvassed the neighborhood added nothing. There were no street cams in the vicinity of the house. Door-to-door questioning had been thorough, but no one had seen anything.

Spanish Town was the oldest and one of the most culturally and professionally diverse areas of Baton Rouge. Most folks knew their neighbors, but no one could recall seeing any strange faces or out-of-place vehicles on the street.

She was about to drive back to Spanish Town to chat with the residents in the nearby houses when Jason Burley plopped into the empty chair a few feet away.

"I can tell by the look on your face that I'm not going to like whatever you're about to say." Wallace waited, not sure what was coming.

"Where is LeAnne?"

"Keeping tabs on Tonya Lennar, the housekeeper who cleaned Marioneaux's house."

Burley nodded as if he was weighing whether to continue. "They stayed up all night at the crime lab, a Saturday night no less, working on your case."

"See, I should be pleased about that, but I know that's just the first shoe."

"I knew you would feel that way. You probably just checked on the early lab reports and you didn't see anything significant in there. Am I right?"

"You being right is not the issue. The issue is why do I get the feeling you know something I don't?"

"Because it hasn't been logged into the case file yet."

"Then how did you get it?" It bothered her that she was getting the information secondhand. "Why did this information go to you instead of into the lab report? Is this how the case is going to happen, with everything filtering down from you to me?"

"Fair questions," Burley said. "The answers, in reverse order, are no, this is not how the case is going to go, at least I hope not, and second, the information is . . . how do I say this . . . politically sensitive. No, that's not strong enough. Let's say it's potentially explosive, so the lab director decided to put it in the police chief's hands first. He sent it to me and I'm here handing it off to you."

"We've got a suspect." She addressed her comment to Trombone Shorty.

Burley grimaced.

"Someone everybody's afraid of."

"Terrified, actually, but so far, you're batting a thousand."

"Before you tell me who, tell me what kind of evidence we're dealing with?"

"Several human hairs were recovered from inside Marioneaux's shirt. They fell down the back of his collar and snagged in the fabric."

Her enthusiasm started losing air. "Suddenly, I'm less worked up about this. Hair is about the least reliable forensic evidence there is. It's on the verge of being inadmissible in a lot of jurisdictions."

"Unless the root bulb is still attached to the hair and there's enough tissue to get a DNA match." He grinned.

"Which there obviously must be, or you wouldn't have come hustling back here to entertain me with all this happy talk."

Burley gave her a lopsided smile.

"And that was pretty fast, from yesterday morning to this afternoon."

"It was a clean, straightforward sample, so they were able to amplify the DNA pretty quickly. After that, a comparison to existing DNA records was a snap. Plus, the Marioneauxs have big-time political connections. Strings were pulled, and this one got jumped to the front of the line."

Wallace thought back to the crime scene. She imagined the killer coming up behind Marioneaux, dropping the slip lock over his head, yanking it tight. One of Marioneaux's hands would have reflexively gone to the slip lock, in a futile defensive move. His other hand, might have reached back to grab his assailant. It was easy to picture the senator scraping his nails across the killer's scalp or even grabbing a handful of the killer's hair. So, it was plausible that a few strands got pulled free and found their way down the back of Marioneaux's shirt.

"So, who's the lucky bastard?"

The remaining joviality drained out of Burley's expression.

"Look, Wallace, this is absolutely your case, but if you don't want to be in on the arrest yourself, nobody's going to hold it against you. In your place, I'm not so sure I would do it, but Chief Shannon says it's your call."

"It's someone I know."

Burley grimaced again.

SIX

The shame game was a delicate business. Come down too hard and you alienate the squeamish and miss a chance to pick up new followers. Too easy and you risk losing some you already had. Through long practice, Eddie Pitkin had developed a workable balance.

During some of his early attempts, mistakes were made. A few had been bad mistakes. But he was a diligent student. From every mistake he learned a valuable lesson, and he allowed those lessons to shape his thoughts and his actions for future encounters.

Goals were served before ego. Principles trumped emotions. Approach with a smile and an outstretched hand, like you were greeting a long-lost friend. Craft your questions carefully and give your targets a chance to say the right thing. Give them several chances. Never ridicule. Never raise your voice.

If they became upset and pushed back—perfect. You never knew what would come out of people's mouths when they felt off-balance and self-righteous. People often revealed the truth of their hearts when they were feeling the right kind of stress.

And always get it on video, make sure the sound was crystal clear, and don't be afraid to publish it. To Eddie, who had reached adulthood before the internet became so ubiquitous, YouTube was almost too good to be true.

It was a slow, methodical process, but it worked. It was the same routine skilled courtroom attorneys used to get what they wanted from a hostile witness. Eddie had been such an attorney back in the day. But now, after having passed through a valley of deep shadow, he had emerged to serve a higher purpose.

Today's target would be tough. Somehow the man had gotten wind that he was on Eddie's list, so he would be on guard. But he was a public figure of sorts, so it was impossible for him to hide and still do his job.

He was also a kind man, and that caused Eddie discomfort. The mission was more important than the feelings or even the reputation of any one person, but Eddie was not oblivious to the sensibilities of his targets. He just couldn't afford to cater to them.

Eddie looked across the expanse of open lawn in front of the church and pulled his hat low on his forehead against the afternoon sun. It was one of those brilliant blue days in late spring when the air was that perfect temperature, where you couldn't feel it against your skin. And the humidity was low—a rarity for Baton Rouge where, for much of the warm seasons, the heat and the humidity were often in the high double digits.

Afternoon Mass had let out several minutes ago. A thinning tide of parishioners streamed around him, heading for their cars.

About forty yards away, his assistant, Marla Krismer, straddled her moss-green Vespa, at the edge of the lot. Marla was very nice looking. Her shoulder-length blond hair and her faintly tanned Swedish skin were difficult to look away from. And she was unmistakably interested in Eddie. At twenty-three, she was also young enough to be his daughter. In fact, she had been introduced by one of Eddie's daughters.

But Eddie was not interested in Marla. He was married. Unhappily, at the moment, but married nevertheless. And while temptations came his way with enough frequency to keep his middle-aged self-image amusingly inflated, adultery was a territory into which he would not cross. He had crossed a lot of lines in his time, but infidelity would not be one of them.

He recognized the opportunities, appreciated the flattery they represented, and then he resolutely turned his mind against them. *I'm old-fashioned,* he thought. *So, sue me.*

He loved his wife and his children and he supposed they loved him back, although he didn't always make himself easy to love—especially lately.

Eddie looked over at Marla again. Her long, delicate fingers danced across the screen of her phone. Then he looked down and read her text on his own phone: "He's left the rectory. Approaching from your right. Thirty seconds." As Eddie rose from the bench he ran through his script. *Stick to the script,* he reminded himself, and then he muttered a quick prayer.

Out of the corner of his eye he saw Marla dismount from her Vespa and move in his direction. Eddie turned to meet his target—a heavyset man with thinning hair and a ruddy complexion. The clerical collar and his easygoing expression gave the man gravity. He was laughing at something one of his companions was saying.

"Father Milton, I'm Eddie Pitkin." Eddie's hand went out. His smile slid into place. The laughter stopped, and the mirth faded from the faces of the priest and the two men with him.

One of the men tried to move between Eddie and Father Milton, but the priest held his arm out, blocking him. Marla was off to the side, her phone camera running.

"It's okay," the priest said as he stepped forward. "Good to see you, Mr. Pitkin." The priest gripped the offered hand with his right and laid his left hand on top in a shepherdly fashion. "I suppose you've gone to the trouble of tracking me down to let me know that you and I are related. Distant cousins, maybe?"

Eddie gave him a sheepish grin. "No, Father. Not me. But there about two dozen other black people scattered across this part of the state who are."

A small crowd was assembling to one side, watching Eddie and the priest.

"Aren't we all related, Mr. Pitkin? Aren't we all descendants of God's first humans?"

"I believe that, Father. Just like you. But it's the more recent branches in your family tree that interest us."

"If you're here to tell me that some of my remote ancestors were slaveholders, I know that already."

"No, Father. Not *some* of them. *All* of them. Every single direct ancestor of yours who was of legal age at the onset of the Civil War was a slave owner. Right here, in South Louisiana."

"If you're looking for wealth to spread around, I'm afraid you've come too late. Whatever land my family used to own has long since passed into the hands of people to whom I am not related. And, as you can see, I am obviously a man of very limited means."

"Understood, Father. But other members of your family are not so limited. In fact, quite a few of them live very well. And they are able to do so because of wealth that was, in the beginning, amassed on the backs of people that your ancestors owned as property. People they used just like they would use a plow or a draft mule or a hay baler and, in some cases, for sex."

"Trust me, Mr. Pitkin—"

"Please Father, just call me Eddie."

The priest went quiet. He and the two men with him stood still. They had all noticed Marla and her phone, but they weren't trying to avoid her. Others in the growing crowd were also recording the encounter.

"Of course," the elderly priest said. "So, trust me, Eddie, when I say that I understand what you're doing."

"Do you, Father? Have you ever been black? Do you know whether any of your ancestors were ever slaves? Have you ever felt persecuted because of the color of your skin?"

Eddie waited for the priest's response. This was a critical moment in the drama. Father Milton would either lose a lot or lose everything.

The priest studied Eddie, then turned to look at Marla and the parishioners who were still gathering a respectful distance away. Eddie could tell the man was calculating what sort of demeanor would play best for the cameras. All of Eddie's smartest targets were politicians, in a sense, and they were skilled at appearing humble when the situation demanded it.

"No. None of those things. And I'm not trying to imply that I've endured the injustices that motivate you. But I do, intellectually, comprehend your motives. I recognize and freely admit the terrible personal and societal transgressions of the past. And I see the effects those events are having on the present and what they foretell for the future. I just don't know if what you're doing—this quest of yours, for reparations, especially on such an individual level—whether it will bring with it the reconciliation that is so desperately needed."

"Nobody knows that, Father. But you and I both know that *doing* nothing *changes* nothing. *My* conscience won't allow that."

"Mr. Pitkin?" The voice came from behind him. It was a woman's voice. One he recognized. He couldn't imagine that someone in the crowd had summoned the police. For Father Milton, that would be a lose-everything gambit.

Without turning, Eddie spoke loudly enough to be heard by the person behind him. "Lovely day, isn't it, Detective Hartman? A lovely day to be outside, exercising one's constitutionally protected rights to speak freely and to peaceably assemble."

"It's also a lovely day to be advised of one's constitutionally protected rights to remain silent, and to know that anything one says can be used as evidence—"

"You can skip the recitation, Detective. I was litigating those rights in federal court when you were still in diapers."

Eddie looked Father Milton squarely in the eye, probing for some sign that this was his doing, but the priest looked genuinely baffled.

When the priest stepped up next to Eddie so that they might face Wallace together, it was Eddie's turn to look perplexed.

"Mr. Pitkin and I are having a civil discussion, Detective, about matters of significance to both of us. I fail to see how this could be of any concern to the police."

"Father, please stand to the side. I won't ask you again." Wallace looked at the officer she had brought with her, silently signaling for him to station himself between the priest and Pitkin.

Eddie shook his head in disbelief. An amused smile slowly blossomed on his face. He turned and shook the priest's hand again, this time laying *his* free hand on top. "It's okay, Father. I've been down this road before."

He stepped forward, freeing two steps of empty space between himself and the priest.

Eddie looked for Marla among the growing crowd. She remained about twenty feet away, recording everything.

"What's this about, Detective Hartman?"

"I'm willing to put the cuffs on hands-in-front. If you'd like to remove your jacket and have it draped it over the cuffs, I'm fine with that too. Can I count on you to be cooperative?"

Eddie smiled and shook his head. "Absolutely not." He shoved his hands into his pockets, then stood stock-still. "Let's go for the full pageantry, shall we? You'll have an opportunity to show off your handcuffing technique and your frog-marching style, and I get to add another viral video to my growing collection. Sounds like a win-win situation."

He knew he was about to break his rule about indulging emotions, but the moment seemed to call for exactly that. Besides, his first time through the criminal justice meat grinder taught him it was better to sail in on a tide of rising emotion than to slink in nursing an attitude of fear and defeat. He stood tall and filled his lungs with a deep, deliberate breath and looked toward the assembled crowd.

"Help me out, folks." His smile was huge and confident. "Should I make this easy, or should we make her work for it?"

Some shouted "Work for it," but some expressed the opinion that Eddie must have done something wrong, otherwise the police wouldn't be on the scene.

Wallace moved around behind Eddie, pulling first one hand, then the other from his pockets and snapping the cuffs around his wrists.

Speaking just loud enough for Eddie to hear, Wallace said, "I made my offer out of—"

"Out of respect for my brother." He laughed and shook his head. "Always, it's my brother. What about respect for me, Detective Hartman? When does that enter the calculation?"

Wallace had given serious consideration to Burley's offer to have someone else make the arrest. Eddie was the much older half-brother of Craig Stephens, one of Wallace's closest friends since childhood. Her being the one to slap on the cuffs was going to stress her relationship with Craig.

But she also knew that Eddie would have an easier time of it if she was the one to bring him in, because no one else on the force would have as strong a personal interest in de-escalating any crisis behavior that broke out. Either way, there would be fallout.

She took hold of one of Eddie's elbows and her fellow officer took the other. Carefully, but firmly, they led the smiling man through the jostling gauntlet of phone-wielding churchgoers and curiosity seekers.

SEVEN

W ord of Eddie Pitkin's arrest had traveled fast. A crowd of "Free Eddie" protesters greeted his arrival at the police building.

Once Wallace delivered Eddie over to the booking process and filed her report, she fled the premises and drove to Mason's apartment. From there, she took the two of them to her mother's house.

After the hassle of the afternoon, Carol Hartman's birthday dinner turned out to be therapeutic. For the first time in days, Wallace was able to let her guard down.

Davis McCone had arranged the party as part of an effort to rekindle an old romance. His wife had died a little over a year ago and his long-ago interest in Wallace's mother had resurfaced.

Wallace and her mother had been widows for several years and both now found themselves with prospects. Carol had encouraged Wallace to be receptive to the idea of having a man in her life, but Wallace had been unenthusiastic until Mason had arrived and taken her completely by surprise. Now Wallace watched with keen interest as her mother dealt with the same possibilities.

"You're probably wondering if she was this argumentative as a child," Carol said to Mason after they had listened to several minutes of heated debate between Wallace and Davis over the Progressive legacies of Huey and Earl Long, two influential but controversial Louisiana governors from the early and mid-twentieth century. "Although you can never be sure whether Davis is really an anti-tax-and-spend person or if he's just pulling Wallace's chain."

"She does seem to have a very well-developed . . ."

"Talent?" Wallace filled in, turning her attention to Mason.

"Precisely the word I was looking for." A smile spread across his face.

"At breakfast one morning, when she was about four years old, she asked her father what sausage was made from."

"Mom, do you have to tell that silly story to every man who's ever shown an interest in me?"

"It would be a shame to waste something I've had so much practice at," Carol said without missing a beat. "Anyway," she continued, turning back to Mason, "he told her, 'Sausage is made from pigs,' so Wallace immediately said, 'That means pigs are made from sausage.' Well, that practically set off World War Three. No matter what Walter said, Wallace would simply not be parted from that bit of deductive reasoning. They went round and round on that point until I was sure there would be gunfire. That was the day her father learned that his was only the second-hardest head in the house."

"Are you saying I'm hardheaded?"

"I can see the logic in Wallace's—" Mason began.

"You stay out of this." Wallace raised her palm in a stop gesture. "Mom, do you really think I'm hardheaded?"

"Wallace, you say it like it's a bad thing."

"Do *you* think I'm hardheaded?" Wallace asked, redirecting her attention to Mason.

"You just told me to stay out of it."

"And now I'm telling you to jump in . . . with both feet . . . on the correct side."

"There's really nothing about you I don't like a great deal."

"Weasel."

"Guilty."

"And smart," Carol finished.

"And handy in the kitchen too." Mason stood, gathering dishes from the table. "This was a wonderful meal. Let me clean up."

"Well, aren't you two just the sweetest pair." Wallace laughed, looking from her mother to Mason.

"Mason, sit. Davis and I made this mess. We'll clean it up," Carol said.

Wallace watched as Mason stacked a few dishes, one on top of the other, relying mostly on his right hand. His left arm was still a bit weak and unsteady from a nearly fatal wound he had suffered several months earlier. The offending bullet had ripped through Mason's left armpit damaging the network of arteries and nerves that fed his arm. Months of agonizing and frustrating rehabilitation had restored a great deal of function. His surgeon claimed he'd had patients who came all the way back from worse damage, but Wallace wondered whether that was more pep talk than prognosis.

"Mom, you and Davis did all the cooking. Let me and Mason clean up." She looked back at Mason and saw him looking at her, smiling. He wasn't the least bit self-conscious about his injury. Wallace liked that about him. He didn't worry about what anyone else thought and he seemed incapable of self-pity.

Just as Wallace reached across the table for Davis's dishes, the doorbell rang. She looked at her mother, then at Davis. Both shook their heads and gave her puzzled looks. Concern clouded her face.

"I'll see who it is." She set the plate down and then moved into the hallway toward the front door. The light inside made it hard to see out through the glass panes of the door. The silhouette of a man standing several feet back, at the edge of the porch, was just visible. As she drew closer she recognized him and her spirits sank.

She had prayed he wouldn't come looking for her, that he wouldn't even call. For a split second, she considered backing away from the door and disappearing into the house. He was turned away, so he hadn't seen her yet. But he had seen her car parked at the curb. He appeared to be looking directly at it.

Wallace slipped out and pulled the door shut behind her. The visitor turned at the sound.

"Craig," she said, hoping she sounded surprised to see him.

"Hey, little white girl." He gave her a half-hearted smile, but worry was leeching the cheer out of his normally upbeat demeanor.

When Wallace was a girl, her family had lived on the white side of one of the streets that marked the borderline between a white neighborhood and a black neighborhood. She had spent a good bit of her growing-up years playing with Craig and his younger sister, Berna, the black children who lived on the other side of the street— something not all of the white neighbors had found charming.

The fact that Craig refused to call her anything but little white girl hadn't helped matters. Craig's mother had spanked him silly trying to make him call her Wallace, but for reasons known only to himself, Craig had stuck to his guns.

"How did you know where to find me?" she asked.

"I called the station. I drove by your house and Mason's apartment. A process of elimination."

"I know this has got to be hard on you and your mother," Wallace said. "How is she?"

"She's dealing with it." Craig sat sidesaddle on the porch railing, one foot on the floor, the other swinging free. He shoved his hands into his pockets. The skirt of his sport coat bunched up along his forearms. "Eddie didn't do it."

"You're talking to the wrong person," Wallace said. "I was the arresting officer and the detective of record on the investigation. I have no control over the issue of guilt or innocence."

"I know. That would be the judge and the jury. But I'm telling you, he didn't do it. This is not the time to close your investigation."

"Who told you I was closing the investigation?"

"You did," he said, his voice rising. "You're already referring to it in the past tense, as if it's all over but the hanging."

Wallace leaned back against the front wall of the house. Table talk and dish clatter drifted out through the screened window to her left. She debated how much to tell him.

"Craig, he's been tied to the crime by some very convincing circumstantial evidence. The word is, the DA thinks she has enough to convict. Are you saying the evidence is wrong?"

"I know what the DA's thinking and I know what evidence she thinks is making this an open-and-shut case. But what I'm saying is that Eddie didn't do it because he *couldn't* have done it. He was at my fishing camp on False River the whole time. I don't use it much anymore, so he's out there most weekends."

Almost from the moment she'd put the cuffs on him, Eddie had remained silent. This was the first Wallace was hearing about an alibi.

"Were you there with him?"

"No, I wasn't."

"What about his wife?"

"He and Renata are having difficulties. The lake house is where he goes to take the ethanol cure." Craig's lips twisted into a sour expression. Disapproval was clear in his voice.

"Could anyone else have been out there, offering to console him during his time of marital discord?"

"I wasn't there, so I don't know. But that's not his style."

"And style points don't count as evidence." She pushed herself away from the wall and took a step toward Craig, tilting her head and looking into his worried eyes. "You know this."

"We've got an audience," he said, staring past her, at the living room windows.

Wallace looked back over her shoulder. Mason and Davis were in the living room.

"Look, before—"

The porch light came on. Wallace raised her hand for quiet. She threaded her arm through Craig's, pulling him with her toward the sidewalk in front of the house. When she looked back at the house,

Davis was standing at the front door, squinting out at them. He turned away when he saw Wallace looking at him.

"Before Eddie's troubles started, all those years ago," Craig began again, "he was a first-rate criminal lawyer. He tried and consulted on cases all over the country and most of his high-profile work was based on the reliability of forensic evidence. A guy with that kind of smarts isn't going to just forget and leave a few stray hairs lying around the scene of his latest murder."

Ironically, as Wallace recalled, Eddie's long-ago troubles stemmed from an evidence-tampering scheme he had tried to pull off in a case on which he was lead counsel. Eddie was convinced his client was innocent. He was also convinced that a certain piece of evidence would be too inflammatory and unfairly bias the jury. Certain that only he was aware of the pesky evidence in question, he had buried it. But it turned out that at least one other person knew of its existence and that person had made sure the deception was brought to the court's attention.

Eddie's fall from grace had been swift and complete. His client was eventually acquitted, in spite of the evidence Eddie had tried to hide, but Eddie was tried and convicted of obstruction of justice— a serious felony in Louisiana. He had been disbarred and spent three years in Angola, the state penitentiary.

"We can debate this all night long and it won't do you or your brother any good. When was the DA notified of this alibi?"

"She hasn't been told. At least, not that I know of."

Wallace took a step back. "Craig, you know you can't just claim the evidence is bad because you think the odds are against it." She looked back at the house to see if they were still being watched. They weren't.

"Look, Eddie's been lying to me since we were kids. I know what that looks like. This time he's telling the truth."

"If so, then either the lab got it wrong or somebody planted that evidence. Framing someone for a capital crime is a dangerous and very tricky business. Are you thinking of someone in particular who'd be willing to try a harebrained scheme like this?"

"We both know that list would be quite long. Eddie's not exactly the darling of the white community and there are even a fair number of black people, me included, who wish he would just stop with this crusade of his." He shook his head. "What I can't figure out is why anyone could honestly believe Eddie would even do something like this."

"I hear you, but others will see things differently. He and Herbert weren't exactly exchanging love letters, over the years. He said things in public that came awfully close to sounding like threats of violence against Marioneaux and his family."

"That sounds more like a motive for Herbert Marioneaux to get rid of Eddie, not the other way around. Besides, Eddie referred to Marioneaux as the kind of person who served no useful purpose in an enlightened society. That's not the same thing as a threat."

"Maybe. But when the DA does her song and dance for the jury, those old hostilities will not be ignored."

"I'm not asking anybody to ignore anything." Craig's voice trembled with barely controlled anger, "I'm just asking you not to close the investigation yet. Eddie's been picked up for something he didn't do and Herbert Marioneaux's killer is still on the street."

"Okay." Wallace raised her hands in surrender and took another step back. She wasn't used to the ire and frustration she was seeing in Craig. "Did anybody else see Eddie up there? The guy at the bait store? Somebody at a restaurant where Eddie paid with a credit card and there was a nice, high-res surveillance camera staring him square in the face as he signed the bill? Maybe with a big, fat time and date stamp across the bottom of the picture?"

"Not that we know of," Craig said, lowering his voice. "He says it was just him and a cooler full of food and beer. He got there on Friday afternoon and didn't leave until Sunday morning. The only place he went was to and from the house and the dock out back, so unless somebody just happened to be doing a field study of the neo-bourgeois southern Negro infiltrating the age-old habitat of the light-skinned rural cracker bird, then it's just Eddie's word against a couple of very inconvenient hairs." Craig pulled his glasses off and rubbed the spot between his eyes with the heel of his hand.

"Craig, do you have to talk that way? You know it creeps me out."

"What can I say?" His gaze was steady, but his voice was not. "If it takes a case of the creeps to keep this investigation going—until things get set right—then so be it."

"Who's representing Eddie, and may I assume he or she knows about this little conversation you and I are having?"

"Tasha Kovacovich, and no, she doesn't know. But she will."

An uncomfortable feeling swept through her. Craig was stepping out-of-bounds. Way out-of-bounds.

"Let me give this some thought. At the moment, that's the best I can do."

"Thanks, Wallace." It sounded more like "thanks for nothing." His smile was weak and doubtful. "Tell your mother I said hello and Happy Birthday."

Without a good-bye, he turned and strode off into the gloom, leaving a heavy sensation in the air between them. It felt like a burned bridge.

If Craig was convinced Eddie was telling the truth, the least she could do was make the argument that it was too early to close the investigation. She didn't want the police department or the DA to get blindsided and played for fools. She called Jason Burley's cell and left him a message with the broad outlines of her and Craig's conversation.

When she walked back into the house, Davis and Mason were sitting in the living room.

"Trouble?" Mason asked.

She shook her head. "Just some repercussions from a case."

"Trouble," Davis said with the barest hint of a smile.

Wallace looked at Davis, then back at Mason. Mason cocked an eyebrow.

"Carol kicked us out of the kitchen." Davis rattled the ice in his drink and brought it to his lips.

Wallace smiled at Mason and squeezed his shoulder as she passed him on her way toward the back of the house. Craig's revelations troubled her, but the sound of dishes being loaded into a dishwasher pushed thoughts of Craig and Eddie out of her mind. A year ago, she wouldn't have been able to shift gears so easily. Back then, once her mind started to wrestle with a case it proved almost impossible for her to shake her thinking loose.

Mason's arrival had changed that. Almost from the moment they started working together, her focus had enlarged to include him.

"Perfect timing," Carol said as Wallace entered the kitchen.

"Can I help you do anything?"

"Push the Start button on the dishwasher."

"Lucky me." She pushed the button and then leaned back against the counter and looked at her mother. A sad expression had taken over Carol's face. "Mom, what's the matter?"

"I had a dream about your father last night." She brushed her palm across the countertop, as if she were wiping away crumbs. Her eyes followed her moving hand.

"Tell me about it." Wallace reached for her mother's hand, but Carol moved away and then sat on a stool next to the stove island.

"We were walking along a crowded street. Suddenly, Walter stopped. 'You go on,' he said. He shooed me away, so I walked a bit and looked back, and he was standing right where I left him, smiling and waving me on. Every time I looked he was a smaller part of the picture, until all I could see was his face. I felt like the crowd would surge and wash him away. I felt so lonely and so sad. And he just had that stupid smile on his face. I knew if I kept going, I would lose sight of him, so I hurried back. I told him I loved him and he said he loved me too. We walked back in the direction we had come from, talking about what we did earlier that day, but before I realized it, we were back where he said he had to stop, and he was telling me to go on."

Wallace scrutinized her mother's face. "You've had this dream before."

Carol's gaze fixed on Wallace for a moment and then she slid from the stool and began rearranging spice jars clustered next to the stovetop. "How would you know that?"

"You don't seem very upset and you usually get weepy at a lost-puppy poster." Wallace took her mother's place on the stool.

"Well, aren't you a regular detective."

"Mom, I'm not sure I believe in signs from above, but at the very least your own subconscious seems to be giving you permission to move ahead with a new part of life. If your mind is couching it in terms of Dad giving you the go-ahead, then go ahead."

"His is not the only understanding I value."

"You don't need my permission to have a man in your life."

Carol propped her elbows on the countertop and laced her fingers together. She closed her eyes and took a deep breath.

"If you're not interested in Davis, just tell him."

"It's not that simple." Carol rested her chin on top of her intertwined fingers and looked at Wallace. "Did you ever wonder what made me choose your father over Davis?"

"Not really." Wallace squirmed, giving her mother a nervous look. "Is this something I need to know?"

"Davis was very certain about things. He had a sense of the way things ought to be and he'd go about engineering situations to meet those expectations."

"Is that a bad thing?"

"I wasn't sure if that left any room for me and my ways of thinking. Everybody has their differences, you know."

"Has he changed, in that regard?"

"Oh, I'm not sure. But at our age it's less threatening. We've both probably figured out who we are. And don't get me wrong. His sort of single-mindedness is probably what made him such a good lawyer."

"Which doesn't necessarily make for a good husband."

"Your father and I were a perfect fit—naturally and effortlessly so. A rare thing."

"But people do change. I'm not the same woman who married Kenny, all those years ago. Mason might not have worked for me back then."

Carol sighed and gave Wallace a tender smile. "You're a lot like your father was."

"Hardheaded, you mean?"

Carol laughed. Her eyes brightened for just a second as she studied Wallace. "And intensely logical, even when the emotional strain makes that tough."

"So what are you going to do?"

"Remind you that logic isn't the only way to reason through a situation. And then haul you up to the front of the house, so we can rejoin our dinner companions." Carol looped her arm around Wallace's waist and pulled her along into the hallway.

"Dinner was wonderful," Wallace said as they joined Davis and Mason on the front porch. "I didn't know you were such a fancy cook, Davis."

"New hobby," he said, pulling a chair around for Carol.

"I think this little to-do is Davis's way of distracting me from being content with my solitary life," Carol said, reopening the subject of their kitchen discussion.

"How hard do you plan to make him work at it?" Wallace asked, taking Carol's statement as a license to pursue the topic.

"You've phrased your question in a way that assumes she already knows the answer," Davis said with a toothy smile. "I'm not yet convinced that's the case."

"I'm not making anybody do anything," Carol objected.

Wallace looked over at Mason. His expression was a mixture of fascination and mild discomfort. His home life growing up had been one of emotional austerity and physical turbulence, and he wasn't accustomed to the casual intimacy so normal among Wallace's friends and family.

"Entirely true," Davis continued. "But she hasn't told me to hit the bricks, either."

Wallace walked around behind Mason's chair and laid her hands on his chest, then leaned over and kissed the top of his head. When he reached up and took each of her hands in his, she could feel the difference in the strength of his grip.

"Davis, what do you want with me, anyway?" Carol asked. "I'm an old woman."

"You've been an old woman since we were kids. Why should that bother me now?"

"If you're trying to be charming, it's not working."

"It worked for Walter."

"You're not Walter."

"Walter's not even Walter, anymore."

"Wallace, are you listening to the way he's talking about your father? Don't you have something to say?"

"Mom, we've got to go." She massaged Mason's shoulders.

"And leave me alone with this man? Even though you know full well, the minute you're gone, he'll probably try something?"

"You make it sound so dramatic. Besides, he looks determined. I don't think us staying will change his game plan."

"When he thinks I can't hear him, he refers to me as 'the widow Hartman.' Before you two arrived, he was out here on the porch, yakking into his phone with one of those silly friends of his. 'I'm paying a call on the widow Hartman.' What kind of talk is that?"

"The true kind?" Wallace frisked herself for her phone and her keys.

"See what happens, Davis? You teach a child to always tell the truth and then just as soon as it's the wrong thing to do it's the first thing out of her mouth."

"You and Mason can't leave before I give Carol her birthday present." He pulled a clumsily wrapped box from the side pocket of his blazer and offered it to Carol on his outstretched palm.

"Didn't I tell you not to buy me anything?"

"You did, and I didn't."

"Then, where did you get this?"

"Stolen goods."

Carol eyed the box with suspicion.

"Just open it," Davis said. "We're not getting any younger, you know."

Carol snatched the box from his palm and began pulling the paper away, the tendons bow-stringing on the backs of her hands as she struggled with the ribbon.

"Careful," Davis said. "It's the last of its kind."

Carol pulled away the remaining bits of wrapping to reveal a small framed photograph of her and Davis as teenagers. They were standing in front of the clubhouse at the city park golf course. She was looking wide-eyed into the camera, her cheeks puffed out like a blowfish. Davis, with an exaggerated pucker, was giving the camera a sidelong glance as he planted a kiss on one of Carol's inflated cheeks.

"Wallace swiped this out of a box in my closet, didn't she? That's why you wanted her here. So she could do your thieving for you. You little devil," she said, smiling at Wallace.

Davis gave her his patented so-what shrug, that effortless way he had of acknowledging he had done wrong but still managed to get things right. He still had the rascally frat-boy attitude that made him such a formidable presence in the courtroom. Wallace had seen a long line of judges fall victim to that little enchantment of his. She watched as her mother studied the picture.

Carol's eyes glistened, then appeared to lose focus. Her gaze drifted to one side and her eyelids gently closed.

"How did you know I still had this?" Her eyes opened and she looked at Davis.

He gave her the shrug again, adding a smirk and a slow-motion eye roll. "Of course, I had no idea where you might have stashed it. For that I needed a little help. And if you must know, and I think you must, Wallace didn't hesitate for so much as a second."

"Well, I have to say, this is a strange sort of a gift. You're giving me back something that was mine all along?"

"I'm trying."

"May I?" Mason asked, leaning forward to look.

Carol handed him the photograph, then sat back in her chair.

Mason studied the image. He turned his head to look up at Wallace and then he looked back at the picture. "Carol, you've certainly perpetuated your good looks."

"Oh, please," Wallace said. "Have you been taking smooth-operator lessons from Davis?"

"Bravo," Carol said as Mason answered with a respectable imitation of the Davis shrug.

Wallace looked from Mason to her mother and saw something in her face she had never seen before. Carol's gaze traveled back and forth between her and Mason, studying their faces, and Wallace could tell that her mother was trying to imagine what a grandchild might look like. A current of alarm jolted through her.

Sensing the tension, Mason tilted his head back and looked up at her, his expression instantly mirroring the worry he saw on her face.

"Mom, we really have to go. Happy Birthday."

Everyone stood, and there was a round-robin of hugs and good-byes.

"This is a good thing you're doing," Wallace whispered in Davis's ear as she and Mason stepped off the porch into the darkness.

They drove in companionable silence, arriving at Mason's apartment building—a nicely restored two-story fourplex on the edge of the Garden District—less than five minutes after leaving the birthday party.

Wallace killed the engine and rolled down the windows. She turned toward Mason with a wistful smile on her face.

"What's going on in that head of yours?" Mason whispered.

"I think my mother is falling in love with you."

"What about you?"

"I might be too. Maybe, just a little." She brightened her smile, hoping Mason wouldn't sense the anxiety beginning to gnaw at her, in the wake of Craig's visit. "A lot happened at that little party."

"I was there, remember?" He turned and reached for her just as her phone lit up.

"Sorry," she said, giving Mason a pained look. "It's Burley." She put the phone to her ear. "Somehow I knew we'd be talking before the night was through."

As she listened, she looked over at Mason and gave him a sad pouty face. After a few minutes, she signed off and put the phone away.

"I can tell from your end of the conversation that my plans for a grand seduction just got back-burnered," Mason said.

"Somebody's unhappy about my visitor during the party. Burley and the chief of police feels the need to chat me up."

"If it's not too late when you're done with the other men in your life, you know where to find me."

She smiled and leaned in for a kiss.

EIGHT

Wallace met Burley in his office—a glass-walled fishbowl a short hallway away from the Homicide Division cubicle farm—and laid out all the details of Craig's visit.

"Just for the record, I don't like this," Burley said.

"Because you're worried about the politics of it."

"Look, the defense has a statutory obligation to formally notify the DA if they plan to use an alibi and they have to show whatever evidence they've got that supports it. They *have* to show it to us. But this is not something that should be done informally by the brother of the prime suspect, the brother who just happens to be a lifelong friend of the principal investigator."

"What's done is done. We can't change it, so let's use it to our advantage. I want to do some snooping around False River and I want to search Craig's fishing camp."

Burley sat back in his chair and folded his hands across his softening middle. "We'll need a warrant, because there's no way Eddie's lawyer is going to allow a consent search of that house."

"Which is why I want you to lead the charge with the powers that be in Pointe Coupee Parish and in New Roads, the little town right next to False River, and make it okay for me to get this done."

"Slow down. Are you sure you want to do this? Once your relationship with Craig Stephens becomes common knowledge—and it will—the perception will be that you're looking for evidence to substantiate the alibi because of your friendship, and that *maybe* you'll be less diligent or objective about looking for or preserving evidence that tends to cut the other way."

"I just want the facts, whichever way they cut. This was not a spur-of-the-moment crime of opportunity. There was no break-in. The victim's cell phone and laptop are missing, but none of the other valuables were even touched. This was an execution and it clearly took planning. And now I have credible information that, at the time of the murder, the prime suspect was someplace else."

"And I'm not questioning your intentions."

"Then why all this pushback? If we have good reason to believe the suspect was at a specific place at the critical time, then we have an obligation to go over that location with a fine-tooth comb."

"It isn't an issue of *what* needs to be done. It's about *who* should be doing it."

Wallace's head snapped up like she'd been slapped. "I see."

"And this has nothing to do with you as a person. You don't ever need to convince me that your motives are pure." With both hands, fingers splayed, he pushed down on the air in front of him. "It has to do with how your connection to Eddie Pitkin will be viewed from the outside."

"And from the inside. You're not saying that, but I can hear it in your voice."

"There are some on the blue team who will think you've gone to work for the defense because your good buddy's half-brother is the one with his head on the block."

It dawned on her what a clever move Craig had made. If she got taken off the case and Eddie ended up being found guilty, she wouldn't have been the one to put Eddie in line for the needle. And

Craig would have moved her out of the picture without the insult of directly asking her to take herself off the case. It would look like she was being replaced because he had tried to use his friendship with her to steer the investigation.

It was also possible that Craig was worried that, of all the possible investigators the police could put on the case, she would be the likeliest to find any damning evidence. By having her off the case, he was trimming the odds of that happening.

He was trying to help her while he was trying to save Eddie and he was willing to take the heat for sticking his nose in where it didn't belong. It was typical Craig—smarter than everyone else and not afraid to suffer for it.

She looked up at Burley. His grimace and his slow nod told her he was thinking the same thing.

"I don't want to be taken off this case."

Burley just stared at her. A tiny smile tugged at the corners of his mouth.

"So what are you going to do?" She crossed her arms and stared back at him.

"Send you upstairs. Chief Shannon wants to put his two cents in."

Wallace couldn't remember the last time she had been on one of the upper floors of the building on a weekend night. The hallways were dim and quiet. She pulled open the door to the chief's office suite and stepped inside. The only light came from his open doorway, across the empty reception area.

Jack Shannon's office was nicely appointed but conspicuously modest. Most of the wall decorations were awards and certificates and photographs of him with local dignitaries. He didn't believe in feathering his nest with the tax dollars of hardworking citizens. Especially when quite a few of those hardworking citizens were police officers who risked their lives for a paycheck and would resent seeing chunks of their money turned into Oriental rugs and cloisonné vases for the exclusive enjoyment of some bureaucrat who no longer risked his life for a paycheck.

"Have a seat, Detective. I'm sure we'd all prefer to be home right now, but for reasons you'll understand in a moment, this case is the department's number one priority. Number one headache too. So, before we move on to the issue of Craig Stephens, I'd like to show you something that was brought to me by the pastor of one of the largest, predominantly African-American churches in town. Right over here, if you don't mind."

He pointed to a seat at the little conference table in one corner of the room. A laptop rested on the table in front of where he wanted her to sit.

"Just click the Go icon on the video. I've already seen it, so I'll let you enjoy it. Then we'll chat."

The video was shaky, but the event it recorded was crystal clear. The cab and the bed of a bright red dual-wheel pickup were loaded with hollering white teenagers, male and female. One of the girls standing in the bed was holding up a wind-stiffened banner tacked to a wooden pole. A game of hangman was crudely sketched in black paint on a white bedsheet. Beneath the unfinished image of the person on the gallows it read:

_ _D IE P I T K I N The only thang missin is good old E D.

Wallace stopped the video, too embarrassed to watch it to the end. She looked at Chief Shannon. She knew this had to be hard on him. He was the first black police chief in Baton Rouge. He had been born and raised in the city and came up through the ranks. It was a proud moment for the town when he took the job. Now, despite prodigious efforts on his part, the specter of racial violence seemed poised to cast its shadow over the community yet again.

It had been less than eight hours since she had arrested Eddie Pitkin and already things were heating up.

"Where did this happen?" Wallace asked.

"Out on Larkens Ferry Road. That truck full of goofballs pulled up next to a school bus full of black children—a church group out on a field trip. One of the kids in the bus shot the video."

"Where do people come up with this shit?"

Shannon shrugged. "Wherever they get it, there must be a lot of it there, because reports like this are popping up all over. It's only a matter of time before there's a physical confrontation."

"Chief Shannon, I know this is a sensitive case. And I know that Jason Burley believes my relationship and my conversation tonight with Craig Stephens have compromised me, and that I'm just adding to the danger."

"That's his theory. It's not my theory. But before we get into that, I need you to focus on this video and all these other reports of unrest that are coming in. In the short time since Pitkin's arrest hit the news cycle, things have gotten really edgy really fast. The street is heating up. The pastor who sent me this video had the good sense to keep it off the internet, but who knows how long that'll last."

In spite of herself, Wallace couldn't drag her eyes away from the image on the screen. The girl with the banner looked high on a cocktail of hatred and glee, her hair blowing wild, her mouth frozen open in mid shout. The rest of the kids in the truck were offering their middle fingers to the children on the bus.

"As you can imagine, time is of the essence. And we're going to be under a fucking microscope. Every single thing we do will get scrutinized and second-guessed in the most public way possible. So, we can't be seen as dragging our feet and we can't be seen as shutting down the investigation prematurely. We damn sure can't be perceived as hiding anything the public or the defense has a right to know, but, at the same time, we can't afford to prejudice public opinion by showing just the inflammatory stuff, either."

Wallace closed the laptop, unwilling to continue seeing the faces in the truck.

"It makes the spot between the rock and the hard place seem desirable, by comparison, wouldn't you say?" Shannon asked.

"There are a lot of things I'd like to say, but none of them would be very productive."

"Let's you and me take stock of things, Detective. I'm putting together a sort of ledger in my head—the pros and cons of you continuing as the lead investigator."

"If you want me off the case, Chief, please, just do what you think is right for all concerned. I won't like it, to be perfectly honest, but you'll have my full cooperation."

"I think what's right for all concerned is for me to tell you about the pros and cons of you being on the case and for you to give this a good hard listen." He smiled to indicate that he appreciated her attempt to let him off the hook.

"Sorry." She smiled back, feeling like she was in the principal's office.

"On the negative side, I'm getting pressure from the boneheads in City Hall to . . . how do I say this . . . put a more optically correct officer in charge of this investigation."

"Jesus."

"He was not among their recommendations. Which brings me to the other negative on my list. And this one, to my way of thinking, is the more important one." He paused until she gave him an expectant look.

"I understand a video exists of you arresting Eddie Pitkin. It's already available on YouTube and every form of social media you can think of. I haven't seen it yet, but that will change just as soon as you and I are done here. My point in bringing it up is that this case and that video have the potential to put a big fat target right in the middle of your back."

"Nowadays, police activity is routinely recorded by citizens. Even before that, blowback from arrests was always a source of danger. It's just part of our job."

"But this case is touching a very raw nerve. Not just in Baton Rouge, either. You're the only detective with a personal connection to Eddie and his family. That's going to intensify public scrutiny of you." He jabbed his finger in Wallace's direction to emphasize his point. "Things could get very dicey."

"If you're asking me whether I *want* you to take me off the case, my answer is no. And if your next question was going to be 'Who would be a suitable replacement?' my answer would be that there's no one on the force I dislike enough to saddle with this."

Shannon chuckled. "We both know that's not true. But look, I don't want your sense of pride to get you killed." He stared at Wallace. When she didn't respond, he smiled and nodded slowly. "Fine. So let's look at the plus side of the ledger."

Wallace knew he was going to keep her on the case. He wouldn't bother taking the time to explain his reasoning in such detail if he had already decided to replace her. She should have felt elated, but she felt only worry, instead.

"Although I'm in the distinct minority on this, personally, I think your relationship with Craig Stephens is an asset. You will be seen as someone who is not inherently predisposed against the suspect, someone who has a foot in both camps, so to speak, more willing to take an evenhanded view of things and conduct an unbiased investigation, someone willing to go where the facts lead instead of leading the facts where the prosecution wants them to go."

"Pardon me for saying so, Chief Shannon, but that's a really subtle point, a really slender reed to hang something this important on."

"It *is* a subtle point, but in today's climate I'm convinced it's important. It'll be the kind of thing that lodges in the public consciousness on an instinctive level, so it will exert a quiet but powerful influence. And, if need be, I've got enough access to the media to make sure that point gets made as explicitly as we need it to be."

Shannon reached around her and raised the screen on the laptop. He studied the ugly picture as it sprang back into view.

"That was an awfully short list of positives, Chief Shannon."

"There's one other thing." He pulled his attention away from the picture and walked over to the window. He turned his head and spoke to her over his shoulder. "Burley doesn't want you on this case, but he also says you're the best person for the job."

Wallace looked back at the picture. She had no trouble staring down a gun-wielding, meth-addled carjacker, but compliments made her feel uneasy and shy. "Thank you," she mumbled at the tabletop.

"I didn't need him to tell me that." He gave her the questioning look again. "But I do need to tell you this. No matter how this investigation comes out, you're going to be one of the bad guys. If Pitkin goes down, you were part of a scheme. If he's ultimately cleared, people will accuse you of shaving points, of throwing the game."

"I know."

"And you can live with that?"

"I *am* living with it. I'm afraid of punishing an innocent man just like I'm afraid of letting a guilty one go free. Those things I could *not* live with."

"That's exactly what I wanted to hear. You'll have whatever and whoever you need to get this done properly. And while I want you to take the time to do it right—meaning zero mistakes—I also want this case out of my hair and out of your hands and on the DA's desk as soon as is humanly possible."

"Understood." Wallace didn't like the look she saw on the chief's face. She could tell he felt sorry for her.

"And, even with the advantages of having you as the shot caller on this investigation, we're still taking a risk." He walked over and stood by her chair. "I'm going all in with this decision. I'm betting everything on Hartman, to win."

Wallace opened her mouth to speak, but he waved her off.

"One last thing. Because we have what appears to be very convincing DNA evidence putting Pitkin at the scene of the crime, standing in very close proximity to the victim, pressure is already mounting to close out our part in this investigation. To just put everything in the hands of the prosecutor and let her and her investigators flesh out what's left of the case." He pushed the computer to the side and leaned against the edge of the little table. "Think of this as a test question. How long do you think I should resist that pressure, Detective Hartman?"

"As long as there's a chance that caving in would look like a rush to judgment." She looked him squarely in the eye.

"I'm counting on you to understand, in very practical terms, the difference between a rush to judgment and a sprint to the truth."

"I think I'm clear on what you're telling me, Chief Shannon."

"I'll want you to brief *me*. Directly." He repeatedly jabbed the first two fingers of his left hand against his chest. "Every evening. I'll want a recap of the previous twenty-four hours."

"Yes, sir."

"What's your next step?"

"I need to get a warrant from a judge in Pointe Coupee Parish, so I can search Craig Stephens's lake house on False River."

"If I'm not mistaken, Burley has been beavering away on that very matter, while you and I have been having our little chat."

NINE

"I'll stay, if you want me to," Mason said, setting his coffee cup in the sink. "I can always reschedule my morning appointments."

They were standing in Wallace's kitchen. He had stopped on his way to his office, bringing the morning paper with him. Together, they had listened to news reports on the radio. As demonstrations in support of Pitkin spread across Baton Rouge, counter-demonstrations demanding Pitkin's swift conviction and execution were springing up as well. There were relatively few of the latter, although Wallace feared that could soon change.

"Thanks, but I'll be fine. No sense in both of us getting carted off by the torch-and-pitchfork crowd." She gave him a strained smile and a gentle push toward the door. "Besides, you've got a jealous mistress waiting for you."

After the case that nearly cost him his life and the use of his left arm, Mason left his years-long position with the DEA and moved from Washington to Baton Rouge to be near Wallace. Two months ago, he had opened his own business—a cybersecurity consulting firm that allowed him to use his background and his government contacts on behalf of private companies.

The new venture—what Wallace had begun to call his jealous mistress—hoovered up nearly every waking minute of his time.

"I'll call . . . someday," she said, giving him a rueful look as he stepped into the carport.

"That's what you tell all the guys." He opened the back door of his car and set his satchel on the floor.

"But I'm lying to most of them."

"Are you sure you're okay?" He climbed behind the wheel.

"I'd say if I weren't. Promise."

Wallace watched through the screen door as he backed out of her driveway.

Once his car disappeared down the street, she walked back into her den to finish reading the news. Lulu, one of her two cats, was napping on top of the paper. Boy Howdy, her other cat, was perched on a windowsill, his head swiveling in short frantic arcs, tracking the movements of the backyard critters.

Wallace pulled Lulu onto her lap and read back through all the stories related to the case. The Pitkin arrest was front-page news. It covered much of page two, as well, and a significant portion of the op-ed page.

The fact that Marioneaux appeared to have been asphyxiated was reported, but the precise details of how that had been accomplished did not appear in any of the stories.

The circumstances of Pitkin's arrest, however, were very public thanks to Marla's YouTube video, which Wallace had watched. It made her feel strange to see herself on camera. And, unfortunately, it showed exactly what had happened: Eddie affably encountering the white priest and his companions, Eddie calmly and logically laying out the facts of his grievances, and then Eddie being arrested, cuffed, and marched off by two white police officers. To anyone who saw only the video but didn't know the whole story, it looked as if he was being smacked down for trying to advance his reparations agenda.

By the time the real reason for the arrest came out, the video had already gone viral and tempers had begun to flare. Judging by the increasingly dire reports she and Mason had listened to, the truth seemed to be adding fuel to the fire. Red-hot rhetoric was spewing from every quarter accusing the police of being part of a plot to silence and intimidate an important figure in the quest for racial justice.

And, thanks to Marla's nice sharp close-up of the laying on of hands, Wallace had become the face of the oppressor—just as Chief Shannon had feared. The paper had run the shot, taken from the video, showing Wallace at the precise moment she was slapping on the cuffs.

She set the paper aside and tried to think through the implications of her newfound celebrity. Mostly, she worried about whether her mother and her younger brother, Lex, a Catholic priest who pastored a parish in the eastern suburbs of Baton Rouge, would become the target of people wanting to strike at her.

The prospect of threats against her loved ones had set off a low current of anxiety that kept her awake for most of the night.

It had been a long time since she had driven out to False River. As its name implied, it wasn't really a river—at least, not anymore. At one time, it had been a bend in the Mississippi. Now it was just one of the many oxbow lakes the titanic waterway had sloughed off when it periodically jumped its banks and carved out new channels over the course of the ages.

For generations, False River had been a getaway for people in the parishes surrounding Baton Rouge. Most of the shoreline was dotted with fishing camps and weekend homes, but there were still a few stretches along the west bank that were thinly populated and relatively undeveloped. Because of that, Wallace knew it was entirely possible for someone to go unnoticed for a few days, even when the lake was thronged with visitors.

Dennis Halsey, one of the department's newest and youngest crime-scene investigators, rode with her. For reasons she couldn't put her finger on, Dennis had taken a shine to her after their first meeting a few months back.

And he was a talker. He had talked Wallace's ear off during the trip out to the lake. Even though her contributions to the conversation were rare and perfunctory, he didn't seem to notice, which left Wallace free to stay lost in her own thoughts.

A few blocks before the road that ran alongside the lake, Wallace pulled into the parking lot of a property management company that handled rentals for most of the houses around the lake.

"I'll be right back."

"No prob." Dennis pulled out his phone to make a call. Wallace could hear him talking before her door was even closed.

It was cool inside the office. A collection of stuffed mallards and trophy-sized largemouth bass studded the grooved wooden paneling behind the woman sitting at the desk beyond the counter. She was about Wallace's age, dressed in khakis and a polo shirt with a name tag that read: MARYBETH. She looked up with an expectant smile.

"I'm Wallace Hartman, a detective with the Baton Rouge police. I'm hoping you can help me with something." She held her credentials toward the woman.

"Is this official business?"

"I'm trying to find out if anyone was in residence at either of these addresses in the last several days."

She offered MaryBeth her card. The addresses of the houses she was interested in were scribbled on the back.

"We respect our tenants' privacy, so I ain't telling any names without a court order."

"I may not—" Wallace began, but MaryBeth cut her off.

"My husband's the chief of police here in New Roads and I tell him the same as I'm telling you whenever he comes sniffing around here looking for information. He thinks I'll play fast and loose with *him* just 'cause I let him play fast and loose with *me*, but that ain't the way I roll."

The woman grinned and stared, clearly expecting Wallace to laugh at her wordplay. Her grin remained frozen in place as Wallace stared back.

"I may not need any names, if the houses were unoccupied." She held the card out again.

MaryBeth took the card, then went back to her desk. "Gimme me just a minute, Detective. May I offer you something to drink?" she asked as she consulted her desktop computer.

"No, thank you."

"Neither of these has been occupied for a few months," Mary-Beth said after a minute of silence. "The one that's just a few lots away was tied up in foreclosure for a while. The bank took it back, and it's just sitting there. They don't want to fool with trying to rent it out, which is a shame, because I still get inquiries about it all the time. Just last week some fella offered me good money to let him have it for a solid month, but the bank didn't even bother to return my call when I let 'em know. The other house, the one to the north, it's a bit pricey for that side of the lake. The fella that owns it, I keep trying to get him to come down on the lease, but he's afraid he'll get a bunch of broke-ass college kids in there who'll trash the place. Which, I get that, but if the house doesn't rent, then he ain't making any money and I sure ain't, either."

"Thank you," Wallace said, making for the door before MaryBeth could share any more clever observations about her and her husband's private life. She would check the houses anyway.

The trip from the rental office to Craig's fishing camp took several minutes. The lake was twelve miles long, nearly a half mile wide, and shaped like the letter C, with the open side of the C facing east. Craig's house was on the west bank, near the middle of the curve, in one of the thinly populated areas. The edges of the old asphalt road, sun bleached to a silvery gray, were crumbling into the grassy shoulder.

One of the houses Wallace had asked MaryBeth about was north

of Craig's place. The other one was a few hundred yards to the
south—the direction she was approaching from.

"Let's check for signs of recent activity," she said, pulling into the
driveway of the southernmost house. She peeked into the mailbox
at the street, then approached the front door, while Dennis looked
inside the dumpster in the carport.

"Empty," he called out, and then moved off to check the side yard
to the north.

Wallace knocked on the front door and waited several seconds.
When no one answered, she walked around to the south side of the
house, looking at the windows and letting her eyes comb the ground
for fresh cigarette butts and other signs that someone may have been
on the property in the last few days.

As she rounded the corner into the backyard, she saw Dennis approaching from the opposite direction.

"Anything."

"Not a thing. But this is a pretty cool place. The lake, I mean.
I've never been out here, before. Have you?"

"Years ago." Wallace stole a quick look northward, toward Craig's
place. Even if anyone had occupied the residence here during the
past weekend, they would have been too far away to be of any help.
"Let's move on?"

They returned to her car and cruised slowly up the road. Craig's
house sat about forty feet back from the road. The thick layer of
loose white shells that formed the driveway made hollow popping
noises under her tires.

The place was at least sixty years old and it looked it. Wallace
had been inside a few times and, while the interior was more up-to-
date than the exterior, the whole business was rather plain. Craig
had told her that he felt nervous about being conspicuous with his
money. She knew he could buy the twenty most expensive homes
on the lake without breathing hard, but he was the private type.
Consequently, his place stayed old and unassuming.

They climbed out of the car. Wallace popped the trunk and Dennis started hauling his cases out. Wallace remained by her open door, one hand on the doorframe and the other on the roof. She looked past the house to the lake beyond.

The breeze blowing off the water carried the faint scent of fish and marsh mud. It was intoxicating. It made her think of all the times she and her family came to the lake during her growing-up summers.

An ancient pickup truck with clattering valves and a collection of grimy junk in the bed trundled by on the road behind her. She listened as the rumble of its engine grew fainter.

"Dennis, let's do a quick check-around and then I'll walk to the house just north of here. You wait here for the deputy who's bringing the search warrant. A key to the front door should be arriving any minute, courtesy of Eddie Pitkin's lawyer."

"Got it." He walked back toward the car.

The shells in the driveway squealed and scraped under her boots as she walked up to the carport. The trash bin was empty.

The carport ended at a storeroom. A breezeway between the storeroom and the house led to a weathered wooden staircase that followed the slope of the yard down to a boardwalk that ended at a floating dock at the edge of the lake. Tubular steel swimming pool ladders disappeared into the water from each end of the dock.

Wallace paused at the top of the stairs and looked across a vacant lot toward the house to the north. The treads of the steps flexed gently beneath her as she descended.

At the bottom, she turned and looked back at Craig's house. Dennis was scrutinizing the side yard to the south. A big screened porch covered most of the rear of the structure—empty, except for several folding lawn chairs stacked against the wall next to the back door.

The wind picked up, so she took an elastic band from her pocket and pulled her hair into a ponytail to keep it from blowing into her eyes. She walked along the boardwalk toward the dock, then looked north again, toward the neighboring house.

It was a newer structure and parts of its dock looked as if they had been recently replanked. The sight line from where she stood to the back porch of the nearby house was unobstructed. Anyone sitting here would be easily visible to someone on the back porch of the other house. Binoculars would probably be needed in order to make a clear identification.

Wallace waded through the ankle-high grass of the empty lot to the other house. Once upon a time, there had been a building on the lot, but brick footings and a rectangular-shaped bare patch were all that remained.

Normally, Wallace would have trudged back up to the street and knocked on the front door. Lot-to-lot shortcuts were the privilege of little kids and longtime neighbors. Strangers were expected to observe basic lakeside etiquette and approach from the street. But because the house was supposed to be unoccupied, she hiked through the yard to the back porch. She tried the door. It was locked.

A gravel pathway led around to the side of the carport. She lifted the lid on the heavy plastic dumpster that was pushed up against the rear wall. Beer cans and fast-food boxes covered the bottom. The containers were recent enough to still have the smell of their contents.

Wallace wheeled the bin into the carport and pulled on a pair of latex gloves. She dumped the trash onto the concrete and poked through it for some clue as to who had left it. Nothing. She pushed everything back into the dumpster and set it against the wall. Before they left, she would bag the contents and haul it in to have it printed. Maybe she would get lucky.

The carport door and the front door were locked. Pleated sheer curtains blocked her view through the panes in the door. All of the other windows were screened and curtained, as well.

When she looked back toward Craig's house she saw a blue Range Rover and a gray sheriff's department SUV with light bars parked out front.

TEN

H ello, Monte. The investigator business must be pretty good these days." Wallace nodded in the direction of the Range Rover.

"Not bad. Not bad," he said distractedly.

Monte was a former East Baton Rouge sheriff's deputy who now worked exclusively as the investigator for Tasha Kovacovich, the lawyer representing Eddie Pitkin. Wallace had prevailed upon the lawyer to have someone bring a key and the security codes to Craig's lake house. She could have called a locksmith, but that would change the state of the locks more than a key would and might obscure something she needed to see.

She also could have forced the door open to execute her search warrant, but that too might damage something that could later turn out to be important, so she had asked for the key. She had gone through Eddie's lawyer to avoid further contact with Craig.

The door from the carport into the house stood open and Dennis was scrolling through the memory on the security system keypad. Monte stood as close to the action as he could without touching the crime-scene tape Dennis had stretched across the threshold, and used his phone to record what the tech was doing with the security system.

"Excuse us, a minute, would you, Monte?" Wallace waited until the investigator moved several paces away. "Have you found anything?" she asked Dennis in a low voice.

"Someone entered and exited several times starting at two o'clock last Friday afternoon, and ending at eight seventeen on Sunday morning. Mostly in and out of the back door. Nothing since then."

"What about between seven and ten P.M. on Friday?"

"The last exit was at five forty-three P.M., followed by a reentry at seven oh eight P.M. After that, the system was set to Home. Lots of activity on Saturday, ending with a final entry at eight thirty-eight P.M. Nothing after that until eight seventeen Sunday morning, when it was set to Away. That was it until I opened it up just now."

"Have you checked anything for prints yet?"

"Yeah. The doorknob and this keypad. When I'm done with this," he pointed at the security system panel, "I'll dust and tape all the doorknobs, fridge handles, faucet taps—all your basic touch points—then I'll do the lawn chairs on the back porch. We might get a few clear shots. Who knows? You got a list of people we need to get elimination prints from?"

"I'll work that up and get it to you. Did you find anything on the keypad buttons?"

"Well, they've obviously been touched, because a lot of activity was inputted, but I couldn't lift anything. That's the first thing I checked after Monte gave me the key," Dennis said, scribbling something on a tablet strapped to his right thigh. "But the buttons were either knuckled or the pad might have been wiped, because everything on it is smudged."

"Well, that's just lovely."

Wallace looked toward the gray SUV parked on the street. "I'll be right back."

"Hey, Detective," Monte called out as she passed him. He eyed her quickly, head to toe. "Tasha K wanted me to tell you that she's happy to play ball on this house-key business because you're trying to verify an alibi. Anything after this, though, you're on your own." He shot her a pained look.

Wallace stared at him like she smelled something bad. She thought about arguing with him, just to set the record straight—that she wasn't looking to prove or disprove an alibi—but she knew Monte was trying to bait her into an argument to see if he could shake some interesting information loose or goad her into saying something imprudent.

"We didn't need her help, Monte. I could have used a crowbar to crack the door open, so the way I see it, by having you bustle on over with the key we're doing you and your client's brother a favor. Not the other way around."

He raised his hands in surrender. "Hey, don't shoot the messenger. You know me. Just call me pushover Monte. But TK? Whoa. I'm actually surprised she rolled over so easy on this. I mean, you know her. A day without making somebody cry is like a day without sunshine."

"Does she know you say things like that?"

"Yeah. Probably." He grinned and then looked back over his shoulder to where Dennis was working.

Wallace knew that Monte was telling the truth about how his boss operated. If Tasha ever asked Wallace to return the favor and Wallace balked, a press conference would be called and everyone with a pulse would get an earful about how playing nice with the police, in hopes of getting to the truth, was a fool's errand. That oppression was the only dividend an investment of goodwill could be expected to pay—or some such nonsense.

In general, Wallace couldn't stand Tasha. But she didn't think she would hesitate to call her if she ever needed a lawyer to defend her in a criminal proceeding.

"Good to see you, Monte. Please tell your employer . . . something nice from me."

"Yeah, sure. You bet." He gave her another quick once-over, then went back to hovering around the door.

Wallace walked toward the sheriff's vehicle. The deputy was sitting inside, with her door open.

"I'm Wallace Hartman. Thank you for bringing the warrant."

"Not a problem, Detective. I'll hang around for a bit, and then if you don't need anything more I'll head back out on patrol. Here's my number in case you need me after that." She handed Wallace a generic contact card with her name and number hand-printed in a blank space.

When Wallace returned to the house, Dennis was coming in from the back porch.

The faint pine scent of household cleaner dampened Wallace's mood. If Eddie had cleaned away signs of his presence before he vacated the premises, he had done himself no favors.

"Shit."

"Yeah, really. How unlucky is that?" Dennis said, sniffing and twitching his nose.

Wallace began a slow, methodical tour of the house while Dennis finished his evidence gather.

All of the windows were locked and none looked as if they had been forced open. It was the same for all of the doors. And they were all wired to the security system.

As Dennis packed his gear, Wallace walked out to the front yard and called Glenn Marioneaux. She got his voicemail again and hung up. The man's unwillingness to participate was becoming irksome.

She grabbed a large evidence bag from her trunk and hustled back to the neighboring house to the north. She emptied the contents of the dumpster into the bag and then returned to her car.

Wallace was beginning to think the search might have been for nothing. It would have been nice to find a newspaper with Eddie's prints and the relevant dates. Or even a bag of newly purchased slip locks.

The security system showed that someone had been in and out of the house from the Friday before until the Monday after Marioneaux was killed, but without something tying Eddie to the lake house at the critical time or pointing an incriminating finger at him, the whole trip looked like a waste. Maybe the trash from the dumpster next door had been handled by someone whose prints were already on file. Someone who might have seen something useful.

They were six blocks from the police station in Baton Rouge when her phone buzzed. It was the department's crime lab.

"Detective Hartman? This is Leola Cassidy. I'm a lab tech in the CSI Division. I wouldn't normally call directly with test results, but I know this case of yours is real touchy, so I thought you could use this sooner than you might come across it in my formal reports."

"Leola, this case is radioactive. You've got my full attention."

"We're still not done examining the victim's clothing, however, on the exterior of his shirt, on the back and shoulders only, we found a fair number of fine, pale glassy filaments."

"Fabric filaments?"

"Insulation."

Wallace pulled into the parking lot of a garden supply store and killed the engine.

"These are relatively short fibers, so I'm thinking it's blown-in insulation. The type you'd find in an attic, not the longer, straighter variety that comes glued to the paper-backed batts you'd see stapled up between wall studs."

"If I brought you fibers for comparison?" Wallace's heart started to race.

"We could determine if the fibers have the same chemical composition and cross-sectional shape, and we could verify the shade and hue of any dyes or pigments that impregnate the fibers. Do you have a source in mind?"

"In fact, I do."

She speed-dialed LeAnne. The call was picked up after one ring.

"Can you pull off the surveillance of Tonya Lennar?"

"Sure. She's just making her cleaning rounds."

"Meet me in Burley's office as soon as you can."

ELEVEN

Jason Burley looked up as Wallace and LeAnne filed into his office. He was on the phone, so he motioned for them to sit.

"I've been watching the news and I read this morning's paper," he said, without preamble, as soon as he ended the call. "I want you in body armor, twenty-four-seven, until this investigation is over." He pointed at Wallace.

"Even in the shower?" Wallace asked.

"Especially in the shower."

She took his reaction to her stupid joke as a sign that he wasn't letting the case get to him.

"We need some help," she said.

"I'm all ears."

"We need a warrant to search Eddie Pitkin's house and cars and we need it really fast. And the lake house on False River will have to be searched again."

"I'm still all ears."

Wallace explained Leola Cassidy's discovery and what she thought it meant.

"So how do you want to divvy this up?" he asked.

"I'll go back out to the lake house and take Dennis with me. Can you and LeAnne and another tech search the Pitkin house?"

"I don't need a chaperone," LeAnne said.

"But you will need someone to run interference for you, because you can bet it's going to be a media extravaganza," Burley said. "So, what are we looking for?" He pulled up the warrant affidavit form on his computer.

"Every piece of clothing from his closet and dressers, anything in a laundry basket," Wallace said, ticking the items off on her fingers. "The lint filter from the dryer, the sink and shower traps, and we'll want the inside of the washing machine swabbed—the filters, the agitator, inner and outer drums, the drain hose, and the standpipe it drains into."

"We need to check the inside of his car," LeAnne said. "And his wife's car, and his eldest daughter's car, especially the surface of the seat belt that would come into contact with the driver's clothing."

Burley gave them a questioning look.

"Plus the trash, inside the house," LeAnne said. "And in the dumpster, with an eye out for lint-roller tapes, discarded clothing, anything that might pick up stray fibers." She looked a Wallace.

Wallace shrugged in agreement.

Wallace hated feeling stupid. She wanted to blame it on all the other things pulling at her—Mason, her mother, the unrest the case was kicking up across Baton Rouge—but maybe she had just missed a trick, plain and simple.

The summer after her junior year in high school, she had worked with her two brothers renovating and restoring older homes in the neighborhoods around LSU. Her elder brother, Martin, had eventually become a home builder and real estate developer. But during those early years, he had stuck to fixing things that were already there, instead of building new things.

Spending all that time with her brothers had been incredible. But the work itself she found frustrating. For the most part, the home-owners they dealt with behaved like spoiled children. They changed their minds every time the wind changed direction, they blamed Martin and his crew for problems that were clearly of their own making, and they pitched a fit over the most inconsequential things.

Martin always handled his clients with a calm, smiling, "Yes, sir," and, "Yes, ma'am." When Wallace had volunteered to slap the shit out of a chronically obnoxious whiner, Martin laughed at her and told her she was cute. On days like that, she had wanted to slap the shit out of him too.

But it had been a learning experience, as well. She had come across all sorts of features in older homes that were rare or nonexis-tent in newer ones. One thing that had been common back then was attic access panels in the ceilings of some closets. They were like trapdoors—usually a two-foot square of plywood resting in a frame crafted from quarter-round baseboard molding. All one had to do was push up on the panel and lay it to the side to gain access to the attic.

Craig's lake house seemed about the right vintage to have such a thing. She should have thought to check for it the first time she went. She had seen the pulldown attic door in the hallway, but it was wired into the alarm system and the alarm system hadn't shown that the attic door was opened during the weekend in question.

Once they arrived back at the lake house, Wallace put Dennis to work gathering evidence from the sink and tub drains and tape-rolling the floor for insulation fibers, while she went in search of ceiling panels in the closets.

She moved down the hallway into the first of the three bedrooms. There was no panel in the ceiling of the closet. There were no pan-els in the closets of the second or third bedrooms, either. She was beginning to feel stupid for the second time in one day.

"Detective Hartman?"

Dennis was calling to her from the utility room, just off the car-port. He was on his knees by a large utility sink, using a crescent wrench to disassemble the grease trap.

"Is that what you're looking for?" With his wrench, he pointed toward a pantry in the opposite corner. "If I hadn't been down here on the floor, looking up at such a sharp angle, I don't think I would have seen it."

Wallace stepped over to the pantry. The top shelf was stacked high with ratty old boxes and a collection of cleaning products. As her eyes adjusted to the light, she could see the corner of a frame above some of the boxes.

The shelves were half-inch plywood squares, resting on one-by-two wooden rails screwed to the pantry walls.

"Dennis?" Wallace said. "Leave the sink for now. We need to—"

"I'm on it." He set his wrench aside and pulled a tape roller from his kit and tape rolled the floor in the bottom of the pantry and for a radius of several feet around the doorway. Wallace bagged the tape strips as he handed them to her.

"Now let's take the stuff off the shelves," she said.

They donned blue latex gloves and then, assembly line fashion, they removed the contents of the shelves. Once all but the top shelf had been emptied, they lifted out the shelves.

"I want that photographed, from above. It looks pretty dusty up there, so if any of those cleaning products have been moved we might be able to tell if they weren't put back exactly on top of their original footprints. After that, I want the tops of the products and the shelf tape rolled. If that access panel was moved, it's possible that stray insulation fibers could have come floating down out of the attic."

Standing on a step stool, Dennis hovered his cell phone camera, with its light on, above and among the contents of the shelf, documenting the items and whatever lay on the surface of the shelf around them. When he was done, they removed the items and then the shelf itself.

Using the rails as footholds, Wallace climbed up to the panel. She pushed on the plywood, expecting it to resist, but it lifted smoothly. Wisps of insulation floated down around her. She pushed out her lower lip and blew the filaments away from her face and then laid the panel to one side of the opening and climbed higher. Once her hips were through, she sat on the edge of the opening and then handed the panel down to Dennis.

"Bag it. We'll print it later."

"Aye, Cap'n," he said, holding it by the edges as he took it from her.

Wallace turned her head to look around the gloomy attic. An oval louvered sidelight in one of the gables let in enough light for her to see. A piece of heavy wire screen was U-nailed over the sidelight, and the screen itself was covered with dust-laden cobwebs. No one had entered or exited that way.

"See anything?" Dennis asked.

"Not so far." Slowly, she turned, scanning the attic in the other direction. The spaces between the ceiling joists were filled with blown-in insulation. Behind her, about twenty feet away, she could see a collection of dusty cardboard boxes, household odds and ends, and old sporting equipment. It was clustered haphazardly on the small plywood apron surrounding the pulldown door in the hallway ceiling.

Pulling her feet under her, she stood and stepped gingerly from one ceiling joist to the next. Standpipes came up through the ceiling and disappeared into the roof, but the openings were too small for anyone to get through. She located the sidelight on the other side of the house. It too was covered with a heavy screen that looked as if it hadn't been touched in forever.

She was about to admit defeat and climb down out of the stuffy space when she saw it in the part of the attic that would be above the rear of the carport. The insulation was piled higher there. It looked the way the ground did after you buried something, when there was too much dirt to fill the hole and it formed a mound.

Carefully, testing each joist with her weight before taking the next step, and using her hands to grab hold of the rafters above for balance, Wallace made her way over. The faint clink of metal on metal came up through the opening in the pantry ceiling as Dennis resumed his assault on the sink trap in the utility room below.

Using a finger-sized flashlight, she studied the piled-up insulation. It looked different from the expanse of insulation surrounding the mound, which was settled and had developed a uniform discoloration. The insulation in the mound itself had obviously been moved around. It was fluffier and parts of it had a fresher color. Carefully, probing with her gloved fingers, she scooped the insulation aside, revealing an access panel, like the one in the ceiling of the pantry.

"Dennis?"

"Right here." His voice carried up through the trapdoor. "What did you find?"

"At the back of the carport, there's a storeroom. See if you can open it. Dust the knob for prints before you touch it."

Wallace scooped away the remaining insulation and worked her fingers into the crevice around the edge of the panel. She pulled it from the frame and total darkness stared back at her. The smell of mildew wafted up into the air around her and somewhere down in the blackness a doorknob jiggled. She shone her light into the opening. Boxes and old bed frames cluttered the storeroom. The rattling sound got louder.

"Detective Hartman? Can you hear me?" His voice was muffled by the storeroom door.

"Yes. What do you see?" she shouted.

"The storeroom door is locked, but it's just a knob lock."

Wallace shone the beam of her flashlight around the interior doorframe. It was *not* wired to the security system.

She filled a small evidence bag with insulation, then retraced her steps to the opening in the ceiling of the pantry and lowered herself into the utility room. She called Burley and LeAnne to tell them what she had found, but her calls went straight to voicemail.

She found Dennis outside. He was hauling a couple of evidence containers toward the rear of Wallace's vehicle. She reached into her pocket and pressed the trunk release on her key fob. The trunk lid popped open just as Dennis arrived at the car.

The sound of a passing vehicle drew her attention, and she

watched as a mud-splattered SUV with a red plastic kayak fastened into a roof rack cruised past, slowing as it approached the house to the north. The right turn signal started blinking and Wallace took off at a fast stride.

As she drew near the other house, her phone buzzed. It was Glenn Marioneaux.

"This is Detective Hartman."

"I know you've been looking for me," he said.

"Where are you, Mr. Marioneaux?"

"On my way home. Sorry I had to skip out on you like that, but I wasn't in the mood for a bunch of police procedure, under the circumstances. You claimed you knew what losing family that way can be like, so I took you at your word and withdrew for a bit, to gather myself together."

"I hope you're calling to tell me you're in the mood right now?"

A loud, sustained car horn sounded through the phone. "Go, goddammit. It's green." A faint chorus of other horns joined Glenn's. "I just got a talking-to from mommy dearest about stiff upper lips and doing the proper things and all that crap. Maybe she'll shut the fuck up if I let you get your hooks into me for a while."

It sounded to Wallace as if the mother-son relationship wasn't as tender as their behavior at the crime scene seemed to indicate. "May I assume you're in okay condition to be behind the wheel?"

"You may. Last night? Definitely not. Today? Just peachy."

"Then let's make a plan. Where would you like to meet?"

"Not at my office. Can you meet me at my home in, say, two hours?"

"That's fine. I might be a few minutes late. Make sure you wait for me." She ended the call just as she arrived in front of the vacant house.

The driver of the SUV had a phone wedged between his shoulder and his ear and he appeared to be rooting around in his glove compartment as Wallace came up to his window. When he raised his head and saw her, a look of panic flickered across his face and he pushed his gearshift into Reverse.

She held up her badge and shook her head. The driver seemed to dither for a few seconds. She drew her thumb across her throat, signaling for him to kill the engine, then motioned for him to lower his window.

He dropped his phone into the center console as his window came down.

"What can I do for you, Officer?" He was white, average build, midthirties. His face was covered with a few days of stubble.

She let her eyes roam freely over the driver and the interior of the cab before she spoke. "I'm Wallace Hartman, a detective with the Baton Rouge City Police. Is this your house?" The smell of pizza drifted out of the window of the SUV.

"Not exactly." The man visibly relaxed. He checked his rearview mirror, then looked through the windshield toward the front door of the house, finally settling his gaze back on Wallace. "Is there some sort of problem here? You're a little out of your jurisdiction, aren't you, Detective?"

"I'm trying to pin down the whereabouts of an individual on a certain day at a certain time."

"Would I be the individual you're referring to?" He smiled. It was the kind of disarming smile she knew some guys practiced in the mirror.

"No. You're not." Out of habit, she continued to scan the interior of the vehicle. The pizza box on the passenger seat was from the same restaurant as the one she had bagged from the dumpster. She looked past the driver's seat into the rear. The seat backs were folded down even though he carried no cargo. "Would you have a few minutes to talk? Right now?" Her gaze locked on to his. "Just pull the rest of the way into the carport. We can chat right here in the driveway."

"Sure. Give me a second."

As he moved forward, Wallace studied the rear of the vehicle. A Louisiana license plate was affixed to the rear bumper. She memorized the number. Someone had finger-traced a message into the film of dust below the rear windshield: "Test dirt. Do not wash off."

"You have kids?" Wallace asked as the man strolled in her direction.

"No. Is that who you're looking for? Kids?"

Wallace pointed toward the inscription on the back of his vehicle.

He snorted. "That was those smartass punks hanging around the service station down the road. They been trying to dog me out of a few bucks to let them wash this baby. That's where I was coming back from, just now. Peter Ecclestone." He extended his hand.

"Peter Ecclestone," Wallace repeated. "Rock of the church, if my altar girl Latin is correct. That's a heavy name."

"I crumbled under the weight years ago." The smile was back. "So, who are we looking for, and how can I help?"

"I take it you've been staying in this house? But don't worry," she said when she saw him flinch. "I'm not going to hand you over to MaryBeth at the rental office."

"I sort of forgot to turn in the extra key, the last time I rented the place."

"And they must not have changed the security codes."

He gave her a sly shrug. "What can I say?"

"You can say if you were here, at the house, this past Friday, between four in the afternoon and ten in the evening?"

"As a matter of fact I was. I usually don't come around here until after I know the rental office is closed for the night, but that day I went a little off my plan. I needed a quiet place to metabolize an extra-heavy dose of some pretty high-spirited vodka. So, I was here from late, late Thursday night until . . . oh, I don't think I left again until just before lunchtime on Saturday."

"While you were here, and conscious, did you happen to notice anyone at any of the adjacent houses, or on the docks behind those houses?"

Peter hesitated, nodding and pursing his lips. "There was a fella at the little place just south of here. That relic right over there." He pointed toward Craig's house.

"Can you describe him?"

"Sure." Ecclestone looked toward the back of his SUV. "Can I get you something to drink? Would you care to sit? I can offer you some pizza. Plus, it's cooler inside."

"No, thank you, Mr. Ecclestone. This is not a social call. Just tell me about the man you saw next door."

"I'm guessing he was in his mid-fifties. Black. Just kicked back on the dock casting a lure out into the water, over and over again. A brew sitting on top of the ice chest next to his chair. You know, just your basic day at the lake."

"You're very observant, Mr. Ecclestone."

"I have to be. I'm an artist. Watercolors, pencil sketches, socially conscious nature and wildlife photography. Things like that."

Wallace had no idea what socially conscious wildlife photography was.

"Is that what brought you out here in the first place?"

"Mm-hmm. You can always find something interesting around these old-time vacation spots. Animal and human."

He tilted his head from one side to the other and eyed her, like he was sizing her up for a portrait. Wallace assumed this was a standard part of his pickup routine.

"I thought about trying to get something down on paper, with that old guy next door. Kind of iconic, you know. But he was too far away to get any detail. I walked partway over there to see if he'd let me sit on the dock and work, but then I decided I wasn't really in the mood to talk to anybody, so I just let it go. Plus, I still wasn't feeling super great."

"Can you remember when you saw him out on the dock?"

"Actually, I saw him a bunch of times. He spent most of the day on Friday out there, and at least part of Saturday morning."

"Can you say what times Friday?"

"Well, he was going in and out, but he was out at least part of the time until early evening. I wasn't watching him the whole time, but I had my camera up on the tripod, so I'd see him out of the corner of my eye, so to speak."

"Was he ever away from the dock for long periods?"

"Nah. A few minutes here and there, but mainly he was just lounging out there. Reading a book, throwing his line out, not catching a damn thing that I could see."

"If I showed you pictures of the person I'm interested in, do you think you'd be able to say whether he was the man you saw on the dock?"

"I can try."

Wallace pulled out her phone and stood next to Ecclestone as she scrolled through a series of pictures she had put together before her first trip to the lake today, in case she found someone who might have seen anybody. A few of the pictures were of Craig, some were of her next-door neighbor Albert Mills and his partner, and two were of Eddie. There were about eight shots, sequenced in random order.

"One more time?"

Wallace swiped through the pictures again.

"Him and him," he said, picking out both pictures of Eddie.

"You sure?" Wallace asked, intentionally putting a note of skepticism in her voice to test his conviction.

"It was a few days ago, but, yeah, I'm pretty sure."

"He's a bit of a celebrity. Maybe you recognize him from TV or the internet?"

"Nah. I don't do TV. And if he ain't on the sports page, I'm not gonna see him in the papers." He shook his head. "He some kind of bygone entertainer or something?"

"Not exactly." Wallace held the picture up for several more seconds to see if Peter would change his mind. "Do you think he saw you?"

"Not that I could tell. I would have been coming from behind and above him, and I only went about twenty or thirty yards in his direction when I decided to bail. He didn't seem to notice me, but there's no way to know for certain."

"There's a lot riding on this, Mr. Ecclestone. I'll need you to drive into Baton Rouge to make a formal statement. At some point after that, you may be called upon to testify in open court. Would you be willing to do that?"

"You gonna be the one taking statements?" One eyebrow went up.

"Did you happen to take any photographs of the gentleman on the dock?" she asked, deflecting his question.

"No. I don't think so." He massaged his chin, looking thoughtfully into the distance. He brought his gaze back to Wallace. "No. Can't help you there. See, before I could make any money—before I'd be able to sell a photograph of somebody—I'd have to get 'em to sign a release form."

"You hesitated, just now," she said, using her standard shake-the-tree technique.

"No, but like I said, I had my camera on a tripod, taking shots through the open window up in the back bedroom. I got some pretty decent images with my long lens. Things happening out and about out on the lake. Clouds, birds, boats cutting up the water." He looked out over the lake. "Did you have a particular time in mind, to do this statement business?"

"Let's agree on between seven and seven thirty this evening." Wallace maintained eye contact until he nodded. "If we need to change the time, here's my contact information." She handed him one of her cards. "How can I get in touch with you?"

With his left hand, he extracted one of his own business cards from his shirt pocket, holding it scissor-style between his index and middle fingers as he offered it to her. "Cell phone, email, website, studio address—it's all there."

It was a cheap, home-print job, done on flimsy stock with tiny perforation bumps along the edges. Wallace studied the information on the card. His studio was in Cavanaugh, a quaint little town about an hour north and west of Baton Rouge.

"I was actually thinking of pulling up stakes, even before you outed me as a trespasser," he said. "This is a good time of year to be out in the wild with a camera, so I've got a list of other places between here and home where I can get some good work done, as I head north back toward Cavanaugh."

"This is important business, Mr. Ecclestone. Not something that can be put off until who knows when."

"I understand." He laced his fingers together and put his hands on top of his head, elbows pointing forward.

To Wallace's eye, it looked like a calculated display of boyish vulnerability.

"You look like you probably know your way around the outdoors. You ever been on a photo shoot way out in the wild areas, Detective?"

"What else do you remember about the man you saw on the dock?" she asked, growing weary of his attempts to turn the interview into a hookup.

"You're really getting my curiosity fired up. Who is this guy? Is he wanted for something?"

"He's someone I'm interested in."

"Then I guess it's your lucky day that I just happened to turn up." He smiled, pleased with himself.

"I don't think so." Her nostrils flared and she shook her head, trying to ward off a smirk.

Peter's eyes lit up at the prospect of a lively go-round of verbal jousting. "Well, somebody here is lucky."

"This place is supposed to be unoccupied." She jabbed her thumb at the house. "But there was trash in the dumpster and it smelled kind of fresh."

Peter's face fell a bit.

"Beer cans are excellent for holding fingerprints. I bagged everything, thinking maybe I'd turn up some prints that were already on file and they would lead me to whoever had been hanging around here."

Ecclestone's eyes tracked up and to the left. One hand came up and rubbed his face, partly covering a sheepish grin. "That might have worked."

"Is that a confession?"

"I plead young and stupid."

"Why don't you just tell me the rest of what you saw, Mr. Ecclestone?" She put an edge of impatience in her voice. "What are you holding back?" Sometimes a stern question could motivate people to overcome any reluctance they might feel about telling the whole story.

His mouth pulled to one side, and Wallace could tell by his unfocused gaze that he was engaged in some kind of internal debate.

"Well, the only thing I can say for sure is that the lights came on in his place, once it got dark." He bobbled his head back and forth a few times. "I could see movement. You know, shadows past the windows, but I couldn't swear who I was seeing. It just looked like somebody moving around in there. And I wasn't really watching the place the whole time. I saw some things, but there were times when my eyes and my thoughts were elsewhere."

"Has there been anyone here at the house with you?"

"Just me," he said, with a nonchalant, can-you-believe-it look.

"Do you know if he left the house that night?"

"Nah. At some point I fell asleep in one of the loungers on the back porch."

"Can you recall whether any vehicles came or went from the place?"

"It's pretty quiet out here, on this side of the lake, so cars and trucks going by, you can hear 'em, but honestly, I can't say if anybody pulled in or out of the place. I know I didn't *see* anything coming or going."

"Do you have anything else for me, Mr. Ecclestone?"

"I'm afraid you've milked this cow dry, Detective."

She looked at his card again, then slid it into the pocket of her shirt. "Thank you. I've kept you out here and now your pizza is probably ice-cold."

"Don't worry about that. It was good talking to you."

Wallace looked toward the house, then back at Peter. "Between seven and seven thirty. The main police building just south of downtown."

"Oh, I know where it is," he said.

"One more thing," she said as Peter turned toward the house.

He looked back in her direction.

"This may be a little out of my jurisdiction." She gestured toward the lake. "But that won't stop me from coming to look for you." She held his gaze until she was sure he understood the unsaid part of her message.

"Good to meet you, Detective Hartman." He turned away and walked toward his dust-laden SUV.

Wallace watched as he opened the front passenger door and leaned in for his pizza. While he was still absorbed in his task, she headed back to her car. She would need to hustle if she intended to meet Glenn Marioneaux.

As she walked, she tried to put her discoveries into perspective. On one hand, if traces of insulation from the lake house attic showed up on Eddie's clothing or in his home or his car and they looked like the same stuff that was on Marioneaux then it was *possible* Eddie had used the access panels in the pantry and the storeroom to get out of and then back into the lake house without it registering on the alarm system. Peter's testimony that he had seen Eddie on False River late Friday would make a sneak-out-through-the-attic operation look *probable*.

Her frame-up hypothesis would get weak in the knees and Eddie's alibi would look less like a GET-OUT-OF-JAIL-FREE card and more like a confirmation that he had not only killed Herbert Marioneaux, but had also conceived and carried out an elaborate plan to do it.

Under those circumstances, Peter's testimony would be critical to the prosecution.

On the other hand, if no insulation was found, then the chance discovery of an alibi witness would bolster Eddie's innocence and put her frame-up idea back in business and Peter's testimony would be essential to the defense.

Either way, the information in Peter Ecclestone's head was extremely important. Given the "zero mistakes" directive Jack Shannon had issued when he decided to keep her on the case, Wallace wanted Ecclestone's statement to be taken under carefully controlled conditions. At a minimum, she wanted Burley and LeAnne on the interview with her, to make sure no questions were left unasked or unanswered.

It was also true that Ecclestone's testimony would have an impact at more than one point in the prosecution. An elaborate plan to commit murder would not only weigh heavily on the issue of guilt or innocence, it would also have a big influence on the sentencing phase.

The killer, whoever it turned out to be, was already eligible for the death penalty, because of Marioneaux's age. Normally, a killer would have to be involved in the commission of another serious crime while committing a homicide in order for the death penalty to be an option. But, under an obscure provision of Louisiana's capital murder statute, if the victim was under twelve or over sixty-five the additional-crime requirement went flying out the window and the likelihood of lethal injection came flying in.

TWELVE

"'m over here, Detective. Just come through the wrought-iron gate and follow the briny smell back to the pool."

Wallace filed past the doors of the five-car garage, making her way to the fence that ran from the rear corner of the house to the side of the lot. From the research she had done over the weekend, she knew Glenn had cobbled together an empire of budget-brand self-storage facilities across the South. Apparently, such businesses spewed geysers of money.

She pushed on the gate, expecting a metal-on-metal squeal, but the hinges were soundless and so smooth that the gate got away from her and banged against the side of the house.

Glenn appeared from her left. "That thing gets away from everybody."

He was in jeans and a white oxford-cloth shirt. The sleeves were turned back to the middle of his thick forearms and he was barefoot. A highball glass with a sludgy tomato-colored liquid and a celery stalk was in his left hand.

"Virgin Mary." He raised his glass toward her. "Can I get you something?" He pushed the gate closed and then moved off toward a covered patio that ran the width of the the house.

Wallace watched him walk away. He moved with the smooth, carefree gait of a cat. "Sure. I'll have what you're having."

"Great. I've got a pitcher out here. I figured you'd feel safer if we met outside. Most people get intimidated by my size. But then, you carry a gun, so you're probably not like most people. Have a seat. Please." With his drink, he gestured toward an oversized Adirondack chair situated alongside a low glass table. He filled a tumbler with the liquid from the pitcher and held it toward her. His hands were so huge the glass and the pitcher looked like toys.

"You probably think I'm an asshole for skipping out the other day, but I couldn't handle what was happening."

"I'm not going to judge anybody for having a strong reaction to the violent death of a parent." She reached up and accepted the glass from him. "But your mother was a bit puzzled about how you expected her to get back to her car."

Glenn's eyes were hooded. His cheeks and the tip of his nose had the blush of broken capillaries that signaled chronic overconsumption of alcohol. "Are you sure you're up for this, now?" she asked.

"We'll see." He took the chair across the table from her. "You probably want to know if I have any idea why Eddie Pitkin would kill my father."

"Actually, the first thing I'd like to know is where you were in the hours before and after the time of your father's death—between seven and midnight." She pulled a little Moleskine notebook from her pocket and set it on the table in front of her.

"But you've already got a suspect in jail. Isn't the evidence against him pretty bad?"

Wallace smiled, her pen poised above a blank page. "Just tell me where you were."

Glenn smiled too. Wallace could tell he was trying to figure out if she was playing with him. She let her smile fade.

"Hah! You're serious, aren't you?" He sat up straight, his eyes wide. He furrowed his brow, the smile still on his face. "I was at church."

"Does this church have a name?"

"The Communion of Saints. You may have heard of it. 'Where every corner is the amen corner.'" Glenn shifted in his seat.

"Right. I've seen the billboards. So, would there be anyone there who'd be willing to vouch for your presence?"

"Quite a few, actually. As you can imagine," he gestured at the house and the pool, "I'm pretty handy with money, so I serve as the chief financial officer."

"That's interesting, but how does that tie you to a place and a time, in front of witnesses?"

"We've got a big congregation and a great many of them come equipped with very large bank accounts, so we move a lot of money. Come collection time, we try to make it look like a casual experience to the folks in the sanctuary, but it's not. There's a very rigid system for collecting, protecting, and accounting for the cash. That takes people, all with precise tasks, all carried out on a strict timetable that begins the moment the ushers are issued their collection plates and doesn't end until the last tally clerk in the counting room has submitted their money and count sheet and I've audited it and the money has been secured."

"Sounds like a casino-style operation."

"Except, in our case, the odds are one hundred percent in the giver's favor. Every penny pays off. Every time."

Wallace studied Glenn's face as he spoke. She couldn't tell whether the enthusiasm lighting up his eyes reflected the conviction of a true believer or the convincing routine of a skilled merchant.

"Can you provide me a list of the people you worked with that night?"

"Sure. But you can just look at the camera footage if you want."

"What footage would that be?"

"The counting rooms are a pretty wired place. Like I said, we move a lot of money."

"Which probably attracts people who'd like to get their hands on it."

Glenn gave her a broad smile. "There is, in fact, a class of people that shops around for churches with loose money procedures, for the express purpose of stealing. They might go to three, four, five different churches on any given Sunday, looking for easy targets."

"I've actually heard of that, but it seems so opposite of what you'd expect in church."

"I wish it were."

"Well, until I can get my hands on the video, why don't you tell me what time you left church and who was the last person to see you there?"

"I have to say, Detective Hartman, this is not the way I pictured this conversation going." He shifted in his seat again and looked at her as if he expected an explanation. "You're starting to make me feel just a little bit uncomfortable."

"Can you remember the time?"

"Oh, I'm going to guess it was coming up on eight thirty, give or take. The last person I know for sure who saw me would have been Molly Sylvester, the head usher. She was getting into her car as I was coming out of the building. I waved. She waved back."

Wallace scribbled the name and the time in her notebook.

"Give me just a moment," she said when she felt her phone vibrate. It was Burley. "I have to take this." She stood and walked along the concrete apron surrounding the pool until she was about fifty feet from Glenn.

"We're just finishing up at Pitkin's house," Burley said as soon as she answered.

"How did it go?"

"Like a goddamn circus. But if we bagged something useful, it'll be worth it. I see you called earlier. You checking up on us, or did you find something?"

"A few things, actually. First, the lake house does indeed have attic-access ceiling panels."

"Shit."

"One in the laundry room, inside, and one in the storeroom, outside. Neither is wired to the security system, and the attic is full of blown insulation."

"Damn, Wallace. That's a fine piece of work."

"We don't know if Eddie actually made use of it."

"Still, you did good."

"I should have thought of it the first time I went out there. Sorry."

"Don't say that. Ride the high as long as you can. There will be plenty of opportunities for this case to mess with your head. I can guarantee it."

"That's already happened." She told him about Peter Ecclestone.

"Let me get this straight. You found possible confirmation of the alibi *and* a way for Pitkin to beat the alibi."

She blew out a long breath. "Looks bad, doesn't it?"

"If we find insulation fibers in the stuff we took from his house today, it's going to look like a date with destiny for Eddie Pitkin." Burley went quiet for several seconds.

"But if we don't, and if this alibi witness bears out, then Eddie Pitkin starts looking like an innocent man."

"He starts looking like a successful plaintiff in a lawsuit against the city for violating his civil rights by arresting him when we should've waited until we had a better handle on the facts." Burley went quiet again. "Fuck. Why can't anything be simple anymore?"

"Jason, don't lose heart. We're not exactly back to square one."

"Where are you now?"

"In the middle of interviewing Glenn Marioneaux. I'm at his house, which is the approximate size of the Taj Mahal."

"And how's that going?"

"My initial reason for wanting to question him was to see if he could point us toward a suspect or a motive. But, with the possibility of a tight alibi for Eddie, the finger of suspicion starts to point at everybody, again, so I'm shaking his tree a bit."

Over the phone, Wallace could hear LeAnne's voice in the background, demanding Burley's attention.

"Before we hang up, there's one more thing." She looked over at Glenn, who was hunched forward, elbows on his knees. His head hung low and one foot tapped rhythmically against the patio.

"Hold that thought," Burley said. "What's the status of this Ecclestone fellow? We need to set up a time for him to come in and make a statement."

"Between seven and seven thirty tonight. But I want you and Le-Anne to be there, and I'll want it on camera as well as on steno."

"We'll be there. I'll have somebody set everything up." He sighed. "So what was the other thing you had?"

She explained about the church videos and asked Burley to send LeAnne to get copies.

Glenn followed her with his eyes as she walked back to her chair.

"So, tell me, Mr. Marioneaux. Why do you think this might have happened to your father?" She resumed her seat by the little table.

"Am I no longer under suspicion?"

"For the moment." She smiled.

"So, are you asking me why I think Pitkin did this?"

"No one has been convicted, yet. If you want to focus on Eddie Pitkin, that's fine. But I'm really just interested in any reasons you can think of that *anyone* might have done this."

"Most of what I know about Pitkin I've read in the papers. This reparations crusade he's got going on, where he uses DNA testing to find family ties between the descendants of white slave owners and the descendants of their former slaves, and then tries to get the white folks to cough up some cash like it's part of the inheritance his people never got . . . seems like stirring up a lot of anger and resentment, if you ask me."

"Do you think his cause is unjust?"

"Well, it's kind of . . ."

Wallace brought the point of her pen to the blank page of her notebook, holding Glenn's gaze as she did so.

"Hey, you know what," he continued, "you've got to admire somebody who thinks that far outside the box."

"Did your father ever have any dealings with him?"

"Nothing that wasn't reported, ad nauseam, in the papers. I mean, back when these guys were going at each other, hammer and tongs, in the media, they hurled a lot of abuse at each other. But my old man had moved on from the frame of mind that motivated the kind of bombs he used to throw at Pitkin."

"Do you believe that was a real change?"

"Can we ever really know what's in the heart of another?" He shrugged.

"Did you ever hear your father express any recent opinions about Mr. Pitkin or his methods?"

"No, not recently. Just the things I already mentioned."

"Did *you* ever have any dealings with Eddie Pitkin?"

"You are full of surprises, Detective. I never know where you're going next. They teach you that little technique at the police academy?"

She nodded, giving him a lazy smile. "The same day they taught me how to recognize when someone is stalling."

"No, Detective Hartman, I do not now nor have I ever had any dealings with the aforementioned Eddie Pitkin." He laughed and shook his head as if he were indulging a silly child.

"Let's assume, just for the sake of discussion, that there's no known suspect in this case. Is there anyone you can think of that would do something like this?"

"Well, half the people in the legislature hated his guts."

"Glenn, your father was murdered. And it wasn't accomplished from some remote distance, like a shooting. The killer had to get up close enough to touch him. And there's evidence the killer stayed to watch him die. It would have been pretty awful. Political rivalry doesn't seem strong enough or personal enough."

"Not to you, maybe. But I'm guessing you don't have a ton of experience pursuing the kinds of agendas that get people all worked up. A lot of folks thought he was swimming against the tide of history, and a lot of others thought he was trying to drown them in it."

"Can you think of anything specific that an individual or group of individuals might have taken as a direct enough threat that it would provoke this kind of violence?"

"I'm not in a position to know what would inspire one person to kill another." Glenn looked at her, then stared into his drink. "Louisiana's a right-to-work state. Some folks consider that a polite term for anti-union. He was in favor of policies that would make it harder to do away with the right-to-work laws. He was also a strong advocate for gender equality and gender identity."

"That seems like a set of priorities that would not typically coexist in the same person."

"Now you're getting the picture." He took a long pull on his drink, refilled it from the pitcher, and then drained it again.

"Anything else?" she asked, skeptical that the senator had fallen victim to union violence.

"I'm not aware of any specific threats. He liked to brag about his little power plays and how he always came out on top. But he never told me anything that sounded dangerous or sinister." He closed his eyes and slumped back in his chair, holding his ice-filled glass to his right temple.

Wallace couldn't help noticing the stark contrast between Glenn's demeanor and that of his mother. Where Dorothy had been a chaotic jumble of anger and grief and despondence, Glenn seemed to be a study in casual indifference to his father's fate.

"Your father was going to hold a press conference this morning. What can you tell me about that?"

"That's news to me."

"I'll be interviewing members of his office staff tomorrow."

"Talk to Garrett Landry. He was my father's chief legislative aide. He'd probably know."

Wallace wrote the name in her notebook and also scribbled a reminder to ask Dorothy about the press conference. "It doesn't appear that the killer broke into the house," she said, changing directions with her questions. "Do you know who had access to the place?"

"Well, him. My mother. He had some woman who came in to tidy up. Beyond that, I wouldn't know."

"Can you think of anyone he might have invited in or brought in with him?"

"Nope."

"What about you? Didn't you have access to the house?"

"I understand he kept a key out somewhere, for the cleaning woman, if that's what you're asking. But I've never been inside the place."

"How could that be?"

Glenn closed his eyes again and brought the glass back to the side of his head. "We weren't that close. Until recently, I was living in Florida. Had been for quite a while."

"What brought you back to Louisiana?"

"When I was a kid, I got sent away to boarding school. After that, college and career. Even though I'm from here, I never felt like I belonged anywhere. But, after all those years away, I started to feel like something was missing. So, I came back to look for it. At great expense, I might add." With his drink hand, he gestured grandly at the house and the grounds.

"This is certainly a beautiful home," Wallace said, slowly taking in the wide expanse of the residence. "Very large for one person."

"You applying for residency?" He laughed, then refilled his glass. "Right up until the day of the move from Florida, I was a married man. For the second time, but married, nevertheless. At the last minute, my wife decided life on the bayou didn't sound as compelling as life in South Beach." His mouth turned down.

"I'm sorry. That had to feel pretty awful."

"My parents never met my second wife. They never even knew I had gotten married, if you can believe that. They knew about the first one, but it didn't last long enough for the folks to get too invested. Then, when Layla came along, things weren't really clicking back here, so . . ."

"Do you know if your father had any other children?"

"None that Momma and I know about." He looked at her and laughed again—a joyless sound that made Wallace uneasy.

"Do you have any suspicions, in that regard?"

"I suspect his marital vows meant little to him. How that translated into his actual behavior . . ." Glenn shrugged and looked off in the distance.

Glenn and his mother seemed sure Herbert was a cheater, but they also appeared uninterested in knowing the particulars. Wallace assumed that made it easier to hide from the humiliation of betrayal. In any event, her line of inquiry seemed to have reached a dead end.

"Tell me again, what it was that brought you to Baton Rouge."

"Uh-oh. Looks like I'm back in the crosshairs. Dear Diary is gonna get an entertaining earful tonight."

Wallace saw hurt in his expression.

"Some things just needed to be cleared away."

She kept her focus on him, sensing his hesitation.

"So, how is my very uninteresting life story of any relevance to your investigation, anyway?" Glenn's voice pitched higher and he seemed to struggle against something that was threatening to have its way with him. His bleak expression begged for a reprieve.

Wallace waited and agonized as the silent seconds ticked by.

"My life had a way of going fine for a while . . . until it didn't." Glenn's voice faltered. "And I could almost predict when things would start to go wrong, almost down to the day and the hour, but I could never figure out why it had to be that way."

"Family things?"

"A friend of mine down in Florida, the pastor at a church I was going to, the place where I met Layla, he suggested I might be working too hard at ignoring things I needed to confront instead."

He looked at Wallace. She could see he was trying to gauge her response to what he was telling her.

"It all seemed a bit New Agey, to me," he continued, waving his left hand airily. "But he kept at it, and after a while it started to sound like there was some logic to it. If you set up a row of dominos, then tip one over, it's easy to see that each one knocks over the next one, all the way to the end. He finally convinced me that emotional cause and effect were not nearly so clear-cut. Something inside you, that you might not even be aware of, could reach into your life and knock things over. Other times, it could be something you are fully aware of, but it affects you in ways you wouldn't anticipate or even notice until it's too late, until the damage is done."

"Sounds like a smart fellow."

"He's big on what he calls forgiveness theology."

"So, did you come back to forgive or be forgiven?"

"Both. It took me a long time to work up the nerve to even attempt something like this."

"You said earlier that you were 'sent away to boarding school.'" She let the statement hang as if it was a question.

"I also said he and I weren't that close."

The afternoon was quiet except for the muted tinkle of ice cubes as Glenn rolled his glass between his palms. Wallace could tell he was weighing whether to continue.

"I could never quite figure out who I was to him." He set the glass on the table and looked squarely at her. "Which do you think would be worse, Detective Hartman? To never have a father or to have one that kept himself out of reach except when he needed to rub your nose in one shortcoming or another?"

Glenn closed his eyes and held his head high, as if he was listening for something. Then he stood and took a few steps. With his back to her, he spoke. "Can you imagine trying to love someone, but never being able to figure out how to get that accomplished?"

"No," she whispered. "I can't."

"What would you do to get that person's attention? Any attention at all?"

Wallace thought she could see where Glenn's questions were leading. She had seen it often enough in the children she grew up around. The ignored child of the self-absorbed parent, the child who was willing to do anything, even destructive things, if that's what it took to get the parent's attention.

"And did you get that attention?"

"Off and on for a while." Glenn looked away. "But when I turned twelve . . . it was gone for good, unless you count disciplinary measures as attention."

Glenn's expression made her blood run cold.

"That was a confusing time. Let me tell you." His voice grew strained. "I kind of went off into a wild, ragged orbit."

"Is that why they sent you away? Because you were getting hard to handle?"

"My oh my, you are a quick study, Detective. But, yes, I did do some things. So they—more precisely, he—stuck me where he wouldn't have to see the problems he'd caused staring him right in the face every day."

Without warning, Glenn hurled his drink against the wall with the runaway gate. Glass fragments showered back around him. He pressed his palms to his face and took a few long, slow breaths.

"Glenn?"

"What's the fucking point?"

"To what?"

"To any of this," he shouted. He looked down at himself, then opened his arms, preacher-style, and gestured at everything around him. "See if you can get your mind around how it feels to find out that the thing you need the most is the thing you hate the most."

Wallace looped her fingers through the toe straps of the well-worn leather sandals he had left next to his chair and then stood, dithering over whether to go near him.

She gave him a wide berth, approaching slowly as if he were a skittish horse, and then held the sandals toward him. "Bare feet and broken glass don't play well together."

"Thank you," he said, still not looking at her. First with one hand, then the other, he held on to her shoulder for balance as he slipped the sandals on his feet.

Wallace stiffened at the unexpected touch, but Glenn seemed not to notice. He stepped back and surveyed the mess he had made.

"Glenn?" She waited until he was looking directly at her. "I admire you for coming back." Her tone was soft. "For trying to fix this."

"And that's about as far as it got. Trying. Just when things were starting to show some promise . . ." He looked past her, his nostrils flared, eyes focused in the distance. "Now you know why I flaked out on you and Mother. Why I found me an out-of-the-way place with long hours and good booze and just crawled on in."

He closed his eyes. With both hands he pulled hard at the hair on the sides of his head. A cry of frustration escaped through his gritted teeth.

"He was a real bastard, and yes, we fought, and it got ugly, and yes, there were times when I just wanted to kill him." Glenn's eyes were brimming and his face was congested with anger. "If there's a hell, he's roasting in it now. But, goddamn him, when he went, he took what I needed with him."

In two long strides, Glenn was at the table. A second later, the pitcher of Virgin Mary hit the wall.

THIRTEEN

Peter Ecclestone was unnerved by his encounter with the detective. He wasn't worried about her turning him in for trespassing, but he *was* worried about her dragging him into something that involved more exposure than he and his little sideline career needed.

Once the detective had cleared out, he'd Googled her name and found the stories about the Herbert Marioneaux homicide. After that he ran through the images on his camera and deleted all the shots of Eddie Pitkin. This was not something he needed to get involved with, especially not something as touchy as what looked to be a race-based execution-style killing. No matter who his testimony helped or hurt, somebody would be gunning for him. Now looked like the perfect time to find a new place to roost for a while—a really long while.

As soon as he was sure she was good and gone, he did a few quick errands that her appearance had put him behind schedule on, and then he returned to the lake house. He backed his SUV into the carport and began moving things out of the house. The loading was almost complete when he heard tires crunching on the gravel in the driveway. Imagining a surprise return of the detective, his mood sank.

Peering between the boxes and the luggage already stacked inside the cargo space of his vehicle, Peter watched as a jacked-up gray dual-cab pickup eased to a stop a couple of feet from his front bumper. Glare off the windshield kept him from seeing who was behind the wheel. The man in the passenger seat looked vaguely familiar, but he couldn't place him. That was usually a bad sign.

Just as Peter was about to close the last of his camera cases, he remembered where he had seen the face. Instead of closing the case, he worked the camera free of its cutout in the foam padding, then popped open the little hatch on the bottom and extracted the memory card.

The man in the passenger seat opened his door and stepped out onto the gravel.

With his left hand Peter brought his paper cup of convenience-store coffee to his lips and drained the last of it. With his other hand he dropped the memory card into the cup and crumpled the cup into a ball.

The man closed the passenger door of the pickup and strode into the carport.

Keeping his eye on the approaching figure, Peter reached for the dumpster behind him. He lifted the lid a few inches and let the cup fall inside. It made a faint kissing sound as it landed on the bag of household trash he had dropped in a few minutes earlier.

Standing forward of the door, the man pulled open the driver's door of Peter's SUV, letting it thump against the carport wall.

"What can I do for you?" Peter asked, acting startled.

The man walked back around the front of the SUV, to the passenger side, and stopped at the rear corner, just a few feet from Peter. The open driver's side door blocked Peter's avenue of escape on his left. The man was blocking his path to his right.

"Get in your vehicle," he said. "You and I got business to discuss."

———

Burley looked nervous. Wallace couldn't remember the last time she'd seen him like this.

Just as Burley had predicted, before he and LeAnne had finished their search of Eddie Pitkin's house Renata Pitkin, Eddie's wife, had called in the camera crews. Renata turned out to be as skilled as her husband at managing public perceptions.

The TV stations must have put a tape of the event on a continuous loop, and in almost no time, it got picked up by the national media. Wallace watched it on the television in the corner of Burley's office.

Renata was standing on the sidewalk in front of her house, with her wide-eyed three-year-old grandchild, thumb in his mouth, peeking worriedly from behind her right leg. She lobbed question after question at the officers. Heartbreakers such as, "Why are you taking our stuff?," "What have you done with my husband?" "We need him at home," "Haven't you-all done enough to us already?," "How do you expect our family to survive with you-all ripping us apart like this?," and "Can anybody explain why you-all think he would have done what you're accusing him of?"

She never cried or raised her voice. She never made a move in the direction of the officers. She just stood there, asking her questions and looking desolate, and resigned, and victimized.

To Wallace's trained eye, it looked like a very garden-variety warrant search, but with Renata's melancholy commentary it would appear to the public like a Gestapo maneuver. Grim-faced officers carried boxes out the front door to a police van parked at the curb. Neighbors clustered at the periphery looking sympathetic.

And now that there was the possibility of an alibi, the whole operation could've been for nothing. Even worse, it could be spun as harassment of a black man who just happened to have an agenda that made white people uncomfortable with their past.

And there was Burley, stage-managing the entire business—barking orders and directing his officers to keep the onlookers at bay.

Wallace looked at him now, sitting on the couch in his office, anxiety practically oozing out of his pores. At one time, all of this would have rolled off him—back when he still felt like he had something to prove. Now, like many in the late stages of their careers, he would just feel like he had something to lose.

It was a subtle change in perspective, but Wallace knew it could have serious consequences. It made cops cautious about all the wrong things. They started thinking too much about the dangers to their careers and their pensions and not enough about the dangers to their persons.

Please let me make it out the door without catching that one special case. The one that spoils the retirement party. The one that excretes a puddle of suspicion all over my otherwise A-plus career. The one that makes it look like I just suddenly decided it was time to "pursue other opportunities" or "spend more time with my family."

In some it provoked depression. In others it proved lethal. More than a few officers were cut down just shy of the finish line because they were working so hard to preserve the hazy future that they took their eyes off the clear and present. Normally, the change came slowly, but it looked like it was happening to Burley right in front of her eyes.

He rubbed the back of his neck and let out a long, slow breath. "Here's what I've got." He spread a handful of scribbled-on pages along the coffee table between them. They were lists of the items hauled away from the Pitkin home. "And by the way, Eddie's lawyer has informally notified the prosecutor that she intends to demand half of the hair sample we used to get the DNA match."

"No surprise there," Wallace said. She had known this would happen. Eddie hadn't been formally charged, yet, so he wasn't technically a defendant—only a suspect. Consequently, the prosecutor did not yet have a legal obligation to turn over the material. But Tasha

K was letting them know she'd be breathing down their necks and wasn't about to let anything slip through the cracks.

"My other news is that Glenn Marioneaux's church doesn't archive those videos. Once the money count is verified and the funds have been deposited, the video file is deleted."

"So something new might already be recorded over the one from the day Marioneaux was killed."

"Maybe not." His voice sounded unhopeful.

"Will they let one of our IT experts examine the drive they store their videos on?" Wallace asked.

"Somebody's working on that now. Oh, one more thing. The phone records for the victim and his family arrived. Do you want to go through them, or can we put somebody else on that?"

"LeAnne can take first crack. If we need extra bodies to interview any names that turn up, I'll let you know. And thanks for helping on that warrant."

"You can only be in so many places at once." He aimed a remote at the television and turned it off.

"Where is LeAnne, by the way?"

"I'm right here," she said, appearing in the doorway.

Burley waved her over to the empty side chair next to Wallace.

"I still can't figure out why Eddie would have done it," Wallace said. "Assuming, for the sake of discussion, that he did do it—that he slipped out through the attic when Peter Ecclestone wasn't looking and killed Marioneaux—for the life of me, I can't understand why. I know they had their differences way back when, but none of it seemed like something worth murdering over."

"The logic of the killer is not always logical. But I get what you're saying. It was a mean-spirited kill. The motive question is bugging me too." Burley leaned back and spread his arms along the top of the sofa. "So, tell us about this Peter Ecclestone." He checked his watch. "Shouldn't he should be getting here about now?"

"He's an artist slash photographer. Lives in Cavanaugh, and he was squatting in the lake house just up the road from the one Eddie was allegedly staying in. He admitted that the only reason he was in the house that day was because he needed a quiet place to nurse a nasty hangover."

"An unreliable artiste who was chemically impaired, to boot?"

"I'm not saying that. Only repeating what he told me." She wandered over to the bookcase against the wall beside Burley's desk. "That said, he picked Eddie out of a slate of pictures I showed him and claimed the face in the pictures is the same face he saw on the dock behind the house late on the afternoon of the day Marioneaux was killed." She let her eyes roam over a shelf crammed with books. "On top of that, he says that after it got dark he saw lights and movement in the house."

"When we got back from executing the warrant on Pitkin's place, I called Chief Shannon to let him know Ecclestone might be an alibi witness," Burley intoned. "He refuses to get excited until we've questioned this guy twelve ways to Sunday and the alibi looks tight as a drum."

Burley leaned back and spread his arms along the top of the couch again, then let his chin drop to his chest.

"You look like Jesus on the cross," Wallace said. "A bald Jesus."

"You trying to cheer me up?"

"I'm trying to bring you down." She offered him a mischievous grin. "You looked so chipper when I walked in, and you know how much I hate it when you're happier than I am."

Usually, Burley could be counted on for a snappy comeback, but there was no banter in him tonight. He looked up, heavy lidded, and gave her what could, at best, be described as an appreciative smile. He puffed out a long breath and then let his head sag, resuming his crucifixion pose.

"Jason?"

Wallace and LeAnne looked toward the office door. It was Curtis Stiles, a former prison guard who had joined the city police and now worked with Burley on special projects.

"I finished that thing you put me on a little while ago."

Burley opened one eye and looked at Stiles. "Come in, Curtis."

Wallace wanted to tell Burley and LeAnne about Glenn Mario-neaux, but he was already focused on whatever Curtis Stiles had brought in. She would roll it around in her head a bit more.

She and LeAnne slipped quietly from the office.

"I've got some details to clean up from the fiasco at Pitkin's house this afternoon, and then I'm taking off," LeAnne announced as they headed into the Detective Section.

Wallace thought about giving LeAnne a pat on the back for handling the search of Pitkin's house, but she wasn't in the mood for the usual mouthful of cynicism she might be handed in return.

"Okay." Wallace flopped into her chair and fired up her computer to check for new reports from the crime lab. "Burley and I can handle the Ecclestone interview," she said, not looking at LeAnne.

"I can be here for that." LeAnne sounded flustered. "I just didn't know it was a for-sure thing."

"And it may not be. We won't know until he shows up . . . or doesn't. So, no point in the whole detective section sitting around waiting for Godot."

"No. I'll stay." LeAnne put her things on her desk, then left the room.

No new forensics reports had arrived, so Wallace pulled out Peter Ecclestone's card and called his number to see how close he was. It went to voicemail.

Does no one answer their phone anymore?

"Mr. Ecclestone, this is Detective Hartman. I'm just calling to make sure you're on the way, like you promised. We're all waiting for you. Don't forget me."

Then she called Dorothy Marioneaux to ask her if she knew why her husband had scheduled a press conference. Dorothy said she was unaware of the event. In response to Dorothy's question about the state of the investigation, Wallace told her only that every bit of evidence was being examined carefully and every avenue of inquiry was being pursued. Dorothy laughed at Wallace's bureaucratic doublespeak and hung up.

Wallace closed her eyes and rested her head on her desk and let the facts of the case march around in her mind, to see if they would lead her anywhere new or interesting.

Glenn had the makings of a motive, albeit a weak motive, and he certainly seemed to be no fan of Eddie Pitkin. Whether that translated into an act of violence and a willingness to pin the whole business on someone else would depend on whether there were darker, uglier aspects to the father-son relationship she had yet to uncover. Perhaps Dorothy could shed some light on the matter.

As for Eddie, things were even more complex. On one hand, if he had slipped out of the lake house, through the attic, and then traveled to Baton Rouge and killed Marioneaux chances were, as part of such a well-thought-out plan, he would have arranged for an unimpeachable alibi. But, as a former criminal attorney, he would know an alibi that looked too pat might smell phony. So, the fact that Eddie hadn't immediately claimed to have an alibi cut slightly in his favor—why would it occur to him to make sure he had one if he didn't know he would need one? Wallace supposed it was possible that claiming an alibi now, one that could be neither supported nor disproved, created the illusion of authenticity.

On the other hand, if Eddie had been at False River at the time of the murder, then his DNA had almost certainly been planted at the crime scene. And if the DNA was planted, then it was equally probable that the fibers found on Marioneaux were also planted. The same would hold true for any fibers that turned up on the material Burley had seized from Pitkin's house.

And whoever had done it had to know when Eddie would be at a place where an alibi witness was a low probability. That would mean they either had access to Eddie's schedule, in advance, or were keeping tabs on him. It also meant they could act quickly once they were sure he was in no position to have a provable alibi.

An operation like that would require at least one person to keep

Eddie under surveillance and send the signal and another person to kill Herbert and plant the evidence.

With so many possibilities in play, there was a good chance at least one juror would balk unless the DA produced clear evidence of a motive. The marching in her head stopped and Wallace smiled.

A wafer-thin sliver of opportunity gleamed at the edge of her thoughts. The evidence already in hand covered means and opportunity. If someone really was trying to put a frame around Eddie, they would be waiting for the right moment to trot out the motive as well. That required action, and action—movement—might make the plotters visible.

FOURTEEN

The overhead light failed to come on as Wallace backed into her carport. Reflexively, she stared up at the fixture, as if by looking at it from a distance she would be able to diagnose the problem.

After she killed the engine, she sat, wondering whether it was a burned-out bulb that she could change herself or the fixture needed to be repaired. Fatigue was getting a strong grip on her. The light could be dealt with in the morning.

She pulled the latch handle and cracked her door open, then pulled it shut again and fished out her phone. Chief Shannon would be expecting her daily report. She boiled it down to the basics, including the fact that Peter Ecclestone was a no-show. Wallace closed with an offer to expand on any points he wanted to discuss further, and then prayed he wouldn't see the message and call back tonight.

For just a second, she toyed with the idea of paying a surprise visit to Mason. She reached for the ignition but stopped short. If she stayed with him, the sleep they both needed would surely be a scarce commodity. She pulled the latch handle.

Before her door was completely open, a hard, powerful hand closed around her left bicep and hauled her from the car. She reached for her weapon, but another hand seized her right arm. As she was pulled backward through the breezeway that led from the carport into the backyard her attacker pushed her elbows together until they were almost touching behind her back. Wallace tried to twist free.

"None of that, now." He spoke in a hoarse whisper. When she struggled, he shoved her hard up against the rear of the house, knocking the wind out of her.

As his head moved up alongside hers, she felt strands of her hair catch and tug in his whiskers. For a split second she thought of Peter Ecclestone and his unshaven face. But the voice sounded wrong.

Almost tenderly, his beard rasped against her neck as he nuzzled up close to her left ear. His voice stayed low and scratchy.

"Just letting you know, baby doll. You've got your sweet little hands on the right man."

She tried again to wrestle free, but he just pushed her elbows closer together. "You're in serious trouble, mister," she wheezed, trying to recover her breath. Her shoulders felt as if they were ripping from their sockets.

He increased the pressure until she gave up a low groan. He pressed his body against her, holding her tight against the house. She could smell the paint and she could smell *him*.

"Not too, too long before the good senator got pushed off the chessboard, I saw the filthy motherfucker you got locked up sneaking out the back of a house just north of Spanish Town. Seems Mr. Pitkin had been paying a secret after-dark visit to the fine upstanding young woman who lives in that house."

"You couldn't come to the police station and make a statement like a normal person?" She struggled to keep the agony out of her voice.

"Too many reasons y'all might have to keep me there."

"Then how am I supposed to do anything with what you're telling me?"

His answer was a sharp blow to her right kidney. The blade of pain collapsed her. She felt the man back away. She heard his rapidly retreating footsteps. Then she was alone.

Wallace raised her shirt and peered over her shoulder at the reflection of her back in the bathroom mirror. A fist-shaped bruise blossomed above her belt line where he had punched her. A dull ache was spreading through her ribcage.

She sat on the edge of the vanity, thinking about what her attacker told her. It would be almost impossible to verify. It would have to be checked out, nevertheless.

What if it hadn't been a lovers' tryst at all, and the woman had simply been Eddie's transportation from False River to Spanish Town and back?

What if it was all bullshit? Assaulting a cop just to deliver bogus information was absurdly dangerous, but perhaps she was being gamed.

Wallace lowered her shirt and tried to figure out when she was going to tell Mason about her nocturnal visitor. If she called him now, the retelling followed by their certain disagreement over filing a police report and seeking medical attention would keep her up for hours. And if she mentioned it to Burley, he would probably force her off the case.

FIFTEEN

Despite Wallace's climbing into bed at a decent hour, sleep had been elusive and fitful for the second night in a row. The throb from the blow to her kidney, and the gnawing guilt over not telling Mason about the attack, kept her awake.

And now she was starting to think evil thoughts about Peter Ecclestone. Seven calls in the last eighteen hours—all unanswered, all unreturned. She knew people had all sorts of reasons for getting cold feet when it came time to give an official statement in a criminal proceeding.

Mostly, they worried that helping to pin guilt on someone dangerous would make them a target for revenge. Clearing Eddie Pitkin didn't point the finger at anyone else, though—at least, not at this point. But Peter had no way of knowing that.

It was certainly possible that Peter was just off somewhere, doing his artist thing, out of reach of any cell signals. But, by midmorning, after Burley had called her several times asking about him, Wallace decided to do something desperate.

She called the Pointe Coupee deputy who had brought the warrant to the lake house, and asked if she would take a look around the house where Peter had been trespassing. Then she called the chief of police in Cavanaugh, the little town where Peter lived, and asked her if she could have someone look in the likeliest places to see if Ecclestone had gone back home and was simply not interested in keeping his promise to come to Baton Rouge.

Wallace explained why she needed to find him and why sooner was much better than later. Melissa Voorhees, the police chief, was not encouraging.

"No, don't call him flaky," Voorhees said. "Flaky people are actually more responsible. The fact is, Peter's kind of a wild spirit. We grew up together, so I know whereof I speak."

"A man's life may hang in the balance because of the information in Peter's head."

"That wouldn't necessarily matter to him. He would see making a statement as requiring him to get involved in something in more than just a superficial way. That kind of thing scares the crap out of men like Peter. If you don't believe me, just ask half the women in Cavanaugh. Hell, you can ask 'em all."

"Doesn't he have a business to operate?"

Melissa laughed. It was a gleeful laugh that actually lasted a few seconds. "His momma set him up in that studio. And I just put air quotes around studio. I mean, Peter's talented, there's no question about that, and he has some pretty loyal customers and a few profitable outlets for his work. But running a going concern? On a day-to-day basis? Maybe not."

"What's your best advice, then? I'm getting stuck in a squeeze play between my boss and Mr. Ecclestone."

"I'll drive by his house and his alleged place of business, and then check with his mother. If I can think of something else useful, I'll do that too. Let me call you back as soon as I know something, but I wouldn't sit by the phone waiting for *Peter* to call *you*."

Wallace had no intention of sitting by the phone. The Capitol building was full of the late senator's colleagues who needed to be interviewed. She stuck her head in Burley's office on her way out, to let him know her plan and to see if he had any news. He didn't.

Marioneaux had been the head of an important committee, so he had office space and people who worked for him. And because of his longevity in the legislature, he had an extensive web of political connections.

His office was surprisingly well-appointed. Long, heavy curtains were cinched with tasseled tiebacks. All of the furniture was heavy dark wood and leather. Vibrantly colored Oriental rugs covered most of the floor, and the walls were loaded with dozens of grip-and-grin photographs of the senator posing with pro athletes and other notables. The faint scent of cologne hung in the air.

Wallace had worked as a messenger in the Capitol during one of her college summers and seen a lot of the offices in the building. Most were nice, but not this nice.

She spent nearly an hour interviewing the senator's intern, as well as Coy Asber, the secretary-receptionist. The intern was new and had nothing of interest to offer. Asber, on the other hand, had witnessed or overheard lots of tense encounters between the senator and his fellow legislators and between the senator and people from the community and around the state, but he felt that none of it was a cause for concern.

"I've only been with Senator Marioneaux for two years, but I've had one sort of clerical job or another here in the Capitol for going on ten years and I can tell you, we've got a lot of big egos and quick tempers in this building. That's just the way it goes around here."

"Was there anyone in particular that came off as always being at odds with Senator Marioneaux?"

"No, not really," Coy said, fiddling with the cord on his desk phone.

"Anybody who nursed a grudge longer than seemed reasonable?"

"No. People who operate that way don't last long in this business. He'd fight with somebody one day and they'd be best buds the next."

"Let's look at his appointment calendar," Wallace said.

Coy hesitated. "I'm not sure I have the authority to hand that over," he said. "I'll be glad to respond to a subpoena, though. Or, if you don't want to do the paper chase and you're not in a super hurry, you can wait for Garrett Landry, the senator's legislative aide—he's really the guy who runs the show around here. If he says okay, then it's okay."

"Where is Mr. Landry?"

"Out of the country on some kind of trade mission. He won't be back until Thursday."

Coy opened the middle drawer of his desk and extracted a business card with Landry's contact information on it and handed it to Wallace.

"Why don't you call him now and ask him?" Wallace suggested. "Maybe we can save some time? And then I'd like you to make a list of the people who seemed to get crosswise with the senator. Especially if it was someone it happened with more than once. I appreciate that this is a contentious place, but it's always possible that somebody ended up keeping their true feelings hidden."

"Sure. I guess I can do that."

"And I'd like to schedule a meeting with Mr. Landry, as soon as he gets back."

"I can put you down for Friday afternoon," Coy said, consulting a calendar book on his desk. "He's booked until then."

Coy called and left a message when Landry didn't answer. After a few minutes of scribbling, he handed Wallace the list she had asked him to make.

"I have to be honest, I feel strange about this," he said as she took the list from him. "It feels kind of like I'm accusing these people of something. They're going to know you got their names from me, and probably feel the same way. If the senator's replacement doesn't want me, my name will be Mudd, around here. I'll probably have to look elsewhere for a job."

"What if I tell them you gave me a list of people the senator spoke with recently and not mention the other stuff?"

"You're alright, Detective. What else can I do for you?"

"You can help me look for the senator's laptop and his cell phone."

"Sure, we can look, but—"

"I know. You want a subpoena before you let me take them away."

He smiled, sheepishly, and gave her a one-shoulder shrug. "But you know what? I don't think we're going to find anything. I distinctly remember he put the laptop into his briefcase when he left here on Friday. And when he walked out the door, he had his briefcase in one hand and the phone stuck between his shoulder and his ear, yakking with somebody."

"You're quite certain of that?"

"Absolutely. The reason I remember is that he waved good-bye, as he was going out the door, and the phone slipped loose. He kind of juggled it and chased after it with his free hand for a couple of steps."

"You don't mind if we look, anyway, do you? He might have come back to the office after you left for the day."

"Sure. We can have a look around."

They spent the next fifteen minutes scouring the office suite, but, just as Coy had predicted, they found neither the laptop nor the telephone.

"One more thing," Wallace said as they returned to the front room. "What can you tell me about the press conference that was scheduled for yesterday morning?"

"Nothing. I mean I know one was scheduled, but he never mentioned what it would be about. Originally, it was going to be in the middle of the week, but he moved it to Monday, at the last minute. I have no idea why."

"Is that normal, that you wouldn't know?"

"Sometimes he told me. Sometimes he didn't. Really, all I needed to know was when it was happening, so I could update his calendar. Garrett would know. He can be hard to get ahold of, but keep trying. He knew everything about everything going on in this office."

Wallace exited through the front entrance of the building, onto the broad limestone plaza that eventually gave way to the long, low steps that led to the street below. Several women clustered a few steps below the plaza, looking up at the Art Deco spire that rose more than four hundred feet above them

"There she is," one of the women said as Wallace neared the edge of the plaza. The speaker pointed in Wallace's direction. Wallace looked back toward the building, to see who the woman was pointing at, but no one was behind her.

"We're here for *you*, Detective Hartman," another of the women said.

The group came up the steps onto the plaza and moved into Wallace's path. They looked angry.

"Detective, my daughter was raped over a year ago."

"That's horrible. I'm—"

"They still haven't found who did it. Do you know why?"

"No. I'm sorry, but I don't."

"Because they haven't processed the DNA from the rape kit. That's why." The woman's voice rose in volume. "They tell us there's a long wait because there's so many cases in front of hers. Meanwhile the dirtbag who did this to her is still out there, going about his merry way, while my thirteen-year-old girl has had the stuffing kicked out of her life."

"I feel terrible for—"

"Everybody says they feel terrible. But nobody does anything. And here you come with your case. Your victim's already dead. He can't suffer anymore. He doesn't care who killed him, and he doesn't have to face a messed-up life every day like my child does."

Wallace took a step back. The woman was angry, but she was also very sad.

"How come some dead white man gets the DNA profiled in his case before my living, breathing, hurting daughter can have her case taken care of? Does that seem right to you?"

"Do you have children, Detective?" another of the women asked.

Questions flew at her from several women at once. They had gathered around her in a loose semicircle. No one was waiting for answers.

"How would you feel if it was your child who was raped?" one of the woman asked.

"How would you feel knowing she was less important than a dead man?"

"How would your *daughter* feel?"

Two members of the state police detail that provided security for the Capitol were hurrying up the steps behind the women. Their purpose was obvious from the determination on their faces. One of the troopers, a woman, opened her mouth to speak, but Wallace raised her hand.

"We're fine," Wallace said to the troopers as they drew near. She showed her badge.

The troopers continued toward her.

"This gathering needs to disperse," the female trooper said. "Now."

"We're fine," Wallace repeated. "These women have something important to say."

"Whatever needs to be said will have to be said elsewhere," the other trooper said. "Disperse immediately."

Onlookers gathered at the margins of the commotion.

"We're not leaving," one of the women shouted at the trooper. "Not until we get some answers." She stood her ground, her arms folded defiantly across her chest. "We have a right to be here, and we have a right—"

The trooper stepped behind the woman and took hold of her

arms. The woman struggled against the restraint. Another lady began recording the encounter with her cell phone.

"Ma'am, put the phone away," the female trooper said.

"Let me go." The woman squirmed helplessly in the trooper's grip.

"Please don't do this," Wallace said. "No one is hurting anyone."

"The order to disperse applies to you as well, Officer," the trooper shouted in her command voice. "If you don't vacate the premises immediately, you'll be subject to arrest and detention along with everyone else involved in this protest."

"This isn't a protest," Wallace shouted back. "It's a conversation."

Footsteps sounded on the plaza behind her. Wallace turned to see four more troopers approaching. Two more were coming up the steps from the street below.

"We want answers, Detective Hartman," one of the women called out. "All of our daughters are waiting their turn. When does justice . . . Let go of me," she growled as the troopers waded into the group and began pulling the gathering apart.

Wallace turned to face the trooper on her left. "This is a mistake," she said evenly, not moving. "Stop making it worse."

One of the women was on the ground, moaning, holding her knee.

Wallace was sitting on a bench on the little patio just outside the east exit of the Capitol. With silent efficiency, Wallace and the group of women who had confronted her had been escorted from the plaza in front of the Capitol. The troopers had spaced themselves evenly across the sidewalk at the base of the steps, preventing the group from re-forming, although some of the women continued shouting from the street, for a while.

After she found a quiet place to regroup, Wallace spent a few minutes subduing her anger and thinking about how similar this had been to her confrontation with Eddie Pitkin and the priest, except that today hers was one of the voices calling for the police to back off. She wondered how the women had known where to find her.

She pulled out the list of names Coy Asber had given her and then took a picture of it with her phone and emailed it to LeAnne, with instructions to start interviewing everyone on the list.

When her phone buzzed a few minutes later she expected it to be LeAnne calling with some sort of pushback about the assignment, but it wasn't.

"Detective Hartman, this is Melissa Voorhees in Cavanaugh."

"Please tell me Peter Ecclestone is standing right there in front of you."

"You're not that lucky. A vehicle belonging to him—"

"I'm not going to like this, am I?"

"Don't jump to any conclusions. I called the sheriff's departments in the surrounding parishes, places where there were areas that might interest Peter, from a shutterbug point of view. His SUV is in the lot at Lake Kilgore Park."

"That's south of False River. He said he'd be heading north, back toward Cavanaugh."

"Peter and the truth are not always on speaking terms."

"How long has it been there?"

"We don't know. But there's no evidence whatsoever of foul play."

"When I saw him yesterday, there was a red kayak in a roof rack."

"I'll ask about that. In any event, it's a big lake. I've been out there a time or two. It has lots of swampy areas along the western edge. Cell coverage is pretty spotty. If he's out there, that's probably why you're not hearing from him."

"Do you think he would have stayed out overnight?"

"He's a bit of a wuss, but you never know. In any event, I just wanted to keep you up-to-date. I'll get back to you on the kayak, and I'll have them keep an eye on the vehicle."

"Thanks, Chief Voorhees."

"Just call me Melissa. Nobody calls me Chief Voorhees except my kids when I'm handing out chores or nagging about schoolwork."

"Will do, and thanks for pitching in on this."

"No problem. I'm just glad it's your case, not mine."

"How does this thing look from way out in Cavanaugh?"

"Like I said, I'm glad it's your case, and not mine."

Wallace stuffed the list of legislators into her satchel and looked up the number for the church where Marioneaux had led the faithful before he got into politics. The current pastor, Stewart Sutton, happened to be in Baton Rouge when Wallace finally tracked him down. He agreed to meet her at noon.

They met on the front steps of a church where he had come to visit a colleague. He sat on the top step. Wallace stood, facing him, a couple of steps down. He was a youthful-looking man in his sixties with sandy hair and a ready smile. After a few minutes, she pegged him as a man who could speak at length without actually saying much.

"Well, like I said, Herbert was enormously popular—a very charismatic individual."

"And maybe that's what's got me a bit hung up."

"How's that?"

"The picture you paint makes him seem universally loved, yet he was murdered. Those two things don't fit together."

"But they don't have to be in conflict unless you're implying that his killer was a member of my congregation?"

"I'm just saying that congregations can be like families. From the outside, everything looks lovely. But inside the four walls of the house, there is always conflict."

"I don't know what to tell you. He remained a member of the church. He attended fairly regularly. Folks appeared to like him just fine."

It sounded like the meaningless jibber-jabber HR departments spouted when asked for an opinion about a former employee.

"Even though he left a career rendering unto the Lord, to seek fame and fortune in the apparatus that renders unto Caesar." The pastor smiled at his own wordplay.

"I appreciate that someone in your position wouldn't want to speak ill of the dead—"

"Or the living."

"But surely you can see that something about this situation doesn't add up."

Something in the pastor's face changed. He sucked in his lips and bit down. "There were some who felt he had . . . strayed from the path."

"What path is that?"

"The path of righteousness. What other worthwhile path is there?"

Wallace didn't need to get sidetracked into a theological debate.

"Did you ever hear anyone express a desire to commit violence against the senator?"

"No, Detective, I did not."

"Then, what did you hear? What led you to conclude that some felt he had strayed?"

"Well, I can't say, exactly."

"You can't or you won't?" She held her hands wide.

"Take your pick. My interpretation of other people's words and actions is just speculation, and I might be wrong. Maybe somebody had a sour expression at the mention of the man's name, or someone turned away too quickly from an opportunity to engage Herbert in conversation. I'm not about to put people under suspicion because of how I feel about their body language. Surely you can see I would quickly lose the trust of the entire congregation. And these people need to be able to trust me. That's a critical understanding that comes with belonging to a pastored congregation."

"What about you, Reverend Sutton?"

"What about me?"

Wallace waited.

"I may not have agreed with all of Herbert's positions—in fact, I was strongly opposed to some of them—but I'm not in the business of violence, if that's what you're asking. I would willingly suffer violence before I would commit it."

Something about the way the pastor spoke made Wallace believe him. Something about him reminded her of Lex, her younger brother, who was a Catholic priest. Vehement and rigorous in defense of his ideals but relentlessly gentle in his actions.

"Let's say I wanted to get my own reading on how Herbert Marioneaux was regarded by his former flock. Who would I speak to?"

"Well, anybody who'll speak to *you*." The pastor tilted his head to one side as if he was considering whether to continue. "You're free to speak to anybody in the congregation who'll talk to you."

After her meeting with the pastor, Wallace returned to her cubicle in the Homicide Division. LeAnne was in the next cubicle, working the phone like a seasoned telemarketer. Wallace saw the list she had emailed LeAnne sitting on the desk, with notes scribbled all over it.

"Any luck?" Wallace asked when LeAnne hung up her phone.

"Nobody's ever the right person to talk to. I've spent all day getting passed around like a porn magazine at scout camp." LeAnne leaned back in her chair and put her feet up on her desk. "It just all seems too petty to matter—squabbling over things like alternative wording in some amendment to the statute on llama farming, or griping about how Marioneaux kept somebody's pet project bottled up in committee instead of letting it come to the floor for a vote."

"Let's split up the rest of the list." Wallace pulled the original of the list from her satchel. "How far down have you gotten?"

"Really?" LeAnne asked. "You're actually going to do some of the scut work for a change?" She reached over and drew a line under the last name she had called.

"Aren't you going to ask me how things went with Glenn Marioneaux, yesterday?" She was learning productive ways to ignore Le-Anne's endless sniping and griping.

LeAnne looked as if she might give Wallace the eye roll that meant she knew she was being patronized.

"So, how did things go with the son?"

"He's got the makings of a motive, but maybe no opportunity. It'll depend on whether our IT people can resurrect that video from the church's hard drive and whether the head usher backs up his claim to have been at church at the critical time."

"What's the motive?"

"He was thin on details, but he was pretty clear that he suffered repeated humiliations at the hands of his father. And that just when he needed a father's attentions the most, he was routinely ignored or dismissed. I got the impression that whatever attention Herbert did give him might have involved violence between them."

"He wouldn't be the first to take down a parent for fucking up their life."

"But he was also pretty clear that, after all this time, he was tired of suffering the emotional fallout from whatever it was that happened and that the reason he moved back to Louisiana was so he could deal with the past and get his personal life back in order."

"Maybe a little patricide was all the therapy he needed."

"If that's the case, it didn't help. The man still has problems. And, to hear him tell the story, he needed something from his father. An admission. An apology and a plea for forgiveness, maybe. Something he seems to think he hadn't gotten yet. Something he would need Herbert alive for."

"And maybe he was feeding you a line of crap to cover up his decision to give homicide a try as an anger management technique."

"Possible. But something else is bothering me about Glenn. He may have a motive for killing Herbert—"

"But not one for blaming Eddie Pitkin. At least not one that you know about."

"Not one that *we* know about."

LeAnne grinned and rolled her eyes. "You really are trying hard. I'll give you that."

"I honestly don't get you, LeAnne. If you feel like you're being excluded, you cause a stink. If you feel like you're being included, you ridicule. The work you're offered is either beneath your dignity or over your head. What, exactly, works for you?"

Wallace groaned inwardly when she realized her mistake. She had recently asked her mother for advice on how to handle LeAnne. "Never ask a chronic malcontent what would make them happy," Carol told her. "It'll always be something that can't be delivered and that will always be your fault."

"What works for me is you not doing the including and the excluding." LeAnne laughed. "If it's a partnership, then we're equal. Nobody hands out the chores. We just get the work done."

"Fine, then. What's next?"

"See, that's what I'm saying. Just by asking that question in that tone of voice, it's like you're *letting* me be in charge, which is really just pretending because you're in charge of who gets to be in charge. It's still *you* at the wheel."

Wallace could feel a headache developing between her eyes. "You've given me a lot to think about. In the meantime, there are only eight names left on this list. I'll take the last four." Wallace ran her finger down the list of names and then picked up her phone and started dialing.

She finished her part of the list first. None of the people she spoke with raised her suspicions and none suggested further avenues of investigation. She pulled her notebook out of her shoulder bag and found the number for Molly Sylvester, the head usher Glenn had offered as someone who could verify the time he left the church the night Herbert was killed.

"This is Molly."

Wallace introduced herself and asked her if she could remember what time she last saw Glenn on the day in question.

"Well, it would have been a few minutes after eight. We have a six-to-seven service on Fridays and the collection is surprisingly strong, so it takes a while to do the count. And I had a client meeting at eight thirty—I put together private energy investments for high-net-worth individuals—so I would have been well on my way by no later than ten past eight."

"Thank you. That's all I really needed, Ms. Sylvester."

"May I answer an unasked question, Detective?"

"Of course."

"I know family members always fall under suspicion in these kinds of cases, but if you want my opinion, I don't think Glenn could do something like this. I've known him since he moved to Baton Rouge. He's a troubled man—there's no doubt about that—but it's himself, not others, whom he targets with his stronger emotions."

"That seems like a very well-informed opinion."

"It is. And I probably shouldn't be telling you this, but . . . we have a peer counseling program at the church. I'm a volunteer."

Wallace understood the risk the woman was taking, so she considered her next question carefully.

"I don't have any specific information that bears on your case, Detective, if that's what you're about to ask."

"Sorry. I was trying to figure out a way to ask without actually asking. Thanks for sharing your thoughts with me."

Despite Molly's opinion about Glenn, there was still a thirty-minute discrepancy between when he claimed he left the church and when she said she last saw him there.

She opened Google Maps and got a point-to-point route and travel time between Glenn's church and his father rental house in Spanish Town. It would take just over twenty minutes. The coroner had estimated Herbert's time of death at approximately eight forty-five Friday night. If Glenn left his church a few minutes after eight, he could have easily been there within the margin of error for the time-of-death estimate.

"People can be such jerks," LeAnne said, slamming her phone down at the end of a call.

"Anything come of your stakeout on Tonya Lennar?"

"A grand waste of time is what it's been so far. She seems to have a big zero for a life outside of her cleaning jobs."

"Then take a look at this."

Wallace showed her the page in her notebook with Glenn's stated time for being at the church and when Molly Sylvester said she last saw him there.

"Interesting. Assuming we're not able to recover the video from the church, how can we use this?"

"Let's make him nervous and see what he does. Here's his work number." Wallace pulled Glenn's card from her satchel and copied the number and handed it to LeAnne. "Call him. If he doesn't answer, leave a message telling him who you are and that, in light of a time discrepancy in his alibi, we need to speak with him and it has to be now."

"And what will you be doing?"

Wallace shook her head and laughed. "Calling his home number and saying the same thing. Unless you want to call his house, and have me call his office."

"Do you really think a stern phone call is going to put the fear of God in him?"

"It will if you mention the media is hounding the department for developments in this case. So, unless we can put this little time discrepancy to rest, our heightened suspicions will inevitably get spun into him being a suspect."

"Oooh. Wallace plays hardball."

"Wallace plays by the rules."

TUESDAY: JUNE 5 AFTERNOON

Wallace pulled to a stop at the apex of the long circular driveway in front of Glenn's home.

"Jesus, who lives like this?" LeAnne said, ogling the broad façade of the dressed-stone mansion. Gas lanterns lit the ornate arch that framed an intricate leaded-glass fanlight above the doors.

"Looks like we've been outflanked. That's Dorothy's car." Wallace pointed to the Cadillac she had seen Dorothy sitting in the day she first encountered her at the house in Spanish Town.

"The mother?"

Wallace nodded and looked over at LeAnne. "She has a way of getting under your skin if you're not careful."

"I can't stand people like that."

Wallace drilled her partner an are-you-kidding-me look.

"Wallace, that was a joke. Get it? I know I'm one of those people."

"Sorry. You caught me off guard. That was actually pretty funny."

However this partnership turned out, Wallace intended to make Jason Burley aware of just how much he owed her for taking LeAnne under her wing.

After the third ring, Dorothy answered the door. Glenn was not with her. Her stare shifted from Wallace to LeAnne and then back to Wallace. The trace of a smirk as she returned her gaze to Wallace made it clear that she was dismissing LeAnne.

"May we come in?"

Dorothy stepped aside, holding on to the massive door, as Wallace and LeAnne crossed the threshold into the foyer—a huge round room with a delicate marble-topped table in the center. A spray of colorful fresh-cut flowers in a Chinese porcelain cachepot sat atop the table, and a circular staircase wound gracefully up the left wall to a second story. A runner, anchored by brass fittings, carpeted the center of the stairs.

Dorothy pushed the door shut and without looking back, she strode from the foyer through a barrel-vaulted doorway into a large room with floor-to-ceiling windows, leaving Wallace and LeAnne to follow.

The furniture in the room was arranged in four conversational groupings. In the distance, Wallace could see into a dining room with a table that looked as if it would comfortably seat sixteen.

"You have no idea what you've done to him, do you?" Dorothy stopped in front of a long sofa and sat.

"We're here to see Glenn, Mrs. Marioneaux. He invited us, and agreed to speak with us." Wallace kept her tone even.

"I can't see why. You've already got that awful man in jail. The one who very nearly ruined Herbert's reputation and who went to great pains to end Herbert's life."

Wallace gave LeAnne an almost imperceptible nod, and LeAnne detached herself from the group and walked deeper into the house.

"Where does she think she's going?" Dorothy demanded, glancing toward LeAnne.

"I was hoping to put this matter to rest as easily as possible, Mrs. Marioneaux. That's why we insisted on seeing Glenn today."

"Bullied him is what you mean."

"Is he here?" LeAnne asked from the other side of the room, about to disappear down a hallway.

"You listen to me. He's had difficulties. And now you come along with your twitchy little nose and poke it in where it definitely does not belong. Shame on you." Dorothy jabbed an accusing finger at Wallace.

"Glenn? Mr. Marioneaux? This is Detective Hawkins. Detective Hartman and I are—"

Wallace and Dorothy turned toward LeAnne. Her cell phone was to her ear. Wallace nodded for LeAnne to continue.

"Please," Dorothy said, appealing to Wallace. "Can't you leave him alone? He's got nothing to do with Herbert's death."

"I understand your need to say that, Mrs. Marioneaux, but others will make that determination." Wallace could hear LeAnne in the background, finishing her call, trying to cajole Glenn into making an appearance.

Dorothy stood and started in LeAnne's direction.

"No, Mrs. Marioneaux. Don't do that. We drove over here in good faith, because Glenn agreed to help us clear up some things. If you can convince him to come down, that would be very helpful."

Dorothy resumed her place on the couch. "He was making progress, but you and your tawdry questions and your sad little suspicions are undoing that."

Wallace let the silence stretch. The only sound was the faint tap of LeAnne's heels on the hardwood floor as she rejoined the group.

"We're not here to dig up the past." LeAnne said, stopping next to Dorothy.

"I don't know what he told you yesterday, but you can't believe everything that comes out of that fevered brain of his." She closed her eyes and leaned forward, elbows on her knees. "Glenn would never hurt anyone. Everybody sees this big, strong man, but he's as gentle as a soul could be."

"Is he here? In the house?" LeAnne asked. "We appreciate that you're trying to protect him, but in fact, so are we."

"Oh, you don't expect me to fall for that line of baloney, do you? I may not be Baton Rouge smart, like the two of you, but I assure you I'm a long way from stupid." The edge was back in her voice.

"But she's right," Wallace said. "Until we can clear up the matter we came here to discuss, the suspicion around him will only deepen."

"Mrs. Marioneaux, this will be easier if we can talk to Glenn here." Uninvited, LeAnne sat next to Dorothy.

"If it leaks out that he's wanted for questioning but that he's refusing to cooperate . . ." Wallace let the threat hang in the air.

"Get out. Your threats might have worked with Glenn, but I assure you I'm not easily intimidated. Unless you intend to arrest him, I want you to leave."

"She blames herself, for not doing anything to stop Herbert's emotional torment of the boy." LeAnne slipped off her jacket and draped it in the crook of her arm.

Wallace pulled open her car door. "And now she's afraid if Glenn keeps talking to us her failure will become public knowledge. She's protecting herself under the guise of protecting her son."

Wallace took a last look at the front of Glenn's house, wondering if he was peering down at them from one of the dark second-story windows. They would have to come up with a new plan for getting an explanation of the time discrepancy.

LeAnne slid into the passenger seat of Wallace's cruiser and pulled the door shut.

As Wallace reached for the door on her side, her phone buzzed. It was Melissa Voorhees, the police chief in Cavanaugh.

"They found the red kayak," Melissa said. "It was nearly two miles out in the swampy area of the park. A couple of fishermen. No sign of Peter, but there was half an inch of water in the bottom of the boat. Rainwater, not swamp water. They know that because the water was clear, not turbid like swamp water would be."

"I knew I wasn't going to like this," Wallace said. She wandered a few steps down the driveway, then looked back at LeAnne, who was busy with her own phone.

"I'm told it rained in the area around seven last night, but not since then," Melissa continued. "That means the kayak's been out there about eighteen hours."

"Was there anything in the kayak besides water?"

"Nope."

"Could it be someone else's kayak?" Wallace asked.

"It could be. But it would need to be someone who is also named Peter Ecclestone, because that's the name stenciled on the hull, just behind the cockpit."

Wallace went quiet. She looked back at LeAnne again. She had told Burley and LeAnne about Peter yesterday afternoon and then Peter had failed to appear as promised. Now he seemed to have vanished from a place he was not even scheduled to be.

"If you're trying to think of a reason for that kayak to be out there without its owner, I can come up with one." Melissa sighed. "Peter may not have been cut out to run a studio, but over the years he's been moderately successful as a part-time weed merchant. It's also rumored, but I have no real evidence of this, that he's branched out into other forms of chemically curated entertainment. If that's the case, then a little bit of worry might be in order. Meth and its various cousins have a way of making people forget who their friends are, especially if those friends develop the kind of sloppy business practices that put them too far past due in paying for the merchandise."

"I hear what you're saying." Wallace's words came out mechanically, but there was no thought behind them. She was just making sounds to hold up her end of the conversation while her mind considered a new possibility. "What are the odds of him getting picked up by some leg breakers at the exact moment I needed him to give a statement in a high-profile homicide?"

"I guess that would depend on how many people were after him. And how motivated they were."

Wallace quickly weighed the pros and cons of exposing her thinking to Melissa and decided to trust her. Peter seemed to have disappeared before Wallace had ever called her, so the chance she might be involved seemed low.

"Did you tell any of your officers—anyone—the reason I'm looking for Peter?" Wallace asked.

"Not a soul. Why?"

"Right after I told my people about him, he promptly disappeared under circumstances that you've got to admit look pretty peculiar."

"You think one of your people is talking out of school?"

"I don't want to think that."

If Peter's disappearance was connected to his extracurricular activities, that was a calamity of his own making. If it was connected to the fact that he could alibi Eddie Pitkin, then there was almost certainly a leak in her department. Wallace felt like hitting something.

"That would be unfortunate, and very dangerous. But don't just toss my theory out the window. Peter's a nice guy, but he plays with a rough crowd. So, it could be that this is a coincidence—something that was going to happen sooner or later—and it just happened to go down at a really inconvenient time for you."

"Can you keep his disappearance quiet for a while? And do you think you could have his vehicle hauled someplace private?"

"Yes, to both questions. I'll have the SUV brought to Cavanaugh. We'll stow it in the police garage."

"If his vanishing act is because of a leak, but the bad guys don't know I know—"

"Then they won't know you've figured out there's a hole in the boat."

"And maybe I can use that."

"I assume you'll want to look over Peter's vehicle, once I get it in here," Melissa said.

"I'm going to owe you, big-time."

"You won't owe me a thing."

"Can you get Peter's cell service provider to notify you if his phone pings any of the networks?"

"Sure. I'll have to lie and say I've got a missing person report, but hey, what's a few more hours in purgatory?"

For about half a minute, Wallace considered going out to Lake Kilgore to look for Peter. But the lake was too big and her resources too few. Plus, with so many other tasks facing her, she didn't have time. Part of her believed Peter would eventually turn up. Another part of her had a funny feeling she'd seen the last of him.

A sudden dread scurried along her nerves. If Peter was missing because he could've alibied Pitkin, then whoever took him was willing to go to great lengths to make sure the frame fit like a custom-made suit.

And if the people behind Peter's disappearance felt like she was getting too close to the uncomfortable truth of their methods, she too might end up missing.

Other problems loomed, as well. Chief Shannon had told Wallace he wanted daily reports on developments in the case, but until she could determine whether there was a leak or ascertain Peter's fate she wouldn't know who she could trust with details about the case. She would have to either avoid her colleagues or start lying to them. Just the possibility of a leak would cut her off from the resources she needed the most.

The worst part was that a very dangerous cat could be let out of the bag at any time. Once Tasha Kovacovich, Eddie's lawyer, became aware the police had found and then lost an alibi witness, she was going to scream bloody murder. She would accuse the police of suppressing critical defense evidence, and public perception would be on her side.

Tasha wouldn't rest until the whole country knew that another black man was headed to the death chamber because of police misconduct. Wallace and Jack Shannon would be lucky to avoid being indicted, much less losing their jobs.

Wallace felt like her world had shrunk to a pinpoint. She needed some perspective.

Colley Greenberg had been Wallace's first partner when she joined the detective division. He had actually been far more than that—a mentor, a role model, a friend. In retirement, he was still all those things, just no longer connected to her day-to-day world.

"This is seriously bad news," he said after Wallace had laid out the sequence of events that led her to suspect Peter Ecclestone's disappearance was due to a leak in the department. "It could all have an innocent explanation, but my instincts are telling me the same as yours."

She looked over at him, struggling to hide her discomfort. He sounded the same as always, but parked in his wheelchair, in the sunroom at the back of his house, he no longer looked the same.

His multiple sclerosis was the relapsing and remitting variety. He would be fine for a while, then it would show up and ravage him and then turn him loose again. Just when Wallace would start to believe they had seen the last of it, the disease came roaring back. And each new episode pulled him visibly closer to the clearing at the end of the path.

"Did you ever have a situation like this?" she asked, dragging her thoughts up out of the well of anxiety, focusing on the reason for her visit.

"Not exactly. Every now and then, some self-aggrandizing asshole would leak stuff to the press, but I never had any reason to think somebody might be in cahoots with the bad guys I was chasing."

"If you were in my shoes, what would you do?"

"Seems to me you can play this two ways."

"Keep everything close to the vest or plant some tantalizing information with the suspected leakers and see where it goes."

He nodded.

"Did you ever do that with me?"

"Do what?" Colley asked.

Wallace could tell from his barely suppressed smirk that he knew what she meant.

"Feed me some bullshit to see if I'd spill it where it didn't need to be? You know, when we first started working together? Just to see if you could trust me?"

He shrugged and laughed.

"Colley, I can't believe you would do that." She pushed her lip out in a pout. "That doesn't seem very partner-like."

He reached across the table and took one of her hands. "I'm happy to see you haven't lost your sense of idealism."

"Hey." She squeezed his hand and sat straighter, trying to look serious. "Do you think I'm hardheaded?"

He roared with laughter.

"Then why did you want me?"

"They tried to talk me into partnering with somebody else, but I was just hardheaded and idealistic enough to know you were the right person for me. Besides, when it was my turn to pick they were fresh out of perfect people."

The room went quiet and Wallace felt herself slipping into a maudlin frame of mind.

"I just *can't believe* I can't trust Burley," she said, breaking the silence, maneuvering the conversation back onto a topic that didn't remind her that she and Colley weren't a team anymore.

"It's got nothing to do with what you believe. It's a matter of what you know and what you don't."

"I know. I'm just saying."

"Yeah, and just saying has a way of turning into just thinking and, before you know it, just thinking turns into just doing . . . doing the wrong damn thing."

Colley was ruthless about never losing sight of the difference between what you knew and what you didn't know and the difference between what you knew and what you merely believed. He had drilled it into her that you couldn't be a worthwhile detective unless you mastered those distinctions.

She missed him when they were apart, and now she was starting to miss him even when they were in the same room with each other. This was going to be harder than she thought.

Her stomach was in knots. She was back in Burley's fishbowl of an office.

"Wallace, we've already been over this." He was digging around in his briefcase, which was open on his desk.

"I'm just letting you know why I think Ecclestone won't come in."

"Then have him picked up, for Christ's sake. This whole investigation turns on whether it looks like Pitkin is the killer or he's just the pretty picture in a frame."

"Understood. But I've been thinking. Even if Ecclestone can put Eddie on False River at the time of death, it may not mean anything. Maybe Eddie didn't put the slip lock around Marioneaux's neck with his own hands. What if he paid someone to do it while he was safely away from the scene of the crime?"

"If that were the case, he would have made sure there were fifty videos of himself singing karaoke in some juke joint in New Orleans." He snapped his briefcase shut. "Do we need to throw some extra bodies at this?"

"I've informally enlisted the help of the police in Cavanaugh, where he lives."

"Informally?"

"The chief of police there fully understands the urgency of the situation, and she's closer to the . . . locus of circumstance than we are."

"The locus of circumstance? What the hell does that mean?"

"It means she knows the guy and his habits. He's sort of been on her radar for a while. She's in an excellent position to keep an eye out for him. And a BOLO was put out on his vehicle, cell service providers have been asked to notify us if his phone shows up, but . . ."

"But what?"

"He's a wildlife photographer. He's known to disappear out where cell signals don't reach."

"What is LeAnne working on?"

"I've put her back on Tonya Lennar, for the moment. And I've got her digging for any connection she can find between Glenn Marioneaux and Eddie Pitkin."

Burley leaned across his desk, his hands flat against the wooden surface. "Wallace, look. Shannon is breathing down my neck, so if this phantom witness of yours doesn't turn up quick he's gonna start breathing down your neck too. And trust me, you ain't gonna like it."

It was almost like Burley and Chief Shannon were a tag team. Within an hour of her conversation with Burley, the chief had summoned her to his office. The knots in her stomach were tightening.

Shannon was standing when Wallace entered his office. He remained on his feet, and he didn't invite her to sit.

"Detective Hartman, correct me if I'm wrong, but I distinctly re-member Burley telling me yesterday that you found a witness who might be able to put Eddie Pitkin at a location too far away from the Marioneaux murder for him to have done the deed himself. Yet, despite the obvious necessity of getting this person's statement on record, it seems that's not being done. Now, am I losing my mind, or are you playing some kind of a game with me?"

"It's neither, sir. The man in question has turned out to be unre-liable, in the extreme. His identification of Pitkin was slightly iffy to begin with, and now it seems he's gone off somewhere. In the town he comes from, he's a well-known flake with ties to a lot of undesirable types. Apparently, unexplained absences are more the rule than the exception."

"And you're telling me you have no idea what has happened to him?"

"Nothing concrete, no, sir." Wallace started gently bumping her palms together in front of her chest. She wondered why the urge to do idiotic things with her hands seemed so irresistible when she was lying and why the things she normally did when she was telling the truth were so impossible to remember.

"Ideas, by definition, are not concrete, Detective, and I just asked if you had any *ideas*."

Wallace remembered playing this game with her father when she was in high school. She would hedge, he would hem her in, she would hedge some more, and he would hem her in some more. This would go on until he had cornered her so tightly that the next words out of her mouth would have to be a lie. Then he would just look at her and, like an electric current, his thoughts would arc across the space between them letting her know that he knew. He never pushed her that last step and made her say the untrue words, but he had no problem bringing her right up to the bleeding edge of the lie, forc-ing her to recognize that he knew she was struggling to be dishon-est without uttering the actual falsehood itself. She had loved him for never making her say the words. She had respected him for understanding that if something was so damned important that she was willing to work that hard to conceal it without violating the trust that an outright lie would entail then he was willing to let her win the round as long as she understood that, whenever he felt it was warranted, he could win the game.

Shannon walked over to the window and looked down toward the street, then up at the sky. "Were you aware that I have two teen-aged children, Detective?"

"Yes, sir. If I'm not mistaken, that's a picture of them on the book-case over there."

"They're wonderful kids," he said, turning back to face her. "I've learned a lot from them, about dealing with people, and how to pick your battles. You know what I'm saying?"

"I believe I do."

"Good. Excellent, in fact. Kids can get you into a lot of trouble. But, at the same time, they can be source of real joy. Just having them around can be like a magic protection against so many bad things. You just have to know when to trust them."

He reached into his desk drawer and pulled out a set of reading glasses and slid them on and picked up a folder.

"One more thing. Were you aware that the Marioneauxs want to make a public appeal for calm?"

"No, sir. No one told me that. But given the sudden rise in temperature in the city, it sounds like a good idea. Will they be taping it, or will it be a live broadcast?"

"Neither. It'll be live and in person from the plaza between City Hall and the theater."

"Pardon my saying so, but that doesn't seem wise. How do we know whether all the people who show up will be fully committed to peace, love, and understanding?"

"It was the Marioneauxs' wish to do it this way. And, to be hon-est, there's no way we can keep them from doing it. If we don't let them use the plaza, they'll find some other place."

"This is a bad idea, Chief Shannon." She was willing to bet Dorothy had hatched this plan to divert suspicion away from Glenn.

"It's their belief, as well as the mayor's and a few others', that face-to-face with the citizens is more authentic and shows courage. They don't want to come across as afraid and aloof, like they were just going through the motions, because that might defeat the whole point of the event. The consensus is that for this to work, it has to be high impact and in the flesh."

"When is this blessed event going to take place?"

"Tomorrow afternoon, at four thirty."

"Then please tell me we'll have the plaza crawling with security."

He thumbed his glasses up the bridge of his nose. "Rest assured there will be plenty of crowd control in place. Overt and covert."

"Could we at least persuade them to do this indoors? Where seating is limited and access is through a metal detector?"

"This decision has already been made, Detective. Please, carry on."

"May I give you my report for the day?"

He looked at his watch, then at Wallace. "The day is not over, but I suppose now will be okay."

Wallace repeated what she told Burley, leaving out her suspicions about a leak. She couldn't imagine Jack Shannon would be involved in something that absurd, but someone connected to him might be.

SIXTEEN

Wallace left the building after her meeting with Chief Shannon. She needed a place to think and organize what she had discovered so far. She sat in her car, raking through Marioneaux's past one more time, trying to fit everything she knew into the basic framework of means, motive, and opportunity.

Means was not an issue. Someone had tightened a slip lock around the victim's neck. No special skill was required to accomplish that.

And while the list of people she thought of as having an opportunity was short, the fact was, any one of an unlimited number of people could have killed Marioneaux, people who had simply not yet shown up on her radar.

It was the same with motive. In a broad sense, Marioneaux had probably pissed off enough people in his life that the universe of possible killers was practically infinite—an essentially meaningless state of affairs.

She started over, going back through her notes on the history between Eddie and Herbert. While it was true that they had spewed a lot of venom at each other over the years, in some strange way each man seemed to need the other. Each functioned as a springboard from which the other was able to launch himself and his mission into the public consciousness.

She turned to her notes on Glenn, but after a few minutes she found her attention refocusing on Eddie. His situation was different, if only because it was noisier.

With Glenn, it looked like a need for reconciliation balanced against a possibility of revenge, with a slightly shaky alibi thrown into the mix.

But with Eddie, a lot of elements were in play. The DNA, the unconfirmed sighting in Spanish Town the night of the murder, the insulation fibers, and the attic exit all rested on one side of the balance. The discovery of an alibi witness and his increasingly peculiar disappearance, along with the possibility of a leak, all weighed heavily on the other side.

She closed her eyes and leaned her seat back, squirming around until she found a position that didn't aggravate the pain in her side, and then let the newspaper version of Eddie Pitkin's life play out in her head.

When she stopped trying to filter his life through the question of why he might have killed Herbert Marioneaux, the opening she had been searching for revealed itself. It had been with her all along. She had been asking the wrong question. It wasn't why would Eddie kill *Herbert*, but why would Eddie kill *anyone?*

She reached for the ignition.

Wallace pulled into the little parking lot that ran along the side of Davis McCone's law office. It was a solo practice housed in a beautiful Hays Town building that dated from the architect's reclaimed-brick and large-pane-window period. She jogged up the front steps, the ache in her side reminding her she still hadn't told Mason about the attack.

Barbara Seeley, Davis's forever secretary, greeted her as she entered the reception area.

"Hi, Wallace. What a nice surprise."

"Do you think he has a minute to see me?" she asked after giving Barbara a quick hug.

"If you hurry. He's got a couple of late clients starting in about half an hour."

Davis looked up from behind his desk and smiled as Wallace entered the office. "How's your mother?"

"I was just going to ask you the same question. Have the two of you spoken since her birthday dinner?"

"We have." Davis's smile got bigger. "And I've been told that I'm a lot to think about. Which sounds like one of those her-people-will-call-my-people situations."

"Well, you *are* a lot to think about. In a good way." A thoughtful smile emerged as she toyed with the idea of having Davis as a stepfather.

"So, what brings you into a place of such low repute?" Davis rose from his desk chair. "I know you're not here for the latest in geriatric gossip."

"I'm calling in a marker," she said, trying to sound jaunty.

"You don't have any markers." Davis laughed. "But whatever it is you want, I'll do it for free." He motioned for her to take a seat on the couch and then sat in one of the side chairs facing her.

"This is something I'd like to keep quiet, for the moment."

"I've got one-way ears. You tell me, and it stays inside. Period." He tapped the side of his head with an index finger.

"All those years ago, when Eddie Pitkin went to prison on that obstruction of justice charge, the evidence-tampering thing, the person who tattled on Eddie—"

"A confidential informant," Davis said.

"And, according to the old news reports I've been reading, it was also an anonymous informant."

"That's correct. And as far as I know, the DA at the time, Colin Gerard, never discovered the informant's identity."

"Is it possible Colin actually did know but for some reason decided to claim it was an anonymous snitch, so there'd be no chance the judge could order them to reveal it?"

"It's a possibility, but it's an incredibly remote possibility. A stunt like that—essentially pulling the wool over the judge's eyes—it would have to be worth risking your license to practice law. The informant's name would have to be something either really valuable or extremely dangerous."

"Can you see where I'm going with this?" Wallace asked.

"Given the hot potato case you're working on, you must think the informant was Herbert Marioneaux."

"And somehow, after all these years, Eddie Pitkin found out and decided to take revenge for having his career ruined, not to mention having to spend all that time in prison."

"Well, it has a certain intuitive appeal. I'll grant you that." Davis nodded.

"A white segregationist putting the finger on an activist black criminal defense lawyer."

"That would've caused quite a rumpus in the community. But, even if you're right, would that be enough for Pitkin to risk going back to prison forever—or even being executed?"

"That I don't know," Wallace said. "But think about it. If it was enough, and the informant's identity has never been known, who would suspect that now, after all these years, Eddie Pitkin had found out?"

"Obviously *you* would," Davis said, laughing.

"But if there was no forensic evidence placing Eddie at the scene, no one would ever tie these two things together. Very clever, don't you think?"

Davis went quiet for several seconds.

"What are you thinking?" Wallace asked.

He smiled at her. "That you're a very inventive thinker and I hope I'm never the one you're looking for."

"Even if you were, I'd probably let you slide if you promised to behave in the future."

Davis went quiet again.

"Seriously, though, something about this discussion is bothering me. I'm flattered you'd want to bounce these ideas off me, but . . ."

"Why you and not my compadres in the police department?"

"The question does raise itself."

"That vessel may be a bit leaky, at the moment, and I don't think I have the time to figure out where the problem is."

"That's troubling. Extremely troubling. Do you feel like you're in personal danger?"

"No more than usual."

"I wish you had just lied and said no. Now, I'm going to worry my old head off. You know, I really wish this was not your case."

"I'll be fine."

"Look, I know you didn't come over here just to discuss your latest theory. You mentioned calling in a marker."

"According to the old newspaper stories, the informant was passing the information directly to the District Attorney, not the police?"

"Colin is in a nursing home now."

"I know. A series of minor strokes." Wallace hesitated. "And this is going to sound heartless, but at this stage in his life it's unlikely he'd be called to account for any shenanigans he might've pulled all those years ago."

"You want me to see if I can get him to cough up a name?"

"Didn't you go to law school with him?"

"I did and we've been friendly over the years, but I don't think that'll cut much ice with Colin."

"If the informant was Marioneaux, then there's no longer a worry it would put *him* in danger."

"My guess is, if Colin knew it was Marioneaux, he would've come forward with that, once Eddie Pitkin was arrested for the murder. He would have offered it to our current DA."

"Would you mind asking him, anyway? Otherwise, I've got some pretty good reasons to believe we've got the wrong guy in jail for doing Marioneaux."

Davis let out a long breath. "You can be very persuasive, you know?" He got behind his desk and flipped through a calendar book. "Come back Thursday afternoon and I'll let you know what I find out." He made a notation on the page in front of him.

"And I'll expect you to let me know when Mom's people call your people."

SEVENTEEN

Wallace stood next to her car, staring at the darkening sky, unsure whether she really wanted to discover what she was about to start looking for.

Melissa Voorhees had called to let her know that Peter's SUV had been towed to the police garage in Cavanaugh, so Wallace drove out, hoping to find something that would lead her to the missing photographer. Hoping, at the same time, that she wouldn't find a dead body at the end of the trail.

After a few seconds, she forced the indecision from her thoughts and strode toward the dingy metal building. She paused when she realized just how strange her investigation was beginning to feel. She had gone to Davis looking for help to show Eddie had a motive, and now she was looking for an alibi witness to show that Eddie had no opportunity. No one would be able to accuse her of favoring one side over the other.

The throb in her side where she had been punched reminded her that the longer she put off telling Mason about the attack in her carport, the more damage she was doing.

Except for the scrape of her boots on the concrete driveway, there was a lifeless quiet to the evening.

She pulled open the door and stepped inside. Strains of forties jazz oozed from an old boom box sitting on top of a rolling tool bin near the hydraulic lift.

The only person in the three-bay garage was a woman in her late thirties, sitting at a small metal desk at the other end of the building, typing away on a laptop. She looked up as Wallace stepped inside.

"Detective Hartman?"

"Only if you want me to go back to calling you Chief Voorhees?"

The woman gave Wallace an easy smile and motioned toward a large plastic ice chest sitting on the concrete in front of the desk. "Water and soft drinks in the cooler. Is this the vehicle you remember?" She rose from the desk and inclined her head toward the SUV one bay over.

Although it was fainter, from being exposed to the rain, Wallace could see the finger-drawn "Test Dirt" inscription in the dust covering the hatchback. The license plate number was the one she remembered. Her eyes fell on the empty roof rack.

"It's back there." Melissa pointed to a red kayak standing on end in the far corner.

The sight of the little boat made Wallace's heart sink. "Thanks for meeting me here."

"Not a problem. It was either this or homework patrol." She cocked her head toward the SUV. "Shall we take a look?"

"Is it open?"

"No, but I have this lovely little slim-jim." She picked up the door-opening device from the desk and walked over to the SUV. "What are we looking for?" Melissa asked, working the thin metal strip between the window and the door.

"Something that points us to where Peter is. Or something that tells us whether his disappearance is connected to my case. What those things might be I might not know until we see them."

"Got it." Melissa popped open the door. "Why don't we unload the back first, then we can do a forensic exam of the interior. I'm the chief of police, but I'm also my little department's only formally trained crime-scene investigator."

Working quietly, they removed everything from the rear of the SUV and stacked it near the desk where Melissa had been working.

"Can we start with prints?"

"This is your show." Melissa opened the large tackle box that held her fingerprinting tools. Wallace watched, in silence, as Melissa carefully dusted every likely and a great many unlikely surfaces inside and outside the vehicle.

"It looks like the interior has been wiped clean," Melissa said after a half hour of steady work.

"That's a bad omen," Wallace said. *Who would wipe a vehicle except someone trying to cover something up?*

"Hold on. It looks like we've got one partial, on the glove compartment latch button," Melissa said. "I'll try to ID it after we're done."

"What about blood?" Wallace asked.

"Hit the lights, would you. The switch is over there." Melissa pointed to the wall behind the desk.

Wallace killed the overhead lights. In the faint glow from the SUV's dome light, she watched as Melissa sprayed the interior with luminol and then climbed out and closed the door, plunging the garage into total darkness. Nothing inside the vehicle fluoresced.

"Well, that's a relief—sort of." Although she didn't feel relieved.

Melissa pulled off her gloves and used a paper towel to wipe the sweat from her forehead. "If Peter's disappearance is related to his drug business, I guess it's possible some of his merchandise might be onboard, although that seems unlikely?"

"Right," Wallace said. "If his suppliers were looking for back payment, I'm guessing they would've already taken this baby apart looking for money or inventory they could reclaim."

"Or sold the vehicle itself. So, do you think it's worth it, to go through all the crap we unloaded?" Melissa asked.

"I do. He told me he had a list of places he was going to visit, after he left False River. I don't know if it was a pencil-and-paper list or just in his head. But maybe he wrote something down that might shed some light on where he is. It's always possible he left his vehicle at the park and went off with someone," Wallace said.

Melissa looked pointedly from the SUV to the kayak standing in a back corner of the garage. "I suppose."

"And maybe someone borrowed his kayak while he was gone, and just abandoned it," Wallace said, feeling like she was grasping at straws.

They opened each box and poked through the contents. It was sweaty work and it was edging into what Wallace assumed was dinnertime for Melissa and her family.

"Keep in mind that Peter's general approach to life had a way of creating circumstances that made his periodic absences more or less a necessity." Melissa pulled the top off a box and peered inside. "So, he was better than average at knowing how and when to hightail it out of town. He could have seen a bad time coming from some of his own screw-ups or because of whatever you wanted him for and he just decided to disappear in a way that would make anyone looking for him think he was out of the picture for good."

Wallace walked away from the box she was rooting through, and sat on the cooler. "You seem to know the man pretty well." Keeping her eyes on Melissa, Wallace stretched her arms forward, trying to touch her toes. She stopped when the knot over her kidney spasmed with the effort.

"We both grew up here in Cavanaugh. Everybody knows everybody."

Wallace kept her gaze on the woman, wondering if there was more to come.

"And yes, we were involved, way back in the Dark Ages," Melissa said. "It was a long, long, *long* time ago. And it was so brief I can almost make myself believe I imagined it. Almost." A mischievous light flickered in her eyes. "You ever know guys like him? A whole lot of charm and a whole lot of penis, but nothing really substantial connecting the two?"

Wallace laughed at the unexpected joke. "I've heard such creatures exist." She stood, trying to ward off a sinking spell. "You seem fairly resigned to his disappearance."

Melissa sat on the concrete floor next to the open box and pulled her knees up to her chest. "Well, like I said, his vanishing acts are not anything new. We've all gotten exercised about his comings and goings before, so it's hard to believe this time is really different." She smiled, but Wallace could see worry lines in her forehead.

"All those times before, did he ever leave his car behind when he took off?"

Melissa shook her head.

Wallace sat back down on the cooler as her mind began to crowd with possibilities.

If Peter's disappearance was was connected to his drug business, Wallace could easily imagine how things happened. A familiar but not-so-friendly face appears in the passenger-side window when Peter is about to pull out of the driveway. Before he can hit the lock button, the door opens and the person attached to the face slides in. A weapon becomes visible. Peter activates his aw-shucks module, but the sheepish look and the tentative smile are met with a shake of the head and a look of sad dismay.

Brother Peter, how come you couldn't just pay me my money when you had it in your hand, instead of trying to string me along? I don't run a fucking finance company. Man, you know that. It's strictly cash-and-carry. But, for you, I made an exception . . . for old time's sake . . . but you took advantage. You fucked half the town, and now you finally got around to fucking yourself. Turn left, at the end of this block.

But if Peter was gone because he could alibi Eddie Pitkin, other questions came back into consideration. Why was Marioneaux killed while the fall guy was way out on False River instead of in Baton Rouge, where it would have been easier to make the frame-up work? To make the frame fit, the plotters would've had to know when Eddie couldn't account for his time. So someone had to be watching him to know when that was. But where had they been watching from?

Wallace took a deep breath. For the second time in one day, she realized she was thinking about things wrong. What was *in* the boxes might be less important than what *wasn't*.

She looked to her left. The police chief's stare and her off-kilter smile told Wallace that Melissa had been looking at her for a while.

"Where on earth did you just go?"

"We're in the wrong place," Wallace said.

"I believe you, but how do you know?"

"There's no camera equipment in any of these boxes."

"I just assumed he had his equipment with him."

"Maybe. But it could still be at the lake house." Wallace propped an elbow on one knee and rested her chin on the palm of her hand. "He went south from False River to Kilgore Park, so maybe, instead of taking everything, where it might get stolen out of his SUV, he left what he wasn't going to use at the lake house."

"And he was planning to pick it up on his way north, toward home."

Wallace nodded.

"But how would that help you?"

"He said he had been taking pictures of the goings-on out on the lake, from the window in the rear bedroom. Even if Peter's not here to tell us what he saw, maybe there's an image in one of his cameras that will."

"I suppose that's possible."

"Although he did tell me that he hadn't taken any pictures of Eddie Pitkin sitting on the dock—"

"And you *believed* him?"

Wallace laughed at her own naïveté. "I did. But I'm thinking about something else he told me. He said he hadn't seen any cars parked along the road by the lake houses. So, just for the sake of argument, if we assume Eddie Pitkin is being framed, then the killers had to be watching him so they'd know when he would have no alibi. But there's no place along the road in front of the house, or the spaces between the houses, for a car or a watcher to go unnoticed."

"Somebody was watching him from a boat. That's brilliant. Wait, you don't think Peter was doing the watching from the house next door, do you?"

"I considered that for a second, but it doesn't make sense to me."

"What if someone asked him to watch but never told him the reason for the surveillance? And maybe Peter didn't ask. Maybe he owed that someone a load of cash and they decided to let him barter away his debt by doing a little stakeout on Pitkin."

Wallace shook her head. "But why would he return to the lake house, where he ran the risk of getting roped into an investigation? Why would he admit to me that he had seen Pitkin at all?"

Melissa nodded. She closed her eyes and took a couple of slow, deep breaths. "This case of yours is getting stranger by the minute."

"Would you happen to know the chief of police in New Roads?" Wallace asked.

"Oh sure. Mike Duncan. All of us Podunk police chiefs around here know each other. When we're not out fighting bad guys we're scheming about how to outfight our big-city brethren for taxpayer-funded grants so we can buy bigger guns and scarier military-style assault vehicles."

"His wife runs the property management company that leases out a lot of the houses on the lake, including the one your good buddy Peter was squatting in."

"And you want me to call him so he can roust MaryBeth in the middle of dinner and have her meet you at that lake house with a key?"

Wallace laughed. Until just now, she hadn't thought about how long it had been since she'd formed a new friendship with another woman. Tonight was strictly business, but Melissa's willingness to stay so late and work so hard on a case that wasn't hers, and her willingness to remain in a good humor, even though she was giving up an evening with her family, had the feel of more than just business. She seemed to be reaching out, so Wallace reached back.

"The tone of your offer tells me you know the chief's wife and that you might find it a little bit fun to drag her out of the house in the middle of dishing out the tuna casserole."

"For some reason, she's always had it in her head that I've got eyes for her husband."

"Have you?" Wallace laughed again.

"Well . . . yes. But it's literally eyes only. No other body parts involved." She raised her right hand in a scout's honor gesture. "Trust me, it was just window-shopping."

"I sure didn't expect to see you again anytime soon." MaryBeth gave Wallace a sharp look.

"It's a surprise to me too." Wallace tried to look appreciative.

"Do you think this is gonna take all night?"

"Thank you for coming out at such an inconvenient time." She tried harder to maintain her smile.

"There you go," MaryBeth said as she finished entering the alarm code. She stood aside to let Wallace enter.

Wallace moved into the hallway.

"Come in, if you wish," Wallace called back over her shoulder as she entered the living area of the little house. "Just don't touch anything, or move anything, in case I need to get a fingerprint tech in here."

"I'm fine right out here, thank you."

Peter might not have had much respect for the nuances of private property rights, but his housekeeping skills were excellent. Wearing latex gloves, Wallace moved quickly through the house, opening every cabinet and drawer and closet. She found no cameras or photography equipment.

She was about to feel a bit bad for hauling MaryBeth out so late for nothing when she remembered the dumpster where she had first found evidence of his presence. Even if he hadn't left any equipment with pictures of the lake, maybe he had thrown something away that would point to his whereabouts.

It was standing against the rear wall of the carport. With one hand Wallace raised the lid and shone her flashlight inside. A tied-off trash bag covered the bottom. On top of that lay a wadded-up paper cup. Wallace wondered about the box for the pizza he had had with him yesterday afternoon. It wasn't here, it wasn't in the house, and, now that she thought about it, there had been no telltale pizza smell inside Peter's SUV when she and Melissa had gone through it.

Maybe it was underneath the trash bag. Wallace threw back the lid and upended the dumpster, spilling its contents into the pool of light on the floor of the carport. No pizza box.

"You do intend to clean that up, I hope."

Wallace stopped momentarily, suppressing an urge to look up and see if MaryBeth was being serious.

She untied the bag and poked around among the contents. Nothing. Just household trash. She grabbed the cup and tossed it in the bag with everything else. As it left her hand, she heard it rattle. She reached inside the bag and snatched it back out.

Holding it gingerly by the rim, she carefully pried it open and turned it upside down. Her heart skipped a beat when a small plastic square about a half inch on a side with a red-and-white paper label tumbled out onto her gloved palm. She was no photographer, but she knew a memory card from a digital camera when she saw one.

Wallace couldn't afford to let anyone in her department examine the memory card until she knew for sure whether there was a leak, so she asked Mason for some under-the-table help. She drove straight from False River to his office. During the drive, the idea that they might be able to mix a little work time and playtime popped into her head. But then she became apprehensive. Once he saw the bruise on her back, he would be angry and hurt that she had waited so long to say anything.

She walked into his office determined to come clean, but the presence of two of his employees working late gave her second thoughts.

"Don't they have homes to go to?" she whispered from the chair across his desk, inclining her head toward the hallway behind her.

"Yes," he whispered back, leaning forward. "But they think you're dangerous, so they probably won't leave me unguarded as long as you're here."

"Can't you fire them?" She scrunched her nose and bit down on her lower lip. She leaned in closer.

"I could, but they're so good at what they do, I'd just have to hire them back, in the morning."

"Perfect. I promise to be gone by then." She inched closer.

"Hey, Mason." The voice came from the doorway behind her.

Mason bolted upright in his chair and peered over her. Wallace leaned back in her chair and ran the tip of her tongue along her upper lip. Mason went pink to his ears.

"I'll be right there," he said, fiddling uselessly with some papers on his desk.

Wallace heard footsteps retreating along the carpeted hallway behind her. She studied Mason as he maneuvered a set of keys from his pocket.

"So, we'll just put this in the drawer, for now." He dropped the memory card into an envelope and slid it into the desk drawer on his right. He locked the drawer and then rose from his chair, giving Wallace an expectant look. She remained seated, smirking at his discomfort.

"I think I can have something for you early tomorrow."

"But that's such a long time to wait. Besides, I have to go to work early tomorrow."

"They're right." He smiled and nodded in the direction of the hallway. "You are dangerous."

Wallace dithered over whether to tell him. He obviously had important work waiting for him down the hall, and distracting him by opening such a troubling and personal can of worms might be bad timing. She gave him an uneasy smile and decided to wait.

EIGHTEEN

Mason's entire staff was in the office, bright and early, when she arrived to see what they'd found on the memory card.

"These are just the images the photographer decided to keep," Mason said, dropping a flash drive into her open palm. They were standing inside his office.

"Is there a chance of recovering any deleted images?" The drive disappeared into one of her shirt pockets. She knew that whenever a camera recorded an image it assigned an address to it, so the camera would know where to look for it later. She also knew that deleting an image didn't actually erase it. It just nicked off the address so the camera no longer knew an image was there. Eventually, as new images were recorded, they were laid down on top of the deleted images. Once that happened, the earlier images were gone for good, but *until* that happened, they were still there.

"We're working on that," he said. "The card was handled quite a bit. Probably moved from one camera to another, so there's bound to be more than just the stuff we pulled off, so far. We should have something for you tonight. If it's after eight, I'll be at home. We can have dinner."

On her way from Mason's office to police headquarters, Melissa Voorhees called. The partial print she lifted from Ecclestone's vehicle hadn't matched anything in any of the fingerprint databases, so it didn't belong to Peter.

After a few hours at her desk, going through the images on the flash drive, Wallace was barely able to keep her eyes open. There were thousands of pictures and looking through them was tedious. Her eyelids were getting heavy and her concentration kept drifting.

"How're you doing, Detective Hartman?"

The voice startled her. She quickly minimized the pictures on her screen, then pulled her feet off her desk and looked behind her. It was Lanny Berto—a beat cop who, as far as Wallace knew, was trying hard to protect and serve but was in just a bit over his head.

"You might not want to sneak up on people like that."

When Berto smiled and jingled the keys in his pocket, Wallace realized she had actually heard the noise at the edge of her consciousness as he came up the hallway, but her fatigue had kept the sound from registering.

She gave him a weak smile. "What can I do for you, Officer Berto?"

"Not a thing. Just passing along information."

"I'm listening. Is this about one of my cases?"

"In a roundabout way."

"Okay." Wallace gave him a palms-up shrug.

"There's more than a few around here that feel like you're putting friendship ahead of doing the right thing. That maybe Mr. Pitkin needs to be wrapped up with a nice big rope and handed over to the DA so she can get down to business."

"And what, exactly, is the right thing, in the estimation of these unnamed others for whom you speak?"

"I don't speak for them. I'm just passing on the scuttlebutt, trying to do you a favor. Me, personally, it's no skin off my nose one way or the other. Just thought you'd want to know."

"What I'd like to know is who these dissatisfied folks are that you're talking about."

Berto scowled and backed up a step. Wallace regretted the words the moment they came out of her mouth. She sounded petty.

"Well, see, I didn't come here to get my*self* in trouble. I was just trying to help *you* out."

Wallace held up her hands in surrender. "And you did exactly the right thing. So, do you think this is just grumbling, or does it sound more like people with a plan of action?"

"No way for me to know. Just don't let your guard down."

"Thanks for the heads-up. I'll keep my eyes and ears wide open."

"You take care now." He turned and disappeared into the warren of cubicles and tables that spread across the room.

Wallace listened as the jingle of his keys kept time with the sound of his footsteps moving down the hallway. She wondered whether her visitor in the nighttime who had left his calling card above her right kidney was one of those dissatisfied colleagues and if maybe Berto was trying to make sure she had gotten the message or to warn her that another visit might be in the works.

"What was that all about?"

Wallace flinched—startled for the second time in two minutes. "Hey, LeAnne."

"A little jumpy today, are we?"

"Officer Berto stopped by to let me know that there are some among us who feel we're making a nuisance of ourselves by continuing this investigation."

"Did that little gargoyle just threaten you?" LeAnne pointed in the direction Berto had taken. "If he did, file a grievance against him. If people make trouble for you, you have to make trouble back."

"I don't think he intended it as a threat."

LeAnne shrugged and dumped her shoulder bag onto the seat of her chair.

"What have you found on Tonya Lennar?"

"She cleans houses, she goes to the grocery store, she goes home, she goes to sleep. If there's anything sinister there, it's very well hidden."

"What about any connection between Glenn Marioneaux and Eddie Pitkin?"

"Still digging. But so far, nothing."

"Did Burley give you the phone records on the Marioneauxs?"

"That's probably why he was looking for me. I'll go track him down. Unless you want to do that and I can take over your vacation-photo scrapbooking operation." LeAnne smiled and nodded at the pictures Wallace had just clicked open on her monitor.

"Thanks, but I'll manage."

After LeAnne took off, Wallace returned her attention to the images from Peter Ecclestone's memory card. He had taken lots of close-ups of insects and individual flower blossoms and one of a long-legged white bird wading through a marshy area. Peter was actually a good photographer, and Wallace kept finding herself engrossed in the quality of the composition and how beautifully some subjects were lit. But eventually the surge of energy that came from her encounter with Berto faded. She gulped down the remainder of her coffee and refocused.

She kept hoping she would find a shot of Eddie Pitkin on the dock behind Craig's lake house. There was a shot of the house at twilight, but there were no faces in the shot—just the house with clouds behind it. The milky glow from a waning gibbous moon shone through a thin spot in the clouds, and once again Wallace found her mind wandering. A few more screenfuls, then she would have to get up and move around to keep from falling asleep.

She scrolled down, bringing up a new batch of images. One by one, she ran her eyes across the pictures. Near the bottom of the screen she saw a series of daylight shots of the lake. It looked as if they had been taken from the back of the lake house where Peter had been staying. She remembered that the dock behind the house had been replanked. In the image on her screen, fresh tan boards were visible, mixed in with the weathered gray of the older planking.

Some of the images seemed to have no obvious subject. She spread the images and let her eyes roam over the elements in the pictures. Houses on the opposite bank, a speedboat pulling a pair of skiers exiting frame left, somebody wiping out on a boogie board. She dragged the images across the screen, chunk by chunk, looking at everything. Near the right edge of one picture she spotted a bass boat, with a lone occupant. It looked about a hundred yards offshore.

Wallace enlarged the shot further, marveling at the image resolution. The occupant was seated in the rear of the boat, right hand on the steering wheel, left hand holding a pair of binoculars to his eyes.

It had been a windy day and the choppiness of the water tilted the boat, so she couldn't be absolutely sure what the binoculars were aimed at, but it looked as if they were pointed toward the shore, a bit south of where Peter took the shot from. The occupant could have been looking back toward Craig's lake house. A registration number was visible on the hull, just below the forward gunwale.

Northlake Cemetery was old and no longer accepting new tenants, but it was still well kept. It had assumed an almost park-like status in Baton Rouge and, for the last half century, had been maintained by the city.

Wallace walked toward the sound of a mower in the distance. A sluggish breeze carried the heavy fragrance of freshly mown grass through the boneyard. It was a cloudless day, so she moved from one patch of shade to another, doing her best to stay out of the baking sun.

As the noise of the mower grew louder Wallace slowed. She wanted to approach the man with caution, but she didn't want him to know she was being cautious.

He had his back to her as he pushed his mower between two rows of headstones. She could see a thick black pouch-style wallet in the back pocket of his jeans. The steel chain fastening it to a belt loop glinted in the sunlight. He had draped a shop rag over his head and pulled a ball cap down on top of it, so the cloth shielded the back of his neck from the sun. He was a wiry man about her height, with thick, gristly forearms. The edge of a blurry tattoo on his right shoulder blade peeked out of the armhole of his sleeveless gray T-shirt. A Buck knife was strapped to his left thigh.

His head was down and he appeared to be focused on the ground right in front of his mower as he jockeyed it forward and backward, angling it this way and that as he mowed between and around the stones. He was very precise and extremely thorough. The cemetery was so large and the man cut with such deliberation, Wallace guessed that by the time he finished, it would be time to start again.

On his present trajectory, he would soon reach the high brick fence that ran along the perimeter. At that point, he would have to turn back in her direction.

She quickened her pace so she could meet him as he made the turn. The roar of the mower covered the sound of her arrival. With his head still down, the man mowed past the end of the row, then pulled back, making a three-point turn to head back in the direction he had come from.

As he began pushing up the row in earnest, Wallace's boot came to rest on the engine housing of the mower, bringing it and the man behind it to a sudden stop. For a full three seconds, nothing happened.

Wallace could practically hear him thinking. He would decide if he recognized the boot invading his field of vision and whether it was friend or foe. Then he would calculate whether, with both hands still gripping the mower handle, he could get to his knife in a useful amount of time. He elected to look before he leapt.

His head inched up. His brow furrowed and his gaze slowed as it moved past her hips and her gun and then stopped entirely, several inches above her belt line, once he became certain the boot belonged to a woman. Wallace's badge placard dangled from a lanyard around her neck. She flipped it around so he could see her ID on the other side.

With excruciating care, the man reached for a lever on the mower handle and turned the machine off. His big hands and his ropy, over-sized forearms were covered with a fine haze of grass and leaf trimmings.

"How are you, today, Mr. Harpin?" She spoke quietly, but, in the sudden silence, her voice seemed loud.

"Officer." He nodded, avoiding direct eye contact and declining to initiate further conversation.

"This feels like a good time to stand in the shade and take a break, wouldn't you say?"

He remained silent, apparently understanding her question was not really a question and not something to which an answer would be welcome. His gaze went over her shoulder, into the distance. Wallace studied him, fairly certain he was engaged in some internal debate over how he should proceed while he figured out what was coming down.

"I brought you a present." She smiled casually and offered him one of the bottles of water she carried with her, holding it by the cap.

"No, thank you."

She continued to hold the bottle in his direction. "You can pay me back out of what's in the cooler you've got in your pickup. Besides, how much cooperation will a bottle of water obligate you for, anyway?" She brought the bottle close to her face and studied the label. "Although it says here that this came all the way from some glacier in South America. Pretty special stuff." She held the bottle back in his direction. The smile was gone from her face.

Mechanically, Harpin's hand came up and he took the bottle, but he didn't open it. Wallace nodded in the direction of a huge oak and Harpin trudged ahead of her.

In the deep shade beneath the canopy of branches, Wallace leaned against the trunk, keeping Harpin backlit, between her and the sunshine.

"Am I in some kinda custody?" His gaze meandered across the loose branches and squirrel-gnawed acorns scattered among the tree roots.

"Would you like to be?"

Harpin looked at the bottle of water in his hand, then back over his shoulder at his silent mower. He pushed his lower lip out and rocked back on his heels.

Wallace pulled out her phone, tapping and swiping her way to the image of the man in the boat on False River. She spread the image until the boat and its occupant covered the screen.

"Is this you?" She held the phone up next to her face, forcing him to come in close for a look, so she could watch his expression as he examined the image on the screen.

She could tell that he was uneasy as his eyes toggled back and forth between her and the phone, eventually coming to rest on the picture.

"Can't really tell. He's wearing a cap and them binoculars he's looking through are covering some of his face."

"Look again. See that registration number on the bow. From that I found the owner—a gentleman by the name of Leslie Hatfield. He runs a boat rental concession on False River."

Harpin scuffed the toe of his stained work shoe against the ground.

"He says that this past Friday he rented that boat to a man who showed him a Louisiana driver's license in the name of Oliver Dale Harpin. As luck would have it, the State of Louisiana has issued only one driver's license to an Oliver Dale Harpin. I looked at the license photo. It looks a lot like you."

Harpin pursed his lips and nodded. They made solid eye contact for the first time.

"Tell me about your little outing."

"Nothing to tell. It's a popular fishing spot. I got a valid fishing license."

"Were you fishing for birds? It's those binoculars that make me ask."

He waited a few seconds before answering. "You don't know a lot about fishing, do you, Detective?"

"I'm more of a hunter."

"Well, see, nice boats got fish-finders. It's like underwater sonar that locates where the fish are schooling. The boat in that picture is a rental. A low-cost rental, at that, so it ain't equipped with fancy electronics."

He paused. Wallace knew he wanted her to ask him to continue, as if by making her drag things out of him he was somehow in control of the conversation.

"And all this has something to do with you and the binoculars?"

"Looking out for pelicans. You know, the state bird? They eat fish. Live fish. Scoop 'em up in them big bills they got. If you can spot a formation cruising low over the water and diving, you know there's fish close to the surface. A poor man's fish-finder." A smug grin spread across his face.

"Seems to me, such an expert fisherman as yourself would have his own boat and fishing equipment."

Harpin laughed and looked back at his mower, then at Wallace. "You priced out any decent bass boats lately? Even used ones might go for more than the substantial sums a memorial garden lawn care specialist rakes in. And you can bet the city don't hand out a lot of cash bonuses to people like me. All that green stuff you see out there—them's grass clippin's, not stock options."

"Tell me about Peter Ecclestone."

"Who?" Harpin held her gaze. "That a friend of yours?"

Wallace studied his face as he spoke. He hadn't flinched at the name.

"He might be a small-time meth peddler," she said. "From one of those picturesque little towns out in the Florida Parishes."

"And what? You think 'cause I do low-end manual labor for a

living that I'd just naturally know every crank dealer in the tri-state area?"

Wallace could hear the edge creeping into Harpin's voice. It might be aggression. It might be camouflage for some other emotion. "Think hard," she said. "This could be a bad time to have a lapse of memory."

"If I thought I could pull off a gig like that, I can promise you I wouldn't be chasing that motherfucking lawn mower all over creation." He snorted and his smug little smile was back.

"What about Eddie Pitkin?"

"That fellow who's in jail for nailing that politician? What could I possibly know about him?"

Wallace continued to scrutinize him. The raspy bark of a fussy squirrel, in the branches overhead, drew his attention. She looked at Harpin's hands, which hung at his sides. Her eyes touched briefly on the Buck knife strapped to his thigh and then moved back to match his stare.

"Good of you to stop by, Detective. You have yourself a good day now." He leaned forward and placed the unopened bottle of water on the ground in front of her and then turned and ambled back to his mower.

She watched him walk away. There was a slight stiltedness in his walk, which she hadn't seen before.

The mower rumbled to life. Harpin's back was to her as he angled the machine between two headstones and started pushing.

As soon as a row of Italian poplars blocked Harpin from view, Wallace reached down and slid a plastic bag over the bottle at her feet.

Once she was back in her car, she emailed the image of Harpin in the boat to Mason, along with a note asking him to see if he could do some quiet digging into Harpin's background.

She opened an email from her mother that had come in while she was with Harpin. "We need to talk," was all it said.

NINETEEN

The gym was crowded and loud. Fluorescent fixtures hanging from the ceiling flooded the place with harsh, irritating light, and the stink of sweat and damp towels and fear was everywhere. The air was full of noise—the iron-on-iron clank of weight machines, expletive-laden shouts of encouragement, groans of effort, the rhythmic tapping of jump ropes, the bloodless slapping sounds of fists striking flesh. Everything echoed, sounding far off and up close at the same time.

Carlton Lister stared through slitted eyes at his opponent across the ring. He fanned the fingers of both hands, then resumed his side-on position, hands curled loosely in the guard position in front of his face.

As his opponent moved left, he tracked the movements of the man's feet and shoulders, looking for the stutter steps and muscle twitches that foreshadowed punches and kicks and head fakes. This was only a practice bout, but Lister took every fight seriously. When someone stepped into the ring he was giving you permission to beat the shit out of him—if you could—and that was always serious business.

Here it comes, he thought. The man lunged. He opened with a straight left, then another left. He feinted a kick with his right leg and then came with a full left leg kick at the ribs instead.

The guy had mastered about a dozen such combinations. Some of them were well thought out and some were even finely executed. But they were easy to anticipate, and that made them ineffective.

The man was, however, big and fast and he could be difficult to hurt. If one of those hot left hands of his ever landed clean on a squarely presented jawbone, Lister knew it would be lights-out, followed by a good deal of reconstructive surgery.

Lister's physical speed wasn't as great as his opponent's, but he could certainly think faster. And once he got into the flow of a bout he could be as quick as he needed to be. Besides, he knew how to deliver a blow with a lot of power behind it—where to strike to inflict maximum pain and damage.

He was also methodical and creative and very attentive. There was never any mistake about when the tide of a fight had turned in his favor. And he wasn't shy about letting his opponents know how things were going to play out. He was a submission artist.

They carried on for a while, exchanging meaningless blows, each trying to maneuver the other into a vulnerable posture.

Lister was getting bored with the fight when he saw his shot. His opponent was starting to work his mouthpiece around in his mouth. This had happened twice before. First to the left, then to the right, then the guy's mouth would open just a touch as the mouthpiece came back to center.

The routine was starting again. Left, now right. And just as the big dumbfuck relaxed his jaw muscles and his mouth began to open, Lister struck. A downward-looping overhand right, snapping the man's jaw all the way open. Then a smooth left hook unhinged the jaw. The big man dropped to his knees and, before he could turn his back in surrender, Lister was on him, swarming punches and kicks until the trainer intervened.

Lister made the trainer work hard to stop the match. He never just stopped on a dime, even though he certainly could have. He always took a few more wild-eyed shots. His opponents needed to believe that once the spirit was upon him it wasn't so easy for him to flip the psycho switch back to the Off position. Although, in truth, he never actually went berserk. The more heated the battle became and the crazier the crowd sounded, the more he geared down.

Lister stared at his erstwhile opponent. He couldn't remember the guy's name. He doubted he would need to.

He slipped out between the ropes, peeling off his gloves as he went.

"Hey, hey, wild man."

The voice came from his right. It was Oliver Harpin.

"Brother, you done a number on the jolly green giant, out there." Harpin jerked his thumb toward the ring as he trotted over, his arm extended, ready for a fist bump.

Lister waited until Harpin was a few feet away, then turned toward the locker room. "What the hell are you doing here?" He nodded, snapping off index finger salutes to some of the men he passed.

"You don't look all that happy to see me."

"Is that right?" Lister turned to face Harpin, forcing the man to pull up short.

"Maybe you and I should spend a little time having ourselves a high-level conference."

Normally, Lister didn't mind putting up with a little of Ollie's jawing. It was a small price to pay for generally excellent work.

Ollie's skills were as limited as his perspective, but he followed instructions with uncanny precision and he could be counted on not to go off-script. Ollie could *do* what needed to be done, he just couldn't *figure out* what needed to be done. He had to be told. Only once, but he had to be told.

At the moment, however, Lister wasn't in the mood for Ollie and his jabbering. He was focused, instead, on getting cleaned up and heading over for a spirited game of hide the jackhammer with his girlfriend's little sister. It was entirely the little sister's idea, but it was a good idea because, just like him, she was a thoroughly committed rough-stuff junkie.

Lister pulled open the door to the locker room and walked through. Ollie, his thumbs hooked into the belt loops on the front of his jeans, scooted in behind him to get inside before the door closed.

"You gonna tell me why you're here, or you just like following me into the shower?" Lister sat on a bench between rows of lockers.

Ollie looked around. "I was mowing out at the cemetery this morning when I got me a visit from somebody asking if I knew Peter Ecclestone or Eddie Pitkin."

"So?" Lister's jaw clenched.

"She can put me at the lake, last Friday."

"She who?" Lister pulled off his outer shorts and tossed them into his locker.

"The cop."

Lister's head inched up. He locked Harpin in a sidelong stare.

Ollie scanned the room again. "That female detective. She's the one who showed up this morning."

"Well now, that's an unexpected development, wouldn't you say?" Lister skinned off his compression shorts and his jockstrap and pitched them into the locker with the rest of his gear.

"She had a picture of me out in the boat." He lifted his cap and smoothed his thinning hair back over an expanse of bare scalp and then reseated his cap.

"And exactly where did that picture come from?" Lister stood and wrapped a towel around his waist.

"How the fuck should I know? Judging by the direction it was shot from, it's a pretty good guess that it come from one of Ecclestone's cameras."

"Well now, that would be a motherfucking miracle, wouldn't it? Because I distinctly remember seeing every piece of his equipment sink out of sight as I was motoring back from Parker's Island." He massaged his forehead above his left eyebrow.

"Well, I'm all out of ideas, then."

"So, tell me. What did you and the detective go on about, during your little graveyard symposium?"

"She showed me the picture, and there wasn't any quibble about who it was. I explained to her how I was just out there fishing. And then, just as casual as you please, she dropped Ecclestone's name into the conversation. Then, Pitkin's. Trying to see if I'd react. But I didn't."

Lister scrutinized Harpin's face, looking for signs of deception. He saw fear but not dishonesty. Ollie was probably holding back, but he probably wasn't telling any untruths. And maybe not any half-truths, either.

"What you thinking, boss?" Harpin crossed his arms across his midsection and began massaging his elbows.

"I'm thinking you should've taped over the registration numbers on the front of that boat, because that's about the only way I can figure she made a connection between you and that picture she's got."

Ollie shifted from foot to foot and Lister noticed he was having a little trouble swallowing. He guessed Ollie was dying to say something stupid like "You never told me to do nothing like that," but the crazy fuck didn't have the stones to try to lay off the blame.

"That's alright, Ollie." Lister gave him a comradely punch on the shoulder—a hard punch. Ollie tried smiling to cover the pain, but he didn't quite pull it off. "Besides, I never told you to do that. Some game warden come by and see that, you could've been in big trouble." He socked Ollie again—a little harder.

"You're right about that." Ollie brightened a bit, in spite of the second punch. "Taping over them numbers? That would've been asking for nothing but trouble."

"So what's next, big guy?"

"Nothing. I just wanted you to know what's what. That's all. She can put me at the lake, but she could probably put a million other people there if she wanted to. It ain't like I was the only one there, that day."

"You're right about that," Lister said with greater enthusiasm than he felt. He rubbed his hands together and gave Ollie a lifeless smile.

"She can't connect me to Ecclestone or Pitkin and she can't connect me to you. So, there ain't nothing to worry about."

"Then I'm not worried." Lister looked toward the ceiling, then let his eyes dart around the room. "You didn't happen to *ask* her where she got that little picture of hers, did you?"

"No way. Uhn-uh. I ain't about to open some can of worms by asking questions I don't already know the answers to. There's no telling where something like that might lead, but it wouldn't be anyplace worthwhile, I can tell you that."

"Then my advice would be for you and me to forget good old Peter and go on about life as if he never existed."

"Sounds like a winner to me."

"Well, good. Now why don't you get on out of here, so I can get myself prettied up for a little bit of fun I got planned for later on."

"Roger that."

Ollie backed up a couple of steps and then turned toward the exit. Lister waited until Ollie's hand came up to grab the door handle.

"So, tell me something. In that picture she showed you, what exactly were you doing?"

Ollie's hand froze just short of the door. He half turned and stared at a spot on the floor a few feet in front of Lister.

"Holding up a trophy fish? Scratching your ass, maybe?"

"I's looking through my field glasses."

Lister waited to see if there was more. Ollie shuffled from foot to foot, cutting a quick glance at the door.

"May I assume you had an innocent explanation for that?" He tightened the towel around his waist.

"You better believe I did. Came straight out with it. And she bought it too."

"I bet she did, Ollie." Lister knew the guy would stand there until he got some signal that he was free to go.

"Well, carry on, soldier."

As Ollie turned and sped through the door, Lister slumped against the bank of lockers behind him. He was sure the photograph itself was just a piece of really shitty luck. The fact that it was discovered, however, wasn't only a bad omen, it was also a weak spot. If the detective had followed Ollie from the cemetery to the gym, it could turn them both into liabilities.

Lister would be glad when he no longer had to deal with the Oliver Harpins of the world. If he was careful, and smart, that time was not far away.

For the moment, though, he was worried. He had no doubt that even if the detective believed whatever Ollie told her about the binoculars, she would eventually figure out the truth. And if she had access to one photograph, she might have access to others. The source of the photograph would have to be investigated. Maybe even eliminated. And maybe the willful detective needed some additional guidance on where to aim her investigatory efforts.

TWENTY

Wallace drove straight from the cemetery to Cavanaugh with the bottle of water Harpin had handled and the paper cup that the camera chip had been inside of.

She gave them to Melissa Voorhees and asked her to compare the partial print she had lifted from the glove box latch in Peter's SUV to the prints on the bottle. She also wanted to know if there were any prints on the paper cup and, if so, who they belonged to.

"I'll be happy to do this." Melissa took the bagged items from Wallace. "On that partial print comparison, it's going to take a while because I'll need to do a manual comparison. I already ran it through AFIS and came up dry. And I don't have the software to compare outside-the-system prints to each other."

"I seem to be putting a lot on you. I'm sorry, but I don't know who I can trust on my end, and—"

"Say no more. I'm glad I can help. And it's not like Cavanaugh is being overrun by a crime wave at the moment. The prints on the bottle, do you want me to find out who they belong to?"

"No need. I was with the owner when he handled the bottle. And

I already know that he's never been printed. But I do need to know if anything you find on the cup can be linked to anyone we're interested in."

"I'm on it, Detective."

The minute Wallace returned from Cavanaugh she was summoned to Jason Burley's office. From there, they moved to one of the small conference rooms on the floor above the Homicide Division.

"Whatever you called me in here for, can't we talk about it later? Glenn Marioneaux's going to be arriving at the courthouse soon to put on his dog-and-pony show and I need, let me repeat, I need to corner him on something."

"You'll have a ton of time after it's over. And this is important. So sit."

Burley brought up a video on his laptop.

After about ten seconds, Wallace reached up and turned the sound off. She couldn't bear to hear the word. She didn't even want to lip-read it, but that was unavoidable. And she would have preferred to live out her life without having to see the effect the word was having. But that was unavoidable too.

The white faces screaming and laughing. The faces of the black kids, some angry, some hurt, the smaller kids taking shelter behind the older ones. The casual savagery of the aggressors raised goose bumps on Wallace's arms.

"Seen enough?" Burley asked.

"Too much." She clicked the Stop button and closed the browser. "You're not showing me this instead of just giving me the 'you need to get this thing wrapped up fast' speech, are you?"

She hoped that by voicing one possible reason for their meeting she could somehow magically keep him from bringing up the other possible reason. The one she didn't want to deal with. The one she didn't have an answer for, because she was no longer sure who she could trust.

"I brought you up here so we could talk without people gawking at us."

Wallace rose from her chair and then sat on the table, facing Burley. She rubbed her arms distractedly, like a junkie.

Burley looked at her for several seconds without speaking. It was the same expectant look all cops knew how to project whenever they had someone on the hot seat.

She willed her dangling feet to be still and she looked at the wall, not trusting herself to maintain an innocent expression if she had to look him in the eye.

"I'm offering you as much help as we can throw at this case," Burley said.

"And I appreciate that," Wallace said. "And I'm putting it to the best use I know how. We've got someone working on the videos from Glenn Marioneaux's church. Thanks to you, we've got forensic techs working overtime to sort through all the stuff that came from Eddie Pitkin's home, as well as everything we snagged from Craig Stephens's lake house, and—"

Burley raised a hand, cutting her off before she could continue her performance.

"Somebody put the idea in the mayor's head that if this case keeps poking along it'll start to look like it's because we're dragging our feet."

"Poking along? Oh, please. It's barely been five days since Marioneaux was killed, and there's still time under the statutory deadline before the suspect has to be charged or released."

Burley waved her quiet. "He's convinced that it's going to look like we're not moving on it because we're certain we've got all the evidence we need to convict, and that all this other stuff is just going through the motions. Because we've arrested a defendant whose skin color and reparations activism automatically add up to guilt beyond a reasonable doubt, all we're doing now is marking time so the public will think we're doing a thorough job."

"Does he think we should be trying to clear Eddie Pitkin's name, instead of digging up the evidence, no matter which way it cuts?"

"It *does* sound like that. But remember, he's got a bigger megaphone than you or I do."

"Is it campaign season again, already?" She crossed her ankles and leaned forward, her hands folded in her lap.

"He's a politician, not a law-enforcement professional." Burley stood and started pacing. "He's terrified the feds will show up and start hectoring us about racial bias in policing, and how civil rights lawsuits brought by the Justice Department tend to leave unique, long-lasting scars on the collective consciousness of a community."

"Oh, this is just beautiful. The investigation is about politics, now, not justice."

"Nobody said that."

"Well, tell me, then, if you were in my position and I had just said to you what you just laid on me, how would it affect your perception of the situation?" She tapped the toes of her boots together.

Burley started to speak, then closed his mouth. "You get more pleasure out of being right than I think is healthy, sometimes."

"As long as you recognize that I *am* right." She followed him with her eyes as he paced in front of her.

"Wallace, please." He raised his hands, palms out. "I'm not lecturing you, and I'm not telling you to let politics influence the pace or direction of your investigation—"

"But just by putting it that way, you're doing both of those things. And you're doing them in a way that will let you deny that you did either of them."

"Let me finish." He blew out a long, tired breath and then flopped into a chair. "What I *am* telling you is that this case is not like anything we've dealt with before. No one can predict what it's going to do to the town, but everyone's pretty sure that it won't be good."

"And?"

"Let's just say I'm worried. About how it's going to affect you, regardless of the outcome."

"I've already been over this with Chief Shannon."

"Just remember, when things are going well everyone will want to have their picture taken with you, but the minute it looks like it's headed south you won't be able to buy a friend."

"What about you?" Wallace instantly regretted the question.

A hurt look flickered across Burley's face. "Just let me know what else you need. Keep me and Chief Shannon in the loop on everything, and I'll make sure you have at least one friend, come hell or high water. And for Christ's sake, find that fucking photographer."

Wallace surveyed the crowd from one of the big south-facing windows on the third floor of the City Hall building on St. Louis Street. Chief Shannon stood to her right. She had wanted to be on the ground, to intercept Glenn when he finished his speech, but Shannon had ordered her to stick with him, so he could grill her about developments in the case.

Every news outfit in Baton Rouge was present. She could see the tall, smoky glass doors of the Theatre for Performing Arts that lined the far edge of the plaza.

A podium on a low stage stood in front of the bronze Pietà in the center of the plaza, and a large crowd had gathered between the stage and the street. Some were probably there out of curiosity, morbid or otherwise, but Wallace recognized what she felt sure were troublemakers. It seemed that, with alarming frequency, all around the country, every time someone grabbed a microphone and called for peace, provocateurs were waiting in the wings, itching to stir up just the opposite.

The plainclothes and undercover officers milling around in the crowd weren't going to intimidate anyone. At best, they might be able to spot problems and keep the more obvious rowdies under control. But she doubted a determined effort to spark violence could be thwarted.

Through an intercom, she could hear Glenn's voice asking for the attention of the crowd. Dorothy stood to his left. He was leaning forward, gripping the podium from the sides.

"Fellow citizens of Baton Rouge, I'm here today to plead for calm. These outbreaks of violence and racial intolerance are not what my father would have wanted—"

Faint laughter rippled across the crowd. Someone hollered, "Yeah, right. Heil Hitler." More laughter erupted.

"And this is not what Mother and I want. This is not the Baton Rouge I know and that we all love. Please, let's have an end to these provocations. No more displays of contempt and hatred."

There was a scattering of polite applause mixed with more heckling.

"Eventually, this chapter in the city's history will be over, and whatever happens between now and then, we will all remember it, and we will all have to live with it. The things that are said and done, now, will never go away. Please, don't set us up for regret."

A more sincere wave of applause came up from the audience. Wallace found herself nodding in approval of the sentiments Glenn was expressing.

"Let's not put ourselves in a position where we're going to have to feel shame over things that were done in anger or in cruelty— where some of us will end up having to avoid others of us, probably forever. We will all still be living here, so please, let's keep it a place where we'll still want to live. Where we'll all be happy to live. Where we don't have yet another generation of children learning to be unkind to others because of their race or the color of their skin."

"You tell 'em, Dr. King," someone jeered through a bullhorn.

A member of the audience turned toward the bullhorn and screamed at the heckler to "shut the fuck up."

Wallace watched as the crowd shifted its focus from Glenn to the people causing the commotion. In the space of a few seconds, what started as a listless assemblage became a lot of bodies in motion as people turned to see what was happening.

With almost military precision, the individuals surrounding the man with the bullhorn formed a circle around him, facing out toward the crowd. They started shouting and shoving and the crowd shouted and shoved back.

The man with the bullhorn started chanting "fourteen eighty-eight"—the Fourteen Words, the credo of the white supremacist, and the eighth letter of the alphabet, *H*, two times, for *Heil Hitler.*

Wallace felt sure the troublemakers were part of Affirmative Action, a group that specialized in disruptive tactics intended to hasten what they believed was a coming race war. She watched as some of the plainclothes officers in the crowd moved toward the center of the disturbance.

As the mob's attention fixated on the man with the bullhorn, the men surrounding him started throwing punches. A man with a bloodied face lunged into the melee, his fists flailing.

Wallace watched as the mass of people heaved and swelled like a wave blindly following the force of a rising tide. She could still hear Glenn's voice, now only a part of the cacophony, begging for calm.

A woman was knocked to the ground, and the crowd flowed over her. Wallace looked toward Jack Shannon. He raised his phone to his ear.

Wallace turned her eyes back to the action in the courtyard. Two officers in civilian clothes were pulling the sagging form of the trampled woman to her feet when someone rushed from the confusion and stomped her lower back. She slumped to her knees as her attacker fled back into the throng.

Hotspots multiplied and chaos leapt through the crowd like wildfire. A knot of uniformed officers hustled Glenn and his mother from the stage, pulling them behind the City Hall building as rocks and bottles flew in their direction. Dorothy clung to her son with one hand, her other hand raised palm out to ward off the flying debris. Wallace saw a scowl of contempt contorting her face.

"Initiate crowd suppression," Shannon spoke into his cell phone. Out of the corner of her eye, Wallace saw him turn in her direction. She could feel his eyes on her, and she didn't have to look at him to know that he was daring her to let an I-told-you-so look show on her face.

Wallace kept her expression neutral and her eyes glued to the ruckus below. Police in riot gear streamed out of the doors of the theater.

The sound of gunshots echoed between the buildings and panic flashed through the crowd as canisters of tear gas trailed smoke over the pandemonium like lazy little comets. The man with the bullhorn droned on, repeating his string of numbers.

People fled into the street and tires squealed on the pavement.

Wallace stalked from the room, ready to explode.

The pressroom was nearly full, but there was not a reporter in the bunch. Dozens of conversations buzzed through the room like white noise. Except for Chief Shannon himself, half the department brass and what looked like most of the detective corps were present.

Mack Bonvillian, the head of public affairs for the department, was ready to gavel a debriefing about the riot into session. Wallace wasn't sure if it was supposed to be a morale builder or if they were simply being fed the party line in the event they found themselves confronted by concerned citizens or members of the media.

Wallace held many of the people she had arrested in higher esteem than she did Mack Bonvillian. The story was that he had used family connections and the remarkably tight fit between his lips and the backsides of everyone above him to rocket up the department's organizational chart. His rise was so fast the soles of his shoes had barely made contact with the grit and grime of the street. Wallace thought of him as the poster child for the out-of-touch career bureaucrat.

She moved down a row of chairs to the empty seat next to

LeAnne as Mack glad-handed a few officers who stood near his lectern. How anyone could be in a smiling mood after what had just happened was beyond her.

"Did you have a chance to go through the phone records for the Marioneaux family?"

LeAnne pulled open a briefcase at her feet and extracted a sheaf of papers and handed it to Wallace without looking at her.

"Anything?"

"Not that I could see. A very busy guy, but nothing suspicious, so far."

"What about a connection between Glenn and Eddie?"

"Nothing, and I don't think there's anything there. At least not anything that's public. We could always start digging around Eddie's family and friends, to see if anybody's willing to talk to us. Were you able to catch Glenn after that disaster in the plaza just now?"

"Gone by the time I got back to where their cars were."

"I'll see if I can catch him at his place of business, after we're done here."

"We've got something more important, at the moment." Wallace lowered her voice. "A potential Eddie Pitkin sighting from the night Marioneaux was killed—in Spanish Town."

LeAnne sat back and her eyes got wide. "Burley must be on cloud nine with this news."

"Burley doesn't know, and let me emphasize this is unconfirmed and from a questionable source."

"This is amazing."

"It's unconfirmed."

"No. This." LeAnne wagged her index finger back and forth between herself and Wallace. "I'm getting the goods before Burley."

"LeAnne, we're partners. And no, this isn't some charm offensive I'm rolling out, to make you feel included," Wallace continued when she saw LeAnne's eyes start to roll. "This is just getting the work done. And since it's unconfirmed and potentially inflammatory, until we can track it down we need to keep it out of the hands of anyone with a political motive to feed it into the media frenzy. Don't tell Burley. Don't tell anyone. This is strictly between you and me."

LeAnne's eyes got big again, and then she nodded. "Okay. Got it."

A muffled pop came from the front of the room as Mack tapped the mic with his finger. "Thanks for coming. We're all busy. It's been a rough day. I'll be brief."

Vigorous applause came from several in attendance. Mack grinned. He paused for effect.

Wallace pulled a pad from her satchel and scribbled instructions on how she wanted the Pitkin sighting checked out. She tore off the page and handed it to LeAnne.

"Sometimes democracy is neat and tidy and sometimes it's messy," Mack began. "What happened earlier today shows that, as a department and as a community, we're willing to take risks in the name of decency and doing the right thing."

A low groan slithered through the room.

"The gunfire? Was that some of the neat part or the messy?"

The question came from an undercover cop sporting two black eyes, courtesy of the plaza mob.

"The gunfire. Hah." Mack smiled and shook his head. "Nobody, I repeat, nobody got shot. We think one of the undesirables in the crowd was firing blanks, trying to start a panic."

"And it worked," Wallace said. "What about the little girl who ran into the street when the crowd started to surge and got hit by the motorist who was rubbernecking his way past City Hall on a street that was supposed to be blocked off? Or the woman who got trampled and stomped when the fighting started? This is what's on the news. This is what we'll be asked about."

She looked around. No one spoke as they waited for an answer. Bonvillian looked toward the floor.

"As per standard operating procedure, for events of this type, an ambulance had been positioned at the precisely correct location. The woman was treated at the scene and released. For the little girl, lifesaving measures were begun almost immediately. After that, she was transited to the emergency room as quickly as the ambulance could safely clear the crowd." Bonvillian's eyes followed his finger down the page of notes in front of him. "And so—"

"And so . . . what do we know about the girl's condition?" It was the officer with the black eyes.

"Despite heroic efforts by the docs, by everyone actually . . ." He shook his head. "Her injuries were simply too great."

"Jesus," Wallace said. "Do we know when the funeral will be?"

Mack cleared his throat pointedly. "The department has a pre-designated representative to attend. And I've personally made arrangements to have a wreath of appropriate size placed at graveside, and for our sincerest condolences to be conveyed, through suitable channels, to all interested parties."

Wallace stared at Bonvillian, unable to choose from among the many responses to his comment that were crowding into her head.

"Is this your way of telling us not to go to the funeral?" she asked finally.

"It's my way of telling you that we've got that covered."

"Got *what* covered?" someone asked. "The department's ass?"

"Why don't we get ahead of the game and just send an appropriately sized wreath to every household in town?" Wallace asked. "That way, whenever somebody gets killed because of police negligence our asses will be preemptively covered."

"Being cynical doesn't help, Detective Hartley."

Every head in the room snapped up, and all eyes were on Bonvillian. Near the front, one of Wallace's fellow detectives motioned for Bonvillian's attention and then whispered something in his direction.

Bonvillian scowled at the whisperer. "What are you saying? I can't hear you."

"Hartman," the detective said louder.

"What?"

"It's Hartman," the detective said, practically shouting. "Her name is Hartman, you bonehead. Not Hartley."

Bonvillian's face went crimson.

"Since you've obviously got a thorough command of the facts, you won't mind if I sneak out and get back to my investigation, will you, Lieutenant?" She smiled down at LeAnne, then turned and threaded her way along the row toward the door.

Wallace had one foot in the elevator when Jason Burley emerged from the pressroom with Curtis Stiles, his special projects officer. Burley motioned for Wallace to wait for them.

"If you're going to tell me I need to go back in there and apologize, don't."

"Mack Bonvillian is a boob," Burley said, releasing a lungful of air through puffed cheeks. "Hold the elevator. We'll ride together." He turned to Stiles. "Curtis, I need you to slip back into the briefing and stay till the bitter end. When it's done I want you to corner Mack and make him give you a list of all the folks who have filed a complaint over what happened on the plaza today."

"Got it," he said and then turned back toward the pressroom.

"That was a huge waste of time." Wallace pressed the button for their floor.

Burley made an exasperated sound that was somewhere between laughing and crying. "How are you and LeAnne getting along?"

"I think she's warming up to me."

"Tell me that again in a month and I'll be less inclined to smirk."

"You think I'm naïve?"

"I think you're my last best hope for her not being a lifelong pain in my testicles."

Wallace laughed at Burley's unexpected candor.

"Look, Chief Shannon is being heavily criticized for the riot." The exasperation was back.

Wallace remained silent. She didn't want to tell Burley that she had tried to talk his boss into doing the event in a less vulnerable forum. She liked Jack Shannon and didn't want to be part of the pile-on.

"I assume you're not telling me this just to spread gossip."

Burley shook his head. "His judgment is being questioned."

"Let me guess. This isn't limited to his buy-in on the location for the speech today."

"Correct. And your name is in play."

"I offered to let this case go, at the very beginning."

The doors opened and Burley motioned for her to follow. "I know, and at the time I was in favor of that. But since then, I've gotten religion."

"Good," Wallace said. "Because this would be the wrong time to switch horses in midstream."

"I'm with you on that too. And even though he's up to his ass in alligators, Shannon will fight for you as long as there are people who will listen."

They stopped at the door to Burley's office. "That's all I wanted to say."

"That and 'hurry the fuck up with this investigation'?"

Burley gave her a tired smile and then stepped across the threshold into his office.

TWENTY-ONE

As Wallace hustled down the hallway toward the cubicle area where her desk was, her phone signaled an incoming text. It was Melissa Voorhees. Several clear prints, all belonging to Peter Ecclestone, had been lifted from the paper cup. Her manual comparison of the prints on the water bottle to the partial print from the glove box latch in Ecclestone's vehicle was still underway.

Wallace spent another hour at her desk, checking updates on the forensics. The insulation fibers she had recovered from Craig's lake house attic matched in shape, color, and composition those found on the back of Herbert Marioneaux's shirt. The report cautioned, however, that the fibers were very common and could be found in many thousands of structures across the country.

Still, she had to consider that the match strengthened the possibility that Eddie had been the one standing behind Marioneaux, dropping the big slip lock around his neck.

She was about to start second-guessing her decision to tell LeAnne about the alleged Pitkin sighting, but unless she started testing the people she worked with there was no way she'd be able to figure out who she could trust. She would just have to keep her eyes and ears open to see if the information ended up somewhere it shouldn't.

Wallace sat behind the wheel of her car, in the lot next to the police building. The evening gloom was deepening. She replied to her mother's email about wanting to talk, letting her know she was on the way, and then she scrolled to Melissa Voorhees's number. She pressed the earbud into her left ear, then touched the number.

"I had a feeling I was going to hear back from you," Melissa said, her voice empty of the energy Wallace had become used to. "A bad feeling, actually."

"I thought you'd want to know about something I found."

"I saw the City Hall riot on the news," Melissa said. "And I heard about the little girl who got struck by the car."

A stab of sorrow at the child's fate kept Wallace from speaking for a few seconds. "I turned up something at the lake house, really late last night, after I left your place." She started the car and eased out of her spot.

"With all this crazy stuff going on in Baton Rouge, how are you doing?" Melissa asked. "Personally, I mean."

"Like I don't even recognize this town anymore. All this hate that's spewing out, everywhere, it didn't just spring into existence over the last few days." She paused at the exit to the lot, then accelerated into the street.

"Strange, isn't it, how people can keep their worst parts hidden until it feels safe to let them show," Melissa said. "They can fool you for years and then, when the circumstances are right, they reveal themselves for what they've been all along. And it's seldom a pleasant surprise."

"The thing I found . . . it has to do with Peter."

The line went quiet. Wallace waited for Melissa to speak.

"Like I said, the other day, I'm glad this is your case, and not mine."

"Inside that crumpled paper cup I brought you? The one you

found his prints on? I found a memory card. Very likely from one of Peter's cameras. It led me to a very rough character named Oliver Harpin. Ever come across this guy?"

"Nope." Melissa let out a long breath. "I'm guessing your police chief is in a serious sweat now, over that brawl." Her voice was unsteady.

"I've debated all day whether to tell you about this." Cruising west, up Government Street, Wallace rattled off the details of where and how she found the card. She heard sniffles coming through the phone.

"He was a real prick, you know," Melissa said. "I mean, really, he was. So why am I getting so fucking weepy over this?"

"Remember when you called to tell me that his vehicle had been found? How you told me it was too soon to jump to conclusions about what that might mean?"

"And I remember you fell for it."

Wallace heard Melissa's breathing grow ragged. Apparently, even a family and the passage of a great deal of time had not completely blunted Peter's effect on her.

"Now it's your turn to fall for it," Wallace said. "At least, until we know for sure what happened to him." She turned right, onto the street where her mother lived.

"Promise you'll call if you find out anything. You know, it was impossible not to like him. Even when you knew it was going to hurt if you got too close. Somehow, he could make you forget that was going to happen."

"We still don't know anything for sure. It's too soon to lose hope. I just didn't feel right keeping this from you."

"It's okay. And I'm okay. Just call me if you find something."

"I promise. You sure you're alright?"

Wallace slowed in front of her mother's house. The pale luminosity from the streetlight made it only as far as the front steps. She could see her mother, in silhouette, sitting on the front porch. The lights were off and she was backlit by the glow shining from inside the house.

"With your alibi witness out of the picture, does this mean you're ready to let the DA take Pitkin to trial?" Melissa asked.

"It means big trouble on the horizon. If the 'Free Eddie' movement ever gets wind of the fact that an alibi witness has vanished after his existence became known to the police but before we notified the defense, the shit is going to hit the fan and I'll be accused of burying the evidence." Wallace turned into Carol's driveway and stopped.

"Even though there's evidence pointing to the fact that he might have disappeared for reasons unrelated to your case?"

"I'll be happy for you to come down and make that case to the public."

"No, thanks. I got an eyeful of what the folks in your town do to the peacemakers."

Wallace walked with purpose through the manicured grass in the front yard and slowly mounted the steps. She could just make out a tentative smile mixed with a hint of sadness on her mother's face and wondered if the darkness was creating the unsettling expression.

"Mom, why are you sitting out here in the dark?"

"He proposed."

For a moment, Wallace didn't understand because she was still disentangling her thoughts from her conversation with Melissa Voorhees. Then she got it.

"Davis?"

Carol nodded, her expression staying the same.

"Wow. It seems so sudden." Wallace studied her mother. "How are you feeling about this?"

Carol looked toward the street. "Confused, flattered, anxious, excited." A self-conscious smile brightened her face. "The same way I felt when your father asked me. And the funny thing is, I expected Davis to ask, but I didn't expect to feel this way about it."

Wallace sat on the floor in front of her mother, her knees drawn up. When it had been just an abstract idea, it had had a certain appeal. Now that it had lurched closer to reality she felt unexpectedly possessive.

"I haven't said anything to your brother Lex. And I have absolutely no idea what I'm going to tell Davis."

"How did you leave things?"

"Up in the air."

"He understood?"

"Well, he didn't make any macabre jokes about the last of the sand running through the hourglass." Carol took a deep breath and let it go. "I'm making this seem so ominous, but it isn't. Davis was as giddy as a schoolboy, and it was a sweet moment." She looked at Wallace and raised her eyebrows. "It's just not something I thought I'd ever need to think about again."

"It's not something I thought you'd ever need to think about again, either."

They both laughed, and the tension drained out of the air.

"Don't worry," Carol said, her smile finally breaking free of its earlier sadness. "I'm not going to put you on the spot and ask you what you think I should do. But do feel free to express your thoughts on this. Mostly, I just wanted you to know."

"You know how I feel about Davis. I'm happy for you, Mom."

The tiny grace note of sadness that had been there earlier crept back into Carol's smile.

Wallace took her mother's hands in her own and stood. "Mason is expecting me for dinner." She tugged gently. "Come with me and you can tell him your news."

Carol shook her head. "You go. This old woman needs to be alone in her head for a bit. But do give this some thought, would you?"

Mason's apartment was on the ground floor of the building. It was a compact space with a lot of fifties charm. The street-facing windows of his apartment were raised, and hazy lamplight shone from inside.

Wallace stood to the side of the windows and scratched softly on one of the screens.

"We shoot burglars in this neighborhood," Mason said from inside.

"Even the ones you're sleeping with?"

"Am I sleeping with someone? I've forgotten—it's been so long." His face appeared in the window, blurred by the screen.

"Keep that up and it could be a lot longer."

He smiled, eyeing her up and down. "You're early."

"I wanted to see if I'd catch you with another woman."

"Then you're late. She's been gone for at least ten minutes."

"Are you sure you're up for another round of company?" she asked, matching his smile.

"Maybe."

"When you know for sure, call my office and leave a message. I'll try to get back to you." She pulled back from the screen and moved along the edge of the building.

"What's your number again?" Mason called after her.

He met her at the side door. Her heart was thudding as she ran through what she was about to tell him.

She paused briefly as she crossed the threshold, pressing a palm against his chest, looking at him with soft eyes.

With one foot Wallace pushed the door shut, and then she looped her arms around his waist, pulling him close and breathing him in. As she held on to him she could feel the weight of the day sliding off of her.

"Dinner smells divine."

"All part of my plan. I've got big ideas."

"Mmmm. Tell me in detail about your big ideas." She squirmed purposefully against him.

After several more seconds, she smiled up at him and then pushed away and walked into his living room.

"How long until we eat?"

"Twenty minutes."

"What is that incredible aroma?"

"Back where I come from, we call it soup." Mason returned to the kitchen. "I've got some things to show you."

"More images from the memory card?"

"That's part of it. The flash drive on the coffee table is everything we were able to pull off the card that you don't already have."

Wallace opened her laptop and set it up on the table. The repetitive *snick-thump* of a knife slicing through vegetables on a cutting board and the clinking of utensils on plates drifted in from the other room. She plugged the drive into her computer.

"That snoop job you asked me to do on Oliver Harpin bore a little bit of poison fruit."

"That was fast."

"It's more show than tell, so it'll have to wait until after dinner."

As she scrolled through the bewildering montage of deleted images rescued from the card, she reeled off the low points of her day—the secondhand threats Lanny Berto had presented to her, the plaza riot.

"Did anything good happen?"

"Davis proposed to my mother." She tried to sound matter-of-fact.

Mason's head popped around the doorway to the kitchen. "Really? And?"

"She told him she'll have to think about it."

"Do you—?"

"Oh my God. Mason, it's him. He's here."

"Who?" He poked his head around the doorway again.

"Eddie Pitkin. I can't believe this." Her gaze was riveted on her laptop screen.

Mason stepped into the narrow space between the couch and the coffee table, drying his hands on a dish towel. He leaned over to look at the image on the screen. The shot had been taken close to sunset with a long lens, but Eddie's face was clearly visible.

"And that's the dock behind Craig's house," she said, pointing.

"How can you be sure? It looks like it could be a dock behind any house on any of a hundred lakes."

"It's a floating dock, with swimming pool ladders on two sides. I recognize it from when I was out there a couple of days ago."

"Open the data file that goes with the picture," Mason said. "Let's see when it was taken."

Wallace patted the couch next to her and then handed the laptop to him.

After a few minutes of trying, Mason handed the computer back to her. "We're going to need some tools that I don't have here."

"Could it be found with what you've got at your office?"

"Assuming the information is still there."

Wallace studied the picture, wondering how it was going to change things. "Peter told me he hadn't taken any photographs of Eddie."

"Well, somebody did, and then somebody deleted it."

"But why leave the memory card inside a cup inside a dumpster? If the point was to get rid of this, why not destroy it? A couple of quick hammer blows and all that's left is powdered plastic."

"Maybe he didn't have time," Mason said. "Does it really matter why?"

"At this point, the only thing that matters is whether we can put a date and time with this image. And it doesn't just matter to Eddie Pitkin." Wallace gave Mason a stricken look.

"I'm listening."

"The only person who saw Ecclestone on the lake and got him to admit to an alibi for Pitkin is me—a police officer."

"And now he's disappeared before his existence was made known to the defense," Mason said, dropping his head into his hands.

"Once this comes out—and it will—they'll be measuring me for a cross."

"Maybe you should out yourself. That way it won't look like you tried to cover something up."

"You saw what happened at City Hall today. The town is like a tinderbox. If I can't offer up this image of Eddie on the lake, with a solid date and time, as some sort of substitute for Peter, you can bet Eddie's lawyer will be all over me and the department."

"Stir the soup. I'll make some calls." He set her laptop on the table and disappeared into the back of the apartment.

Wallace could hear Mason's muffled voice through the closed door of his bedroom. It seemed like circumstance continued to conspire against telling him about the attack at her house—which was now nearly forty-eight hours in the past.

Lost in thought, Wallace stood and followed the low murmur of the bubbling soup toward the kitchen. She could still hear Mason's voice through the door. As she turned the corner, another sound crept into her consciousness. It was just like the one she had made to get Mason's attention when she arrived for dinner—the low, deliberate rasp of something scratching across one of the window screens in the living room.

Her stomach dropped and a rash of goose bumps sprang up on her arms. The ambush in her carport flooded into her thoughts.

She concentrated on the sound. She couldn't see the screen from where she stood, which meant that no one at the window could see her. Her sidearm was lying on the seat of the big chair at the far end of the coffee table, in the living room. The single floor lamp illuminating the room was in the corner, right next to where the sound was coming from.

If she walked back into the room, she would be clearly visible to anyone standing outside the window until she was able to turn off the lamp. Mason's voice had gone quiet. The soup and the scratching noise were the only things left on the soundtrack.

The noise stopped.

Maybe it was a moth fluttering against the screen. Maybe she had only imagined it.

It sounded again. Only this time it was a louder, more insistent, ripping noise.

She heard Mason's voice again. It took on an urgent tone and then went quiet. Wallace heard the bedroom door open.

Mason appeared in the archway that led from the dining nook into the kitchen. With one hand, Wallace reached out and pulled him into the kitchen with her. She raised a silencing finger to her lips.

Something thudded dully onto the floor in the living room.

A baffled expression took over Mason's face. He tried to pull away in the direction of the sound, but Wallace tightened her grip. She had a moment of vertigo as the situation took hold of her. She pulled Mason close enough to whisper in his ear.

"Where's the breaker box?"

He tensed. "The wall, next to the fridge. Right behind you," he whispered back.

"Not one fucking sound." Without letting go of him, she turned and pulled open the little gray door covering the panel. With a single swipe of her hand, she pushed every switch, plunging the apartment into darkness. Except for the hammering of her heart, the hiss and burble of the soup and the pale glow of the gas burner were the only sensory inputs she registered.

Wallace closed her eyes and waited, focusing her senses outward. Mason's chest expanded against her as he breathed. At the outer limits of her hearing she heard the faint scrape of shoes running on concrete.

The door to one of the upstairs apartments opened and then slammed. Tipsy laughter and footsteps floated down the interior stairwell. The door leading from the building's small lobby opened, and suddenly she could hear the laughter filtering in through the screened windows. The happy sounds moved steadily toward the street.

"Someone cut the screen on one of the front windows and dropped something inside."

Silently, Mason opened the cabinet beneath the sink and pulled out a flashlight. On his hands and knees, he peeked around the doorframe. The glow from the streetlamp highlighted a ten-inch slit in the screen. He swept the beam of the flashlight along the baseboards beneath the front windows and let out a long, slow breath. "Someone is sending you a message. Lucky us, it's not the explosive kind."

Wallace looked around the doorframe to where Mason was shining his flashlight. A noose fashioned from yellow nylon rope sat on the floor below the cut.

"Shit." She reversed into the kitchen and stood with her back against the refrigerator.

"Indeed." Mason extinguished the flashlight. "Somebody knew you were here. You're being followed."

Wallace pulled open the refrigerator door and shoved the pot of soup inside, and then she reached over and turned off the gas.

"We're getting out of here." Her eyes were adjusting to the low light. She could see Mason in deep, shadowy grayscale.

"We need a plan to shake off anyone who might want to follow you."

"I'm thinking."

Mason slipped from the kitchen and disappeared in the direction of his bedroom. "I'll throw some stuff into a bag. Meet me at the side door."

"I'm going to flip the breakers back in a minute," she whispered. "So don't switch on any lights."

Wallace moved quietly into the front room. Standing to the sides of the windows, she pulled them down and latched them and then drew the curtains. She fumbled around until she found the cord to the lamp and unplugged it.

With quiet efficiency, she pulled her shoulder holster from the chair and fastened it in place and then closed her eyes, listening once more for any threatening sounds. All she heard was the shuffle of Mason's shoes against the hardwood floor in the back of the apartment. She called for a taxi to meet them in twenty minutes at an intersection several blocks from Mason's apartment.

She stuffed her laptop into her shoulder bag, then moved quietly back into the kitchen and threw the breakers back to the On position.

The compressor motor in the refrigerator kicked on, filling the little galley kitchen with a low hum, but the apartment remained pitch-black.

"Ready," Mason whispered from the dining area, a few feet away.

Wallace met him at the side door. "You go in front of me, toward the back of the lot. When we get to the alley, turn left. After that, let me go in front."

Mason reached for the doorknob, but Wallace grabbed his arm and shook her head.

Holding Mason back with one hand, she opened the side door, crouched low, and then peeked around the frame in both directions.

"Now," she whispered, waving him through.

Mason slipped past her into the night. She pulled the door shut and tested it to make sure it was locked. She offered up a quick prayer of thanks for the clouds that blocked out the moon, and then took off after him.

Once they reached the alleyway at the back of the lot, Wallace pulled Mason into a hard left turn and they ran for about thirty yards through the sickly yellow glow that fell from the ancient sodium vapor streetlight that extended from a utility pole at the midpoint of the alley. Abruptly she moved onto a nearly invisible path that led between two houses on the other side of the alley. They stopped and waited. From their cover, Wallace could see back into the dimly lit alley. No one showed up.

They waited nearly a minute longer as Wallace watched and listened intently for pursuers who might have stopped short of entering the alley for fear of being seen.

When she was satisfied no one was close behind, she tugged on Mason's sleeve and they moved along paths she vaguely remembered from her growing-up years. Twice more they stopped and listened.

Ten minutes after leaving Mason's apartment, they were climbing into the back of a taxi.

"Baton Rouge General," she told the driver. "The ER entrance."

"Somebody you know got troubles?" The cabbie caught Wallace's eye in his rearview.

Wallace nodded, twisting her mouth into an expression of worry.

The cabbie bobbed his head and returned his attention to the road ahead.

Wallace leaned against Mason. By unspoken agreement, they remained silent, keeping their intentions and their plans to themselves. Six minutes later she and Mason climbed out of the taxi into the bustle and clamor around the emergency room.

They spoke little as Wallace led them through the maze of corridors and stairways that connected the different parts of the hospital, finally emerging at a deserted waiting room on an upper floor. Seating units with three or four seats separated by armrests lined the walls. They moved into the dim rear of the room and sat side by side.

Wallace called her brother, Lex, and explained that he and his mother needed to go someplace safe for a few days. Then she turned toward Mason.

"Why does this keep happening?" she asked after she ended the call.

"Why does what keep happening?"

"You being in danger because you're connected to me."

"It's a dangerous job you do." He shrugged and smiled.

"But it's not your job. You took yourself out of the danger zone when you left the DEA to start your own company."

Wallace remembered the conversation when Mason told her about his decision. It was time to move on, he needed a new challenge, he wanted more control over his life, he wanted to be near her on a daily basis.

All of those reasons were true, but they weren't the whole story. The grim reaper had come uncomfortably close—Mason's diminished left arm was a constant reminder of just how close—and lurked on the sidelines for a long time. He hadn't put that reason into words, and Wallace hadn't pushed him on it. She assumed that at some point, when he felt the time was right, he would bring it up.

She looked over at him, and she could tell he knew what she was thinking.

"I took myself out of the danger zone years ago, when I quit being a border patrol agent and became an analyst."

"And then you stepped inside my orbit and nearly lost everything."

"Hey, there are no guarantees. We both know that." He reached over and took one of her hands in his. "And besides, I'm starting to think you may be worth the risk."

Wallace wanted to smile, but she couldn't. With the fingers of her other hand, she reached out and touched his face.

"I've been keeping something from you," she whispered, her voice faltering.

A perplexed look descended over Mason's face.

She faced away from him and raised the back of her shirt.

"Monday night, when I got home. Someone was there to meet me."

"Whaaat?" He drew the word out into a long syllable as he took in the bruises. "Who was this someone?"

"I don't know." Her eyes stung and a heavy feeling blossomed in her chest. "He said he had information relevant to my case."

"And the only way to get you the message was to beat you up?" His voice rose and he sat back, shaking his head.

"He grabbed me from behind so I couldn't see him. Knocked the wind out of me to keep me subdued while he said what he came to say. Then he kidney-punched me, so he could get away without me being able to follow him."

"What are the chances he's the one who dropped the noose through my window?"

Wallace's face crumpled and her eyes started brimming. "I can't bear to think I've made you a target."

"You should have told me the minute this happened."

"I know. I'm sorry."

Gently, Mason snaked his arm around her waist and pulled her close. *Thank you*, she thought. *Please don't give up on me.*

"Next time something like this happens, you've got to tell me. It'll make me worry, but I'll worry more if I think you're hiding things from me."

Wallace nodded, pulling his arms tighter around her. After a couple of minutes, she was able to let go of some of her anxiety and she relaxed into him. When a wave of fatigue threatened to drag her under, she sat up with a start and turned to look at Mason.

"What's going on in that head of yours?" he asked.

"I need to disappear for a bit."

"We both need to. I doubt that whoever's on your tail is really interested in me, but they could certainly try to use me to get a tighter grip on you. I'll just need to find a place where I can work while I'm away."

"That won't be a problem." She stood and strode to the other end of the room, pulling her phone from her pocket as she went.

"Our ride's here." They were waiting in an alleyway between a wing of the hospital and one of the parking decks. She reached down for Mason's hand and pulled him to his feet.

A maroon SUV idled at the mouth of the alley. The window slid down. Melissa Voorhees was smiling and shaking her head.

TWENTY-TWO

Well, it looks like you and me are becoming regular friends, Detective Hartman." MaryBeth turned the key in the lock of the carport door to the little lake house situated on the east side of False River. "Although, I have to say, if you'd give me just a bit more notice, I could get myself prettied up a little better for all these girls' nights out you keep inviting me to. And maybe we could start going someplace a touch livelier than, you know, vacant lake houses."

MaryBeth pushed the door open and stood to the side. Wallace and Mason and Melissa filed past, into the house.

The sharp scent of chemical cleaner almost masked the faint mildew smell that all the houses near the water eventually picked up if they weren't opened on a regular basis.

"I feel bad about getting you out so often, after closing time," Wallace said. "We appreciate you doing this on such short notice." She turned to shake MaryBeth's hand.

"No problem at all," MaryBeth said, giving the offered hand a perfunctory shake. "My husband never had any reason to stash witnesses in out-of-the-way places, before, but I watch TV. I know things can be different up in the city."

Wallace had instructed Melissa to tell MaryBeth that they needed the house to keep a witness safe from the media. They had chosen a place on the more populated east side of the lake so Mason wouldn't stick out so much, in case he had to leave the house.

Lights started coming on as Mason and Melissa moved deeper into the house.

"Will we need to sign any more paperwork?" Wallace asked. "Or is everything in order, on the contract?"

"All our ducks are in a neat little row. No worries there. And I know you don't need me hanging around, so I'll be heading out."

Wallace looked around the house. It was an open floor plan with two bedrooms opening off the main living area. The entire back of the house was windows that opened on to a screened porch. She walked out onto the porch. Dock lights were visible up and down the shoreline. Midseventies Steely Dan, barely audible, drifted across the lake.

"Wallace?"

She turned. Melissa was standing in the doorway to the porch.

"I'm going to wait in my car, so you two can say your good-byes."

Wallace nodded. She wanted to say "thank you," but that seemed inadequate for all the things Melissa was doing.

"This is a good plan," Melissa said, squeezing her hand. "I'm sure Mason will be fine. It's you I'm worried about."

She looked at Melissa, trying to think of a way to reassure her without sounding trite. "Let me tie up a few things with Mason and I'll be right out."

"Take your time."

Wallace watched her walk back through the house toward the carport door.

"Mason?" She stepped back inside.

"Back here." His voice came from the bedroom at the back of the house.

She found him sitting at the little desk next to the double bed. The furniture looked like castoffs from a motel. His laptop sat open on the desk.

"Grab a chair from out there. I want you to see this before you take off."

She trudged out of the bedroom and returned with a chair from the dining table.

"Is this what you dug up on Oliver Harpin?"

She turned the chair backward and straddled it, her elbows propped on the back.

"On paper, Harpin is as clean as you thought, at least in terms of an actual rap sheet."

"Which may mean he just hasn't been caught, yet."

Mason nodded. "His name, however, is very much on the radar in terms of his associations."

Wallace's eyes widened. "He must be connected to some pretty interesting people."

"Allow me to introduce you to one of them." He clicked a video into motion. "This is courtesy of a friend of mine in the FBI who's part of the federal task force that deals with hate groups. It was taken at a farm way east of here, about twenty miles before you get to the Mississippi line."

The video opened with a wide shot of a man standing on a long wood-floored hay wagon in the middle of a large grassy field. The wagon was being used as a stage.

Mason ran his finger over the screen, indicating the crowd in front of the wagon. "I'm guessing, given the number of people in the bottom of the frame, that the camera must have been about a hundred feet from the platform."

The stage was draped in red and black. The microphone at the front gave off a brief squeal of feedback as the man approached. He had an easy grace about him. The others on the stage with him kept a respectful distance. He wore jeans and a black short-sleeved cyclist's shirt that clung to his chiseled physique like a second skin. With an approving smile, he surveyed the crowd, then he closed his eyes and raised his right hand, palm out, like a preacher calling for silent prayer. The crowd went still. When he opened his eyes, his smile was gone, replaced by anger. The camera zoomed in for a waist-up shot of the speaker.

"Storm clouds are gathering, my friends."

The roar of the crowd drowned out his next words. He paused, his nostrils flared, and the curl of his lips hinted at the earlier smile. After several seconds, he motioned with both hands for silence, and began again.

"Storm clouds are gathering, and they are threatening to become a permanent part of our world." He motioned for quiet again as a scattering of applause erupted.

"This cannot be allowed to happen." He looked down, drew in a slow, deep breath, then stared out over the assembly.

"As the world around us changes, so must we. And the most important thing we must change is our attitude about certain matters. I have never counseled taking the law into our own hands. But in theory and in fact, each and every one of us enters this world a law unto ourselves, and we entrust a limited amount of our individual power to our elected officials. In return, we demand that they exercise that power on our behalf, to achieve our goals, to produce the decent kind of life we want.

"But doing this is wise only when that power is secure in the hands of a competent government. One that recognizes and understands its obligations to we the people. One that is ready, willing, and able to use that power for its intended purpose and *only* for that purpose. That's the deal. But what happens when the government violates the terms of the deal? What happens when the law is allowed to fall into the wrong hands?"

He nodded holding his hands out, palms up, in a questioning gesture.

"Responsible citizens must *reclaim it*," he intoned into the microphone.

The crowd erupted. This time the man did not motion for silence. He let the noise continue until it died out on its own.

Wallace watched in uneasy fascination as the speaker continued, touching on all the mad, worn-out ideas used to justify violence in the face of social change. Something about him seemed familiar, but she couldn't put her finger on it.

"The power was ours to begin with and it's our right to take it back," he said in a quiet, even voice, stabbing his right index finger skyward for emphasis.

There were scattered shouts of agreement mixed with the blatting of aerosol air horns.

Wallace glanced over at Mason. He looked tired.

She turned her attention back to the video. As the man on the stage continued his speech, the person running the camera occasionally cut away to zoom in on different parts of the crowd. It didn't look like a typical gathering of the master race. Aside from a certain uniformity of skin tone, Wallace saw a few things that surprised her. Mixed in among the skinheads and the camo and the neck tattoos were a fair number of people—men and women—who looked as if they might practice medicine or be members of a country club. But the more well-heeled listeners reacted to the speaker with the same enthusiasm as their down-market compatriots. The spirit of the moment was clearly upon them all.

"So, hear me," the man thundered, both hands pointing out over the crowd. "What's ours is being hijacked—stolen by criminals." He paused, his eyes becoming intense. "By a growing class of destructive America-hating agents eager to seize the levers of power for their own godless agenda." He looked out over the crowd. His eyes were hooded, as if he was daring anyone to disagree.

"Dangerous times are at hand, so don't be afraid to provoke the outrage of those smug, self-righteous bigots who try to smear you and me with that label, because we won't be bullied by their hatemongering. Don't be afraid to do what needs to be done, whenever and wherever that need arises. And never forget our overriding goal, our guiding light, our ultimate principle: restoration, not reparation."

The clapping and shouting was thunderous, and the crowd chanted the man's closing phrase over and over. He soaked in the applause and, after several seconds, the video stopped on the image of the speaker holding his arms high, his fingers beckoning the applause.

"Somehow I'm not surprised that Oliver Harpin is connected to this kind of crowd."

Mason continued to stare at the screen. "Not just this crowd, he's connected to this guy in particular. It's a tenuous connection, but a connection, nevertheless."

"Who *is* he?" Wallace asked, leaning forward to study the image of the man's face.

"Carlton Lister."

"Who the hell is Carlton Lister?"

"Former sheriff's deputy. Released for overzealous use of generally unlawful methods of physical restraint."

"Choke holds?"

"Among other things. He was also a former prison guard. Again, released for similar reasons."

"By the looks of that video, he's definitely found his calling."

"And he's as smart and as violent as they come. College educated, from a good school. At one time he had pursued a career in federal law enforcement, but if I'm understanding the double-talk I got from the Fibbies, he was unable to get past the psych evaluations."

"You said this video was shot in Louisiana. Where is Lister from?"

"Baton Rouge. He's homegrown."

Wallace sagged in her chair. "Did your friends in high places happen to mention when it was that he delivered this dissertation on political theory for citizen militias?"

"Yesterday."

"You're kidding me." She stood and took a few steps away from the desk. "How did your pal at the FBI get his hands on this video?"

"It's a woman. She was the camera operator. Very deep cover. According to her, Lister is about to go on tour to deliver this message to groups of the faithful all around the southern part of the state. What you saw was the warm-up round."

"Jesus Christ." She dropped onto the bed and lay back with one arm under her head and the other draped across her forehead.

"According to the FBI, Lister's law-enforcement background, especially the fact that he was ejected for being too enthusiastic about the use of physical force, gives him a lot of credibility among the white supremacist crowd—among the party faithful, as well as the fence-sitters, the window-shoppers, and the undecided. He's also something of a local legend among the cage-fighting crowd."

"I've never heard of him."

"Probably because you're not heavily involved with the mixed martial arts scene."

"I'm not involved at all. That kind of thing scares me."

"Sure it does." Mason twisted his mouth into a skeptical look. "Remember who you're talking to. I've seen, firsthand, what happens when you play cops and robbers for keepsies. I don't think it's possible for you to convince me that you're afraid of anything. Although, in this case"—he pointed at the screen—"I would actually feel reassured if I thought you were at least a little bit concerned about the danger this implies."

"I think you're underestimating my fear factor just a bit."

"Even tonight," he said, "I never got the impression you were afraid for *you*. For me, yes. For your mother and your brother, of course. But for you, not so much."

"Mason, I'm not in the mood to have this debate again." Her eyes roved over him from head to toe. "The day you got shot, you nearly died and I had to watch you nearly die. That scared me."

"And you, you're still *on* the front lines. Still dealing with *this* kind of thing." Again, he jabbed a finger in the direction of his computer. "That scares *me*. Every day."

"I know," she whispered. "But I can't stop. Not now. Too much is at stake."

"Just promise me that you'll devote some very precise thinking to everything that's at stake."

Wallace stood, a hurt look on her face.

"That didn't come out right," Mason insisted, raising his hand to protest before she could speak. "It sounded like a roundabout ultimatum, but that's not what was in my head or in my heart." He stood and took her hands in his. "I need you to think about *you*. That's all I meant."

She nodded. "I know." She squeezed his hands, then pulled away. "Did your connections have anything else on Harpin?"

"Indirectly. According to my friend in the FBI, there's been an uptick in reported hate crimes over the last several days. And almost from the minute Eddie Pitkin's arrest hit the news cycle, the chatter from the hate groups and the professional agitator class has risen in frequency and volume. This homicide and your investigation have inflamed groups like this. Judging by what's in the chatter, that riot at City Hall will look like a church service compared to some of the plans being noised about."

Wallace moved to the window. "My investigation? Has there been anything . . . specific mentioned in all that chatter?"

"If you're asking whether your name has surfaced, the answer, as of just before we got here, is yes. That little bit of joyous news was in one of the emails I checked on our ride out here. I just didn't want to discuss it in the car. And yes, I had asked specifically if your name was floating out there."

"Did your source happen to mention what was being said?" she asked, trying to maintain a stony expression.

"You're not being nominated for Miss White Supremacist."

"I assumed as much. Anything I can use?"

"You've become a person of interest. Consternation is being expressed over why this investigation isn't being closed. Why someone who is clearly guilty of murdering a white lawmaker is being coddled by the police. Whether alternative justice for Eddie Pitkin is in order, in the event he's acquitted or goes unprosecuted."

Wallace pointed at the laptop. "Was it Lister who mentioned my name?"

"He's one." Mason opened an email and read a list of names.

"I've never heard of any of those people."

"There are others. Individuals whose real identities are unknown at this point."

"Is Carlton Lister the top of this ugly little food chain?"

"Not by a long way." Mason shook his head. "But his star is rising. For the moment, however, he answers to others. Folks who have managed to remain in the shadows—the people who control the money and the strategy behind a lot of this movement. Your good buddy Oliver Harpin? He's a hanger-on around the Lister campfire. Less than an insider, but more than a wannabe. Prone to violence. Considered to be very dangerous."

"Where is Lister now?"

"Nobody knows."

"Boy, you guys are *really* quiet," Melissa said as they drove away from the lake house. "The walls of these old places are so thin you should be able to hear a headboard banging against the wall from across the lake."

Wallace smiled at Melissa's attempt to pull her out of her melancholy mood.

"It's possible we were on the back porch, where it would have been harder to hear."

"Nope. I checked." She laughed.

Wallace laughed with her.

"We were just talking." Wallace looked over at Melissa. "He's terrified for me. I'm worried that he's terrified."

"What's your next move?"

"Disappear, stay alive, find the truth."

Melissa smacked the heel of her hand against the side of her head. "Stupid me. I should have thought of that." She drummed her fingers against the steering wheel. "You big-city cops."

Wallace leaned her head back against the headrest and stared at the ceiling. The rush of light and dark from the lights of the oncoming cars as they approached and passed played shadow games across the fabric of the headliner. The unaccustomed sense of real fear was threatening to break loose inside her. She closed her eyes, willing the emotion away.

"I may need your help again," she said in a low voice. "No one close to the case knows you and I are as connected as we are. An advantage for me, a danger for you."

"I'm a big girl. I'll let you know if I can manage it or not."

After a few minutes of quiet time, Melissa broke the silence. "So what do you want me to do with you right now?"

"There's a car rental place in St. Francisville, which is on your way home from here. If you could drop me off at one of the chain motels nearby, that would be great."

TWENTY-THREE

Wallace's smoke-free rental car smelled a lot like smoke. But at least she was invisible, for the moment.

To stay that way, without arousing suspicion, she would need to continue her status reports to Burley and Shannon, even if it meant more fabrications and more meaningless blather. It needed to look as if she were still going about things in as normal a way as possible.

If her name was being mentioned by the people in the video Mason had shown her and if her movements were being monitored by the person who brought her the noose, then she had to consider the possibility that all of those people were connected. And she could no longer afford to think of Peter Ecclestone's disappearance, if it was related, as just a *killer* covering his tracks. It might be a *movement* trying to cover its tracks.

The part that didn't make sense was that a band of white supremacists might be responsible for Marioneaux's death. At best, the jury was still out on whether Marioneaux's abandonment of his segregationist past was genuine. His most recent activities and rhetoric had been tarted up with all the standard ecumenical catchphrases, but based on her research, there were still plenty of people out there who believed that deep down, when he was out of the public eye, the new Herbert was the same as the old Herbert. That, in the legislature, he was a stalking-horse, biding his time, waiting for an opening to strike a blow for whatever divisive tactics he and his kind were constantly dreaming up. So, why would the skinheads even be interested in taking down a man like that?

She was just plugging her earpiece in when her phone buzzed. She looked at the screen. It was Craig Stephens. She knew she shouldn't answer it, but she also knew he wouldn't be calling if it weren't critical.

"I don't think it's a good idea for us to be talking to each other right now," she said without waiting for him to speak.

"I'm pretty sure it's a terrible idea. But I think you should know that somebody at the parish jail fucked up. Eddie got put where he shouldn't have been and a few of his low-melanin fellow inmates, the ones who take a dim view of his politics, got about three unsupervised minutes to shine their shoes on his face."

Wallace yanked the car to the curb. She felt sick.

"They ruined his left eye."

"Oh, Craig, no. Where is he?"

"Baton Rouge General. They really messed him up. The docs are keeping him under observation for a few days."

"When did this happen?"

"About two hours ago."

"Craig, I—"

"I don't know where you are on this case, but I think you need to be closer to the finish line."

"Just listen."

"I'm not asking for miracles. Not asking for promises you might or might not be able to keep. Just . . . hurry . . . please."

Wallace could tell he was struggling to maintain his composure but failing. She had never seen him cry. When they were twelve, they had been walking home from the city park when they were confronted by a pair of slightly older white boys who thought Craig needed a tutorial on the proper relationship between black males and white females.

They fought the boys together, but Craig took the brunt of the attack. The older kids hurt him, but he hadn't shed a single tear. When his sister, Berna, died, it was the same—sad, hurt, but in control. Wallace couldn't fathom why this business with Eddie—a half-brother who had caused so much trouble in the family—was affecting him so deeply, and she felt strange that, after all these years, she wouldn't understand this about him.

She was about to speak when she saw that Craig had already hung up. The phone buzzed again. It was Burley.

"I just found out what happened to Eddie," she said before Burley could say anything.

"I don't suppose you've found Peter Ecclestone yet."

"Still working on it. Has the press gotten wind of this screw-up at the jail?"

"You better believe it. And the question is floating out there whether this was done intentionally." Burley went quiet for several seconds. "There's going to be a press conference in about an hour, to try and calm the waters. Chief Shannon wants you standing next to him when he and the sheriff take the podium. And speaking of Chief Shannon, he called to ask—very politely—'where the fuck' is the briefing he was supposed to get from the chief investigator last night."

"Can you tell him that I'm in the field and that I feel like I'm getting a clearer picture of what this case is about and that I'm still looking for Peter Ecclestone and that if I come in for a press conference I'll lose my grip on a very important thread."

"Are you serious? You want me to call a man whose credibility, not to mention his career, is about to blow up in his face and you want me to feed him that pile of bull crap? Let me rephrase that. You actually want *me* to make that call?"

Wallace wanted to tell Burley about the deleted picture of Eddie that Mason had found on the memory card from Peter's camera, but she still didn't know where that information might end up or what effect it might produce.

If she told Burley about the picture now and news of its existence leaked out, people would start asking questions, like who took the picture and where this person was. An unavailable Peter Ecclestone would amount to a tacit admission that Wallace had found and then lost a witness who had evidence crucial to the defense. She wasn't interested in speeding that plow.

Plus the picture, without any time or date information, would be useless. She and the department would be accused of trying to cover up her mistake by offering a picture whose value couldn't be supported.

"I can't be there for the press conference," she said finally.

"I'm pretty sure it was a direct order, not an invitation with an R.S.V.P. option."

"Would you call an undercover officer out of an in-progress field operation just as she was on the verge of nailing her target?"

"You're a plainclothes detective, not an undercover officer."

"I can't come in. Opportunities will be missed. I'm operating under the original priorities Chief Shannon established. That's all I can say, at this point."

The line went quiet again.

"Tell me where you are?"

"I'm not in a position to discuss that, at the moment."

"Are you in a department vehicle?"

"I'm not in a position to discuss that, either."

Wallace and Burley had been crosswise enough times in the past that she could imagine exactly what was going on with him—an aggressive posture, a barely contained explosion building behind his eyes, an uneasy quiet that inevitably preceded a gathering storm.

"I'm willing to take a beating for missing this press event," Wallace said. "Please tell the chief I'm sorry. I have to go now." She touched the End Call icon on her phone.

Her first priority was to do a quick drive-by to eyeball her house and Mason's apartment. A break-in at either place would have triggered an alarm and a police response, but there might be lesser transgressions she needed to be aware of.

Her personal vehicle was still parked at the curb near Mason's apartment. As she cruised by she could see it was undisturbed. Continuing down the street, she glanced over at Mason's apartment. Other than the cut in the screen that the noose came through, there appeared to be no damage.

As she drove, she wondered why whoever was behind this little campaign would even be interested in intimidating her. It would do no good to frighten her off the case, because there was a long line of detectives who could replace her. Unless they thought she had some unique knowledge or ability, the same reasoning applied to killing her. The pool of state, local, and federal law-enforcement officers was too big to murder out of existence. It was another piece of the puzzle that didn't make any sense.

Nothing was out of place at her little bungalow in the Garden District. No pile of ashes from a cross-burning, no cut screens or broken windows or doors swinging free. She wished she could see the back of her house, but she didn't want to go back there and look. Someone might be watching her house, and she didn't want to blow the disappearing act she had gone to so much trouble to put in place. She had left the cat feeders full, so Lulu and Boy Howdy would be fine for a few days.

Cruising along the street, she saw her next-door neighbor Albert Mills, pushing a lawn mower—the old-fashioned type that didn't have a motor. He paused to wipe his brow with the hem of his shirt and then looked in her direction as she drove by, but he showed no sign that he recognized her.

The smell of the cut grass floated on the warm summer air through her partially lowered window. Normally a happy fragrance, this time it reminded her of the graveyard.

TWENTY-FOUR

Wallace needed to stay out of sight, but she couldn't stay out of circulation and still do what she needed to. Unannounced and unexpected appearances would at least keep people from knowing what her next move was going to be. That gave her a degree of cover from whoever was trying to scare her. If she stuck to that and to people she knew she could trust, maybe she could go unmolested until she wrapped things up.

She moved quickly through the scattering of tourists milling about in the lobby of the Capitol building and made her way to the elevators. Her call-and-hang-up ploy confirmed that Garrett Landry was indeed in the office.

The elevator ride was short. As the doors dinged open she turned left and approached the late senator's office. She listened at the door for a few seconds, her hand on the knob. No voices, but someone was moving around. She opened the door and stepped inside.

A man was standing in front of the secretary's desk. His back was to her, and he was stacking piles of green paper into a cardboard file box. Wallace could see that he was too heavy for his frame. On one side, his white dress shirt had come untucked from his slacks and the tail hung down, covering one of his back pockets. A battle-scarred overstuffed garment bag, folded in half, was slouched over the arm of a chair against the wall to her left. A navy blazer was folded on the seat of the chair.

"Is that you—" He stopped in midsentence when he saw her.

"Are you Garrett Landry?"

He looked at her intently, clearly unhappy at the intrusion. After a few seconds, a dawning look rose in his eyes.

"You must be the detective."

"I must be."

"Sorry I didn't call you back, but things have been kind of chaotic, as you can imagine."

Wallace looked around the office, then back at Landry.

"I thought we were going to get together tomorrow afternoon, Detective . . ."

"Hartman. Wallace Hartman." She offered him one of her cards. "Today works better for me."

He took the card, then offered his hand but kept his gaze focused on the card. "Garrett Landry." He looked at Wallace, then back at the card and then laid it on the desktop. "Forgive my appearance. I've been on the road all day."

"That's not important, Mr. Landry. I just need a little bit of your time. I'll try not to step all over your afternoon."

"Sure," he said, his demeanor softening a bit. "You don't mind if I work while we chat, do you?"

He turned away, not waiting for her to answer, and pulled out his phone. He spoke to her over his shoulder. "I taxied in from the airport, so I don't have my car. Let me just text my ride that I'll be a little later than we'd planned." Landry thumbed the screen of his phone for several seconds, then dropped the phone in a front pants pocket. "I've been thinking about what you might want to know, but I haven't come up with any way I can be of much help."

Wallace glanced around the office for a place to sit. The only chair that didn't have something piled on the seat was the chair behind the desk where Landry was working. A transition was clearly under way. She wondered why the change was happening so fast.

"Sorry," Garrett said when he saw her looking around. "Let me—"

"I'm fine," Wallace said. "Sit if you like. I'm fine to stand." She waited a beat. "My condolences for the loss of the senator. It was a shocking thing. I imagine this has been hard for you."

"Thank you for saying that." Landry moved in the direction of the empty chair. He stopped short and decided to lean against the desk instead. "It's a strange feeling, being connected to someone who's been murdered." His tone had an almost clinical detachment to it.

"How long had you been working for him?"

"Just shy of two years. I was a law clerk for one of the state appellate judges here in Baton Rouge for two years before that."

"So, you're an attorney."

"I've got the degree and I've passed the bar, but I've managed to avoid practicing a single day, so far. Politics is more my ambition. Plus, the law firm treadmill looks somewhat unattractive these days. Making partner is more like chasing your tail than a bankable career."

"Law clerks usually rank pretty high in their class in law school."

"Number twenty-four," he said with a mouth-only smile. "Not Supreme Court material, but decent."

"How did you get the job with Senator Marioneaux?"

"His son, Glenn, and I knew each other growing up." He shrugged. "Never hurts to have a connection."

Wallace did a quick calculation. If he and Glenn had been contemporaries, then law school was clearly a later-than-usual career choice.

Landry nodded, smiling, obviously sensing her thoughts. "You've noticed I'm not as youthful as some who might be only four years out of law school. After college I took a gap year that lasted nearly twelve years."

"That sounds interesting."

"I came into a rather substantial trust fund the day I graduated.

With a lot of very careful planning and judicious decision-making I managed to blow it all in six years, instead of the usual two. I hung on for a while after that. There are still a couple of barely profitable dive shops down in the Keys, with my name over the door, that I let slip through my fingers. But most of it either went up in smoke or went up my nose." With an index finger he pressed one nostril shut, and made a sharp sniffing sound.

Wallace decided to have a seat behind the desk, after all, so she walked around Landry and sat. He turned and was now looking down at her from across the desk.

"Mr. Landry, I need you to think really hard about the questions I'm going to ask you." She rested her palms on the desk, her fingertips drumming gently on the wood.

"I guess we've gotten the small talk out of the way." He looked at her, letting his eyes wander just a bit. The barest hint of an approving smile flickered across his lips.

Wallace waited a few seconds, watching him watch her. "Were you aware of any threats to Herbert Marioneaux's life?"

"Not specific threats. No."

"Then tell me about the nonspecific kind."

Landry perched, sidesaddle, on the front edge of the desk. "He was never fully able to shed the reputation he carried with him from his . . . earliest days."

"Did that translate into people threatening his life?"

"It translated into the kind of hate mail that would make most people lock themselves in their houses and not come out without an armed escort."

"I'd like to see those letters."

"Pull on your boots and gloves, Detective. They're all in a landfill somewhere."

"You're kidding me."

"He refused to take them seriously. Said they were just bumpkins with more mouth than brains. Stupid people blowing off steam or goofballs flaunting their ignorance, so he ran them through the shredder."

"Did he ever report them to the police?"

"Not that I know of."

"What about the sergeant at arms for the legislature? Or the state police detail here in the building?"

"Same answer." Landry leaned toward her. "Look, he just wasn't the type to be easily intimidated, and he didn't want people to think that he could be. He figured that if he reported the letters it would end up in some newspaper somewhere and make him look scared and weak—like he was hiding behind the police and couldn't take care of himself. Impression management was very important to him."

"You read some of these letters."

"He showed me a few."

"Did any of them make reference to any specific method by which the sender might go about taking the senator's life?"

"One letter writer seemed to show a marked preference for knives. Which could mean he was a hunter."

"Sure. Field-dressing a deer carcass requires a good bit of blade-work."

Landry looked surprised that she would know that.

"Anything else come to mind?"

"There were also the usual threats of beatings and the like. My guess is that a lot of them came from the same individual or small set of individuals."

"Anything exotic or particularly out of the ordinary?"

"Not in any of the ones he showed me. It wasn't like individual words and letters had been cut from newspapers and magazines— nothing that dramatic. They were mostly just amateurish baloney, from what I saw."

"Can you remember when the last of the letters showed up?"

"It's been a few months, at least. They seemed to be seasonal, coming in bunches. Another reason he thought they must have been mostly from the same individual, somebody with blocks of free time at regular intervals throughout the year. All the ones he showed me were typed, so there would've been no way to track back to anyone from the handwriting."

"Anybody ever show up here at the office with an attitude that raised a red flag?"

"Politics is a sharp-elbows business, Detective Hartman—as I'm sure you know. Campaign donors can get testy when they think they or their money are being ignored or forgotten. So, of course, there were shouting matches from time to time. But you can be sure there's half a dozen of those going on in this building at this very minute. It's the typical give-a-little-expect-a-lot mentality that's always snapping at the heels of the elected official."

"Can you remember the names of any of the people who were involved in those meetings?" Wallace pushed a piece of paper across the desk toward Landry and offered him her pen.

Landry looked at the paper and pen, then at Wallace, but made no move to begin writing. "I'll have to give that some thought. None of it's been recent, and to be honest, I can't recall any names at the moment."

Wallace assumed Landry was lying. He'd gone to the trouble of making a lengthy point of how shouting matches cropped up but was now unable to summon the name of a single individual involved. That seemed unlikely. But she wasn't ready to start pushing yet. She still needed his cooperation.

"What can you tell me about the press conference Senator Marioneaux had scheduled for this past Monday?"

"I knew the time had been blocked out on his appointment calendar, but I didn't know what it was for. Sometimes he would set something up, just to have the press ready and waiting, in case some new initiative or project looked like it needed an assist from the Fourth Estate. But he might just as easily call it off if it turned out the announcement would've been premature."

"He had also scheduled an interview with Barry Gillis, a reporter from one of the TV stations, for the Sunday before."

Garrett rolled his eyes at the mention of Gillis's name. "Then my guess is it was something he and I would've discussed on Saturday, but . . ." He lifted one shoulder, then let it drop, and gave her a rueful smile.

"Speaking of the senator's calendar, I'd like to take a look at that, if you don't mind."

"Sure," he said, pointing. "Coy told me you'd want that. Let me get where you are, and I'll pull it up. It's digital."

Wallace stood and Landry slid into the chair and then typed and clicked his way past a log-in to the desktop screen—a sunset shot of the Baton Rouge skyline with the bridge in the background. Dozens of icons populated the screen.

"Here we go." He clicked on the calendar icon, typed in another password, and opened the application.

Wallace had watched carefully as he navigated his way to the calendar, but his fingers moved too quickly across the keyboard, so she hadn't been able to see what the password was.

"How far back does this go?" she asked.

"Years. All the way, I think. For as long as he was in the legislature. You want me to print you a copy?"

Wallace pulled a flash drive from her pocket. "Let's put it on here." She handed him the device.

Landry copied the calendar and handed it back to her.

"Who maintained the senator's appointment calendar?" she asked, slipping the drive back into her pocket.

"It was an open calendar. He put things in and took things out. I did the same. So did Coy. It was a fluid document, because his schedule could be unpredictable, subject to change at a moment's notice. Why?"

"Just wondering. Did everyone with access have a password?"

Landry smiled guiltily. "Yes, but we all used the same one."

"How were things with you and the senator?" Wallace asked.

"In what regard?"

"How was your relationship with Mr. Marioneaux?"

"Excellent, in every respect. I've known him practically my whole life, and I looked up to him as a young boy. I'm pretty sure he was disappointed in my choices after college, but he had a tendency to hold everybody to the same standards he held himself to."

"So, your family was close to his?"

"No. Just me. Glenn and I were friends growing up. We met in grade school. My folks had a lot of money. Still do. Glenn's family was one generation away from sharecropping."

Wallace allowed a startled look to cross her face.

"I don't mean that literally, but you get what I saying. Poor and working-class would have been a high reach for Glenn's grandparents."

"Yet you looked up to Glenn's father. That's interesting."

"He was a rather unusual man. Turning labor capital into education capital and then into social capital typically takes at least three generations to accomplish, or so the social science gurus in the academy tell us. Herbert Marioneaux did it in one." Garrett raised an index finger to emphasize his point.

"Apparently, not everyone shared your admiration for him."

"Not everyone took the time to know him. He made mistakes and, like all of us, he started life as a victim of his upbringing, but he managed to . . ." Landry pursed his lips and bobbled his head as he searched for the word. "To rectify his thinking and his actions. And he was quick about it. Something most people never even attempt, much less actually do." He stepped from behind the desk.

"I have to admit, you're challenging my long-held notions about the man. That's something I did not expect." Wallace offered Landry what she hoped was an engaging smile.

"And you're challenging my long-held notions about the police. Something *I* didn't expect."

Wallace bunched her shoulders and widened her smile. Landry smiled back.

"I can see why you would be so enchanted with him," she said. "What I can't see is why it took you five days to come back from that little junket you were on."

Landry's posture stiffened. His nostrils flared and his eyes widened. Slowly, he rubbed his palms together and then tilted his head back to look down his nose at her. A black expression hardened on his face.

Wallace kept a steady gaze on Landry and stayed quiet.

"If there was something I could have helped with, I would have been home on the first plane out of there. Glenn and I spoke the day after it happened, and he told me that it looked like the case was solved, already. That the police had arrested a suspect and from what he told me the evidence looks pretty conclusive."

"As a lawyer, you probably know that until the evidence has been tested in court sometimes those looks can be deceiving."

"And as you probably know, I won't have a role in those court proceedings. I'm an outsider to the case, with no useful information to offer. Why *would* I come running back?"

"Moral support?" Wallace waited, but Garrett just stared at her. "What about this office?"

"What about it? I'm not the only member of his staff."

"But you're the most important one, yet the last one to make yourself available to the police. I've already spent time with everyone else because they were all here."

"Detective Hartman, do I need to point out just what an absurd statement that is? If you interviewed us one after another, then, by definition, somebody would have to be last. Surely you're not implying that my place in the queue is of some evidentiary significance. If so, I must have missed that day in law school when they trotted out the age-old principle that you're presumed innocent unless you happen to be last in line to be interrogated by the police."

"I'm sorry. It's just that, given your evident admiration for the man, you seem rather unconcerned. On a personal level, I mean."

"Are you passing judgment on how I express my emotions?"

"Of course I am." She studied him carefully as he stood before her, in front of the desk. A low murmur of conversation and laughter grew louder as a group of people moved along the corridor outside the office door. Wallace made a point of running her eyes over Landry's doughy face, then his hands, eventually locking him into an eye-to-eye stare.

"What is it you think I do for a living, Mr. Landry?" her voice barely above a whisper. She pushed her hair behind her ears, then laced her fingers together and lowered her hands gently onto the desk, never breaking eye contact.

Landry shifted from foot to foot. His hands hung loosely at his sides, then took up momentary residence in his pockets, finally coming to rest as he crossed his arms over his chest.

Outside, in the hallway, the chime of the elevator sounded. As its doors opened, the number of voices grew briefly more numerous. The chatter ended abruptly as the doors slid shut. The rough drone of an airliner's engines faded from the soundscape, leaving silence in its place.

"I collect information and I pass judgment," she said into the stony quiet of the office. "And at the moment, I'm judging you to be a bit of an artful dodger."

"Based on nothing, as far as I can see."

She nodded. "But it's what *I* see that counts. You don't want to fool yourself into believing otherwise."

"I get it, now." He took a step toward her and then leaned forward, resting his hands on the front edge of the desk. "This stern Buddha face and these cryptic, menacing utterances are just you shaking my tree, trying to see if something falls out." He chuckled.

"I do that, from time to time, it's true. But that's not what's happening here. You're hiding something. You can tell me now or, one way or another, I'm going to rattle it loose."

TWENTY-FIVE

Wallace grabbed a pair of sunglasses from her satchel on the floor and slid them on. She kept her phone to her ear, pretending to be involved in a call, while she studied the faces and vehicles she could see through the windshield and in her rearview and side-view mirrors. After a couple of minutes of watching the street, she stowed her phone, then started the car and pulled into traffic.

Her conversation with Garrett Landry was going to bug her until she could figure out what—or who—he was hiding.

She drove aimlessly around the Capitol and then through Spanish Town, at every turn keeping an eye on the road behind her. She checked the clock. She still had time.

Wallace pulled into the parking lot alongside Davis's office. She sat for a minute checking her surroundings. No cars moved past, and no one was on the sidewalk, on either side of the street. She grabbed her satchel and strode quickly from her car, up the steps, and through the front door.

The outer office was empty, but the door into Davis's office stood open.

"Knock, knock," she said, presenting herself at the threshold.

"Come in, come in," Davis said, moving around his desk to give Wallace a quick hug. He motioned her toward the sofa against the wall of windows that looked out on to a shaded patio, as he pushed the door to his office shut.

"I can tell by the look on your face that you and your mother have been talking."

Wallace laughed. "I'm not sure what to even say."

"Are you surprised?"

Wallace cocked her head and thought for a moment. "That you asked? Not really. That it happened so soon? Maybe a little." She felt a flush rising in her cheeks as she took a seat on the sofa. "But that's all you're getting from me." She pointed at herself. "This daughter will not be breaking faith with her mother by spilling any beans that are not hers to spill."

"Duly noted." Davis laughed nervously as he lowered himself into his desk chair and swiveled lazily back and forth.

"But I do have some secret inside information that I am willing to share."

Davis hunched forward, over his desk. "Do tell."

"I've taken myself into protective custody," Wallace said.

Davis sat back, his eyes narrowed. "Protection from what? From whom?"

His face remained impassive as Wallace outlined the events of the previous night.

"Please tell me you're taking this seriously," he said. "That you're taking precautions."

"Of course I am." Wallace smiled and patted her gun.

"That is not what I meant," he said, raising his voice and looking at her as if she had lost her mind. "Why aren't you working with a partner? Surely Jack Shannon isn't so stingy that he'd force you to go solo in a situation this dangerous."

"Until I figure out whether there really is a leak in the department, I've kind of been keeping to myself." Wallace shifted uneasily. "But I hate lying to Burley and Chief Shannon."

Davis waved both hands in an emphatic stop gesture. "The truth is what you're after and honesty is not always your best tool for getting it. Sometimes you have to lie. If that's what's keeping you safe, then lie until you're blue in the face. You can always apologize and ask forgiveness, later."

Just hearing Davis say the words that vindicated her thinking made her feel better about what she was doing.

"So, your mother's gone underground." He chuckled. "Well, at least she'll have a story to tell." He stood and walked over to a small refrigerator hidden inside a walnut-paneled cabinet and pulled out a couple of bottles of sparkling water. He held one in Wallace's direction and cocked an inquisitive eyebrow.

"Sure. Thanks." She reached for the bottle as he crossed the room toward her.

"I suppose it's time we got down to the real reason you're here."

"I'm guessing if your visit with Colin Gerard had been a complete waste of time you would have called and said so. So, please tell me our former DA had something interesting to say about who he thinks outed Eddie Pitkin for obstruction of justice." She held up both hands, fingers crossed, then sprawled into a corner of the sofa, arm spread along the top.

Davis pulled his tie loose a bit. "Well, it's not good news. It's not bad news. It's just information."

"I'm listening," Wallace said, her enthusiasm waning.

"To be honest, I assumed he would tell me to take a hike. That, friends or not, he wouldn't even entertain the idea of having the conversation."

"Davis, you're killing me with all this preamble."

"He swears he never knew the name of the informant. And I got the impression he would have at least told me if he knew the person's name, but he was pretty insistent."

"Not even a hint?"

"Wallace, you know the secret code of the political class in Louisiana. Don't say it if you can nod it. Don't nod it if you can wink it. Colin wasn't saying, he wasn't nodding, and he wasn't winking. And before you ask," Davis said, holding up one hand, "the man appears to be fully compos mentis. All those strokes have taken a toll on his body, but his mind is as sharp as ever." Davis leaned back in his chair and propped one foot on an open drawer.

"You know, even though it benefits me, as a police officer, I find this whole anonymous informant business unsettling, from a due process point of view. It's just a little too police-state for me."

"Agreed. But, as you know, reliability is key to the value of an informant. Colin told me that whoever it was seemed to have access to solid information about a lot of other crimes and that those were the first ones the informant tipped him off about."

"I don't remember any of those other cases."

"No reason you should. They were all small potatoes—minor-league, police-blotter material." Davis clasped his hands behind his head. "Just back page, Saturday edition kinds of things. But the source, whoever the hell it was, was never ever wrong. So, by the time the evidence of Pitkin's misdeed got tossed over the transom, the anonymous tipster had built up a strong enough record of reliability that the DA was able to convince the judge that the information would support a warrant for going after such a high-profile defendant."

"How was it that the informant communicated with the DA?"

"Email."

"That simple?"

"Not so simple, actually. The informant used what's known as a Mixmaster anonymous remailer."

"I'm guessing all those big words mean the identity of the sender and the point of origin were untraceable."

"So I'm told. But in the initial contact, the sender set up an authentication system, so Colin would be able to verify that subsequent emails were from the same person."

"Is it safe to assume that system was never made public?"

"Almost. If it had been, of course, it would have been easy for anyone to send messages to the DA through a remailer and make them look like they were coming from the informant. However, the authentication system *was* revealed to the defendant and his attorney. Because Eddie was such a well-known and widely disliked figure, the judge required the DA to do an in-chambers disclosure."

"That seems so risky. Wouldn't that cast doubt on the authenticity of future messages?"

"Colin told me that Judge Hargroder didn't give a damn about hypothetical future cases. He didn't want Pitkin's case getting kicked back on appeal, so he ordered everybody to keep their traps shut and then he made Colin cough up the goods. That way they could all agree that the message putting the finger on Eddie came from the same source as all the others. And, of course, neither Eddie nor his lawyer was in the mood for a contempt citation, and they weren't about to start biting the hand that was feeding them, so they gladly went along with the judge's order to stay quiet."

"Were there any further revelations, after the Pitkin case?"

"Not a one. Eddie Pitkin got nailed and then the well dried up. Colin swore to me that, as far as he knew, that particular informant was never heard from again."

"So, it would be a safe bet that Eddie Pitkin was the informant's real target from the get-go. Everything before that was just priming the pump and once that was accomplished he or she just went back to their regular life."

"That was the speculation at the time. Although you and I both know that informants sometimes cease operations for other, less pleasant reasons."

"Surely Colin had his suspicions. He must have been curious as hell."

"He did and he was. A lot of us in the profession were curious. But, as you requested, I asked him point-blank if he thought it was Herbert Marioneaux. He just laughed and shook his head." Davis grinned and toyed with a heavy binder clip that was sitting on his desk. "He absolutely hated Marioneaux and I got the impression he would have enjoyed the irony of it."

Wallace smiled half-heartedly at the anecdote. She had other questions she wanted to ask, but the concerns her conversation with Garrett Landry had raised bumped those questions out of her head for the moment. She turned to look out through the windows, wondering whether to trouble Davis with her thoughts.

"You look distracted," Davis said.

"Just puzzled. Earlier today I interviewed Garrett Landry, the legislative aide for Herbert Marioneaux, and I've got a strange feeling about him."

"Anything you'd care to discuss?" Davis stood and walked to the windows overlooking the patio.

"He's hiding something. He was a childhood friend of Glenn Marioneaux, Herbert's son, and he idolized the senator. Had since he was a boy. Plus, he felt like Marioneaux had given him a second chance in life after he had essentially pissed away his first one. But Landry was out of the country on a bullshit business trip with a few functionaries from some state agency when Marioneaux was killed and he didn't come back until today. That's several days he stayed away when the father of his lifelong friend, the man he considered his mentor, had been murdered."

"Why do you think that means he's hiding something?" Davis looked down at Wallace.

"He didn't seem shaken up about Marioneaux's death. I never got a sense that he was grieving. In fact, he barely said a word about the investigation—something everyone in Baton Rouge seems to have a strong opinion about." Wallace looked at Davis, then turned her gaze back toward the patio.

"That might make him an ass, but I can't see how that points toward deception." He breathed in heavily through his nose, his shoulders rising and then falling as he exhaled.

"He claimed that the senator got some pretty nasty hate mail," she said, watching a starling as it pecked at the seeds in the tray of a hanging bird feeder.

"As do all politicians, I'm sure." Davis massaged his chin and his lower lip with his index finger.

"And that, occasionally, meetings in the senator's office could turn into shouting matches, when constituents or donors felt they weren't being properly served. Yet he couldn't remember the name of a single individual involved."

"I get it. You would think that after his idol got murdered he would have gone back over Marioneaux's appointment calendar and tried to dredge up some of those names," Davis said, turning away from the window and walking back behind his desk.

"And offered them to the police days ago," Wallace added. "Plus, I find it almost unbelievable that he would not have been in the room when at least some of those folks were getting hot under the collar. At a minimum, *those* names would be extremely unlikely to slip his memory." She sat forward, closing her eyes and pinching the bridge of her nose.

"Maybe he's afraid that if he mentions a name, the name of somebody he believes is harmless, he'll put that person in your gunsight."

"But unless he was certain that every single person who ever yelled at the senator was innocent, he could be unwittingly protecting the killer of the man who gave him a new lease on life." Wallace opened her eyes and looked over at Davis, a pained smile on her face. "That doesn't make sense to me. Unless . . ."

"Unless Landry's protecting someone he cares for more than he cared for Marioneaux."

"Exactly."

"The son, Glenn, his childhood friend." He hesitated. "That *is* troubling."

"Given their history, it's possible Glenn and his father got into it, in Herbert's office."

"So, what's your next move?"

"For this and other reasons, I'll stay on Glenn, but first, I need to find a nice quiet place to go through the senator's calendar and make a list of other people that need to be talked to." Wallace rubbed her eyes with the heels of her palms and let out a groan of frustration.

Through the closed office door, Wallace heard the sound of the front door opening.

"My next client," Davis said, checking his watch and shrugging into his suit coat.

Wallace stood and picked up her satchel, moving toward the office door.

"This way, if you don't mind," Davis said. He opened the door that led from his office out to the tree-shaded patio. "It's the preliminary stages of a divorce case and my client, well, she's a bit shy at the moment."

"Aren't you worried the neighbors will talk if they see one woman fleeing out the side door just as another comes waltzing in the front?"

"At my age, I'd be way past flattered."

Wallace threaded her way through the potted plants and metal furniture. In one corner, a mimosa tree that had been newly planted and shorter than her when she was a teenager now towered above her and the brick wall that surrounded the patio. The furniture had been repainted several times over the years and a few new planters had been added, but, for the most part, nothing had changed. Not even the vaguely menacing Green Man fountain built into the rear wall, still spitting his endless stream of water into the algae-filled pool. She couldn't remember the last time she had been out here. It gave her a sense of safety and permanence to see that some things never changed. Unwilling to let go of the feeling too quickly, she stopped and took a quick look around before she pulled open the gate that led to the parking lot.

She climbed into her car and set her satchel in the rear foot well on the passenger side. The tide of suspicion had grown turbulent again, and it was giving her a headache.

Maybe Glenn had erected this façade of a son struggling to come to terms with an agonizing past to conceal his true game—murdering his father for pissing all over his life.

Or maybe Marioneaux actually had been the informant who sent Eddie Pitkin to prison for evidence tampering and Eddie had found this out and killed Herbert in a fit of revenge.

Davis had agreed that both theories held water. But Wallace knew both couldn't be right.

Garrett Landry had looked suitably unnerved when she left him. She would let him roast for a while and then apply some more pressure.

Reaching back into her satchel, she pulled out her tablet and plugged in the flash drive with the late senator's calendar. She began paging through it, starting with the date of his death and then moving backward in time.

Herbert Marioneaux had been a remarkably busy man. Beginning at 8:00 A.M. and often going until well past 8:00 P.M. every weekday and some weekends, the days were divided into six-minute increments. Each increment was color-coded and filled in with a name or a task. Sometimes stretches as long as two or three hours were blocked off with notations such as "Floor Action" or "Committee Hearing."

As she studied page after page, the dull pain of tedium concentrated itself between her eyes. The idea that every name and event on the calendar would have to be checked out was dispiriting.

After looking back through several weeks of calendar entries, she set the tablet aside and pulled out the phone records.

LeAnne had organized the information into groups according to the names of the individuals the senator had called or received a call from. The groups were ordered alphabetically, and the calls were in date and time sequence. Names that had already been checked out were noted.

Nothing pointed a finger at any of the people the senator had spoken with, so Wallace set aside LeAnne's summaries and began looking back through the call logs themselves.

Between the phone logs and the calendar, there seemed to be virtually no unaccounted-for time during the senator's workdays. If he wasn't in a meeting with someone, he was on the phone with someone.

She picked up her tablet again and started looking at the calendar and the phone records side by side. One by one, she compared the dates and times of the calls to the entries on Marioneaux's calendar, looking for some pattern that might tip the balance toward Eddie, or Glenn, or some third possibility.

Once she got into the flow of the task, it began to go quickly. By the time she had worked her way back through everything, she had found five points at which the late senator had been more than just busy—he had been something of a magician at multitasking. On those dates and times, and only in those instances, Marioneaux appeared to be simultaneously on a call and in a meeting. And the calls were lengthy, covering virtually the entire time for each of the meetings. All of the calls in question were with a company called the LPGroup. Three of the meetings were with a man named David Jasper and two were with a woman named Mona Navarette.

Wallace quickly cut and pasted the calendar into a Word file and searched the entire document for Jasper and Navarette. Other than the entries for the meetings that coincided with the phone calls with the LPGroup, neither person's name appeared again. The LPGroup did not appear anywhere on the calendar.

From the 4-1-1 operator, Wallace got telephone numbers for Jasper and Navarette, and called them. Both were home, and neither remembered having ever been in a one-on-one meeting with the senator. They both sounded quite elderly, and both were members of the church Marioneaux had pastored years ago. Other than occasional after-church chitchat, neither had spent any time with him since he left the ministry to pursue his political career. And neither could offer an explanation of why their names had been on Marioneaux's calendar, unless maybe he had intended to get in touch with them but ended up not doing so.

A quick internet search showed that the LPGroup was a local firm, owned by a woman named Lydia Prescott. Under the "Team" tab on the website, Lydia was the only person listed. The name seemed familiar, but Wallace couldn't remember where she had heard it. A quick Google search refreshed her memory. Lydia was the woman who had been killed during a carjacking on the same day Herbert Marioneaux was murdered.

Wallace pulled out her phone and called Shirley Cappaletti, the detective working on the Prescott murder.

"Cappaletti here. Speak."

"Cappy, this is Wallace Hartman."

"Hey, Wallace. What's up?"

"That day we ran into each other in the police garage, you said Lydia Prescott operated a boutique research firm. Who else worked with her?"

"Nobody. It was a solo operation and, like I said, she ran it out of her house—pretty much a virtual business."

"Did you happen to find any records about her current clientele or projects underway?"

"Nada. The whole shebang was on her laptop, which has probably gone to computer heaven by now. We checked every pawnshop in the area. Nothing. Same for her phone. No external backups. Nothing in the cloud we could find, and I looked really, really hard."

"What about her house?"

"Clean as a whistle."

Wallace's mood sagged. "Email?"

"If she had a personal account, we don't know what it is. She definitely had business email, but there's nothing there. Her account used the old POP technology. Whenever she checked email, the messages migrated off the mail server onto whatever device she was using. Once the device goes missing, so do the messages that had already been looked at."

"What about new emails coming in, after she was killed, that haven't been looked at?"

"Well, I keep checking, but there's nothing interesting. A few new client inquiries. What's got you so curious, all of a sudden?"

"Phone records in the Herbert Marioneaux case I'm working on show some sort of connection to the LPGroup. I'm just doing due diligence. Running every rabbit down its hole."

"Well, Lydia did all sorts of research, including campaign consulting, so I'm not surprised a politico like Marioneaux would get in touch with her. Do you think the connection goes beyond that?"

"I don't know. If I find something more, I'll slide it your way."

Wallace closed Lydia's site and then pulled up the official website of the Louisiana legislature and studied the biographical sketch of Herbert Marioneaux she found there. Finally, the mist was starting to clear. The disappearance of Herbert's and Lydia's computers and cell phones had to be part of an effort to obscure any connections between the two of them.

Wallace checked her surroundings again. Except for the car of the client who had come in as she was leaving, everything looked the same as it had when she arrived at Davis's office. She started her car and pulled out of the lot.

TWENTY-SIX

Wallace parked on one of the side streets in Spanish Town, not far from the Capitol building. The shadow of the monolithic structure deepened the gloom around her. She quickly made her way inside and took the elevator up.

The reception area of Marioneaux's office suite was much tidier than it had been during her early afternoon visit. Except for the computer and the telephone the desk was completely cleared, and all of the boxes were neatly stacked in one corner. Wallace heard movement in another room. No talking, just the rustling of papers, then footsteps approaching.

Garrett Landry backed into the office from the hallway that led deeper into the suite, his arms stacked high with boxes. As he cleared the doorway, he turned. He jumped when he caught sight of Wallace, upsetting his cargo.

"Shit." He swayed and dipped, trying to stay under the boxes. "I didn't hear anyone come in." He set the boxes on the edge of the desk. "I'm afraid I'm on my way out, Detective." He stuffed a slim briefcase into the outside pouch pocket of his garment bag and zipped the pouch closed.

Wallace studied Landry's face for signs of distress, but all she could see was annoyance.

"Since I was here earlier, my investigation has suddenly become so much more interesting."

Landry moved back in the direction of the hallway, then turned his head and spoke over his shoulder. "You're not required to give me updates, Detective." He looked her up and down. His mouth formed a prim expression of distaste, and then he turned away and resumed his progress down the hallway.

She spoke loudly, to make sure her voice followed him. "Because I know how close you were with the late senator, I'm working on the assumption that you have a strong desire to help me get this investigation finished up. That way you won't have to worry about me keeping you under a microscope."

He came back up the hall and stopped just shy of the doorway. "You're not one for subtlety, are you?"

"Fresh out today."

"Well, just so we're clear, I'm not worried about you or your little microscopes. Why would I be?" Landry gave her a steady stare.

Wallace waited until he turned away again. "Why didn't you tell me the senator was gearing up for another campaign?" she asked.

Landry stopped again and looked in her direction. He rubbed the fingers and palm of his right hand across his mouth, massaging his jawline.

She got to five-one-thousand before he spoke.

"It wasn't a for-sure thing that he was going to do it," he said, lumbering haltingly through the statement.

"Who else knew?"

"How could I possibly know the answer to that question?" He looked down the hallway toward the back of the office suite. "He and I didn't spend every waking minute together, and he certainly didn't tell me everything."

"Did Glenn know? Did Dorothy?"

"You'll have to ask them. Besides, I can't see what difference any of that makes. Once a person gets elected to office, their first and most important priority is to get reelected. That's not exactly breaking news." He raised his hands, palms out, and scowled as if to say his point was beyond argument. "So if the big lightbulb-over-the-head idea that got you bustling back over here is that Herbert got knocked off by a political rival—someone who was willing to use any means necessary to become the all-important senator from no-place-important Louisiana—I'm afraid your powers of deduction have deserted you."

Wallace smiled inwardly at Landry's attempt to nudge her suspicions down the wrong trail.

"I think we both know that term limits would've kept him from seeking another term as senator. And my powers of deduction keep insisting this is something you should have told me. Don't you think so too?" She raised her eyebrows and offered him a thin-lipped smile.

"If I say yes and then say I'm oh, so very sorry, do you think that will hasten the end of this interview?" A faint glimmer of sweat shone at Landry's hairline.

That was not the response she had been expecting. Surely he wanted to know how she had found out about Marioneaux's campaign plans. If the shoe were on the other foot, that would have been the first question out of her mouth. The fact that he wasn't asking meant that he already had a pretty good idea how she found out. If he knew that, then he would also know he had just gone from being an object of interest to the subject of frank suspicion. *Perfect.*

"Tell me about David Jasper and Mona Navarette." she said.

Landry looked toward the ceiling, then tilted his head to one side. After a few seconds, he looked back at Wallace. "Those names ring a faint bell, from when I was little, it seems like. I think they may have been in the congregation of the church we went to sometimes. The one where the senator was the preacher."

"Have you had occasion to think about them lately?"

"No." He snorted and rolled his eyes. "Why would I?"

"Tell me about Lydia Prescott."

For the smallest fragment of a second, something changed deep inside Landry's eyes. His gaze faltered, as if his thoughts had turned inward, and then his face resumed its original expression. It was only a fleeting micro-expression, but Wallace was certain of what she saw.

"Never heard of her."

Landry's posture became nonchalant and he gave Wallace a bored look. "Listen, Detective Hartman, I appreciate what you're doing. I wouldn't want you to think otherwise. But if you don't mind, I need to get moving. Someone to replace the senator will be chosen soon and I've got to be able to manage the transition. If I can make myself appear to be useful and if I'm lucky, maybe I'll get to keep this job."

"Are you sure?"

"About keeping my job? Of course I'm sure." He maintained unwavering eye contact.

"Are you sure about Lydia Prescott?"

He closed his eyes again and sighed audibly, letting his head and shoulders sag. He shook his head and smirked, as if he were trying to keep from laughing at her. "Look, Detective, a lot of folks come through this office on a pretty much constant basis. Constituents, lobbyists, businesspeople, religious leaders, other politicians, consultants of every size and shape." His voice rose in pitch as he named each group. "You name it, they've been here. It's endless. Okay?"

Wallace waited to see if he would continue his performance. She hadn't mentioned that Lydia Prescott was a consultant. Maybe it was just a coincidence that Landry had included consultants in his list of the pesky flies buzzing around the senator's office.

He gritted his teeth and he raised his hands, shaking the air in front of him in mock frustration. "It's just the pitter-patter of little minds. And it never stops. You get what I'm saying? There is absolutely no way I could remember them all."

Wallace could see why he was so attracted to politics. He had a natural talent for the smooth lie and the convincing bluff. But two could play that game.

"Do you recall what I said earlier about you hiding something and me rattling it loose?"

Landry blew the hair off his forehead in an exaggerated display of resignation. "Yes, Detective Hartman, how could I possibly forget such a terrifying experience, especially when it happened such a short time ago?"

"Since I saw you last, I got a judge to green-light one of my specialists to do a little snooping in the late Senator Marioneaux's calendar. And not the flash drive version you gave me. With an assist from the head of IT for the legislature, she's been rooting around the server where the online version is maintained."

Landry's face remained blank, and for a moment Wallace thought he would see through her lie.

"I don't believe you." His expression didn't change, but he shifted from foot to foot.

"But you will."

Wallace waited for Landry's comeback, but he remained silent. She could tell that, for the first time, he felt unsure of himself.

"I know the calendar was altered, *after* the senator's death," she said.

"So."

"And I know you did it. Only you and Coy Asber and Marioneaux had the password. Coy didn't do it. I called him before I came back up here, just to make sure."

Landry was no longer looking at her.

"Don't you want to know what we found?"

"First of all, you had no right—"

"The judge gave me a warrant. That's all the right I need." She stepped toward him. He took a step backward. Wallace waited for him to challenge her. The beads of sweat at his hairline were heavier.

"Every entry for Mona Navarette and David Jasper was a postmortem entry. The time and date of every one of those entries coincides with a phone call between the senator and Lydia Prescott. She was his campaign consultant, wasn't she? She was helping him test and shape his campaign messages. He was going to hold a press conference last Monday, but he was killed before that could happen. Whatever he was going to announce, I feel certain it was something the late Lydia Prescott helped him with. So tell me, Garrett, are you sure you want to stick with your story from earlier, that you have no idea what that press conference was going to be about?"

She watched him dither over how to proceed. His shoulders sagged and he looked as if he might cry. He closed his eyes and nodded, slowly.

"Let me show you something," he said, blowing out a huge breath through puffed cheeks. He stepped past her, reaching toward a file cabinet against the front wall of the office.

Wallace heard the grunt of explosive effort and the world went black.

TWENTY-SEVEN

The bonging of the elevator bell cut through the fog in her head. The room was dark. Wallace raised herself to her hands and knees. The carpet felt rough against the palms of her hands. A heavy throb radiated from the back of her head. She heard the elevator doors slide shut.

Her first thought was that she had no place to stay, no fresh clothes to change into, and that she hadn't eaten all day. *Shut up*, she told herself, pushing the pointless unbidden worries aside. *Focus on what you need to do next.*

She felt sick to her stomach. She rolled onto her side and lay still while she untangled her thoughts from the pain and the nausea.

Vaguely, Wallace remembered hearing Landry's footsteps as he fled the office, the closing of the door, the metal-on-metal thunk of the bolt gliding into place, the sing of the key sliding from the keyhole—a maneuver that would not confine her, only delay her momentarily as she fumbled for the lock in the dark. *He was a thinker, that one.*

She tried to sit, but the nausea struck again, like a bully not yet willing to accept victory, so she decided to stay on her side for a bit longer.

Wallace wondered how much of a head start Landry had. His blow to the back of her head meant that he was deep in desperation mode, maybe even panicking. The fact that she was able to form that realization made her believe the muddle in her head was clearing.

The light shining under the door from the hallway was enough to let her to make out her surroundings. The receptionist's desk stood about a foot in front of her. Grabbing the front edge, she steadied herself and stood. The room spun hard left. She leaned heavily on the desktop to keep from lurching. Slowly, she slumped to her knees and closed her eyes, pressing her cheek against the cool wooden panel that spanned the front of the desk. She felt herself slipping away.

TWENTY-EIGHT

By the time she recovered enough to give chase, the idea of running after Garrett Landry seemed futile. Surely he was out of the building by now.

Wallace realized she needed help and she needed to move fast. She looked around the vacant office suite. Except for the ringing in her head, the building was quiet.

She called Melissa Voorhees and asked her to notify the major public transport facilities that Landry was a fugitive and that if he attempted to board he was to be detained and she was to be notified. She also asked Melissa to put out a BOLO on Landry's automobile and to text her Landry's address and plate number from the state's DMV database.

Then she ransacked the senator's office. As quickly as the nausea would allow, she went through every box, drawer, closet, and cabinet in the place, looking for anything that would shed light on the identities of the other players in the scheme Landry was part of. The search proved futile.

Her phone buzzed. It was Melissa.

"I did everything you asked, except get the info on Landry. I'll text that in just a bit. In the meantime, I've been instructed by Mason not to say that I'm worried about you, so you can be my witness that I didn't say it."

"How's he holding up?"

"Like a rock. He misses you and he's worried about you, despite his protestations to the contrary. My husband and I took him dinner, before you called, earlier. He's quite a guy, and my God, is he ever smitten with you-know-who."

"I needed to hear something exactly like that, right about now." Melissa's words brought a tiny smile and a lot of energy, but the nausea was returning, so Wallace lay on her side on the floor in Marioneaux's office and closed her eyes.

The throb at the back of her head reminded her that, for the second time in three days, she had taken a beating and was concealing it from Mason. The shot of energy she felt a moment ago was overwhelmed by the anxiety over how he would react when she finally did tell him.

"Listen, I've got some actual news," Melissa continued. "That partial print from the glove box in Peter's SUV matched one of the prints on the water bottle."

"That's interesting. Not surprising, though, at this point."

"You sound like you're in the middle of something."

"Deep thought," Wallace said. "The landscape is changing fast, and I'm trying to figure out what it all means."

"One more thing, then, and I'll let you go. Joe Hanna, one of the geniuses in Mason's office, found the data file for the picture of Eddie Pitkin on the dock at False River. It indicates that it was taken at a time that would have made it virtually impossible for Eddie Pitkin to be in Baton Rouge when Herbert Marioneaux was killed."

Despite the disorienting nausea, Wallace's mood perked up again. "That's excellent news."

"Only partly excellent," Melissa said. "Without the camera and the photographer, Joe said the image and the data file are vulnerable, because there's no way to know if the camera's internal clock and calendar were set to the correct time and date."

"Terrific," Wallace said.

"If you need any more technical help while Mason is in exile, he said you can go straight to Joe."

Wallace scribbled down Joe's number and address as Melissa read it to her.

"Is there anything you need me to do?"

"Tell Mason I miss him too, and that I love him."

With the new information from Melissa, some things were starting to fall into place. Colley Greenberg had drilled it into Wallace from the beginning: If A is connected to B and B is connected to C, then A is connected to C. The connection might be murky and it might not even be useful, but it was there, and high-grade police work demanded that it be examined.

Eddie Pitkin's picture on the memory card, whenever it was taken, connected him to Peter Ecclestone. And Ecclestone was connected to Oliver Harpin by the image of Harpin in the boat near Craig's dock and by Harpin's fingerprint on the glove box latch in Peter's SUV. So, Pitkin was connected to Harpin.

And assuming the data file was correct and that Eddie was at the lake when Marioneaux was killed, the hair and insulation fibers at the crime scene had to have been planted as part of a frame-up. From there, it was a short jump to the inference that Peter had disappeared because he could spoil the plot by providing an alibi for Eddie.

Any remaining doubts about the existence of a plot were put to rest by the inconsistencies she had discovered in the senator's calendar and the attempt to cover them up—not to mention the dense knot of pain in her head.

With Eddie safe in the hospital, the pressure was off to deliver her newfound discoveries so that the charges could be dropped and Eddie could be set free. With the possibility of the leak still in play, showing her cards now would let the conspirators know exactly how much she knew.

Clearly, Eddie Pitkin was connected to Herbert Marioneaux by their long-ago fights in the media over issues of race and segregation and, more recently, by the planted evidence found on Marioneaux's body. And the late senator was connected to Garrett Landry by employment and personal history.

The chain of connections led clearly from Harpin to Ecclestone to Pitkin to Marioneaux to Landry. And based on the information Mason's FBI contact had passed along, Carlton Lister was connected by way of Harpin.

There would be others. Individuals she had not yet encountered, with roles she did not yet understand. And someone had to be the mastermind.

Garrett Landry had the brains, but Wallace didn't like him as the shot caller. He had panicked at the mention of Lydia Prescott's name—the wrong temperament if you're the one with your hands on the levers.

If she was right that Landry might be protecting Glenn Marioneaux, then perhaps Glenn was the man with the plan and all of his emotional displays were just so much blather intended to confuse the issue. And with Dorothy protecting Glenn, perhaps she too was part of it.

Wallace pulled herself up from the floor and sat in Marioneaux's massive desk chair. The maroon leather squeaked as she shifted around, trying to find a comfortable position.

The most intriguing connection she saw was between Herbert Marioneaux and Lydia Prescott, the dead campaign consultant. Given their linkage, it seemed probable that whoever had killed the senator was responsible for Lydia's death, as well.

The big question that all of this raised was why any of this was happening. The connection to Carlton Lister implicated issues of race, but how and to what end?

Landry had been hiding more than the fact that Marioneaux was planning a new campaign. He had also hidden the fact that it wasn't going to be a campaign to remain the senator from noplace-important, as Landry had called it.

The trajectory of Marioneaux's career made Wallace fairly certain he'd be aiming for higher office. Congress was a possibility, but elections for the U.S. Senate were too far in the future to be gearing up for now and the House seat in his district was in the hands of a shoo-in incumbent.

Wallace was willing to bet a lot of money that Marioneaux was getting ready to run for governor. But being electable in the sparsely populated southeastern rural districts of the state was not the same as winning in the more politically and racially diverse urban precincts—areas he would need to carry if he intended to make a serious run for the governor's mansion.

Given the stubbornness of his early reputation and the persistent skepticism of the pundits, Marioneaux would have needed a lot of help to convincingly rebrand himself. Enter Lydia Prescott, political consultant.

Of all the names floating through her head, Garrett Landry and Oliver Harpin seemed to be the most strongly connected to the plot and reasonably findable. If they didn't pan out, Glenn would be next on her list.

Wallace stood. Her head ached and her back was still sore where she'd been kidney-punched. She looked around the office, wondering if she was about to do the right thing. She flipped open her little notebook to the page where she had written the home address and tag number for Oliver Harpin—information she had gotten from the DMV the day she tracked him to the cemetery—and committed it to memory.

She checked her weapon. It was time to enter the belly of the beast.

Wallace headed south out of the front doors of the Capitol building, then turned east at the lowermost boundary of Spanish Town. She was walking a big loop through the neighborhood, approaching her car from the east—the opposite direction from which she had left it.

The opening vocals of "Doolin-Dalton" floated low and plaintive from the open window of a passing car.

From behind a tall hedge, a little girl shrieked and then laughed and shrieked again, like she was suddenly it in a game of chase.

Wallace was hungry and her head was killing her and she was almost too tired to keep worrying about whether anyone was dogging her trail. But this was the wrong time to get careless. If there was a leak in her department, then it was possible whoever might be following her was a fellow officer—someone trained to avoid being seen.

But, given the events of the last few hours, she was no longer opposed to being followed. She just wanted to know if it was happening and, if possible, who was doing it.

As she hiked deeper into the part of the neighborhood that was close to the freeway, the foot traffic thinned to almost nothing. About a block from her destination she found herself alone on the street. Moving slowly, she dragged her gaze in short, deliberate arcs across everything ahead of her and she stopped abruptly at random intervals to check her back trail.

She turned the final corner, onto the street where her car was parked, and felt very smart for having taken such an indirect route. In this rapidly gentrifying neighborhood, the car parked at the curb, about fifty feet ahead, looked very out of place with its bad paint and extensive dent collection. Maybe it was nothing—just the vehicle of a poor relation come for a visit or a holdover from Spanish Town's less prosperous days.

But the car was pointing away from her and in the low light from the streetlamp she was just able to make out the tag number.

Harpin.

A tremor of fear skittered up her back. She slid into the shadow of a tree overhanging the edge of the sidewalk.

Her mind struggled to understand Harpin's presence here and now, less than half a block from her rental car. It couldn't be a coincidence. How had he known where to find her?

After a few moments of reflection, it was as if the helter-skelter strands linking remote parts of a spider's web lit up and the connection from Harpin to Landry became clear.

During her first visit to Landry, he had texted someone, telling her he was letting his ride know he might be late leaving the office. He had actually been alerting someone to her presence in his office—signaling that the scare job at Mason's apartment hadn't worked, that she was still pursuing the investigation.

If that had brought Harpin onto the scene, he would have seen her leave the Capitol earlier today and he would have followed her to Davis's office. A rush of alarm caused her breath to catch when she realized Davis might be in danger.

If she had led thugs such as Oliver Harpin and Carlton Lister to Davis's doorstep, she could never forgive herself. And it would break her mother's heart.

She backtracked a few steps, then turned around and walked toward the corner, pulling her phone out as she went. She called Davis's number. It went to voicemail. She left a message, telling him the situation and insisting that he get someplace safe. She prayed he was already at home, in his gated community that had enough security to protect an embassy.

Wallace stowed her phone and looked up the street, calculating her next move.

As she approached Harpin's car again, she reached inside her jacket and unsnapped the strap on her holster. She wrapped her hand around the grip of her gun.

The car was about thirty feet ahead. But something was wrong. She stood in the shadows studying the situation until she could figure out what was bothering her.

Light shone back through the rear windshield from the streetlamp up ahead of the car. The silhouette of the front passenger seat was clearly visible. The silhouette of the driver's seat was not—as if the driver's seat was leaned back, below the level of the rear dash. It was a position she referred to as eyelid surveillance because, on a stakeout, reclining the seat always led to sleep and the study of the backs of one's eyelids.

Wallace approached the car with caution, wondering if she had already been seen. Perhaps Harpin was not even in the car but was on the street, watching her dither over what to do.

She picked up a rock from the gutter and tossed it toward his car. It crashed onto the roof with a bang. Then she pressed the panic button on the key fob of her rental car, letting the lights flash and the horn whoop a few times.

Nothing happened. No sudden rocking of Harpin's car. No head popping up. No one came running toward either car. No one came out of their house to see what was going on.

During the commotion, Wallace moved quickly to the passenger side of Harpin's car, staying below the windowsill.

Through the rear passenger window she saw him.

His seat had been reclined and he lay motionless, his head slumped over to his left. Wallace crouched low and pulled open the front passenger door. A dried rivulet of blood traced a sinuous path from behind his right ear down into the collar of his denim work shirt. The window and windshield on his side of the car were clean. No exit wound. It would have been a small-caliber weapon, maybe firing hollow points. A gun, with a silencer, lay on the floor just in front of her. Harpin's right arm had flopped, palm up, across the console.

Wallace wasn't buying suicide. Landry's rash move must have triggered a tactical retreat among the conspirators and the scene in front of her was part of a cleanup operation. She wondered if Landry was also in line to be scrubbed.

The stink from the mountain of garbage covering the backseat didn't quite cover the sharp smell of spent gunpowder. The scratchy sound of insect feet inside the trash made her skin crawl.

She held her ear against Harpin's chest for a full minute. Nothing. She laid her palm across his forehead. It was cool to the touch. She tried to bend one of his fingers toward his palm, but already she could feel the rubbery resistance of rigor mortis.

TWENTY-NINE

Leaving the scene of Harpin's murder without calling it in went completely against Wallace's training, but he was beyond help and the call would expose her phone and her location to the 9-1-1 operator.

With Harpin out of the picture, Wallace shifted her focus to Garrett Landry. She arrived at his house to find newspapers piled on the porch and his car in the carport. The hood was cool.

She walked to the rear of his house where she assumed the bedrooms were and phoned him. He didn't answer and no lights came on.

Back on the front porch she sat on the cool gray-painted wood and leaned against the white clapboard wall. A velvety quiet lay over the neighborhood, but in the far distance, at the edge of her hearing, she caught the warble of police sirens and the grating claxons of fire trucks. The sounds came from several directions at once.

She felt her phone vibrate. It was a text from LeAnne:

Glenn into psychiatric care facility. Dorothy less friendly than before. Where are you?

Good question, Wallace thought. *Where am I? Temporarily lost.* She shoved her phone into her pocket without responding to the text.

With no information to help her locate Landry, Wallace once again began the laborious process of reexamining what she knew.

The image of Eddie on the dock, even though it was vulnerable, still leaned toward Eddie's innocence. But his shaky alibi, the existence of an escape route through the attic, and the presence of insulation on Marioneaux's shirt all pointed toward Eddie having had an opportunity. If a jury wanted a motive before they'd convict, revenge would probably be enough.

Wallace's mood sank further when she realized how cunning the plotters were. Marioneaux couldn't deny being the informant. And even if he hadn't been, the real informant would never step forward and reveal his identity. The plotters only needed to make it *look* like Marioneaux was the informant—and that Eddie had found that out.

Barging in on someone in the wee hours was not usually the way to win friends and influence people. And Mason would probably kill her for abusing his employee Joe Hanna, but she was running out of options

"Hello?" The voice was hoarse with sleep.

"Joe. This is Detective Hartman. Mason said I could get in touch with you if I needed any more technical help."

"Uhn-huh?"

"I'm on your front steps."

"Seriously? You *are* serious. Jesus. What time is it?"

"It's late . . . or early. Listen, I'm sorry, but this is important."

"Gimme a sec."

Two minutes later he joined her on the porch. "Go back to sleep, honey," he said before pulling the door shut behind him. "It's just some woman who needs me and says she can't wait."

The guy was a saint, Wallace realized.

He turned to face her. "Okay, Detective Hartman. What can I do for you?"

"I need to know how the Mixmaster anonymous remailer works, and here's why."

Joe nodded as Wallace recounted what she had learned from Davis.

"This happened years ago. So, here's my question. With all the advances in software technology since then, could someone trace a message back to the sender now, even though it was untraceable back then?"

"No. It can't be done. But *I've* got a question for *you*. There's more than one kind of remailer, so how do you know the originals were sent using the Mixmaster?"

"The information I'm telling you was relayed to me secondhand, by someone I sent to interview the recipient. He was just reporting to me what the recipient said."

"But that's my question. How could the recipient know which type was used? The sender would know, *maybe*, but there's nothing in the message when it arrives that would tell the *recipient* which one was used."

She was confused. Why would Colin Gerard make up a story like that? Perhaps Davis had been wrong and Colin's medical problems were affecting his cognitive abilities after all. Maybe Colin had let something slip that he shouldn't have. Had he known who the informant was and been privy to his methods all along?

"And yes, I'm sure about this," Joe said. "I can practically see the question forming in your head."

Wallace supposed Colin could have been the one to finger Pitkin and that the whole anonymous informant story had been a charade to cover his own secret campaign to rid the city of what many considered a troublesome personality. Could someone like Colin be connected to the plot to frame Eddie Pitkin?

She had been up for more than twenty hours and had had only four hours' sleep in the last forty-eight. The fatigue felt like a physical thing occupying space in her head. Even so, the questions and possibilities multiplied. She felt like the answer was close, like it was about to show itself. Then nothing. Without warning, the blizzard of ideas chasing around in her head ground to a halt.

She leaned against a porch railing and dropped her face into her hands. "Thanks, Joe. I promise not to bother you again."

"You okay?" He ran his hands through his unruly curls.

"Yeah. I'll be fine."

"Well, if you need me, don't hesitate." He gave her a questioning look, then slipped back into his house.

Wallace returned to her car, more puzzled than when she had arrived. *Just let it go. Think about something else for a minute and then come back to it.*

She started driving, paying no heed to where she was going. Just turning randomly, trying to quiet her mind without falling asleep at the wheel.

The first thought to disturb the newfound quiet took her by surprise. Besides herself, not one blessed soul on the entire planet knew where she was at this moment—in a strange neighborhood, in the middle of the night, driving around with no destination in mind, with a blinding headache courtesy of a man who had cracked her in the head and then disappeared.

What kind of life was this that she was leading? What kind of person spent her time chasing after people who hated her, while taking elaborate measures to isolate herself from the people she loved and who loved her? The wisdom of Mason's words from the night before, urging her to think about everything that was a stake, seemed so obvious.

When she looked at things in that light, it seemed clear that all of the most basic assumptions about the who and the what of her life were ripe for serious reexamination.

And with that thought, the lock in her head sprang open.

———————

Wallace called Melissa Voorhees and arranged to meet her at a point halfway between Baton Rouge and Cavanaugh. Then she called Davis. He didn't answer, so she left a message that she needed his help, that she would meet him at his office between nine thirty and ten.

She needed to make one other stop in between.

A strange, hollow fear crept inside her.

THIRTY

Wallace felt like she was standing at the edge of the roof on top of a very tall building. In front of her, nothing but the abyss. Behind her, a man with a gun. In the last fifteen minutes, Burley had called and called and called, each time hanging up when her voicemail prompt kicked in. Then he texted her:

> Word leaked this a.m. that we lost alibi witness. Tasha K demanding your head on a platter for suppressing evidence and agitating for a criminal investigation. Unhappy people with signs gathering around our building. Your name on some. Good day to avoid work and media. Shannon may get boot. Maybe you too.

Wallace knew Tasha was pulling a stunt for Eddie's benefit, and she knew it would work. The public would see one more white cop hammering down on an innocent black man.

Just as she was about to get out of her car, her phone buzzed yet again. It was Barry Gillis, the TV reporter who had called her six days ago, sniffing around for inside information about the Pitkin investigation. She turned her phone off without waiting to see if he left a message, and then did a slow, methodical survey of the area around her and Davis's office.

No one was on the street. She exited her car and headed quickly up the front steps.

She pulled open the door and stepped inside. The sound of heels clicking on hardwood sounded from her right. Barbara Seeley, Davis's secretary, was pushing a metal cart with dozens of hanging files.

"Hey, Wallace. Good to see you. Just go on in. He's not doing anything important. Probably just reading the sports page."

Wallace crossed to Davis's office, knocked, then went in. She pushed the door shut with her backside and stayed leaning there until Davis raised his eyes from the desk and saw it was her.

His expression was a mixture of concern and relief. "I've seen the news. My guess is the media will be staking out your house, maybe your mother's too. You can stay here, as long as you like, and you're welcome to one of my spare bedrooms."

Wallace closed her eyes and took a deep breath.

"It's been quite a night," she said, still leaning against the door. She opened her eyes.

"I can only imagine," he said. "Well, you were smart to call me. No one will think to look for you here and you can wait till things calm down a bit before you wade back into the mess."

"I need you to promise me something," she said, letting her gaze wander around the office for a few seconds before settling on Davis.

"Whatever you need. Just name it."

"Promise me you're not going to do something stupid. Something that will make this harder on me than it already is."

Davis sat straighter in his chair. His look turned quizzical.

"I know."

"You know what?" He looked mystified.

"I know it was you." Her eyes were burning. She was having trouble swallowing and her breathing was ragged. "You were the informant who put Eddie Pitkin behind bars."

He let out a tired laugh and dropped his head into his hands. His voice was soft and conciliatory. "I'm afraid you've made a mistake, kiddo."

"No. There's no mistake." She studied his face, wondering how long he would continue his pretense.

Davis's mouth pulled to one side and his eyebrows bunched together in a look of strained apprehension.

He stood and moved around the desk in her direction.

She shook her head and raised her hand, signaling for him to stop. "I talked to Colin Gerard this morning, before I came over here."

"Excellent. I hope the old bastard is doing well," Davis said. He slouched against the side of the desk, his hands in his pockets, jingling the change and the keys, the look of concern frozen on his face.

"He's doing well enough to remember that he never told *you* something that you told *me*. He said he told you about how the snitch who fingered Eddie used an anonymous remailer to send his information. But he never told you that it was the *Mixmaster* remailer. He couldn't have because he never knew himself. No one could've, except possibly the informant who was doing the sending."

Wallace stood away from the door and moved into the center of the office, keeping her eyes focused on Davis. "One of Mason's colleagues, an expert in these things, assured me that only the sender could know exactly which remailer was used."

"Did you ever consider the possibility that, way back then, the Mixmaster was the only type of anonymous remailer in existence, and maybe that's how I knew?"

"Of course I did. After I talked to Colin, I kept trying to find another explanation that made sense. Any little thing that would let me believe something else was going on. And let me tell you, I tried and I tried some more." She took a deep breath. "But it *wasn't* the only one. You know, I almost couldn't make myself look it up. My hands were actually shaking when I Googled that bit of information."

"Fine. So I embellished my story with a few big words." He looked down shyly. "Was it wrong to try and impress you with some high-sounding technical terms? And, besides, what possible difference could it make?"

"If that was the only thing, I don't think I would be here right now. But the day I tried to persuade you to ask Colin Gerard for help, I told you I had good reason to believe we had the wrong guy in jail for the Marioneaux murder. Do you remember that?"

Davis looked down at his feet. He scuffed the toe of one loafer against the Oriental rug that covered the floor.

"You never asked what made me believe that."

Wallace waited for a reaction, but Davis just looked up at her with an almost expressionless face.

"Eventually, when I thought back through that conversation, I realized that you hadn't asked. So, I had to ask myself why a man like you, a lawyer who makes his living by being relentlessly inquisitive about the facts, why you wouldn't want to know what caused such a momentous development in my thinking. I could think of only one reason. You already knew. You knew because the leak in my department had already gotten word to you that I had found an alibi witness. You knew and you forgot to make yourself act curious."

Davis took a deep breath. "Wallace, please, sit. Your mind seems to be swinging from one slender vine to the next." He gestured toward one of the armchairs in front of his desk. "I think this case has had an effect on you. And that's nothing to be ashamed of. It's a common occupational hazard in your profession."

The gentle smile on his face made Wallace think back to when Davis and his wife had been the emotional support system for her and her mother and her surviving brother. She had expected this confrontation to be difficult, but she had underestimated how sad it would make her feel.

Davis's kindly gaze remained steady, his hand still pointing toward the chair.

"At first, after I figured out you were the informant and that Eddie wasn't the killer, I couldn't understand why Marioneaux had to be killed. But all my thinking up to that point was based on the assumption that Marioneaux's personal evolution ended once he let go of his youthful bigotry. I mean, really, how much can one person change? It never occurred to me that he might aim for yet more distant horizons."

"Wallace, please. I know this wild chain of insights must seem totally logical to you, but it isn't. Listen to yourself. Surely you can hear how irrational this is starting to sound."

"So, I asked myself," she continued as if Davis hadn't spoken, "what was Marioneaux going to announce at last Monday's press conference that would make him a target for murder? What was Lydia Prescott helping him with? What was Garrett Landry trying to cover up? The answer, of course, is the very thing that made Eddie Pitkin the perfect fall guy. Marioneaux was about to announce a run for governor."

Davis had the benign smile of a psychiatrist trying to maneuver an unstable patient away from her delusions.

"He was going to run for governor and he was going to have some sort of reparations plank in his platform. He saw himself as someone who could steer us through a difficult pass. He and Eddie Pitkin, once sworn enemies, were about to end up on the same side of that issue."

Davis laughed quietly and gestured again for her to have a seat. "Wallace, that's quite a tale you've cooked up. But even if everything you say is true, why would I possibly care enough about any of that to be involved in murder?" He gave her the sweetest look she could remember.

She had just accused him of something horrible, yet he remained so composed. How could he still look at her with such unflinching affection?

A wry, welcoming smile blossomed on Davis's face. He shrugged as if to say this was all going to be okay. He reached for her with one hand and gestured toward the couch with his other.

The warmth in his expression held her transfixed and a tendril of doubt began coiling itself around her conviction. She wanted to smile back at him. She wanted so badly to take his hand. Instead, she spoke.

"Oliver Harpin didn't die."

Davis tensed. His hands drifted to his sides, and he assumed a casual slouch against the side of his desk.

"Who?"

Wallace heard his voice pose the question, but she saw his face fail to produce the correct expression to go with it.

"The bullet . . . it struck the mastoid process . . . that hard knob of bone right behind the ear." Unconsciously, her finger moved to the spot behind her own ear. "He's got a depressed skull fracture and he's stone deaf in his right ear, but he's very much alive and he's been chattering away."

"So who is this Harper fellow?" Davis asked, his tone less sure-footed, his gaze steadfast on the floor.

"Enough," she murmured. "Please."

"Wallace . . . I watched you grow from an infant. Watched in utter amazement as your mind developed into this remarkable thing it has become. Even now, after all these years, you still astonish me." He pushed his lower lip out and shook his head with the smug confidence of a proud parent.

"I couldn't make the facts stop pointing straight at you," she said, struggling to swallow, her eyes brimming. "As you might imagine, it was almost impossible for me to even think these thoughts."

For the first time, Wallace imagined she saw something akin to regret in Davis's face, but it was fleeting. He stayed perched against the edge of his desk, his arms folded across his chest, his eyes drifting up to meet hers, smiling and slowly nodding as if he were listening to a fascinating story about somebody else.

"I had hoped you would be taken off the case. Or that your efforts could be deflected long enough for this to play out as originally planned. When it became clear those things weren't going to happen, I thought the noose through the window would do the trick. Given your history with Mason, I assumed that if your investigation posed a clear danger to him you would gladly give it up rather than put him in the line of fire again. I should have known that trying to frighten you would only increase your resolve. A miscalculation on my part. After your second visit to Garrett Landry, yesterday, I knew I would have to take extraordinary measures to protect myself and to protect you."

"So, you're the one who put Oliver Harpin on my tail. You orchestrated today's revelation that I had found and then suppressed Peter Ecclestone."

"If our little enterprise was going to be found out, and there was a growing likelihood that at least some parts of it would be, I didn't want it to be you that did the finding. There are some who would have insisted on great harm to you and your family. *That* I could not allow."

Wallace wanted to ask him why he was involved in this nasty business at all, but it seemed like such a foolish question. A question that implied there could ever be an adequate answer. She stared at him instead, hoping he might still be able to convince her she had it all wrong.

When he looked back up at her, his expression broke her heart. She wasn't sure what she expected to see in his eyes—fear, remorse maybe, but not the casual defiance she saw staring back at her.

"When Garrett Landry came to us with Herbert Marioneaux's idiotic plans something had to be done. If his approach had shown promise, other states would have felt pressure to follow suit. It would have spread like an infection and so much that's true and good would be destroyed in the name of chasing this . . . this fashionable insanity."

Wallace stared at him, a hopeless tangle of emotions welling up inside her. "Is Carlton Lister part of the true and good?"

"Carlton Lister is an unfortunate necessity. An awful individual practically summoned into existence by the forces he's being used to thwart." Davis wrinkled his nose as if he smelled something disgusting. "A distasteful type who proved to have the common touch—

that uncanny ability to translate highfalutin political ideas into the idioms and slogans the man on the street seems to enjoy shouting.

"Once Marioneaux approached that ill-fated campaign consultant Lydia Prescott, the danger became too great. Swift and complete containment of his poisonous vision was our only option."

"Doing nothing was still an option. No?"

"No," Davis said. He paced in front of his desk. "An entire economy would be ruined to pay for the sins of the long dead."

His hands went back into his pockets, and the jingling started up again. "A whole culture would have been thrown into perpetual chaos because of the wreckage caused by a terrible mistake we rectified more than a hundred and fifty years ago."

The circle of his pacing widened until he was in front of the cabinet that concealed his little refrigerator. "So, no, doing nothing was not an option."

Wallace tensed as she saw him reach for the door with his left hand. Davis grimaced, then smiled and raised his right hand in a comic don't-shoot gesture. The door came open. From where she stood, Wallace could see the tops of half a dozen bottles of sparkling water. She relaxed.

Just as he had the day before, Davis stuck his hand into the refrigerator and picked up one of the bottles. He smiled and raised his eyebrows in a question. He bent forward slightly and lowered his hand, ready to toss her the bottle.

She released a pent-up breath and then shook her head.

He shrugged again and the bottle disappeared back into the little refrigerator. His hand went deeper and stayed too long.

The bluish metal of the pistol caught the light. Wallace rushed toward him, but he was too far ahead of her. The gun thundered and the back of his head flew away.

She was on her knees beside him, quaking with grief.

"I lied," she whispered, her face close to his, her chest heaving as she squeezed her eyes shut—trying not to see, trying not to think. "I'm sorry. Please forgive me."

THIRTY-ONE

When the crime-scene crew arrived they found Wallace on the patio, just outside Davis's office. Burley and Shannon arrived along with them. The wire Melissa Voorhees had brought her, a few hours earlier, was on the seat cushion of one of the patio chairs. Wallace was perched on the rim of the little pool, in the shade of the mimosa tree, her legs drawn up, her chin resting on her knees. She watched as the water streamed from the Green Man's mouth.

Wallace had barely listened as Burley told her he knew why she had gone off on her own. Less than an hour ago, he had caught Curtis Stiles, his special projects officer, taking phone pictures of case-related documents and figured out Stiles was leaking information.

Wallace remembered seeing the man slide into Burley's office just as she was leaving the day she and Burley and LeAnne were rehashing the search of Eddie Pitkin's house. Before signing on with the city police, Stiles had worked as a prison guard with Carlton Lister, where they discovered their shared commitment to segregationist causes. She assumed Stiles was behind her being accosted her at her home, and maybe even the group of women who had confronted her at the Capitol.

Burley offered to drive her home, to get her away from the scene, but she shook her head and turned away without speaking. When Mason arrived a half hour later, she was still sitting in the same place.

Lying to Davis about Oliver Harpin had been the right thing to do. Still, she hurt. She was shocked that she had been so utterly fooled for so long and that someone she thought of as family had turned out to be so unworthy. But the pain went deeper than that. She had loved him. And love ripped away, even misplaced love, hurt like nothing else in this world.

She tried to block out everything going on around her, but the murmur of familiar voices intruded at the edge of her hearing— Mason and Burley talking to each other.

"I'll do it," Mason said. "I'll ask her."

"Wallace?" Mason was squatting in front of her.

"Not now. Please." She turned away, raising her hands to the sides of her face like blinders.

"I know you don't feel like—"

"You couldn't possibly know how I feel." She squeezed her eyes shut. Her trembling hand covered her mouth.

"You're right." He spoke in a low voice. "I couldn't. I don't." He moved behind her and sat on the rim of the pool. He laid his hands on her shoulders and then rested his cheek against the base of her neck. "I'm sorry, angel, but this isn't over yet."

"Oh, it's over." Her voice broke, her eyes stung. "Just look inside that office. It's over."

Mason let his hands slide off her shoulders and down the outsides of her arms. He circled his arms around her waist and pulled her closer. At first, she resisted, but then she relaxed.

He took a long breath and then slowly let it go. "Remember the video? The one my contact in the FBI took of Carlton Lister preaching to the choir from the back of a hay wagon?"

"Can't we talk about this some other time?" Her hands came up to cover her ears.

Gently, Mason rocked back and forth. "Remember how I told you she said Lister was about to start traveling, delivering a call to arms to the faithful?"

Wallace tensed.

"We heard from her again. This morning."

She pushed Mason's arms away and turned to face him.

"Did she happen to mention where Lister's next stop is going to be?" Her jaw tightened and the light drained from her eyes.

Mason nodded.

THIRTY-TWO

Lister sat on the little campstool, his back against the warm aluminum siding of the barn.

It had been a long night. After bidding farewell to Ollie and disposing of Garrett Landry's body on Parker's Island in the middle of the mighty Mississip, he had returned to look for the detective, the old man's wishes to the contrary notwithstanding. But she had slipped into the wind. Others would have to deal with her now.

In about six hours, the next rally would begin and he would be there to fire up the crowd.

In a few more weeks, he could begin to shed the ballast of old men who were once so useful but were now increasingly timid and out of touch. And he would be on the front line of a refocused movement—a movement that could begin to sail out of the shadows.

It would be a dangerous time. Transitions always were. Stepping into the open made one an easier target and those against him were many and violent and well organized.

For a while, he would have to stay on the move. He smiled at the irony that some in the civil rights movement, back in the fifties and sixties, had lived this way, never sleeping in the same place two nights in a row, keeping word of their movements under wraps until the last possible moment. An inconvenient but necessary tactic in the face of dangerous change.

Burley had offered Wallace the option of standing down on the chase for Carlton Lister. Her look had been enough to convince him that was not going to happen.

She had left him and others in the department working hard to keep a lid on Davis's suicide for as long as possible. Once the story got out—once Lister knew their nasty little game was over—he would surely disappear, burning every bridge behind him as he went.

From the front passenger seat of an East Baton Rouge sheriff's department SUV Wallace stared across the pasture to her right. They were parked on an old farm access road. It was little more than a dirt track running just inside the tree line on property adjacent to a cattle ranch owned and operated by Coco Beckwith—a longtime sympathizer with causes that drew inspiration from the Third Reich. They were over a mile from Beckwith's ramshackle farmhouse.

LeAnne and another deputy were in the backseat.

Wallace brought a pair of field glasses to her eyes and looked across Beckwith's land toward a cluster of metal buildings.

She could see Lister perched on a canvas and metal-frame stool, leaning back against a faded barn, his hands folded in his lap, the sun on his face.

Wallace consulted her watch. Lister had been there nearly twenty minutes. He had arrived with two other men—both of them openly carrying weapons. They had chatted for a while and then left Lister alone.

LeAnne had tried to eavesdrop on their conversation with a parabolic microphone, but the wind through the foliage and their low voices produced an unlistenable signal-to-noise ratio.

"It almost looks like he's asleep," Wallace said

"Is he armed?" the deputy in the driver's seat asked.

To Appomattox and Beyond

TO APPOMATTOX AND BEYOND

*The Civil War Soldier in
War and Peace*

Larry M. Logue

The American Ways Series

IVAN R. DEE   *Chicago*

Library of Congress Cataloging-in-Publication Data:
Logue, Larry M., 1947–
    To Appomattox and beyond : the Civil War soldier in war and peace
/ Larry M. Logue.
        p.   cm. — (The American ways series)
    Includes bibliographical references and index.
    ISBN 1-56663-093-2 (alk. paper). —ISBN 1-56663-094-0 (pbk. :
alk. paper)
    1. United States.   Army—History—Civil War, 1861–1865.
2. Confederate States of America. Army—History.   3. United
States—History—Civil War, 1861–1865—Social aspects.   4. United
States—History—Civil War, 1861–1865—Veterans.   I. Title.   II. Series.
E492.3.L64   1996
973.7'42—dc20   95-30217

For Barbara

Contents

Preface

THIS BOOK SHIFTS the perspective on the Civil War and its aftermath from generals and politicians to the ordinary soldier. The literature on rank-and-file Rebels and Yankees has grown in recent years, and we can begin to take stock of their later lives as well as their wartime experience. Three million men served in the war, a larger share of the population than in any other American conflict, and more than 600,000 died, likewise the most in our history. The horror and exhilaration of combat affected everyone involved, and echoed throughout their lives. The sheer numbers of Civil War veterans ensured that their needs and convictions would carry special weight.

Mutual animosity between North and South had been smoldering for decades before the fighting, but two events caused resentment to flare into open conflict. In October 1859 the antislavery activist John Brown and twenty-two followers seized the federal arsenal at Harpers Ferry, in what is now West Virginia. Brown had hoped to touch off a widespread slave revolt, but federal troops and local militiamen quickly retook the arsenal and captured Brown and six surviving supporters. All were tried and hanged within a few months, but shock waves from the incident lasted much longer. Many Southerners believed that the Northern subversion they had long feared was now at hand, and they lashed out at potential threats. Southern governments stockpiled weapons and revived dormant militia companies; Southern citizens assaulted some Northern-born neighbors and sent others fleeing for their lives.

The final spark came in the fall of 1860. By then, political parties could no longer bridge sectional differences; the Democrats, the one remaining national party, had split apart in the summer over federal policy on slavery. Northern Democrats nominated Stephen A. Douglas for president, while Southern Democrats chose the current vice-president, John C. Breckinridge. Abraham Lincoln was the Republican nominee, and a group of older politicians who still hoped to avoid disunion formed the Constitutional Union party and nominated John Bell for president. With the Democrats' North-South coalition gone, Lincoln received enough votes to win the election, but the result signaled the final breach in the Union—Lincoln carried every free state but no slave states. Convinced they would be powerless against a hostile government if they remained in the Union, Southern "fire-eaters" demanded secession. South Carolina withdrew on December 20, 1860, and by February 1 six other states had followed suit. Before month's end the seven states had formed the Confederate States of America, with its capital in Montgomery, Alabama, and Jefferson Davis as president.

All this happened before Abraham Lincoln took office; Democrat James Buchanan was president until March 4, 1861. Believing he had no authority to use force to prevent secession, Buchanan hoped that a last-minute compromise might somehow emerge. None did, and the newly inaugurated Lincoln inherited a critical situation at Fort Sumter in South Carolina. The fort's federal garrison was caught between a dwindling stock of supplies and the Confederate artillery of Charleston harbor. When Lincoln announced his intention to resupply the fort, Davis gave the order to fire, and the Union garrison surrendered on April 14, 1861. In response to the attack, Lincoln called for 75,000 militiamen and ordered a blockade of Southern ports, acts that Southerners in turn took to be a dec-

laration of war. Virginia, Arkansas, Tennessee, and North
Carolina cast their lot with the seceded states, and the enlarged Confederacy moved its capital to Richmond, Virginia.
Both sides organized armies remarkably quickly, and the
first major battle took place at Bull Run, Virginia (known to
Southerners as Manassas) on July 21, 1861. The Confederates
routed the overconfident Yankees, making it clear the war
would be long and costly. Indeed, for nearly two years the
armies fought to an appallingly bloody stalemate. The Union's
plan to take control of the Mississippi River proceeded
steadily, if slowly, under General Ulysses S. Grant, but the
early campaign to capture Richmond was a failure. George B.
McClellan brought a large army close to Richmond in the
spring of 1862, only to be driven back with sharp counterat-
tacks by General Robert E. Lee. In September, Lee's own
foray into Union territory was turned back at Antietam,
Maryland, in a battle that killed six thousand men in one day.
Lincoln used the modest Union success as a pretext for an-
nouncing his plans to issue an Emancipation Proclamation,
declaring that all slaves in Confederate territory on January 1,
1863, would be free.

The military deadlock continued: after their success at
Antietam, Union forces were badly beaten at Fredericksburg
and Chancellorsville, Virginia, in December 1862 and May
1863 (though in the latter battle the Confederates lost a
revered commander, General Thomas "Stonewall" Jackson).
But decisive events were around the corner. In the West, Grant
captured the vital Confederate stronghold at Vicksburg, Mississippi, on July 4, 1863, and the Mississippi River was soon in
Union hands. In the East, Lee attempted another invasion of
the North but was defeated at Gettysburg, Pennsylvania, beginning his retreat on the day that Vicksburg fell. Much hard
fighting remained, but now the North had the upper hand.

In early 1864 Grant became general-in-chief of all Union armies and took command of the assault on Richmond; he assigned William Tecumseh Sherman to overcome Confederate resistance to the south and west. While Grant attacked Lee in Virginia, Sherman closed in on Atlanta; news of his capture of the city in September helped Lincoln win re-election two months later (against George McClellan). Sherman and his army then set out on their "march to the sea," an expedition meant·to break Southerners' spirit by laying waste to the countryside. In December 1864 Sherman's men reached Savannah, having cut a swath of destruction through Georgia; they then turned toward South Carolina to continue the job.

Meanwhile, Grant was tightening the noose around Lee's Army of Northern Virginia. Attacking, pulling back and moving southward, and then attacking again, Union forces wore down a Confederate army already decimated by casualties, hunger, and desertion. Confederate officials abandoned Richmond in early April 1865, and Lee surrendered at Appomattox Court House on April 9. Confederate armies elsewhere would follow suit in the weeks ahead, but the war was to take yet another key casualty: on April 14 Confederate partisan John Wilkes Booth shot and fatally wounded Abraham Lincoln.

It appeared at first that Lincoln's successor, Andrew Johnson, would favor harsh treatment of ex-Confederates. Soon, however, Johnson made clear his support for restoration of Southern white supremacy, putting him on a collision course with congressional Republicans. From 1866 to 1868 Johnson and Congress fought over Reconstruction: Congress enacted guarantees of civil rights for Southern freedpeople, Johnson vetoed them, and Congress overrode his vetoes. In 1868 the House of Representatives impeached Johnson and the Senate came within one vote of convicting him; the remainder of Johnson's term saw a truce in the fighting, and his successor, Ulysses S. Grant, was a Republican who was less at odds with Congress.

By 1870 the former Confederate states had met Congress's requirements for ensuring freedpeople's rights and had been readmitted to the Union, but conservative Southern whites would not tolerate the Republican-dominated state governments. In state after state, exploiting Republican weaknesses where they could and using violence elsewhere, Democrats overthrew Republican rule. Congressional Republicans had less interest in and control over Reconstruction than in the 1860s; an economic depression beginning in 1873 and scandals in Grant's administration occupied national politics, and the Republicans lost control of the House of Representatives in the 1874 election. As part of the compromise that resolved the disputed 1876 presidential election, the new president, Republican Rutherford B. Hayes, removed federal troops from South Carolina and Louisiana in 1877. Reconstruction ended with the quick fall of these last Southern Republican governments.

Until the final years of the nineteenth century, there were no more wars to distract Americans from the memory of the Civil War. In April 1898, amid a public outcry over Spain's treatment of its Cuban subjects and following the suspicious explosion of the American battleship *Maine* in Havana's harbor, the United States declared war on Spain. The war lasted less than four months and produced fewer than four hundred battle deaths before an overmatched Spain surrendered. The United States inherited control of Cuba and ownership of the Philippines and other distant possessions; Americans increasingly turned their gaze outward, away from the sectional conflict of an earlier era.

These central events shaped the experience of those who fought in the Civil War. Who they were and how they responded to the developments of their era will be explored in the chapters to follow.

To Appomattox and Beyond

1

Raising an Army in the North

NORTHERN SOCIETY WAS rapidly changing on the eve of the Civil War, and some of these changes affected the way Northern men would view military service. One clear sign of change was the extraordinary rise of Northern cities. The nation as a whole was growing—each decade from 1790 onward, the American population increased by about one-third, the fastest growth rate in the world. But cities were growing much faster. The population of New York, the nation's largest city, rose by nearly 70 percent in the 1850s, surpassing a million; Philadelphia, the next largest city, grew by 39 percent to more than a half-million.

Some newer cities exceeded even these rates. Buffalo, which had only 8,000 people in 1830, grew to more than 80,000 by 1860, and Newark, New Jersey, which had not existed as a town in 1830, passed 70,000 just thirty years later. The most remarkable increase occurred in Chicago, which went from a few cabins in 1830 to more than 100,000 people in 1860. Smaller cities and towns likewise flourished throughout the North. The South had New Orleans, whose growth was similar to that of Northern cities, but only one in ten Southerners lived in cities and towns on the eve of the Civil War, compared with more than a third of people in New England and the Mid-Atlantic states.

Just as they always had, most Americans still lived on farms and in the villages that served them, but farming could no longer provide a living for everyone in a population that doubled every twenty-five years. The adventurous could still find farm land to the west, but cities, especially Northern cities, were the great magnets of opportunity. Antebellum cities were built on commerce: the nation's population passed 30 million in the 1850s, and feeding, clothing, and otherwise supplying this many people created an immense flow of goods through cities like Buffalo and Philadelphia, with money to be made at every step. The cities also had manufacturing, though not yet an industrial revolution. Large, mechanized factories employing armies of workers were found primarily in the textile industry; most other manufacturing took place in small shops where a master craftsman or merchant watched over a few workers. But here too there was money to be made for people willing to put up with the overcrowding, crime, and appalling death rates that plagued the cities.

And on they came, young people leaving the countryside to become bank clerks or dockworkers or shoemakers, immigrants coming from western Europe to become weavers or day laborers, and African Americans fleeing the South to become porters or domestic servants. Yet cities did not bring prosperity to all newcomers. Work that was plentiful and steady in good times could become sporadic in a slow season and disappear in a depression. On the eve of the Civil War the North had just emerged from one such depression, touched off in 1857 by the failure of a major investment firm and the collapse of wheat prices. Merchants, bankers, and manufacturers cut back or closed down at times like these, and there was no unemployment insurance for clerks or ironworkers or anyone else whose wages ceased. Unpredictable bouts of unemployment were a hard fact of life for men and women in the North's commercial economy.

Another lesson had to be learned by those who wanted a living wage in the world of urban commerce. Rural Americans had taken for granted that people made most of their own decisions, within limits set by nature. Farmers decided what and when to plant, storekeepers decided what supplies to order, and success depended on providence and one's own industry. Likewise, tailors, blacksmiths, and other village artisans had controlled production in their shops. But working for wages involved an entirely different set of conditions. When an employer offered work, employees worked by the owner's rules. Employers decided the hours of work and the tasks to be done, and they owned the place of work and often the equipment the workers used. In exchange for wages, workers had to give up much of the control over life that they or their parents had enjoyed. Labor unions sometimes challenged employers' worst abuses: workers demanded and won a ten-hour day in many industries, and twenty thousand Massachusetts shoemakers struck in 1860 to protest low wages. But unions faced bitter opposition from owners and public officials and were usually crippled by economic depressions. Most workers had to cope as individuals with the new rules of work.

Self-control was the approved method for individuals to deal with the demands of wage employment. Self-discipline was nothing new in antebellum America: the New England Puritans had preached against idleness and waste in the seventeenth century, and Benjamin Franklin had promoted rigorous self-discipline in the eighteenth century. But the overwhelming emphasis on self-denial in the nineteenth century was unprecedented. Social reformers, educators, writers of guidebooks on child-rearing, and ministers pleaded with Americans to reject temptation, reminding them of the consequences of indulgence in sex, drinking, gambling, and idleness. Prominent men and women insisted that every act of self-indulgence broke down character as well as the body (in men, for example, every sex act drained away vital fluid), and would lead to crime or insanity.

Influenced by this conviction, officials of penitentiaries, insane asylums, and poorhouses tried to indoctrinate residents in self-discipline. Public officials insisted that poverty, for example, was "the result of such self-indulgence, unthrift, excess, or idleness, as is next of kin to criminality." School officials were similarly determined to teach "habits of regularity, punctuality, constancy and industry in the pursuits of business."

Parents in the growing middle class worked long and hard to inspire self-control in their children. Unlike farmers, most urban fathers spent the day away from the household, working for pay, and it became the mother's job to instill in sons and daughters a conscience for self-regulation. By doling out or withholding affection and approval, mothers (occasionally reinforced by their husbands) cultivated the "tyrannical monitor," as one nineteenth-century American called his conscience. Parents wanted a properly functioning conscience to be an internal brake on their children's impulses, to head off wrongdoing before it could begin. Parents and advice-givers agreed that only through self-control could people achieve happiness and success: everyone must religiously avoid wasting energy, money, and time. If people heeded this advice, they would have little trouble with the time and work demands of employers.

Was this approach successful? It was preached most urgently in the Northeast, and evidence from several Northeastern communities shows that premarital pregnancies declined in the nineteenth century, one hint that Americans accepted reformers' preaching on sexual restraint. Yet there are also indications of strong resistance to the dictates of self-control. Historian Anthony Rotundo argues that middle-class boys in the nineteenth century were strongly inclined to impulsive violence and vandalism; other evidence of resistance comes from strikes by workers, many of whom refused to embrace employers' definitions of self-discipline.

The North showed other signs of change before the Civil War. The outside world was coming ever closer, even for people who lived far from the cities. Telegraph lines stretched from coast to coast and into most communities, and railroad construction was booming. More than twenty thousand miles of rails were laid in the 1850s, bringing most Northerners within two days' travel of one another. Northern farmers had become more involved with the wider world and were now producing most of their wheat, corn, and livestock for sale; a few decades earlier, most crops raised outside the densely settled New England states had been for home use. And Northerners, like Americans in other regions, were a restless people. Young men and older families alike, especially when they had little land or other wealth, moved frequently from place to place in search of a better living. Historians studying nineteenth-century communities have found that as many as half the residents moved away each decade.

Yet many Northerners clung to old habits even as they did business with the outside world. Many rural and small-town families did not move about, and they were the core of neighborhoods of friends and relatives dependent on one another for farming help, church fellowship, and socializing. Farm women, even when their husbands raised crops for sale, continued to produce butter, eggs, and clothing for exchange and home use. When the crops were harvested and sold, men would often take their favorite rifle and hunting dogs and head to the woods, seeking game as had generations before them. These men would also take up arms for their country. About 100,000 men had volunteered for the war against Mexico in the 1840s. Most of the soldiers had come from south and west of the Appalachians, but war fever had caught up communities everywhere. Most towns thus had at least a few Mexican War veterans who could entertain young people with their exploits in the most recent war.

But Americans distrusted regular armies, and they even refused to take militia duty seriously. Communities were supposed to ensure that their adult males were ready for emergency military duty, but militia responsibilities had become mainly a source for officers' titles and an excuse for getting, in the words of one observer, "supremely drunk" at periodic drills. As the sectional crisis deepened in the late 1850s and early 1860s, a number of states tried to revive their militia units.

Secession came quickly on the heels of Abraham Lincoln's election. South Carolina, where secessionist sentiment had been strong for years, voted to secede in December 1860, forcing its neighbors either to join it or risk having to take up arms against fellow Southerners. By February 1861 six states chose to join South Carolina. On April 15, the day after Fort Sumter fell to Confederate forces in South Carolina, Lincoln issued a call for 75,000 state militiamen. After four upper South states joined the seven that had already seceded, the President recognized that his call-up would scarcely produce an adequate army. On May 3 Lincoln asked for 60,000 additional volunteers for three years' service in the army and navy. Congress, meeting in July, authorized 500,000 more volunteers, and when Union troops were routed at Bull Run before the month was out, lawmakers called for another half-million troops. Mobilizing troops was still seen as a state and local responsibility, so federal officials assigned troop quotas to the states and counted on them to do the rest.

At first the states were largely successful. Governors called for smaller communities to raise companies (about one hundred men each) and larger areas to raise regiments (usually ten companies). Local patriotism then took over. Lawyers or merchants ran newspaper advertisements and printed posters such as this one from Massachusetts: "War! War! War! . . . All citizens are requested to meet at the town hall this evening to see what can be done." At such a rally a local band would play patriotic anthems; politicians, visiting dignitaries, and perhaps a Mexican War veteran would exhort the crowd to stand up for their state and their Union; and local men would come forward. The volunteers would elect their officers, who were often the organizers of the recruiting, and make ready to go to war. Local women would be busy too, making flags, collecting supplies, and even sewing uniforms in these days before the Union adopted standard-issue blue. Within a week or two the new company would be ready for its send-off. Again the brass bands would play, the women would formally present their flag to the troops, farewells would be said, and the soldiers would be on their way to be mustered into federal service. By early 1862, 700,000 troops were thus mobilized for the Union army, and the War Department began to close its recruiting offices.

But by the summer of 1862 it became clear that more soldiers would be needed and that they would be harder to recruit. The war was going well in the West: the army and navy had taken fifty thousand square miles of territory and had captured Memphis and New Orleans on the Mississippi River, though the formidable defenses of Vicksburg remained in

Confederate hands. But in the East the Union campaign to take Richmond had gone miserably. General George McClellan's Army of the Potomac, after advancing close enough in May to hear the Confederate capital's church bells, fell back under sharp attacks by what McClellan wrongly believed was a much larger Confederate army. By July the assault on Richmond was abandoned by a high command convinced that McClellan's failure of nerve had cost a chance for a quick end to the war.

But it was not strategic failures alone that alarmed federal officials. The human toll of Civil War battles was beginning to hit home: in the western Battle of Shiloh, 13,000 Union soldiers had been killed, wounded, or captured; in Virginia the Union lost 5,000 men at Seven Pines, and McClellan's army suffered 16,000 more casualties in the Seven Days' Battle that led to the Richmond campaign's abandonment. Thousands more died of disease, and it would not be easy mobilizing more troops among civilians who were well aware of these losses. Lincoln called for 300,000 more soldiers in July, but it was clear that the days of the patriotic rush to war were over.

To fill their quotas under this new call, state and local officials inflated the traditional payment of soldiers' bounties. Once meant primarily as a discharge payment, the bounty now became a bonus for enlistment. The federal government allowed only a $25 advance on its bounty, but state and local governments added amounts averaging about $100 to coax men into new volunteer companies. If this did not work, the federal government threatened to intervene. In July 1862 Congress ordered the states to activate their militia units (and empowered federal officials to do so if state leaders dragged their feet), and to draft enough militiamen to cover any shortfall in meeting troop quotas. Most states met their 1862 quotas with volunteers, but some had to resort to militia drafts. In several places where support for the war was lukewarm, mobs attacked and occasionally killed the militia's enrolling officers.

Yet African Americans, the one group eager to go to war with or without bonuses, remained unwelcome in the army. The eminent black spokesman Frederick Douglass condemned "the pride, the stupid prejudice and folly" that compelled Northerners "to fight only with your white hand, and allow your black hand to remain tied." But the prevailing mood among whites was expressed by a Pennsylvania soldier, who predicted that if blacks were allowed in the army "our own Soldiers will kill more of them than the Rebs would." As a result, the government's early policies on black troops were halting and contradictory.

But as casualties mounted and Northern morale worsened, the prospect of black troops taking up the burden of fighting became more appealing. Lincoln's preliminary Emancipation Proclamation in September 1862 endorsed a war to change Southern society, and the final version of the Proclamation on New Year's Day officially authorized African-American troops. Some black regiments had already been organized in the West, and one unit had seen action. Now, in 1863, recruiters began to enlist thousands of African Americans as Union soldiers.

But the need for men seemed endless. The mobilization crisis of 1862 repeated itself in the spring of 1863. Vicksburg still stood in the West, and Union forces had been badly beaten at Fredericksburg, Virginia, late in 1862. Worse still, the government had accepted some two-year recruits early in the war, and these troops were about to go home. As a result, Congress enacted a full-scale military draft in March 1863. Federal provost marshals were to visit congressional districts and identify men aged twenty to forty-five who had not joined the army. Their names were then to be drawn by lot to fill any shortfalls in their districts' volunteering.

Men subject to the draft did, however, enjoy some alternatives to service. They could still volunteer and avoid the stigma of being a conscript. Otherwise, to avoid joining the army, they could pay a $300 "commutation" fee that exempted them until the next draft (a provision which was largely repealed in 1864). Or they could hire a substitute, who would exempt them from future drafts as well. Fewer than 10 percent of the men whose names were drawn were in fact conscripted into the army; the rest volunteered, left for parts unknown, were exempted for medical reasons or as family providers, or bought their way out.

The draft, especially its exemptions for those who could afford them, dramatically intensified opposition to the war. Workers angrily protested in cities and towns from the Midwest to New England. In New York in 1863, Irish workers attacked draft officials and wealthy-looking men and then turned their fury on any African Americans they could find, seeing in them the cause of the war. The New York riot killed more than a hundred people and injured three hundred others. But the draft also had its intended effect on enlistments: although only 46,000 men were conscripted into the army, 800,000 others enlisted or reenlisted after the draft went into effect.

In all, nearly two million whites and almost 180,000 African Americans served in the Union army, or about 35 percent of the military-age population of the North. Who were they, and why did some join while others stayed away? The first answer to this question is *youth*. Studies of Northern enlistments have consistently shown that the highest rate of enlistment was among men in their late teens: 40 to 50 percent of them joined the army, whereas enlistment rates dropped to well under 20 percent among men over age thirty. Historian Reid Mitchell has argued that soldiering offered young men a definitive passage to manhood, which helps to explain the enthusiasm of young men early in the war. When word came of Fort Sumter's fall, James Snell, for example, "could not controll my own feelings . . . and would have shouldered my gun and started . . . had it not been for the earnest entreaty of my Parents." But this opportunity was bound up with patriotic duty for young soldiers. An Ohioan knew that he "would prove one of the most neglectful of sons" unless he risked his life for "the good form of government for which [his grandfather] gave seven years of the best of his life, [and] which has made me what I am." In this respect Union soldiers were like soldiers in most volunteer armies—young and eager to demonstrate their manly patriotism.

But we must remember that this war had a character of its own. James Snell's recollection of nearly losing control is an important clue to understanding Northern soldiers. The concern with self-control that was so prominent a feature of Northern society appears repeatedly in the writings of Union soldiers. They longed to achieve self-discipline: a Massachusetts soldier declared that a fallen comrade had been "absolutely cool and collected. . . . It is impossible for me to conceive of a man more perfectly master of himself." Inner discipline was also how Union soldiers defined themselves in contrast to others. A Union general believed that the war's cause was Southerners' "lawless and malignant passion," and soldiers often wrote of their need to punish the South's rebelliousness, to impose the discipline that Southerners had rejected. White men likewise contrasted themselves with black soldiers in their own army: where whites were supposed to be cool and controlled, one white officer believed that his black troops were "affectionate, enthusiastic, and dramatic beyond all others."

Other clues to understanding Union soldiers come from the characteristics of those who served and those who did not. Overall the Union army contained about the same percentage of farmers, skilled laborers, and other workers as did the adult male population, but aggregate comparisons overlook differences in age, property holding, and so on. Several studies comparing soldiers with noncombatants in Northern communities have found that Northerners' decisions were heavily influenced by their economic situation. When age is held constant, it becomes clear that, in areas where commerce predominated, artisans, unskilled laborers, and even white-collar men (and their sons) were more likely to serve than were farmers; where farming dominated, men with little or no property (and their sons) were especially likely to enlist.

There were, of course, individual and group exceptions to the enlistment findings. Oliver Wendell Holmes, Jr., who would later become a Supreme Court justice, and Robert Gould Shaw, son of a wealthy Boston family, served in Massachusetts regiments. And immigrants, especially the Irish, were less likely to enlist: some had not applied for citizenship and thus were not subject to the draft, and those who did serve often encountered hostility from native-born troops. But in general, Northerners with reason to worry about their livelihood—who depended on the whims of business cycles and employers or on small plots of land, sometimes owned by a landlord—were more likely to respond to the economic incentives offered by military service.

Did local politics also affect Northerners' enlistment decisions? It makes sense to suppose that, in communities that supported Lincoln's Republican party, loyal Republicans would eagerly join the army and insist that their neighbors do likewise, and that Democratic communities would discourage enlistment. Some studies have indeed found that draft evasion and desertion were more frequent in places with lukewarm support for the war, and their Democratic sympathies may have contributed to immigrants' reluctance to enlist. But a study of two New Hampshire towns has shown that men in the Democratic town were *more* likely to enlist than those in the Republican town. Local political climates thus appear to have been a less consistent influence on Northern men's enlistment decisions than was concern for their livelihood.

The monetary incentives for enlistment became impressive as the need for men became more urgent. In 1863 the federal government raised its enlistment bounty to $300; together with state and local bounties, volunteers could easily receive much more than the $460 yearly earnings of an average worker. With more modest bonuses already in effect for some time, and with payments for enlisting plus provisions for buying one's way out of service, it is clear that recruitment acted as an economic market for most of the war.

The importance of this market is demonstrated by the treatment of African-American soldiers. Primarily to make black troops more acceptable to hostile whites, the army refused to allow African Americans to participate as equals in the recruitment market. Blacks often received less bounty money than did whites, and recruiters sometimes refused to pay black soldiers the bounties they were owed. Moreover, until late in the war, blacks received half or less, depending on rank, of whites' monthly pay. Nonetheless, 38,000 blacks from the free states enlisted, and 140,000 Southern blacks defied white Southerners' harassment and threats to their families and joined the Union army.

Again largely to make black troops palatable, Union officials decided that black regiments should have white officers and took special care in selecting them. Convinced that black men needed extraordinary leadership to make them into adequate soldiers, and aware that black units would face hostility, army officials created special examining boards for black units' officers. The War Department had largely replaced officer elections with examinations in white units as well, but candidates for black units received exceptional grilling on army procedures and general knowledge. Forty percent of candidates failed the test, and the failure rate would have been higher except for a special school created to prepare candidates for the test. The poor quality of officers, which often crippled the effectiveness of white units, was undoubtedly a lesser problem among the United States Colored Troops.

A wide assortment of men joined the Union army, but there were patterns we can identify among them. Those who fought for the Union tended to be young, to be (or to have a parent who was) in an occupation with an uncertain future, and to be concerned with self-control. How did military service meet the needs of such men? A few soldiers frankly admitted that economic insecurity drove them to enlist. Historian David Blight, examining the career of Charles Brewster, has argued that enlistment in a Massachusetts regiment was Brewster's "effort to compensate for prior failure" as a store clerk "and to imagine a new career." Other soldiers, however, spoke of patriotism and duty in referring to their enlistment. Some historians have concluded from such sentiments that wage earners, needing opportunities in a commercial, free-labor society, gladly fought against a South they saw as an aristocratic, slavery-bound threat to their livelihood. But in rural areas, small farmers were the men most likely to enlist, and most cared little about jobs for wage workers.

Military-age men probably thought as much about what they had to *sacrifice* as what they had to *gain* by going to war. If he enlisted, a master shoemaker who had been put out of business by shoe factories was not giving up the same security as was a prosperous wheat farmer. Henry Bear of Illinois was explicit about this kind of reasoning: "I studied the cost and measured the way before I enlisted." As bounties surpassed $400 or $500, the economic sacrifice lessened, and more financially secure men could be induced into the army. But the backbone of the Union army were men for whom the dangers of war were not a bad trade for a tenuous future in a shop or on the farm.

Perhaps the most famous cliché to emerge from the Civil War is the accusation that this was "a rich man's war and a poor man's fight." Those making this charge against the Union army had an inkling of the truth, but it was not exactly the poor who predominated in the army; craftsmen and clerks were also common in the ranks. Union recruitment, with its bonuses and loopholes, opened an alternative to an insecure world of work. A cliché that has also come down to us is that the Civil War was a conflict of "brother against brother." Besides its literal meaning—there are innumerable cases of brothers fighting on opposite sides, from generals on down the ranks—does this phrase also tell a larger truth? Were the two armies essentially alike?

2

Mobilizing a Confederate Army

A UNION OFFICER voiced a common opinion about Confederates when he described them as conspirators "who plotted and labored for the overthrow of the Republic." He was partly right: for decades before the Civil War, Southern political leaders had struggled to ensure that the federal government would protect what they saw as their right to property, including slaves, and to an orderly society. But Southerners vehemently denied that they staged a rebellion. In their view they were merely reacting to a chain of events that threatened to produce a Northern tyranny and lead to the destruction of Southern society. Using the federal power to hand out offices and other favors, Lincoln's Republicans would curry favor with the border states and upper South where slavery was weakest. Winning over state after state, Republicans would finally control enough states to end slavery by constitutional amendment. Secession, fire-eaters insisted, was no more a rebellion than was the revolution of 1776, when Americans likewise severed ties with a government that threatened their liberties.

Nevertheless, Southerners were far from unified. The South, from the Mason-Dixon line to Texas, was dominated by farming. Agriculture was at the heart of nearly every local economy, and even Southern cities were largely collection points for cash crops. But farming divided rather than united Southerners. A minority of Southerners, most numerous near the Atlantic seaboard and in the deep South, made their living by raising crops for sale—tobacco in tidewater Virginia and North Carolina, rice along the South Carolina and Georgia coasts, cotton in the lowlands from Georgia to Texas, and sugar in Louisiana. Most cash crops were labor-intensive, and most of the laborers were slaves. Owners of large numbers of slaves called themselves planters and formed the local elite. They traveled to Southern cities for business and to the North and Europe for pleasure, sent their sons to college, kept order in their communities, and held political offices.

But moving away from the plantation belts, one would find less and less of this income-producing agriculture. Landholdings and slaveholdings became smaller in Southern uplands and piney woods; typical farms might be eighty or ninety acres with a few slaves rather than the thousand or more acres and dozens of slaves on some "black-belt" places. Many upland families owned no slaves, and an increasing number did not own the land they farmed. Small farmers might put in a patch of cotton or tobacco where possible, but their first priority was sustenance. Upland farmers typically concentrated on corn, wheat, and livestock, using the labor of husband, wife, and children, and nonslaveholders might hire a few slaves or white farmhands. In addition, wives produced butter, eggs, and clothing to use or to exchange with neighbors.

Farther still from the plantation belts were the Southern mountain communities. The Appalachians and their foothills cut through the western parts of Virginia, the Carolinas, and Georgia, and the eastern parts of Kentucky and Tennessee. Mountain folk rarely saw a slave; most mountaineers lived in isolated settlements, raising their crops in valleys and hollows.

Lowlanders despised these mountaineers, and they returned the favor. Plantation elites, central governments, and the wars they made were alien to mountain people. Yet the South's various classes of farmers coexisted. To be sure, there were class tensions in the antebellum South. Planters' contempt extended beyond mountaineers to include their own poorer neighbors, while plain folks' resentment of this disdain could flare into violence: an arrogant planter might have a barn burned or a slave murdered by a resentful neighbor. Though set after the war, William Faulkner's story "Barn Burning" illustrates a long tradition of common whites' resentment. In it a sharecropper, jealous of his "wolflike independence," twice strikes back at wealthy landlords' contempt by burning their barns.

But these tensions were usually kept in check by common interests. Small farmers could ordinarily count on wealthy neighbors for cotton ginning or the loan of a slave or two at busy times. Planters in turn needed commoners' votes for public office. And perhaps above all, planters upheld an ordered society. Planters were always on the lookout for signs of an uprising among their slaves or a threat to community order. The signs might be distinct—a stranger seen talking to slaves—or more indirect—gamblers or liquor-sellers moving into a town, for example. When they saw danger, planters moved quickly, often without benefit of the law. They would typically organize a vigilance committee, investigate the threat, and punish offenders with banishment, whipping, or hanging. Planters' vigilance made it clear that disobedience and dissent were not tolerated in their communities.

Punishing deviance obviously aided slaveholders, but it benefited nonslaveholders as well. It helped them in the present: reminders of slaves' subjugation encouraged even the poorest whites to feel superior to blacks, and affirming obedi-

ence assisted white men in maintaining authority over their
wives, who were expected to obey husbands in much the same
way as slaves did masters. And planters' rule promised to benefit nonslaveholders in the future: hard work and a few good
harvests might enable a small farmer to buy a slave or two and
thereby to benefit from the rigidly maintained slave system. In
exchange for a few considerations such as voting, helping to
build roads, and serving on juries, planters would thus combat
all threats to white men's chance to farm their land and rule
over their families as their forefathers had done.

As a result, planters could portray themselves as guardians
of the Southern way of life, a way that was deeply rooted in
personal relationships and tradition. Southern diaries and letters are filled with exchanges of visits lasting for weeks, trips
to town for medicine for ailing neighbors, and deathbed vigils
for fellow church members. Southerners tolerated only the
slightest governmental regulation of their daily lives, but they
eagerly embraced the intricate obligations of kinship and
friendship. Providing money and hospitality to relatives hon-
ored one's heritage, reaffirming "the old fierce pull of blood,"
as Faulkner put it. Favors to and from friends affirmed the
importance of judgments about character as a key to social
life. Private responsibilities were as central to Southern life as
public responsibilities were marginal, and Southerners had little use for distant governments or the reformers who dis-
pensed advice to Northerners.

Men found this social world filled with challenges to their
manhood. Status and reputation were paramount among
Southern men, who never tired of competing at gambling,
hunting, and drinking to establish a manly reputation. But a
hard-won reputation could be ruined with one unanswered
insult, and men had to be ready to respond with a challenge to
a fight or a duel. Fistfights and knife fights between poorer

Southerners and duels within the gentry allowed men to defend (and for victors, to enhance) their manhood. Despite the efforts of state legislators and reformers who insisted that dueling was "the product of a barbarous age," the resort to violence was difficult to resist for young men obsessed with masculinity and honor.

Masculinity could also be demonstrated in military service. Southerners had made up a large part of the Mexican War army, but the peacetime United States army, amounting to about sixteen thousand troops stationed at remote western outposts, offered few opportunities for military distinction. Southerners had long been as lackadaisical about militia service as were Northerners, although Southern militia training became more spirited after Virginia and Maryland militiamen helped to put down John Brown's raid on Harpers Ferry in 1859.

Secession spurred still more military preparations, and the new Confederate Congress called for 100,000 one-year troops in March 1861. Volunteers overwhelmed local organizers, and new companies applied for arms and equipment faster than state governments could supply them. Following the capture of Fort Sumter, the Congress authorized 400,000 more soldiers (who could enlist for three years in exchange for government equipment, or for a year if they equipped themselves); by August the Confederacy had about 200,000 men under arms.

Mobilization proceeded in much the same way as in the North, but if anything Southern emotions were even more fevered. For one thing, Southern leaders expected an invasion, and they vigorously encouraged a sense of urgency in resisting a Northern assault. A Mississippian warned against "the tide of Northern fanaticism that threatens to roll through the South," and a newspaper spelled out the consequences if the invaders were to win: Southerners would lose their government, their slaves, and their right to vote, suffering "the grossest humiliation, to break down the stubborn pride and manliness native to the Southern breast." The need to neutralize Unionism also intensified Confederate recruiting. Unionism was a complicated sentiment. Not surprisingly, many people in the Southern mountains, convinced that their states were governed by "bombastic, high falutin, aristocratic fools," as one North Carolinian put it, remained loyal to the Union. But some of the South's most prosperous slaveholders, especially cotton planters along the Mississippi River, were also skeptical of the cost of secession. Secessionists eventually prevailed in eleven slave states (Delaware, Kentucky, Maryland, and Missouri remained in the Union), and then built on their victory to overcome opposition to enlistment in the new army. Confederate recruiters found a hostile reception among mountain folk, who often sent a large number of soldiers to the Union; elsewhere, by staging torchlight processions, holding rallies, and banishing and otherwise intimidating Unionists, Confederate supporters did their best to subdue dissent and inspire an enlistment fever.

Women were also instrumental in persuading Southerners to enlist. While Northern women encouraged and supplied Union troops, young women in the South were especially insistent that men join the army. Southerners' exceptional concern about manhood bred insecurity, which in turn made men vulnerable to taunting, especially by women. Women had little genuine power in Southern society, but they were protected (outside the household, at least) from violent retaliation for insults. Women's demands and criticism, especially when aimed at would-be suitors, thus became standards of manhood. In Arkansas the future African explorer Henry Stanley, uncertain about the army, received a petticoat in the mail from a young woman; in Richmond it was said that the "ladies are postponing all engagements until their lovers have fought the Yankees"; and in Mississippi a woman challenged noncombatants to "be men once more, and make every woman in the land proud of having you as protectors."

All these forms of prodding, plus the excitement generated by success at Manassas (the Confederate name for Bull Run) in July 1861, produced thousands of companies for the Confederate army before the year was out. But Union forces scored key victories in the West during the winter, and General McClellan's army threatened Richmond in early 1862. The Confederate government now faced a manpower crisis: about half the troops in the field had enlisted for a year, and their terms would soon begin expiring. In April, faced with few choices, the Confederate Congress enacted the first national draft in America. The new law extended the term of the one-year men to three years, and required most other men aged eighteen to thirty-five to serve for three years. Exemptions were available for Confederate and state officials, for men in certain occupations such as railroad worker, telegraph operator, clergyman, or teacher—and for those who could hire a substitute.

Not surprisingly, the law was greeted with dismay among a populace that detested coercion. The words "usurpation" and "despotism" occasionally appear in the reactions of soldiers and politicians alike. The recollection of a Tennessee soldier is especially telling: after the draft took effect, he wrote, "a soldier was simply a machine, a conscript." To him and many of his comrades, the draft stripped military service of its distinction as an act of honor. Other Southerners, however, believed that the volunteer army had allowed too many men to stay at home, so that coercion was perfectly acceptable. "Good for conscription," wrote a newspaper editor, and a Mississippi soldier agreed that conscription "will pull a goodly number of [men] from around the fireplaces." Like the Northern draft, Southern conscription filled the ranks. Relatively few Southerners were actually drafted into the Confederate army, but large numbers of men volunteered or hired a substitute. In 1862 the army showed a net gain (even after casualties) of 200,000 men. Still, in the long run the draft's inequities harmed the Confederate cause. Congress abolished substitution at the end of 1863 amid reports of widespread abuse, but lawmakers had already made another change that provoked fresh outrage. Responding to stories of plantations whose owners and overseers had left families unguarded against the supposed threat of slave attacks, Congress exempted from the draft one white man on each plantation with at least twenty slaves. Only a few thousand men took advantage of this exemption, but its class favoritism further aggravated soldiers' anger. James Skelton's resentment of planters who were "living at home enjoying life because they have a few negroes" was a typical reaction, while his brother expressed a grimmer assessment: "They intend to kill all the poor men." The twenty-slave exemption, which was eventually reduced to fifteen slaves but not eliminated, drove the wedge deeper between soldiers and the home front.

In all, about 900,000 men served as Confederate soldiers, or about 60 percent of those eligible (the draft eventually included men aged seventeen to fifty). Why did some Southerners join while others did not? When they explained their reasons for enlisting, Confederates described a patriotism that was often interchangeable with that of Union soldiers. One Confederate officer, for example, cited the need to "maintain inviolate the principles and rights of the Constitution," and another declared that he was preserving "Republican government in America." Since they expected the war to be fought on Southern soil, many Confederates added that they had joined the army in order to protect their homes and families. A Virginia soldier asserted that he was "defending what any man holds dear—his home and his fireside," and a Mississippian made a list of his motivations: he was fighting "for my wife & child & relatives and friends & country."

One historian found that the majority of soldiers on both sides made some mention of patriotic reasons for enlisting, and two-fifths had a political motivation such as states' rights or protecting the Union. Home defense as a motive was, of course, much more common among Confederates. But another study of Civil War letters and diaries concluded that personal concerns outweighed Southerners' references to duty. Two-thirds of Confederates made more allusions to personal glory, excitement, and the end of their enlistment than they did to patriotism or political ideals. And Union soldiers were not much different—most of them had at least as many references to personal concerns as to their duty.

Cultural historian Michael Barton's examination of the writings of men in both Civil War armies reveals that they held the same central values. Soldiers' most frequently mentioned concern was morality, followed by other personal values such as religious devotion and patriotism; political principles such as freedom and individualism were mentioned far less often. But though they *ranked* their values similarly, the two sides' *attachment* to them differed. Northern enlisted men were more concerned with self-restraint than with expressing emotions or evaluating character. Coming from a society in which self-control was ceaselessly prescribed as the key to achievement, Yankees tended to keep straightforward records of events; Southern soldiers, coming from a society that prized character and reputation, devoted much more of their letters and diaries to evaluating the kindness, bravery, and morality of those around them.

Southerners even wrote more condolence letters to their comrades' next-of-kin, for these letters were the ideal means of expressing admiration for a soldier's character. Where a typical condolence letter on the Union side commended a soldier as "cool and collected," a letter about Joseph F. Moseley of Mississippi focused on entirely different qualities. A comrade wrote that Moseley had "inspired Confidence, secured friends, that he 'grappled to his bosom with hooks of steel.' . . . His devotion to the cause of the South partook of that lofty enthusiasm which was chivalry itself."

There were highly visible exceptions to these tendencies. Robert E. Lee insisted that habits of self-control be instilled in his sons, and Stonewall Jackson was notorious for his relentless self-discipline. But these leaders were noteworthy for self-control *because* they stood out from their countrymen (and perhaps because they had attended the U.S. Military Academy at West Point). The self-control that many Northerners found essential had made only modest headway among Southerners.

Yet written testimony tells only part of the story. An important similarity between the characteristics of Southern and Northern soldiers was youth. Confederate enlistment rates could approach 80 percent among men in their late teens and twenties, but they fell steadily among older men. It made little difference whether young Southerners were single or married with families; the law, pressure from their neighbors, and their own enthusiasm brought them into the army.

But Southerners were unlikely to forget they were fighting a war to preserve their way of life, including the right to own slaves. Since slaveholders saw themselves as the special target of the Yankee invasion, and since slaveholders had always purged their communities of danger, they might be expected to be the likeliest candidates for participation in this war. Studies to date show that slaveholders (and their sons) did indeed take up their burden. In Mississippi, the greater the number of slaves held, the more likely a man was to enlist; similarly, in east Tennessee and tidewater North Carolina, slaveholders were more likely to become Confederates while smaller farmers and nonfarmers fought for the Union.

To underscore their belief in responsibility and in the unity of classes, a number of wealthy Southerners enlisted as foot soldiers: John Dooley, son of an affluent Richmond family, signed on as a private in the First Virginia Regiment, and Henry Clay Sharkey, a future member of Congress whose family owned more than fifty slaves, enlisted as a private in the Eighteenth Mississippi. (Even so, they kept some of the trappings of status—wealthy Confederates, including Private Sharkey, customarily brought along a slave or two as personal servants.) Despite the repeated condemnations of planters for their unwillingness to defend their own cause (they were "rusting in inglorious ease," according to one commentator), the evidence shows that planters and their sons did assume their usual role of eliminating a danger to their society.

With the intense legal and social pressures to join the Confederate army, how did more than a third of eligible men manage to avoid serving? Some obtained exemptions under the draft laws, but exempt men probably comprised less than 10 percent of the military-age population. Those who neither enlisted nor were exempted illustrate the tenuousness of Southern class cooperation. The war was another instance of the slaveholding gentry taking the lead in fighting a threat to the social order, but this time they first asked and then required other men to join them. Many Southerners refused from the start to follow the gentry's lead.

Militia rolls from several Mississippi counties show that between one-sixth and one-third of the military-age men who had lived there in the summer of 1860 were gone by the fall of 1861. Neither at home nor in the army, these men had left their county, probably for the West or the North. Before there was a draft, and while Confederates were still jubilant over their first major victories, a sizable number of men had already decided that the gentry's campaign was not for them. Some had had no choice: Southern communities drove away many Northern-born residents and outspoken Unionists as warfare approached. Other emigrants lived near the Mississippi River or the seacoast, and undoubtedly feared waterborne Yankee raiders; for still others, the demand that they leave their homes and join this crusade snapped their fragile ties to the gentry. Men who remained uncommitted during the war's early months would see their options narrow: Confederate officials eventually restricted travel, and enrolling officers combed the countryside to find eligible men for the army.

Union and Confederate soldiers thus shared some essential characteristics—primarily youth—and values—primarily a favoring of personal concerns over politics—but there were crucial differences in their motivations and attitudes. Northerners tended to enlist when their own circumstances offered little economic security, when army life was a fair exchange for a livelihood that might be eliminated by an employer or a landlord. Southerners, by contrast, were more likely to enlist if they already had economic security. Yankees threatened to take away their slaves, and though poorer Southerners enlisted at higher rates than poor Northerners joined the Union army, slaveholding was a special incentive to enlist in the Confederate army. Northern and Southern soldiers were also prepared to react differently to their experiences. Conditioned to exercise self-control, many Northerners would try throughout the war to restrain their emotions. Conditioned to express emotion in a world dominated by personal relationships, Southern soldiers would continue to dwell on their feelings and on the personal traits of friend and foe.

3

Union Troops Go to War

THE MEN WHO JOINED the Union army knew about death. Indeed, most would have witnessed at least one death in their own family. More than one-third of antebellum American children lost a brother or sister before reaching age fifteen, and an additional one-fourth saw a parent die. And death was rarely hidden away in some public institution. Particularly when the dying person was an adult, relatives and friends would gather around the deathbed in the hope of witnessing a "good death." Americans longed, as the author Herman Melville put it, "to expire mild-eyed in one's bed." When they did, observers were reassured both about the departed spirit and about their own fate.

But young men were seldom anxious about the prevalence of death. Youths did die in antebellum America: a young man might be killed in a train wreck, die in a brawl, or fall prey to an epidemic disease such as cholera. But his odds of dying were remote. Mortality estimates show that a twenty-year-old male in this period had better than a 90 percent chance of surviving until he was thirty. The young men who went to war were used to seeing deaths among children and the elderly but were unaccustomed to facing their own mortality.

Before they confronted death on the battlefield, however,

recruits faced other new experiences. Their journey from home took them to a "camp of instruction," where they were to become soldiers. Many of the recruits had never been this far from home, which made the experience novel enough, but enlisted men were also required to take orders and do menial chores. Habits of self-control inculcated in Northern society should have made following orders easy, but soldiers drew a distinction between serving in a people's army and working for an employer. One soldier pointed out that in the professional peacetime army, "officers follow the army for a business and the men for a living," but "in the volunteers we are all enlisted for a certain time and . . . I don't think it necessary to be so strict or exact." Most officers had no prior military experience; they were usually from the same community as their enlisted men, and, at least early in the war, they had been chosen by their men for the position. As a result, officers found they had to earn their soldiers' obedience rather than take it for granted. The Union officers most likely to gain respect were those who put the safety of their men first, as did George Mc-Clellan, those who dressed and acted as if they were no better than their men, as did Ulysses S. Grant and William T. Sherman, or those who demonstrated personal courage in battle, as did eleven-times-wounded Colonel Edward Cross. Officers who were arrogant or incompetent, on the other hand, quickly encountered various forms of retaliation. Soldiers had numerous ways of harassing unpopular officers, ranging from mocking orders to defecating in an officer's unoccupied tent to physical assault.

Having to do menial chores increased soldiers' resistance to orders. Most recruits had done chores as boys, but few expected that patriotic service would consist of endless rounds of gathering firewood, preparing food, digging latrines, and clearing brush. Marching drill took up a large part of soldiers' time in camp, and it was particularly tedious. Drill was meant to make some headway against recruits' resistance to discipline and to encourage teamwork, but soldiers hated it. "The first thing in the morning is drill, then drill, then drill again," wrote a soldier. "Then drill, a little more drill ... Between drills, we drill and sometimes stop to eat a little and have roll-call." Even so, inexperienced officers often had reluctant men colliding with each other in formation and losing control of their horses in cavalry drills; supposedly attentive soldiers frequently burst into laughter at officers' attempts to give orders.

But camp life also provided plenty of reminders of soldiering's deadly side. Many recruits had brought their own rifles or shotguns, but the army supplied weapons as quickly as factories could turn them out and purchasing agents could buy them overseas. Union troops received a variety of firearms during the war, from smooth-bore muskets to breech-loading rifles, but the dominant weapon was the rifled musket. This was a muzzle-loader in which powder and bullet had to be driven down the barrel and a firing cap attached to the hammer before a shot could be fired. Although this process took seventeen steps, the grooves that spiraled down the inside of the barrel represented a technological advance over weapons used as recently as the Mexican War. The rifling allowed use of the famous "minié ball" (named for Claude Minié, one of its developers), which was actually a bullet with a hollowed-out base. When the gun was fired, the base expanded and gripped the grooves, and the bullet came out with a spin that made it much more accurate than the ball from a smooth-bore musket. In theory, the effective range of a rifled musket was nearly five hundred yards, versus less than one hundred yards for the smooth-bore.

Yet the guns were only as accurate as the soldiers firing them. Union troops got little target practice: officers were frequently as intimidated by musketry drill as were their men, especially since muskets could and did blow up in the faces of their users. And in an army this large, ammunition was often scarce, not to be wasted by shooting, as one unit did, at an effigy of Jefferson Davis. As a result, much of the small-arms fire of Civil War battles consisted of inaccurate fire from potentially accurate weapons, made worse by the pall of smoke that quickly obscured battlefields. Leander Stillwell of Illinois, for example, "was trying to peer under the smoke in order to get a sight of our enemies" at Shiloh, Tennessee, in 1862. When he told his lieutenant what he was doing, the officer screamed "shoot, shoot, anyhow." It is little wonder that a New York soldier reported seeing no more than one-third of shots hitting a stationary target in a rare target practice, or that historian Paddy Griffith estimates Union troops, firing under battle conditions, took two hundred shots for every one that hit an enemy soldier.

The war's most devastating killers appeared long before Union troops came under fire. Army camps brought together thousands of men in crowded and unsanitary conditions that were ideal for the spread of disease. Soon viruses and bacteria spread measles, smallpox, intestinal disease, and typhoid among the soldiers, and mosquitoes brought malaria; camp hospitals quickly filled, and physicians, who knew little about the cause of these diseases, were powerless against them. Soldiers died without ever seeing a battlefield, and regiments shrank in size. A soldier from Maine wrote that "though we enlisted to fight, bleed and die, nothing happened to us so serious as the measles." In the 125th Ohio and 12th Connecticut regiments, disease killed and disabled more than one-third of the original complement before either regiment fought a battle.

Recruits' prevailing attitude was disillusionment with these unexpected realities of the army, but soldiers also managed to shape camp life in ways that would last throughout the war. Long encampments were common, especially in the winter, and homesick soldiers tried to create a semblance of domestic life. Basic literacy was common among nineteenth-century Americans, and soldiers spent much of their time reading and writing. Their first priority was correspondence: men wrote letters under every conceivable condition, from first thing in the morning to lights-out at night to huddling on the battlefield, and they eagerly devoured responses from home. An observer estimated that a typical regiment sent 600 letters a day, and as many as 45,000 letters passed through Washington each day for the eastern armies. Soldiers read other material too, from newspapers to adventure stories in "dime novels" to the Bible and Charles Dickens. Some soldiers organized literary associations with their own lending libraries; a Massachusetts regiment early in the war maintained a library of more than five hundred books.

Most regiments had a chaplain who encouraged wholesome reading (and usually was the librarian) among his efforts at moral guidance. Chaplains held religious services, baptized converts, officiated at burials, visited the sick and wounded in the hospital, wrote and read letters for illiterate soldiers, and handled the mail. More broadly, religion offered guidelines for men away from parental supervision for the first time, and it promised God's protection for those fighting in a cause they believed was righteous. There were also occasional religious revivals in the Union army.

But as compared with the Confederate army, organized religion had only a limited impact on Union troops. Much of the problem was the chaplains' own shortcomings. Although many were conscientious, soldiers' comments suggest that a number were not up to the task. Chaplains received $100 a month—privates were paid $11 early in the war and $16 by the end—and a common assumption was that preachers "who can not make a good living at home, are the ones who strive to secure the position for the money." Soldiers' comments on sermons reveal some chaplains' inability to communicate with their troops. One chaplain "discussed *infant baptism* and closed with an earnest appeal, touchingly eloquent, to *mothers*," and another "preached doleful Sermons to the men about the hardships they will have to encounter, the Sickness & death and all the difficulties." Conscientious chaplains were equally critical of opportunistic colleagues. One chaplain complained that early in the war "men who were never clergy of any denomination" were appointed, and sometimes "the position was given to an irreligious layman." Historian Gerald Linderman has argued that chaplains' failings and the war's carnage, which came to seem increasingly random and senseless, caused many soldiers to doubt their early belief that the war represented the working of God's will.

If organized religion did not often meet soldiers' needs, music certainly did. Soldiers liked to listen to army brass bands, but they were positively obsessed with singing. They sang on the march, in camp, on the battlefield, and in the hospital; if Union and Confederate troops were within earshot, they might join together in a song. Patriotic morale-boosters such as "John Brown's Body" and "Battle Cry of Freedom" were highly popular among Union troops, but their real favorites were songs about home. "Home, Sweet Home" was probably the leading song on both sides, and so reflected soldiers' homesickness that bands were often forbidden to play it. But such expressions of longing could not be suppressed. Soldiers sang "My Old Kentucky Home," "When Johnny Comes Marching Home," and "When This Cruel War Is Over," the last of which sold a million copies of its lyrics. Songs allowed

an expression of emotion appropriate to the moment, an expression that soldiers could control and that drew them together.

Since the army was the gateway to manhood for many of
the recruits, they concentrated on activities that bridged the
gap between boyhood and adulthood. Sports allowed soldiers
to display their physical prowess, and they took part in individual competitions such as foot racing and boxing as well as
organized sports, especially baseball. Indeed, the mingling of
soldiers from different regions was instrumental in spreading
baseball beyond its origins in the urban Northeast. In the winter, competitive urges were satisfied by organized snowball
fights, distinguished from child's play by their roughness.
These fights sometimes served as military exercises: officers
might lead one regiment against another with bugles blaring
and flags flying. Hard-thrown snowballs, sometimes containing stones, could and did cause injuries. In a battle between
two New Hampshire regiments, a participant reported that
"tents were wrecked, bones broken, eyes blacked, and teeth
knocked out—all in *fun*."

Union soldiers were also caught between the youthful im-
perative to flout the rules of behavior and the mandate to exert
manly self-control. Some, like Cyrus Boyd of Iowa, tried to
cling to the ideals of self-discipline. Boyd condemned his comrades' eagerness "to abandon all their early teachings and to
catch up with everything which seeks to debase," and he resolved to "keep the mind occupied with something new and
keep *going all the time*." Other soldiers, however, viewed army
life as an invitation to return to boyhood, and devoted themselves to seeing how far they could go in rule-breaking. Soldiers made an art of swearing—one private "wished the
whole God damned Army and Navy and every other God
damned thing was in hell"—and they were equally obsessed

with gambling. Union troops played poker, a dice game called chuck-a-luck, and held cockfights, and would gamble anytime, anywhere. Witnesses told of poker hands that were completed under enemy fire, and soldiers were known to bet on the results of courts-martial for men caught gambling.

Practical joking allowed men to risk punishment and to embarrass unpopular soldiers. Pranks ranged from dumping water on a sleeping soldier to hazing new recruits to dangerous stunts such as mixing gunpowder with a soldier's pipe tobacco. But the masculine ritual that most exasperated authorities was drinking. Soldiers would drink any liquor they could get their hands on, from aged whiskey to the rawest "tanglefoot." Drunkenness triggered fights and caused injuries, and not only among enlisted men: an Illinois soldier noted one day that "Major Mellinger was so drunk that he fell off his horse." Frustrated commanders tried to cut off liquor supplies and punish drunkenness by tying offenders to a tree or making cavalrymen carry a saddle around the camp, and chaplains ceaselessly preached against the evils of drink. But liquor, in addition to its appeal as forbidden fruit, allowed soldiers some escape from the horrors of battle and the tedium of camp life. Soldiers' drinking and their resentment of those who tried to stop it appear to have increased during the war.

Soldiers thus viewed the camp as an exotic place where they could simultaneously take part in and escape from the dictates of manhood—but they also wanted it to be like home. Since most men in a company came from the same community, a soldier's companions were constant reminders of home, but a key feature of home life was missing—women. Soldiers occasionally saw women—female relatives visited regiments, and women nurses cared for soldiers in hospitals—but a typical complaint was that "I havent to say the real truth spoken three words to a femail sins I left home." One choice was to try an imitation: a number of regiments held dances with some of the men dressed as women. An Ohio soldier described a dance in which a comrade named Conway "has for a partner a soldier twice as big as himself whom he calls Susan. As they swing, Conway yells at the top of his voice: 'Come round, old gal!'"

Other soldiers were not interested in imitations. Some, especially if they had been well-to-do civilians, were received in nearby residences, even in the South. A soldier from Minnesota reported an evening spent in a planter's house, "conversing with the old gentleman's daughters & enjoying ourselves hugely. It is a long time since I was in a private house and as the 'gals' are quite sociable I enjoy the treat 'right smart.'" More often, soldiers went to prostitutes. Despite commanders' efforts (which once included dunking several prostitutes in the Mississippi River), prostitutes in camps and in nearby towns provided countless soldiers with "horizontal refreshments," to use the popular term. Venereal disease quickly appeared among the troops and became so serious that army officials in occupied Nashville opened a hospital for infected prostitutes in 1863. It is estimated that one in twelve Union soldiers contracted venereal disease during the Civil War.

Eventually camp life came to an end as new recruits prepared to go south for the first time or combat veterans broke camp for the next battle. The journey might begin by train or waterborne troop transport, but sooner or later troops would go on the march. Marching offered the excitement of impending battle, but it also made soldiers miserable. First-time marchers quickly discovered they were overloaded and would have to throw away cherished items from home, a process known as "simmering down." Some simmering-down had already occurred in camp, but now soldiers got down to the bare minimum. In the wake of marching soldiers lay discarded cavalry sabers, dress coats, books, and blankets. But marches were still a trial. They usually took place in the warm months, when southern heat and dust alternated with rain and mud. Marching was, of course, especially painful in ill-fitting shoes. A Connecticut soldier declared that "my gait was somewhat like that of a lame duck, but I waddled along . . . as fast as the remainder of our crew."

After the men finally arrived at the front, they began the ritual of preparation for battle. They received food rations and ammunition allotments, usually sixty paper cartridges containing powder and a bullet, plus a like number of firing caps. As the hour of battle approached and the troops took their assigned positions, the commanding officer would make a speech. These exhortations varied, but they were generally versions of this colonel's succinct instructions: "Now boys is the time to write your name. Let every man do his duty. Follow me!"

What happened next also varied widely. Sometimes Union troops would be ordered into a frontal assault on Confederate positions; on other occasions they would receive an assault behind fortified defenses; or they might exchange fire with enemy troops across a cornfield or in the woods. The assignment that soldiers feared most was the assault, in which they were called on to advance on the enemy's position in a series of lines, stopping several times to fire a volley of shots and reload, and then finish with a bayonet charge into the enemy lines. All too often, however, the outcome of an assault was a bloodbath. The Confederates had accuracy problems with their muskets (which were often captured from the Union), but they were nonetheless able to shoot down frightful numbers of attackers. Repeated assaults at Fredericksburg in 1862 resulted in nearly thirteen thousand Union dead and wounded among the Army of the Potomac, twice the Confederates' loss;

at Cold Harbor in 1864 the same army lost seven thousand
men in a single assault, five times the enemy's casualties.
Union assaults seldom overran Confederate defenses, and they
produced a special horror among men who had been unaccustomed to seeing their age-mates die, much less be cut down in
such numbers.

Soldiers likened an assault to charging through a storm of
lead. One charging Yankee "thought it was raining bullets,"
and another leaned into the gunfire "the same as I would go
through a storm of hail and wind." When an assault was over,
whether or not it had routed the enemy, the aftermath was
singularly terrifying. The faces of the dead after one battle
looked "as if they had seen something that scared them to
death." Another battlefield was so littered with corpses that
wagons had run over them, leaving them "mangled and torn
to pieces so that Even friends could not tell them." At Second
Bull Run in Virginia, corpses lay "with their brains oozing
out; some with their face shot off; others with their bowels
protruding; others with shattered limbs." Soldiers filled their
battle accounts with these graphic descriptions in an attempt
to come to terms with the slaughter of their comrades.

Paddy Griffith argues that more reliance on double-time
assaults, in which troops do not assist the enemy by stopping
to fire and reload, and on the "Indian rush," in which soldiers
dash from sheltered spot to sheltered spot, would have made
assaults more successful. But soldiers hated to receive fire
without shooting back, and the Indian rush was hard to control with a large army. Instead, although soldiers came to declare that "we dont mind the sight of dead men no more than
if they was dead Hogs," they also grew more insistent on digging in for their own safety.

Volunteers had come to this war believing that courageous
soldiers took the enemy's fire and kept moving forward until

the foe retreated; if wounded, soldiers were to leave the field with a minimal display of pain. When the carnage of frontal assaults proved the folly of this belief, soldiers forced a change in tactics. Although early in the war some officers and enlisted men alike had sneered at trenches as a passive substitute for real fighting, most enlisted men came to prefer digging in to making frontal assaults. Indeed, Grant's army dragged its feet at any repetition of the Cold Harbor assault, and the rest of the campaign for Petersburg and Richmond was fought largely from trenches. Trench warfare had its own dangers, especially from sharpshooters who picked off unsuspecting soldiers at long range, but troops found these risks preferable to the wholesale slaughter of an assault.

Although soldiers fought as members of fiercely loyal groups and depended on comrades for their lives ("small-unit cohesion" in the language of military scholars), they also found battle to be an intensely personal experience. Soldiers were astonished at the mass confusion of the battlefield— some soldiers got lost, others panicked, troops with no idea of where to go got in the way of those who did know where they were going, and friend and foe blended into one another in a wildly changing melee. At the same time the senses were heightened during a battle. A private from Massachusetts wrote that "the air was filled with a medley of sounds, shouts, cheers, commands, oaths, the sharp report of rifles, the hissing shot, dull heavy thuds of clubbed muskets, the swish of swords and sabers, groans and prayers." And battles often turned into desperate personal combat with the enemy. These close-quarters fights provided most of the acts that were awarded medals, such as Samuel Eddy's shooting of a Confederate who had pinned him to the ground with a bayonet, and the horseback charge of an artillery sergeant at Gettysburg, slashing with his sword at onrushing Confederates.

Troops were acutely aware of those who "showed the white feather" and ran away during a battle. Straggling was most common early in the war, when untested volunteers found themselves unable to face enemy fire. If they had previously hidden their doubts with boastfulness, shirkers received the special scorn of their fellows. A Wisconsin soldier declared that "the story about Lawtons being so brave was all a hoax. As soon as the battle [of Shiloh] commenced he was making for the river about as fast as his legs would carry him." Straggling could also become contagious. In the same battle a general reported having seen "cowering under the river bank when I crossed from 7,000 to 10,000 men frantic with fright and utterly demoralized."

But the troops whose performance was scrutinized above all others were the African Americans who took to the field beginning in late 1862. There was still considerable Northern hostility to a war against slavery, and whites at the front and at home doubted blacks' ability to make good soldiers. Some whites believed that blacks lacked the strength of character to fight in the face of enemy fire; others were convinced that blacks would fight too well—their unrestrained passions would lead them on a rampage against their former masters.

In reality, black troops fought with distinction beginning with several skirmishes in early 1863, but it would take major battles to win over skeptics. In May 1863 two black regiments were ordered to attack a well-fortified Confederate force at Port Hudson, Louisiana, on the Mississippi River. Without artillery support or reinforcements, the black troops advanced against Confederate fire several times until it became clear that the enemy could not be dislodged. This was yet another failed assault for the Union, but the African-American troops had fought gallantly despite suffering 20 percent casualties.

Less than two months later, black troops faced a Confederate assault at Milliken's Bend, upriver from Port Hudson. Confederates reached the Union lines and fought the black troops hand to hand. When the enemy gained an edge, two companies of whites ran away, but the black troops held their ground; with the help of gunboats they forced the Confederates to break off the attack, but the black troops had suffered 35 percent casualties.

Then on July 18, the Fifty-fourth Massachusetts (Colored) Infantry led an assault on Fort Wagner outside Charleston, South Carolina. This was the elite among black regiments, led by Robert Gould Shaw, son of a leading antislavery family, and included two sons of Frederick Douglass. As the Fifty-fourth advanced on the fort, it was squeezed onto a narrow strip of land between a swamp and the ocean, making the troops an easy target for Confederate muskets and cannon in the fort. Shaw was killed, 40 percent of his soldiers died or were wounded, and the survivors were forced to retreat.

But doubts about blacks' ability and willingness to fight were all but extinguished. Full equality was not around the corner: African-American troops continued to receive shoddy weapons and inferior medical care, and there were reports of Union troops assaulting and shooting at black soldiers. Yet the *New York Times* acknowledged the beginning of a "prodigious revolution [in] the public mind." Advocates of equal rights pointed to the difference between black soldiers' valor on the battlefield and their treatment elsewhere; as a result, by the end of the war some states had empowered blacks to testify in court and to qualify for poor relief, and a few cities had ended segregation of their streetcars.

For black soldiers and whites alike, the days after a battle

were a special form of misery. The end of a battle meant the
start of the grisly task of tending to the wounded and burying
the dead, who were often the friends and relatives of those
doing the burying. Comrades or stretcher-bearers helped
some of the wounded to the nearest cart or ambulance wagon,
and the rest made their own way to the tent, barn, or farmhouse that served as a field hospital. For further treatment or
recuperation, soldiers would eventually be moved by rail to a
general hospital far behind the lines. Civil War hospitals were
more dangerous than the battlefield: more deaths from
wounds and disease occurred there than in battle. As disease
performed its grim weeding-out of more susceptible men,
sickness actually decreased—the rate of illness among soldiers
dropped by 40 percent during the war. Nonetheless, twice as
many Union soldiers died of disease as were killed by Confederate fire.

The creation of a hospital system to treat sick and wounded
soldiers was a remarkable achievement. Starting with almost
nothing, federal officials put together an organization that
treated more than a million soldiers, operated more than two
hundred general hospitals, and employed thirteen thousand
physicians. The effort was aided by the United States Sanitary
Commission, a quasi-official group of physicians and women
reformers who investigated medical conditions in the army
and advised officials on improvements. The commission also
raised money to buy medical supplies for the troops and re-
cruited women to serve as nurses in army hospitals.

Hospitals were nonetheless frightening places for sick or
wounded soldiers. Knowing little about the causes of disease,
the most physicians could do was to administer substances
that seemed to stimulate the body to rid itself of the disturbance. Typhoid, for example, was often treated with calomel,
a compound of mercury that stimulated the bowels, and

malaria with ipecac, a plant extract that induced vomiting. In spite of these treatments, some soldiers managed to recover. But it was the handling of wounds that was most associated with Civil War hospitals. The minié ball that was the mainstay of Civil War troops made a particularly menacing wound. Large, soft, and relatively slow-moving, the bullet usually lodged in the body, bringing along bits of clothing and hair and nearly always causing an infection. Due to soldiers' inaccuracy and to their eagerness to stay behind fortifications, two-thirds of wounds were in the limbs rather than the torso; this was fortunate because it avoided high-risk chest and abdominal surgery, but it also created the dilemma of what to do with shattered and infected limbs.

Physicians were caught between advocates of "conservative" treatment who urged saving a wounded arm or leg whenever possible (and risking the spread of life-threatening infection) and advocates of amputation to stop infection. Accounts of amputated arms and legs piled outside hospitals caused a public outcry and produced a shift toward the conservative approach by surgeons, but rough handling of wounds in the field and enormous numbers of wounded continued to encourage amputations. Union surgeons cut off thirty thousand arms and legs during the war, under conditions such as these reported by a witness:

> As a wounded man was lifted on the table, often shrieking with pain as the attendants handled him, the surgeon quickly examined the wound and resolved upon cutting off the injured limb. Some ether was administered and the body put in position in a moment. The surgeon snatched his knife from between his teeth . . . , wiped it rapidly once or twice across his bloodstained apron, and the cutting began. The operation accomplished, the surgeon would look around with a deep sigh, and then—"Next!"

But hospitals were not only places of torture. Physicians did what they could to relieve pain, liberally dispensing opium and morphine (and creating addicts in the process). They also made occasional, if haphazard, headway against infection. Although the actual nature and spread of infection would not be known until after the war, physicians did notice and sometimes made use of the disinfectant powers of substances such as iodine and carbolic acid.

And human compassion could be found in hospitals. Indeed, it was here that soldiers found the clearest reminders of home. Several thousand women worked as paid or volunteer nurses in Union army hospitals, and "we fell into maternal relations with [the men], ... addressing them individually as 'my son,' 'my boy,' or 'my child.'" If anything, the patients were even more eager for the mother-son relationship, and soldiers slipped easily into addressing their nurses as "Mother." Soldiers longed for the nurturance and moral authority they associated with womanhood, and so a nurse, according to an observer, "was almost an object of worship by those wholly excluded from home influences."

The absence of women's influence added insult to another kind of confinement for soldiers. Nearly 200,000 Union troops were held at one time or another as prisoners of war in the South, most of them in the war's later years. At first prisoners were exchanged under commanders' informal arrangements; if there were too many prisoners to hold until an exchange was negotiated, they were typically released on promising they would not resume fighting until notified they had been officially "exchanged." The two sides formalized this practice in July 1862. But the agreement broke down in 1863, chiefly over the issue of black troops in the Union army. The Confederate government authorized enslaving captured black soldiers and executing their white officers for inciting a slave revolt. The

North held up exchanges to discourage Confederates from carrying out their policy; when the South refused to include black prisoners in any exchanges, trading of prisoners virtually ceased, and each side was forced to house an exploding population of captives.

Soldiers' most bitter condemnations of the war concern prisons, largely because, according to one ex-prisoner, "we felt our manhood crushed to the very earth." Men had expected to serve by codes of honor and courage and to show self-control in the army, but prison life denied them the chance. Conditions in Southern prisons were appalling; a Confederate government that did not have the resources to feed and supply its own troops was in no position to care for an enormous prison population. The best-known Confederate prison was by far the largest, near Andersonville, Georgia. Built in early 1864 as an unsheltered stockade for 10,000 men, Andersonville held 33,000 prisoners by the summer. Rations bore little resemblance to food, and sanitation and medical care were primitive; upward of 100 prisoners died each day at the peak of the prison's crowding.

For decades after the war, survivors would denounce everyone connected with the prison, but they were especially distressed by what it did to human behavior. Most soldiers had come to the army intending to demonstrate manhood, but nonhuman references abound instead in prison descriptions. "The animal predominates," wrote an Andersonville prisoner, who described his fellow prisoners as "so many snarly dogs" and "hungry wolves penned together." Another inmate admitted becoming "more like a Devil than a man." Honor and courage gave way to the law of the jungle as gangs of thieves took over the prison. The prisoners themselves eventually rounded up the ringleaders, hanged six, and beat to death three others. Little wonder that twenty years after the war an ex-prisoner called his confinement "a long, dark night of lingering horror."

The handling of prisoners was not the only aspect of army experience that changed during the course of the war. The makeup of the Union army changed, as did the attitudes of the soldiers themselves. By 1863 the army was the product of a whittling-down process. The men who were most vulnerable to disease had died or been discharged, and some who could not stand the horrors of combat were also gone. Civil War battles produced symptoms, such as difficulty in breathing or severe depression, that we now associate with combat fatigue. Army physicians often concluded that men with such symptoms were insane, prompting one doctor to declare that "the number of cases of insanity in our army is astonishing." Rigid rules on discharges, however, limited the number of men released for combat stress. Some soldiers took desperate measures to escape combat. Self-mutilation, such as shooting off a finger or shooting oneself in the foot, was a common occurrence when the war was going poorly for the Union.

But by far the most common way out of the war was desertion. Approximately 200,000 Union soldiers deserted during the war. Men were especially likely to desert if they had had no compelling reason to enlist until bounties and substitute pay became lucrative, or if they did not belong to what historian Judith Hallock calls cohesive communities. In her study of two New York townships, Hallock found that desertions were considerably more common among soldiers from the township that had a high rate of population turnover and provided little public assistance to soldiers' families, compared to a more generous and tightly knit neighboring township. Cohesive communities were more likely to shame deserters back into the army, and community aid gave soldiers less reason to fear for their family's sustenance.

Deserters were also men who were willing to risk punish-ment. An estimated two-fifths of Union deserters were caught and returned to their units. Early in the war, deserters, like those guilty of lesser offenses, typically were punished by their commanders. A deserter might be branded with a "D" on the hip or the cheek, have his head shaved, or be drummed out of the service. The rate of desertion kept climbing, however, and punishments became harsher as the war continued. Deserters were now routinely court-martialed; soldiers who had de-serted to attend to their families were often imprisoned at hard labor, but repeat offenders or men who had gone over to the enemy could receive a death sentence.

The Union executed 267 soldiers during the war, and more than half were for desertion; numerous others were subjected to a mock execution with a last-minute reprieve. Military punishment of whatever sort was always conducted in full view of the offender's comrades. In an execution this included the prisoner's entire regiment, brigade, or division (a brigade was three to five regiments, a division two to five brigades). The prisoner (or prisoners, because multiple executions oc-curred), an armed party of guards, a firing squad, and a chap-lain were brought before the assembled troops while a band played the "Dead March." The prisoner was then seated on a coffin or placed standing beside an open grave and had his final words with the chaplain. The charges were read, the fir-ing squad put into position, and the order to fire given. The volley did not always kill the prisoner, however, and authori-ties learned through experience to have a second and some-times a third squad ready for another volley. Indeed, a convicted deserter from Pennsylvania was still standing after the first volley, remained sitting against his coffin after the second, and fell dead only after the third squad had fired. Following an execution, the assembled troops were marched

past the body for a full appreciation of the wages of disobedience. Yet the lesson began to lose its impact because soldiers became acclimated to death in all its forms. The idealistic civilians of 1861 and 1862 were in the later years battle-hardened
soldiers, toughened against emotion, drawn together by shared
danger and suffering, and alienated from those who did not
share their experience. "Men can get accustomed to anything,"
wrote a corporal from Rhode Island, "and the daily sight of
blood and mangled bodies so blunted their finer sensibilities as
almost to blot out all love, all sympathy from the heart."

One's comrades, however, were an exception to the feeling
of alienation. Foremost among these were a soldier's messmates—men belonging to small groups that chose their own
members and cooked and ate together. No loyalties in the
army were fiercer than those among messmates: they were
known to call their group a family and their messmates brothers, and a poem by a Union army private maintained that
"there's never a bond, old friend, like this—We have drank
from the same canteen."

There was also a solidarity among enlisted men that went
beyond the mess and the regiment and could even cross
enemy lines. Officers did all they could to prohibit fraternization between Union and Confederate troops, but informal
truces persisted, and probably increased, throughout the war.
A mutual respect for fighting ability grew year by year, as did
mutual empathy for the plight of the common soldier. When
their lines were close enough, soldiers frequently called a truce
and talked, traded, swam, drank, and gambled together.

But as acts of fraternity increased, so did acts of hatred.
Ideals of honor and courage had largely given way to doing
one's duty and staying alive, and though Union troops had
great admiration for veteran foot soldiers on both sides, they

took no pity on anyone who seemed not to share their values. This included new recruits and support troops, whom front-line soldiers assumed were "bounty-jumpers" (men who enlisted to collect a bounty, deserted, then enlisted again elsewhere). A New York combat veteran, witnessing a bombardment of men he assumed were bounty-jumpers, had this reaction: "I saw men fall, saw others mangled by chunks of shell, and saw one, stuck fairly by an exploding shell, vanish. Enormously pleased, I hugged my lean legs, and laughed."

The enemy also included unsupportive people back home. Soldiers detested the "carpet knights at home": antiwar Northern Democrats, whom one soldier labeled "cowardly skunks," and businessmen and politicians "scrambling for wealth or for office." A Wisconsin soldier expressed the wish that Robert E. Lee, whose Army of Northern Virginia invaded Pennsylvania in 1863, "could have had a month more among the people of Pennsylvania" to acquaint them with the hardships of war.

But soldiers could only fantasize about punishing Northern ingrates. When Southern soldiers and civilians aroused antagonism Union troops could fully unleash their fury. Northern soldiers went south with a low opinion of Southerners—most believed that Southern society consisted of a few aristocrats ruling over slaves and a degraded population of white farmers—but few Northerners anticipated fighting civilians as well as soldiers.

Soldiers presumed that the main function of civilians was to stay out of the way of the armies; to people in the South, however, Union troops were invaders, so Southerners engaged in a host of partisan activities. Some men became guerrillas, dropping their usual occupation and joining armed bands to harass Union troops, then melting back into the countryside. Confederate officials were ambivalent about such bands—the government officially recognized guerrillas in the Partisan Ranger Act of 1862, then reversed itself in 1864 at the urging of Robert E. Lee and others—but guerrilla leaders attracted sizable followings in states such as Missouri, Virginia, and Tennessee, where there were large numbers of Union as well as Confederate sympathizers. Guerrillas such as William Clarke Quantrill, "Bloody Bill" Anderson, and John Singleton Mosby became heroes to Confederates and a scourge to federals. Avoiding open combat between equal forces, guerrillas ambushed Union troops and murdered Unionist civilians. There were reports of victims with their genitals cut off, and members of Anderson's band carried scalps in their bridles.

Union soldiers were especially angered by the ease with which guerrillas vanished into the civilian population. Guerrillas often operated out of their homes, and when confronted, according to an Illinois soldier, "they are good union men & unless you catch them in the very act you dont know who they are." When guerrillas were away from home, Confederate supporters fed and sheltered them, then pleaded innocence to Union soldiers; families often switched loyalties depending on who held sway in their neighborhood.

Nor, Union soldiers thought, could they trust Southern women. Soldiers expected women to be nurturing and submissive, and Southern women often were, nursing and feeding Union troops when they were in need. But other women were openly defiant and occasionally dangerous. Women jeered at Union prisoners, spat at the flag, and cursed occupying troops; they took shots at, and occasionally killed, Union soldiers, led Yankees into guerrilla ambushes, and rode as guerrillas themselves. Union troops thus operated in a murky world in which social roles were turned upside down, everyone seemed to be the enemy, and sudden death could come from anywhere.

And so Yankee soldiers acted less and less from civility and more from hatred for civilians. "Foraging" evolved from taking crops, livestock, and firewood that ill-supplied troops needed, into full-scale pillaging. William T. Sherman formalized the practice for his march through Georgia and the Carolinas that began in 1864, but Union soldiers across the South had already started turning foraging into punishment. Depending on their mood and on the reputed Confederate sympathies of their target, Union foragers took corn and grain, confiscated livestock, and broke into houses for clothing, furniture, and jewelry. Officers expressed only token disapproval. Victims who were particularly defiant might have their houses burned. Union troops found that burning an enemy's house both demonstrated the army's power to exact vengeance and underscored the owner's powerlessness.

Yet there were restraints on these Union soldiers' attacks on civilians. In the twentieth century we are accustomed to hearing reports of assaults on enemy women, especially rape. Union troops did commit rape in the Civil War, and eighteen soldiers were executed for the crime. Executions are only the vaguest clue to a crime's prevalence, but historians have concluded that surprisingly little rape took place during the Civil War, and that there was even less against white women. Union soldiers could simultaneously humiliate Southerners and show their hatred for African Americans by raping black women who were under whites' control, and there are reports that some soldiers did so. Yet Union soldiers, disillusioned as they were, retained some self-control and some reverence for womanhood.

Few restraints were evident, however, in soldiers' treatment of guerrillas. Union soldiers adopted the guerrillas' own tactics, using informers, wearing civilian clothes to infiltrate guerrilla bands, and torturing and executing prisoners as they caught them. To bolster their confidence against guerrillas' intimidation, Union troops adopted language from their hunting days. A colonel in Missouri referred to his assignment "of hunting and in some cases exterminating bushwhackers," and another officer boasted that "my men say they can track the bushmen like a dog would a deer." Fighting guerrillas became an eye-for-an-eye struggle of stealth and vengeance.

Atrocities by Confederate regulars similarly triggered the wrath of Union troops. Soldiers' respect for persistence in doing one's duty did not extend to wanton killing. After the introduction of black troops, some Confederates went beyond their government's threats and shot down captured black soldiers on the spot. Documented instances of such murders were isolated until a massacre of black soldiers occurred at Fort Pillow, Tennessee, in April 1864. General Nathan Bedford Forrest and his Confederate cavalry captured the fort and then killed as many as a hundred black troops among the garrison. News of the killings infuriated African Americans throughout the army, and Union troops, black and white, occasionally gunned down Confederate captives with a cry of "Remember Fort Pillow!"

Yet despite their bitter disillusionment most Union soldiers still clung to a few ideals they could separate from the battlefield. On the same evening that messmates vehemently denounced cowards and profiteers back home, they might also wipe away tears as they sang "Home, Sweet Home"; soldiers usually exempted their own families from condemnations of the home front. Or a soldier might take a gold watch from a dying enemy and then write home about his duty to save the Union; there was no appreciable decline in soldiers' expressions of patriotism even as they abandoned rules of civility.

Patriotism and duty were, however, pushed to the limit in 1864, when men with three-year enlistments from 1861 were scheduled to go home. Taking no chances, the federal government offered a month-long furlough, a bonus, and other incentives to induce soldiers to reenlist. Approximately 100,000 men declined the offer and served out their enlistment, but nearly 140,000 others signed on for three more years. A higher percentage of men thus reenlisted than had enlisted in the first place, and historians generally emphasize the importance of duty to comrades and country in convincing soldiers to reenlist.

Yet patriotism probably had little to do with the high rate of reenlistment decisions. For many soldiers the lure of furlough was irresistible. As one Ohio officer put it, it was worth trading "three years more of hell" for "thirty days of heaven— home." Bounties were also enormously attractive to men whose families were going hungry in their absence, but the government used threats as well as enticements to persuade the undecided. Soldiers who were vocal in discouraging reenlistment faced arrest, and men who refused to reenlist were to be classified as "non-veterans" when they were discharged. Most of those who reenlisted undoubtedly did so for this combination of desires and pressures that the government had cleverly exploited.

In 1865 a soldier in Sherman's army wrote that "the experience of twenty years of peaceful life has been crowded into three years." He and his Northern comrades had seen young men die in numbers they could not have imagined earlier, and few of them were good deaths. They had also suffered from fear, hunger, and disease in ways that were inconceivable before the war, and that, in their view, no one else could ever understand. Yet soldiers had also influenced the way the war was fought. Their growing resistance to frontal assaults forced commanders to modify their tactics, and soldiers' evolving detachment about inflicting suffering helped to make possible Sherman's march through Georgia and the Carolinas. And black soldiers, besides being instrumental in the siege of Petersburg, the defense of Nashville, and other late-war battles, erased some of their white comrades' racism and inspired new resolve among jaded white troops. On several occasions whites raised a cheer for black soldiers' performance, and one white officer paid blacks a soldier's tribute: blacks' gallantry, he declared, "will have established their manhood."

Enlisted men were in a poor position to gauge the course of the war. Union troops saw by 1865 that Confederate soldiers were ragged and demoralized, but Yankees were often little better off. Soldiers were passionately interested in knowing when the end would come, but most of their information came from rumors they had long since learned to distrust. Their concerns were also personal—how they had performed in the most recent fight, whether they would survive the next one, whether they would find something better than hardtack (an essentially inedible biscuit) for their next meal, and how to get some decent shoes. Sherman's soldiers, for example, were preparing in North Carolina for yet another campaign when the latest round of rumors proved to be true: the Confederates were surrendering, and the war was over.

These were the experiences of the victors. Fighting for a nation of immense resources whose economy boomed during the war, Union soldiers nonetheless acquired physical and psychological scars from the fighting. How did their experience compare with that of Confederates?

4

Confederates at War

FEW CONFEDERATE RECRUITS expected to meet an honorable foe. The North, they believed, would copy the practice of the British in the American Revolution: Yankees would search the streets and the saloons to produce an army "filled up with the scum of creation" and would probably add a "hireling host" of European mercenaries to plunder the South. The Southern army, by contrast, made up of "the best blood of the grand old Southland," would have little trouble defeating this rabble.

To get the chance, however, the recruits would need to become soldiers, which meant putting up with camp life. Like Union troops, Confederate soldiers went to camps of instruction for initial training and later made camp for wintertime lulls in the fighting. While they were there, officers tried to instill discipline through drill and rules for behavior, but they fell into a contest of wills with their soldiers that was probably sharper than in the Union army. For one thing, among the Confederate officers there were more professional soldiers. At the beginning of the war, experienced Union officers were kept in the regular army while their Southern peers were resigning to train Confederate volunteers; other Confederate officers came from military schools, almost all of which were in the South. These trained officers were especially likely to demand military discipline among their troops.

But Southern enlisted men were especially poor candidates for this discipline. They came from a society that prepared white men to give orders, not take them. The result was, a Virginia soldier concluded, "an individual who could not become the indefinite portion of a mass, but fought for himself, on his own account." Such an individual reserved for himself "the right of private judgment" on orders he received, and he had a familiar standard of unacceptable treatment—being ordered about like a slave. A Georgia volunteer thus complained that "a private soldier is nothing more than a slave and is often treated worse," and another soldier declared that he was "tired of being bound up worse than a negro."

Confederates elected their officers: companies voted for lieutenants and captains, who in turn chose regimental officers. The government tried to phase out the practice, but it lingered in some units until the war's end. When one of these public servants ordered a soldier to dig a latrine it was bad enough, but when he had the soldier thrown in the guardhouse for disputing the order it was an affront to a man's honor. A Tennessee private thus refused to take part in a drill and then threatened the officer who tried to reprimand him; a Louisiana soldier responded to an order by insisting he was a gentleman and drawing a sword on his lieutenant; and another soldier, threatened with punishment for disobedience, called the officer involved "a damned coward," promising that "if you will pull off your insignia of rank I will whip you on the spot."

Confederate soldiers did not, however, hate all officers. Historians Joseph Frank and George Reaves found that only a few more Confederates than Yankees complained about their officers' military competence at Shiloh. Pete Maslowski's sample of soldiers' testimony found that Confederate enlisted men appreciated their officers' personal interest in them. But that appreciation could quickly explode into rage when an officer betrayed the mutual respect that Southern soldiers expected.

Confederate enlisted men also resisted limits on their off-duty behavior. Gambling was as popular in Confederate camps as it was among Yankees: some Southern soldiers would take a chance on anything, from the roll of dice to the outcome of a louse race. Drinking was similarly widespread. Commanders punished soldiers for drunkenness and banned the sale of liquor in or near their camps, but the prohibition only inspired more ingenuity in finding and smuggling liquor. One company brought in liquor in a hollowed-out watermelon, and a Tennessee soldier smuggled in a supply of whiskey in the barrel of his gun. Another soldier recalled that "in each regiment there were a few men who could find a stillhouse if it was within twenty miles of the line of march."

Like Northern units, Southern companies consisted of friends, relatives, and neighbors from the same community (at least until attrition forced consolidation of units late in the war), but Southern soldiers felt the same dissatisfaction with their all-male world as did Yankees, and they tried the same remedies. Some Confederates made do with polite social visits or all-male dances, but others preferred to defy their commanders and seek sexual satisfaction with prostitutes whenever they had the chance. It is impossible to determine whether Confederates went to prostitutes as often as did Yankees, but it is likely that Southerners had fewer opportunities: they were less often camped near cities, many of which were in Union hands anyway, and runaway inflation made Confederate money worth less than Union greenbacks. Yet commanders were certainly convinced that prostitution was a major problem. Their response was to take action against the women: some officials investigated the character of camp followers, including cooks and laundresses, and one general ordered a sweep of a Georgia town, with orders to banish or imprison women of suspicious reputation. There is little evidence, however, that any of these measures worked.

Confederate officials never fully came to terms with the right of private judgment. To be sure, the army had its advocates of iron discipline: Stonewall Jackson refused to lighten court-martial punishments of his troops, and Robert E. Lee asserted that "hundreds of lives have been needlessly sacrificed for want of a strict observance of discipline." But day-to-day dealings with touchy enlisted men discouraged officers from harsh punishment. The soldier who called his officer a "damned coward," for example, was not punished for his outburst, and in the case of one Louisiana private caught sleeping on guard duty, a court-martial imposed a light sentence on the grounds that he had been drunk that night. What one historian has called the Confederates' "prevailing custom of leniency" undoubtedly came from the knowledge that Southern men could and did rebel against severe punishment, especially from unpopular officers. Virginia soldiers, for example, refused to submit to punishment by the "tyrannical" General Charles Winder, and General Allison Nelson's men fired into his tent, thereby convincing him to release two comrades from punishment.

But appealing as defiance of authority was, Confederate soldiers were also as eager as Yankees to duplicate features of family and community in camp. Confederates likewise formed messes, whose bonds were recalled by a Virginia veteran. A soldier, he wrote, "learns to look upon [his comrades] as brothers; there is no sacrifice he will not make for them; no trouble that he will not cheerfully take. Fellowship becomes almost a religion."

Soldiers had a variety of ways to replicate the larger community as well. Some armies published newspapers, which could be handwritten sheets such as "The Pioneer Banner," published by Alabamians, or printed papers such as the *Missouri Army Argus*. Other soldiers arranged formal entertainments, which might be a concert by a regimental band or a burlesque staged by soldier-actors. Military theatricals could become elaborate: programs were occasionally printed, costumes and makeup improvised, and civilians invited. And Confederates were as preoccupied as Yankees with music, both formal and informal. Bands frequently accompanied the theatricals, and Louisiana and Kentucky companies performed an opera in 1864. Southerners also sang at every opportunity, supplementing songs such as "Home, Sweet Home" and "When This Cruel War Is Over" with "Dixie" and "The Bonnie Blue Flag."

Confederates engaged in most of the same sports as did Yankees—ball games, boxing, foot races, snowball fights, and so on—but Southern soldiers were especially devoted to hunting. As we have seen, many Northerners had hunted as civilians and some adapted hunting language to warfare, but Southerners held a special reverence for this ritual that allowed both competition and male companionship; moreover, they had an extra incentive to hunt when rations worsened during the war. Soldiers took whatever opportunities they could find to hunt in spite of the restrictions of army life. Prohibited from using valuable ammunition to hunt, Confederates stalked rabbits and partridges with clubs and climbed trees in search of squirrels. Soldiers would even break ranks in a drill or on the march when someone spotted game. A Virginia soldier recalled that when a rabbit burst into view, "regardless of officers' commands, the soldiers with one shout would start after him. . . . A strange characteristic of the Southern army was their insane desire to run a hare." Religion was a feature of Southern communities about which soldiers were initially ambivalent. Evangelical religion—built around humans' personal relationship with God and preoccupied with overcoming sin and achieving an assured salvation—was a pillar of Southern communal life, but it could run afoul of masculine culture. Young men expected preachers to rail against sin, but they also expected the chance to act like men, especially in the army. If this meant a friendly game of cards and a drink or two, and maybe answering an insult with one's fists, that was what men did; few young men expected to die soon, so there was plenty of time to make amends. As a result, the most vivid descriptions of Confederate sinfulness came from chaplains who were appalled by what they saw and heard. A Mississippi chaplain complained that among his comrades were "the most vile, obscene blackguards that could be raked up this side [of] the bad place. . . . From early morn to dewey eve there is one uninterrupted flow of the dirtiest talk I ever heard in my life." Chaplains would have agreed with another Mississippian that "it is an uphill and discouraging business preaching to Soldiers," and many resigned; by 1862 it was estimated that only half of Confederate units had a chaplain.

But however much Confederates tried to replicate the society they had left, they were also anxious to get into the field and get on with the fighting. Infantry drill, which filled Southerners' days as it did Yankees', made Confederates equally impatient to get out of camp. Frustrated officers drilling reluctant soldiers produced scenes of exasperation similar to those in the North. In a Virginia company, "the luckless captain, losing what little self-possession he had, blundered more and more and generally ended up tying his company in a hard knot."

And Southern soldiers were nearly as unprepared to shoot effectively. Like Union troops, many Southern recruits brought their own weapons, but Confederate authorities had a much harder time replacing them and equipping men who were unarmed. Few weapons were manufactured in the Confederacy, so the government had to buy most of its guns in Europe and try to run them through the Union blockade of Confederate ports. Some states had adequate supplies of guns and a few had surpluses, but governors refused to allow Richmond to distribute their extras. As a result, Confederate soldiers early in the war were armed with a bewildering array of weapons—flintlock muskets that would not fire in the rain, hunting rifles, smoothbore muskets, shotguns, and pistols—and many men were still unarmed. The lack of guns was worst in the war's first year: western commanders reported in the winter of 1861–1862 that up to half their troops had no weapons.

Supplies improved by the next year as Southerners captured large numbers of Springfield rifled muskets and began receiving shipments of the similar English-made Enfields. By 1864 more than 80 percent of soldiers in the Army of Tennessee, for example, had the potentially accurate rifled musket. But even though many Southerners had been good shots with their own weapons, they had little chance to develop much skill with the new guns. Confederate officers were as reluctant as Northerners to use up ammunition and risk accidents in target practice, and Southern soldiers were likewise hampered by battlefield smoke. Rebels' small-arms fire was probably more accurate than was Northerners', but Paddy Griffith has nonetheless estimated that Confederates fired a hundred shots for every one that hit a Yankee.

A number of Southern recruits never got the chance to test their prowess against the enemy. Disease attacked first, racing through Confederate camps and killing a larger proportion of soldiers than in the North. More Confederates came from rural areas with no exposure and thus no immunity to common diseases, so Southern units would typically lose more men before engaging the enemy. Southerners who survived this first assault by disease went through most of the same preparations for battle as did Yankees: sometimes a train trip toward the next campaign, more often a march during which soldiers finished "simmering down" to the minimum of equipment. When they had reached the place where the generals expected a battle, the troops received their ammunition and rations and were stationed to attack or to hold a position. The commanding officer would give his speech, and the troops would wait for the battle to begin.

In major battles Confederates were more likely than Union troops to be ordered into a frontal assault. As with Union assaults, Southern troops would be arranged in two or more lines that were supposed to keep a good distance apart. Occasionally Civil War armies attacked in columns rather than these broad rows, but commanders preferred to send their troops elbow-to-elbow against the enemy, with orders to finish with a bayonet charge.

Historians are divided about why Confederate leaders were especially anxious to use assaults. They do agree on the South's commitment to offensive warfare. A Richmond newspaper insisted that "waiting for blows, instead of inflicting them, is altogether unsuited to the genius of our people"; Confederate President Jefferson Davis endorsed "the one great object of giving to our columns capacity to take the offensive"; and a Confederate officer longed for warfare that "hurls masses against . . . the enemy's army." And Southerners acted on their commitment: they were the attackers in eight of the war's first twelve major battles. But the cause of these views is less clear. The South's aggressiveness has been variously attributed to West Point training, to the successful use of assaults in the Mexican War, and, in an intriguing study by Grady McWhiney and Perry Jamieson, to the influence of Europe's fierce Celtic people on the American South. Other historians have pointed out that in smaller engagements Union forces were just as likely to attack as were Confederates.

There is little disagreement, however, about the cost of their assaults to the Confederates. In the eight major battles with the South as aggressor, the Confederates had nearly one-fourth of their men killed, wounded, or captured, while the Union lost only 15 percent of its troops. Confederate generals deemphasized but never abandoned assaults later in the war. In 1864 John Bell Hood lost more than eleven thousand men in two frontal assaults near Atlanta, then lost five thousand more in an attack at Franklin, Tennessee, while the defending Yankees were losing one-third as many soldiers.

Since Confederates were especially committed to the assault, it is appropriate to view a typical charge from a Southern viewpoint, though the experiences were similar whichever side was on the offensive. Waiting for the order to charge was a special ordeal, especially for untested soldiers. Men who had "seen the elephant," the popular term for undergoing combat, might appear calm and even catch a nap if the waiting dragged on, but new soldiers were usually tormented with doubts about their performance. No one knew if he would be killed or wounded, of course, but untested soldiers did not even know if they would be paralyzed with fear; this is why officers promised to shoot anyone who broke ranks during an assault. If the Yankees were already firing their artillery, the fear was that much worse: one soldier under cannon fire recalled his hair "standing on end like the quills of a porcupine." The command to advance was a kind of liberation. Soldiers could now take on those Yankees whose guns and bayonets they could see while they waited. The attackers marched in their lines, often across an open field, and they could not wait to take their first shot. Officers, realizing that stopping to fire a volley made soldiers better targets, frequently pleaded with their men not to shoot, but firing at the enemy was crucial for a soldier. "With your first shot you become a new man," wrote a Confederate. "Personal safety is your least concern. Fear has no existence in your bosom." The charge quickly became a combination of grim determination and sudden shock. A Tennessee officer recalled that "I do not remember that on our way across the open space, a command was given or a word spoken. 'Where is the enemy?' I kept asking myself." And then "the fence before us became transformed into a wall of flame." As the Yankees fired on the Orleans Guard of Louisiana, a volunteer measured his progress by his downed comrades: "Porce down . . . Gallot down . . . Coiron, arm shattered . . . Percy wounded." A Mississippi lieutenant acknowledged only one honorable way out of this horror: "The first wounded man I recognized was my Uncle Henry's eldest son, cousin James Mangum. He had been shot in the face. I wanted to help him [but] everyone was moving forward. . . . We just had to get at those Federals who were shooting us."

Any semblance of coordination usually disappeared in an assault. The carefully separated lines often collapsed into a disorganized crowd. Soldiers seldom used their bayonets; if enough Confederates reached the Union lines, the assault would probably end as did the Orleans Guard's ("A ragged stand up volley at the Unionists and they scramble off"). But more often, attacks ended like another assault witnessed by the Guard. This time a regiment disappeared over a rise toward the Union position, and soon "the decomposed line tumbled back over the crest again. Men scarcely could be recognized . . . shirts covered with blood . . . faces disfigured with hideous wounds."

Unsuccessful attackers might be ordered to regroup and try again the same day or on following days. When the fighting ended, a mixture of exhaustion, shock, and depression overcame the soldiers. Fatigue was overpowering after a battle, and men often collapsed at night amid corpses that were too numerous to bury. But soldiers also had to come to grips with the carnage they had participated in. Writing about what they saw after a battle, Confederates expressed the same horrified wonderment as did Yankees. A Georgia soldier, for example, described a field where "stiffened bodies lie, grasping in death the arms they bravely bore, with glazed eyes, and features blackened by rapid decay. . . . The air is putrid with decaying bodies of men & horses." And win or lose, soldiers' emotions easily slid into depression. Confederates were especially forthright in admitting their despondency. John Taylor of Tennessee, in retreat from Murfreesboro, watched as "tears traced each other down [the] manly cheeks" of his comrades, and a Louisiana soldier saw that there were "tears stealing down the cheeks of nearly all present" at a prayer service for the dead. The feelings themselves were shared on both sides: nearly three-fourths of the soldiers studied by Frank and Reaves expressed despair after the Battle of Shiloh.

The trauma of battle for unharmed men, however, paled beside the terror and misery of the wounded. Wounded men might lie on the battlefield for hours, sometimes for days, before stretcher-bearers reached them; if the army was in retreat when they were picked up, they would have to endure a long, rough ride before getting medical attention. On the retreat from Gettysburg, an officer in Lee's army saw that "torn and bloody clothing, matted and hardened, was rasping the tender, inflamed, and still oozing wounds" of men riding a wagon; he heard one man cry, "For God's sake, stop just for one minute; take me out and leave me to die on the roadside." Wounded men were little better off when they did reach a hospital. Confederate physicians, like their Union counterparts, had already been fighting a losing battle against disease when they were overwhelmed by combat casualties. The crisis was worse in the Confederate army, which had one surgeon per 324 men compared with the Union's one per 133 (though local physicians helped the Confederates when they could). Confederate surgeons also had to make do with fewer supplies than did Union physicians.

But given medical science's ignorance of the causes underlying disease and infections, shortages of physicians and supplies could prove a blessing. Wounds crawling with maggots, for example, horrified both victims and physicians, and Union surgeons scrupulously removed maggots when they appeared. Yet maggots are efficient cleansers, eating infected tissue while leaving healthy flesh alone. Neglect by frantically overworked medical personnel may thus have saved Confederates such as John Dooley, who lay for days after Gettysburg with maggot-infested wounds. Indeed, despite the difference in physicians and supplies, the Confederate death rate from wounds appears to have been only marginally higher than the 15 percent estimated for Union troops.

Confederate surgeons often performed heroically under impossible conditions. Like Union physicians, some were drunks and some were uncaring, but others were praised as "constant [and] kind" and "a true friend and a Christian Soldier." Hundreds of Southern women served as nurses and hospital matrons, brushing aside initial resistance to their crossing the barrier between female and male worlds. They filled the same maternal role as Northern nurses did, and drew this praise from a Virginia soldier: "May God ever bless them, from the maiden of sixty to the young girl in her teens, [as they] moved like ministering angels among these sufferers." But no amount of care could heal the despondency of some hospitalized soldiers. An observer described the typical sight of a soldier who "had grown hopeless and despairing" in the hospital. "He had lost all control over himself and would cry like a child." Soon he would die "because he had not nervous force enough to hold on to the attenuated thread of life."

Imprisonment caused a different sort of despair among Southern soldiers. Where sickness and wounds made them helpless at the hands of Southerners, capture put Confederates at the mercy of their enemies, leaving them vulnerable to insults and dishonor. The Union housed its prisoners in a variety of forts and stockades, and its policies were guided less by available resources than by reports of conditions at Confederate prisons; indeed, the Union commissary-general of prisons returned $2 million to the federal treasury at war's end. As the Confederacy cut rations for the prisoners it held (and for its troops in the field), the North did likewise for its prisoners. Northern officials and civilians nonetheless believed they were pampering their captives, and they were galled by tales of "sleek fat rebels" in Union prisons. Southerners, for their part, were angered by what they saw as deliberate mistreatment of prisoners in a land of plenty.

Southern prisoners were highly sensitive to the attitude of their captors and were quick to commend officials they saw as honorable. The commandant of Johnson's Island in Lake Erie was praised as "a good friend to the prisoners," and former prisoners paid for a bust to honor the Camp Morton, Indiana, prison head. But far more often inmates denounced Northern prison officials as vicious and corrupt. Officials were accused of shooting prisoners without provocation, soliciting bribes and then punishing the takers, and encouraging African-American guards to humiliate inmates.

Prison stories on both sides were typically exaggerated, but the North did have its own version of Andersonville in the stockade at Elmira, New York, built in 1864 and described by a Texas inmate as "hell on earth." Prisoners, characterized by a camp official as "pale and emaciated, hollow-eyed and dis-spirited," were crowded into barracks and tents that gave little protection from the bitter winter of 1864–1865. Scurvy, dysentery, pneumonia, and smallpox were epidemic, and 25 percent of Elmira's prisoners died, a rate lower than Andersonville's toll of more than 30 percent but nonetheless much worse than the chances of death in battle. Trapped between the continual presence of death and the hope of a prisoner exchange that never came, many inmates of Northern prisons shared the dejection of this North Carolina soldier: "Oh, God, how dreadful are these bitter feelings of hope deferred. I sink almost in madness and despair."

Confederates who stayed out of prison and the hospital underwent changes as well. Southerners became as battle-hardened as Union troops. Samuel Foster, a Texas officer, reported that artillery fire "amounts to nothing. Shelling don't scare us as it used to"; another soldier admitted that gruesome sights "do not affect me as they once did. . . . I look on the carcass of a man now with pretty much the same feeling as I would do were it a horse or hog." And like Yankee soldiers, Confederates began to resist reckless tactics. Soldiers knew that frontal assaults as they were practiced made them easy targets, and their tolerance for such tactics declined.

As early as 1862 a Texas soldier declared that he was "satis-

fied not to make another such charge" as the one at Gaines's
Mill in Virginia. Soldiers' opposition to assaults became increasingly bitter: Samuel Foster charged that John Bell Hood
"virtually murdered 10,000 men around Atlanta" in 1864.
And the men did not simply complain. At Ezra Church,
Georgia, in the same year, the Confederate commander acknowledged that "the attack was a feeble one," and at nearby
Jonesboro a regiment refused to attack because "the men
seemed possessed of some great horror of charging breast-
works." These troops would later participate in the charge at
Franklin, but this would be an exception to soldiers' increasing reluctance to serve as cannon fodder. Like Union troops,
Confederates dug trenches more often as the war went on.
Enlisted men wanted to fight, in the words of a Virginia soldier, in "a very thin gray line . . . back of a thin, red line of
clay." The high command continued to feel otherwise, which
inspired this cheer in the Army of Tennessee: "Hurrah [de-
fense-minded General] Joe Johnston and god D—m Jeff
Davis."

As defeats mounted and Union troops occupied more of
their territory, more Southerners turned to guerrilla warfare.
Guerrillas were not, of course, regular soldiers, but a substantial number of men became guerrillas at one time or another,
and their activities occupied troops and officials on both sides.
Indeed, there were guerilla attacks *against* as well as *for* the
Confederacy, but there were differences between the two
kinds of assault. Anti-Confederate attacks more easily shaded
into pure thievery. Renegade bands, frequently dominated by
Confederate deserters, roamed through areas as far apart as
the North Carolina mountains and the piney woods of southern Mississippi. Sometimes driven by hunger and sometimes
by criminal intent, these bands descended on houses and settlements, stealing anything of value and occasionally shooting

those who resisted, with little regard for victims' political sympathies.

Pro-Confederate guerrillas, who operated closer to Union armies, also did their share of pillaging and terrorizing, especially when they came across Unionists' dwellings. But they had partisan motives that caused them to see themselves as distinct from marauders. Most partisan guerrillas were young men who had not previously been in the Confederate army. William Clarke Quantrill was in his mid-twenties when he formed his guerrilla band; "Bloody Bill" Anderson, the leader of another Missouri band, was twenty when he was gunned down in 1864, and Joe Hart, a notorious guerrilla leader in northwestern Missouri, was eighteen at his death. As historian Michael Fellman points out, guerrillas rejected army discipline for a fancied role as knight-errant, protecting Southern citizens from Yankee savagery. They could tip their hats to women and dutifully write to their parents about their exploits because they were convinced they were simply answering the Yankees, atrocity for atrocity. Determined "to wage the most active war against our brutal invaders," guerrillas ambushed Union soldiers, murdered Unionist civilians, ransacked houses, and attacked churches, typically citing some provocation by the other side to justify themselves.

Guerrillas and renegades provoked increasingly brutal reprisals as the war went on. In 1863, for example, Union cavalrymen surrounded a number of guerrillas in Missouri, "and within fifteen minutes we had exterminated the whole band" except for three wounded men reluctantly taken prisoner. In another incident, Union troops in Tennessee put out the eyes of a captured guerrilla, cut out his tongue, dragged him from a horse until he was dead, and tied his body to a tree. For their part, Confederate troops in the North Carolina mountains, after using torture to extract information from local women, rounded up and shot thirteen suspected Unionist marauders, aged thirteen to sixty.

Battle-hardening among regular Confederate soldiers shaded into hatred for anyone who did not share their role, but with some differences from the Northern experience. Since there was widespread deprivation at home, Southern soldiers were slower to condemn the civilian populace in general than were Northerners; on the other hand, Confederates were quicker to denounce profiteers, those "cowardly scamps" who, according to a Tennessee soldier, preferred to "retire to their feathered couches . . . and ponder in their minds in what maner they can swindle the country."

Indeed, Confederate and Union soldiers had fundamentally different relationships with civilians. Yankees were in enemy territory: if they were exasperated by civilians' treachery, they could retaliate by looting and burning and then insist that the civilians had brought it on themselves. Yet these same civilians were the people Confederates were fighting for. Even if some civilians had more food than soldiers did, most were hardly wealthy; Confederate commanders discouraged plunder, and most of their men let civilians alone. Some soldiers, however, assumed that their country should support its defenders, and they tore down fences for firewood, commandeered livestock, and raided fields and gardens. Civilians were outraged: North Carolina's governor denounced the "half-armed, half-disciplined Confederate Cavalry" as a "plague worse than all others," and a Mississippi farmer lamented, "Lord deliver me from our friends."

Some Confederate soldiers did get the chance to confront Northern civilians. The best-known encounter was General Lee's invasion of Pennsylvania in the summer of 1863. To demonstrate that Confederates were honorable soldiers and not plunderers, Lee tried to keep his men on a tight rein. The soldiers themselves reacted to this glimpse of enemy territory in much the same way as did Yankees in the South. Some Southerners expressed surprise at Pennsylvania's prosperity and admired its people, echoing some Yankee comments on the South. Other Confederates, however, recited criticisms that were essentially a script for Civil War soldiers. As Reid Mitchell points out, if you wanted to disparage your enemies, you sneered at their cleanliness and the appearance of their women. Yankees did it in the South, and now it was the Confederates' turn. A North Carolina general declared that Pennsylvania residents were "coarse and dirty and the number of dirty-looking children is perfectly astonishing," and another soldier claimed that the state had "the largest collection of ugly dirty looking women I ever saw."

When they could avoid the watchful eye of their commanders, many of Lee's soldiers acted in much the same way as they believed Yankees did on Southern soil. Some Confederates could not resist the temptation to take whatever they could carry. A Virginia officer wrote a letter from Pennsylvania, "sitting by a fine rail fire"; he reported that "in spite of orders, [the men] step out at night and help themselves to milk, butter, poultry, and vegetables." Some Confederates went further: to underscore their prowess, they rounded up ex-slaves and free blacks for sale into slavery. These soldiers were willing to defy their leaders to assert Southern power and avenge what they considered to be Yankee cruelties in the South.

As they retreated from their foray into Pennsylvania, more and more of Lee's soldiers thought about religion. Despite the disillusionment, even resignation, of many Confederate chaplains during the early phase of the war, the continued bloodletting sparked a religious revival that swept the Confederate army. In the fall of 1862, after a northward thrust had been turned back at Antietam, Maryland, religious services in Lee's army began to draw ever larger and more enthusiastic turnouts, and the chaplains who were still on hand found they could hardly keep up with requests for prayer services. Local clergymen helped with the preaching, and soldiers showed increasing interest in the religious literature that was distributed in camp. This revival was interrupted by the campaigning of 1863, but it resumed with increased enthusiasm and spread to the western armies in the winter of 1863–1864. Soldiers across the South built scores of chapels in their camps, crowded into them or stood outdoors for services, and converted in large numbers. Preachers would report a hundred conversions in a good day, and one estimate puts the total number of Confederate converts at 150,000. "I have never seen such a spirit as there is now in the army," wrote a Texas chaplain in 1864, and a Louisiana surgeon reported that "from daylight until the late hours of the night nothing is heard but hymns and praying."

Although revivals did occur in the Union army, they were overshadowed by the Confederate awakening in both extent and fervor. Union army conversions have been estimated at about the same number as Confederate converts, but the Union army was more than twice as large. Nor did revivals occur on either home front to match those in the Confederate army.

Why was this awakening primarily a Confederate army event? The revivals have often been attributed to defeat and death: defeats such as Antietam in 1862 and Gettysburg and Vicksburg in 1863 seemed to many Confederates to be God's punishments for their sins, and the carnage on the battlefield made soldiers aware of death's closeness. Yet Lee's army won a major victory at Fredericksburg, Virginia, in late 1862. This victory failed to slow the Confederate revivals, and its appalling Union casualties, which caused commentators to label the battle a "massacre" and a "disaster" for the Union, did not touch off comparable revivals on the other side. Not until the following spring did the more modest Union army awakening begin in earnest.

Historians assume that the accumulation of defeats contributed to the resumption of revivals in 1863–1864, though a Confederate victory at Chickamauga, Georgia, in September 1863 did little to impede the religious urgency. Historian Drew Faust has offered another explanation that helps to account for Confederates' exceptional spiritual interest. The personal, salvation-based religion that was so familiar to Southerners was an ideal remedy for combat stress. The façade of indifference that constituted battle-hardening reduced the outward show of fear, but many soldiers remained inwardly horrified at combat's waste of human lives and terrified of their own death. Instead of denying these emotions, evangelical religion allowed believers to acknowledge and transcend them. A personal assurance of salvation offered reason enough for enduring the mind-numbing terror of warfare: Southern soldiers would thus stand in the rain or in ankle-deep snow for a chance to hear sermons or wait patiently for a preacher to break through a frozen pond for baptisms. The whole thing was simple, according to a Tennessee soldier, who wrote to his wife that "the Cauze of [God's] being my friend [is that] I have ask him for his blessing." Death had lost its terror for him because "we will meat in heaven where there is no ware."

Northern religious beliefs, on the other hand, more often emphasized the individual's duty to state and nation; Union soldiers seldom referred to God as their friend. Reminders of duty did comfort soldiers like Pennsylvanian Milton Ray: "If it is [God's] will that I should sacrifice my life for my country then the Lord Jesus will receive my spirit. Pray that I may be a faithful soldier of the cross and of my country." Yet this belief attracted proportionally fewer soldiers than did the assurance that God was reaching out to provide a personal assurance of salvation to each Confederate believer.

But the consoling power of religion had its limits, even among Southern soldiers. The continuing toll of defeats, combined with worsening shortages of supplies, eventually pushed soldiers beyond the reach of preachers' assurances. Religious enthusiasm among Confederates subsided, especially in the West. Few mentions of chaplains have been found in late-war writings of soldiers. Virginian Alexander Hunter explained: "It is hard to retain religion on an empty stomach; a famine-stricken man gains consolation from no creed." Soldiers did not so much reject religion as exhaust its ability to explain what was happening to them. Many Southern soldiers grew weary of preachers' promises and retreated once again into their battle-hardened shell, convinced they had suffered enough in this war. As Hunter put it, "They had such a hell of a time in this country that the good Lord would not see them damned in the next." Others, convinced they had suffered far too much, gave up on the Southern cause and deserted.

Confederate troops found a number of compelling reasons for deserting. Soldiers might conclude that the Confederacy had abandoned them first: rations were chronically inadequate and were periodically reduced even further, shoes and clothing were constantly in short supply, and soldiers seldom saw a paymaster. Or they might determine that the war was hopeless. A Georgia soldier decided he had seen enough when the Confederates had to abandon Chattanooga, Tennessee, in September 1863: "There is no use fighting any longer no how, for we are done gon up the Spout."

But an especially urgent reason to desert was hardship at home. Many Southern wives were accustomed to a vital role in farming and were prepared to take over while their husbands were in the army, and others received help from neighbors and relatives. Being shorthanded, however, compounded problems that would have been overwhelming even with a husband present. Salt (an essential preservative) and other supplies ran short, causing prices to soar, and armies on both sides routinely helped themselves to the crops that families managed to raise. Wives pleaded with their husbands to return: "Before God, Edward," wrote Mary Cooper of North Carolina, "unless you come home, we must die." A Mississippi soldier, recipient of a similar plea from his family, pointed out that "we are poor men and willing to defend our country but our families [come] first."

And so men left, singly and in groups. Soldiers slipped away from camp at night, dropped out on the march, and refused to return from furloughs; an estimated 104,000 Confederates deserted during the war. Richard Reid's study of North Carolina deserters suggests the potency of home-front conditions in inspiring desertions. Desertion rates were especially high among men in their late twenties, who typically had young children at home, and among men from the northeast part of the state, the area most threatened by Union troops. Desertion was also common among the reluctant soldiers who joined in 1863 and 1864, though leaving had little to do with fear of combat: 70 percent of North Carolina deserters had served for more than a year. Bessie Martin's study of desertion among Alabama troops shows high desertion rates in poorer counties, and historian Victoria Bynum has found that belonging to female-headed households, which had been shorthanded even before the war, raised the likelihood that men in a North Carolina county would desert or evade the draft.

Confederate officials tried to stem the tide of deserters with increasingly severe punishments. As in the Union army, Con-

federates at first depended on public humiliation to deter misbehavior, including desertion. Later, however, leaders overcame their aversion to harsh punishment and increasingly
sentenced deserters to execution. There are no Southern statistics to compare with the Union army, but Confederate authorities may have been harsher on deserters than were Union
commanders. In two multiple executions in 1864, twelve deserters were shot in Georgia and twenty-two were hanged
after being caught in Union uniforms in North Carolina. But
desertions increased right along with executions, and by 1865
the Confederate army had more men absent (most of them
without leave) than were present for duty.

Indeed, the Confederacy had only 160,000 "effectives" in
early 1865, and the number was dwindling rapidly. Why did
anyone remain in the army under these circumstances? The
South had no reenlistment crisis comparable to the Union's in
1864, because in February its Congress simply extended the
terms of three-year men. This act surely encouraged more desertions, but a number of soldiers also took part in symbolic
"reenlistments" to raise morale (and to earn furloughs). Simple duty and patriotism explain much of soldiers' persever-
ance: a Confederate general, for example, felt "honor bound
to fight to the bitter end, unless authorities should direct
otherwise."

Yet there were other motives woven into patriotic sentiments. In a North Carolina study, desertion rates were especially *low* among merchants, professionals such as physicians
and lawyers, and men from slaveholding areas; deserters were
likewise uncommon among slaveholders in Alabama and in a
regiment from Virginia's "black belt." Men from the Southern
gentry undoubtedly fought on because they could not bear the
destruction of their society—an ordered society with proper-
tied gentlemen at the top, setting an example of leadership for

all white men. Yankees promised to take away their property and their right to lead, and to make blacks equal with whites—a society not worth living in. Other soldiers found their loyalty to state and country mixed with loyalty to comrades. Deserting a doomed cause was one thing, but abandoning comrades, the only people who truly understood what soldiers had endured, was unthinkable. And so men made agonizing choices between conflicting ways of surviving, conflicting duties, and conflicting loyalties.

The Confederate armies that surrendered in the spring of 1865 were a shadow of their former strength. Four regiments of the Army of Tennessee, for example, had once numbered more than 1,000 men each; when they surrendered in North Carolina in late April the four regiments amounted to 179 ragged soldiers. They and other Confederates turned in most of their weapons, signed an oath of allegiance to the federal government, and made their way home as best they could. Where possible they took riverboats or railroads, but most Southern transportation had been wrecked during the war; many officers still had their horses, but the majority of ex-soldiers had to walk home, begging for food or breaking into army storehouses as they went. Sixty thousand Confederates were also released from Northern prisons and awaited transportation southward.

5

Union Veterans in Postwar America

UNION SOLDIERS WERE still in the army even though the fighting was over. The federal government intended to demobilize most of the million remaining soldiers, but they would have to be assembled in places where their discharge records could be processed and they could be paid. The two main armies—the Army of the Potomac and Sherman's Army of Georgia—were to go to Washington, D.C., and then to their original mustering-in camps, after first marching in a mass parade in the capital.

Northern soldiers also had to endure one more shock—the assassination of Abraham Lincoln on April 14, 1865. The shooting enraged Union troops and led to reprisals against Confederates, but commanders controlled vengeful soldiers until they again turned their attention homeward. Sherman's army had much the longer journey to Washington, and officers, competing to be the first to complete the trip, drove their exhausted men northward in some of the most grueling marches of the war.

Union soldiers were ambivalent about going home. Although they had continued to revere their own homes and families even as they became alienated from the home front in general, two worries nagged at soldiers when going home became a reality. They feared that the war had changed them too much. Charles Willis of Illinois suspected that his army experience "unfits me for civil life. . . . I have almost a dread of being a citizen, of trying to be sharp, and trying to make money." Willis was certain that "citizens are not like soldiers." Going out into this alien world created another dilemma— leaving the only people who truly knew what a soldier's life was. Sergeant Richard Reeves, for one, admitted that "it seemed like breaking up a family to separate."

In the armies marching to Washington, some soldiers were also less than thrilled about the Grand Review in the capital. "We are tired & sick of Reviews already & never wish to see another as long as we live," wrote a Connecticut soldier, and another called the parade "our grand foolery." But these were young men who had just saved the Union; they did not mean to let a few misgivings and some formalities prevent them from resuming their lives.

The Grand Review was a panorama of the Union military experience. Like the army, it was enormous—200,000 troops marched down Pennsylvania Avenue on May 23 and 24, 1865. The parade also reflected regional differences within the army. Habits of self-control had made their greatest inroads in the Northeastern states, and the greatest admirers of discipline in the army were Easterners, from New Yorker George Mc-Clellan to Eastern enlisted men. Westerners were more in-clined, as an Eastern soldier complained, to "laxity of discipline and personal appearances." The animosity contin-ued after the Confederate surrender, as Eastern and Western soldiers got into brawls on the march to Washington.

In the Grand Review the predominantly Eastern Army of the Potomac marched on May 23 in new uniforms with pol-ished brass and white dress gloves. The next day Sherman's soldiers, nearly half of whom were Westerners, showed their disdain for discipline. They paraded past the president and other high officials much as they had marched through Georgia—in shabby uniforms and ruined shoes, carrying some of their booty, including cattle, live chickens, a litter of pigs, and a goat. According to an observer, Sherman's men "chatted, laughed and cheered, just as they pleased, all along the route of the march."

The Review also reflected the army's official view of the war as a white men's crusade. During the war both armies represented in the Review had included African-American troops, but only a few black soldiers (employed as teamsters or manual laborers) appeared in the parade. Official discomfort over the exemplary contribution of black troops would endure for decades.

The War Department found another role for black soldiers that it thought was more appropriate than marching in parades. Recognizing that most whites would probably refuse to serve past the end of the war, and believing that soldiers' rations and pay would help men who had recently been slaves, federal officials decided to keep large numbers of black troops in the army for duty in the South. While white soldiers were collecting their pay and making final preparations to go home, black troops were on their way to the land from which many had escaped. The troops were to keep the peace and to assist the recently created Freedmen's Bureau in protecting ex-slaves' rights. Most black soldiers were still under the direction of white officers; the few African Americans who served as officers during and after the war were primarily surgeons and chaplains.

Black soldiers were sometimes successful in their new assignment: an observer in the South noted that "when colored Soldiers are about [whites] are afraid to kick colored women and abuse colored people in the Streets, as they usually do." But black soldiers were just as often unable even to protect themselves against resentful Southerners. White gangs assaulted and murdered black troops in a number of Southern towns, a Virginia resident tried to poison a black unit's well, and some South Carolinians ambushed a train carrying a black regiment.

Under these conditions, signs of strain appeared between black enlisted men and white officers. Chafing at peacetime duty, officers occasionally vented their frustration by harshly punishing their men, and the troops sometimes fought back. One black regiment forcibly freed some of its members from punishment, and another group of soldiers exchanged gunfire with its officers after a dispute over discipline. The mutinies were put down and the participants imprisoned or executed, but the incidents show that black soldiers had become schooled in activism as well as in warfare. An observer noted that "no negro who has ever been a soldier can again be imposed upon; they have learnt what it is to be free and they will infuse their feelings into others." Indeed, a significant number of Union army veterans were among the African Americans who became legislators and members of Congress while the Republican party controlled Southern states in the late 1860s and early 1870s.

Eventually black units were demobilized, but ex-soldiers were hardly safe from whites' wrath. In May 1866 a white mob in Memphis attacked newly discharged soldiers, killing forty-six and injuring more than seventy others. And if they went north, African-American veterans could anticipate hostility from Northern whites.

Black veterans, however, were not the only soldiers who faced a suspicious Northern society: civilians were as ambivalent about veterans as the soldiers had been about coming home. Civilians were glad that the war was over, but they feared the worst from men who had been living by the dictates of war rather than the rules of civilization. The author Nathaniel Hawthorne worried that "when the soldiers returned the quiet rural life of the New England villages would be spoiled and coarsened," and a newspaper editor acknowledged "the belief that the army has acted as a school of demoralization."

Returning soldiers provided some evidence for these fears. Ex-soldiers looted and brawled in New York, Washington, and elsewhere in the summer of 1865; former soldiers, upset at being denied a promised bonus, went on an arson spree in Madison, Wisconsin, in 1866. Prison officials across the country reported a sharp increase in inmates, asserted that most of them were ex-soldiers, and blamed army life for the crime wave. Historians have generally agreed that the war corrupted soldiers and thus contributed to postwar crime. A more complete look at the evidence undermines this explanation. Crime did increase after the war, but the country experienced crime waves in the 1850s and during the war as well. The homicide rate, which should reflect the activities of army-trained killers, steadily *fell* after the war and showed a steep rise only in 1870 before falling again. Indeed, the sharpest rise in all crimes occurred in 1870. Why criminal tendencies bred by military service would have revealed themselves in a single outburst five years after Appomattox is difficult to explain. Also of note is that many crimes following demobilization were *against* soldiers: thieves and swindlers often descended on soldiers' discharge points, robbing and fleecing veterans of their mustering-out pay.

A problem that lasted longer was soldiers' addiction to drugs and alcohol. Army surgeons' sympathy for suffering patients had led them to dispense morphine freely, creating an addiction in many of the recipients. After the war, physicians gave additional morphine to already addicted veterans and introduced others to the drug in order to treat the lingering pain of wounds (and occasionally to relieve the aftereffects of combat stress). There were numerous civilian addicts as well, but morphine dependency nonetheless became known as "the army disease," and in 1879 an army surgeon estimated that 45,000 veterans were addicted to morphine.

Public misgivings about the character of returning Union soldiers thus had some basis, but they were nevertheless exaggerated. Criminals and addicts were a small fraction of the roughly 1.5 million Union soldiers who survived the war and had not deserted the army. Yet even men who returned without criminal tendencies or addiction encountered a mixed reception. Evidence indicates that if they were white, and if they reached home soon enough, veterans at least found employment. Rhode Island took a census in June 1865, when about half its soldiers were back from the war—some discharged during the war for disability or expired enlistments, plus the first men mustered out following the surrender. In a sample of men from this census, there are no appreciable differences between the occupations of white veterans and civilians.

The fortunes of African Americans, however, were different. Black veterans in Rhode Island were four times as likely to be unemployed as were white *veterans*, and five times as likely to be jobless as black *civilians*. White soldiers who were discharged early enough could find work in the vigorous wartime economy, but black men were closed out of most occupations that benefited from war production. When a black veteran came to Providence or Newport, he had to compete with other African Americans for whatever work became available for porters, day laborers, or other unskilled workers.

Veterans who came home later in 1865, whether they were black or white, had a more difficult time. Roughly 300,000 sol-

diers were discharged each month at the height of demobilization in mid-1965, and by the year's end nearly a million
men had been released. Information comparable to the Rhode
Island census is unavailable for these later returnees, but there
is evidence that increasing numbers of veterans were going
jobless. Situation-wanted advertisements began appearing in
newspapers, and the United States Sanitary Commission,
which had assisted in medical care during the war, opened
employment bureaus to place veterans in jobs. In New York,
veterans formed their own employment agency. Yet veterans
poured into the cities faster than jobs opened. In August 250
veterans staged a march in New York, with banners proclaim-
ing "Looking for Bread & Work," and the following winter a
city official reported seeing several hundred veterans, "homeless, houseless, and hungry," with "no food, save the cold vict-
uals obtained by begging."

This crisis passed; employment became available for some
of the seekers, while others traveled west and south, taking
work as farmhands, teamsters, miners, or whatever else they
could find. We must remember that the North was still
largely rural. Many discharged soldiers shared the experience
of Lieutenant Leander Stillwell, who hitched a wagon ride
from the train station and then walked the last nine miles
to his parents' farm in Illinois. The next day Stillwell was
out cutting corn, feeling "as if I had been away only a day
or two, and had just taken up the farm work where I had
left off."

But trouble could still develop for soldiers who returned to
home and family. There is evidence of a high postwar divorce
rate among officers who had served with the U.S. Colored
Troops, and some states likewise showed a sharp rise in di-
vorces, led by Ohio's 40 percent increase from 1865 to 1866.
On the other hand, as usually happens after a war, most states

also recorded an increase in marriages—Ohio, for example, had nearly a 40 percent increase in the number of marriages in the same year.

Veterans' joblessness and psychological problems eventually aroused considerable sympathy—newspapers in the first year after the war carried numerous descriptions of destitute ex-soldiers and described veterans' suicides—but these troubles by themselves inspired little government action. Many veterans did, however, have a problem that was widely recognized as deserving of public help—physical disability. More than 200,000 soldiers had returned with wounds, and many other veterans continued to suffer from diseases they contracted in the army, from chronic diarrhea to tuberculosis. It had long been a principle of American government that disabled veterans were entitled to public aid, and Abraham Lincoln had underscored the commitment with a promise "to care for him who shall have borne the battle." To fulfill this obligation, the federal government expanded on the two customary methods of caring for disabled soldiers.

Pensions were the usual form of compensation for war wounds. Poor and disabled veterans from previous wars had received pensions, and in 1862 Congress authorized pensions for Union soldiers. A veteran could receive $8 to $30 a month, depending on rank, for "total disability" incurred in the line of duty (or a portion of these amounts for partial disability), and soldiers' widows could also qualify for a pension. Lawmakers soon began to amend the payment provisions, adding new categories of payment for specific disabilities such as loss of a hand, loss of a foot, loss of a hand *and* a foot, and so on. Applying for a pension could be cumbersome (if a soldier's disability was not obvious, for example, a physician would have to verify it), and many veterans were unaware of pensions, so relatively few ex-soldiers applied at first. Fewer than 10 percent of

Union veterans were on the pension rolls through the 1860s and 1870s. A change in the law in 1879, however, dramatically opened up the pension system. Until then, payments began when a claim was approved by the Pension Bureau, and were dated from the time of application and not from the soldier's discharge (or his death, in the case of a widow). For example, a soldier who learned about pensions in 1875 and had a claim approved the next year would receive nothing for the ten years he had been out of the army. Pensions that were retroactive to the date of discharge or death would attract thousands of new applicants, a fact understood by pension attorneys and claims agents. These individuals assisted veterans and widows in submitting applications in exchange for a fee, and they led a campaign for retroactive pensions in the late 1870s. Although pension attorneys were roundly detested as "the worst class of vermin that ever infested the body-politic," politicians of both parties were intrigued by the voting power represented by disabled veterans. Republicans sought to solidify the loyalty of ex-soldiers to the party of Abraham Lincoln, and Democrats, restored to national potency after the readmission of Southern states to the Union, wished to affirm their own patriotism. As a result, Northern members of Congress voted almost unanimously for the "arrears bill" of 1879, which authorized lump-sum retroactive payments to current pensioners and those filing new claims before mid-1880. The retroactive payments averaged roughly $1,000, and veterans filed more than nine thousand new claims a month in 1879 and 1880, versus about sixteen hundred a month previously; the proportion of veterans who were on the pension rolls more than doubled during the 1880s.

Yet even a generous pension system could not meet the needs of all disabled veterans. Federal officials had for some time recognized that some veterans were homeless or so disabled that they required institutional care; before the Civil War the government had operated homes for soldiers and sailors who were disabled or had served at least twenty years. Local governments and charities, including the Sanitary Commission, operated shelters for needy soldiers during the Civil War, and by war's end a number of politicians, business leaders, and social reformers were calling for a permanent asylum for volunteer soldiers. One advocate insisted that disabled ex-soldiers "should have a nation's gratitude, a nation's care, and a place in the nation's household, a seat by the nation's fireside." Congress agreed, and in March 1865 it authorized creation of a national asylum for Union veterans. By the end of 1870 branches had opened in Maine, Ohio, Wisconsin, and Virginia, and had admitted more than 3,200 ex-soldiers. About 1,400 veterans entered the homes each year in the 1870s and early 1880s; when old age was classified as a disability after 1884, yearly admissions nearly doubled, and more branch homes were added to the system. A number of Northern states established their own soldiers' homes in the 1880s, and some admitted soldiers' wives and widows as well as the veterans themselves.

Ex-soldiers applied in person or in writing to the homes, and were admitted, if space was available, when the management had verified their service record and, in the early decades, determined that their disability was war-related. The homes furnished barracks for sleeping quarters and provided residents with medical care, food, uniforms, and other supplies. The men spent their time tending their institution's farm, reading in the library, working in the laundry or blacksmith shop, or, in the early years, taking classes. They could leave the institution when they felt able and could return with permission.

But this was not a carefree life. Government officials were as wary of ex-soldiers as was the rest of society. The Sanitary Commission, which initially had been skeptical of soldiers' homes, warned that the institutions would fill up with "foreigners, the reckless and unrelated, those who have hitherto been afloat, . . . or [those who] have least natural force to provide for themselves." Even though veterans' advocates tried to differentiate ex-soldiers from inmates of poorhouses, they could not help viewing veterans as akin to other nineteenth-century dependent groups who were generally assumed to be suffering from a moral weakness that could be cured by instilling self-discipline. Since ex-soldiers were already familiar with army discipline, the ideal policy for soldiers' homes was to give them more of it. The only way the homes would work, the Sanitary Commission believed, was to make them "military in their organization, control, dress, [and] drill." Residents thus arose to reveille, ate at mess tables, were organized into companies, and were given furloughs and honorable or dishonorable discharges.

But many residents of soldiers' homes did not consider themselves to be military men—they were civilians who had had their health ruined while fighting for the common good. Union soldiers had grudgingly tolerated military discipline in time of war, but they were unlikely to accept the same regimentation to please a staff of administrators. A chaplain at the home in Dayton, Ohio, explained the residents' attitude: "They want to forget the past. Their series of affliction, the breaking up of their families, and their mental and physical disabilities, put them in a position which causes them to absolutely hate anything military. . . . They feel that military discipline is irksome."

As a result, residents often resisted the homes' discipline, in ways that ranged from trivial defiance to outright challenge.

They stole from the kitchen, missed roll calls, and got drunk, which annoyed the managers, and they protested the handling of pensions, which made management furious. Soldiers' homes often withheld part or all of the payments due to resident pensioners, seeing the policy as essential to proper discipline. According to one home's managers, "as soon as they receive their quarterly payments [many residents] go outside and spend it all on drink." Residents often saw it otherwise. They believed they had earned their pensions just as they had earned admittance to a soldiers' home, and the managers had no right to take their money.

Residents thus protested individually and in groups: in Maine in 1869 and Pennsylvania in 1891, sizable groups of residents walked out to protest pension withholding, and the managers of the Wisconsin state home declared that "no one thing during the life of the Home has done so much to create friction among the members and cause them to become dissatisfied" as had the pension issue. Indeed, samples of federal and state soldiers' home residents from the 1880s and 1890s show that the higher a veteran's pension, the more likely he was to leave after only a few months in a home. Managers did keep the upper hand: they could hand out punishments ranging from revocation of furlough privileges to a dishonorable discharge, so order prevailed in the homes. The cost, however, was bitterness among residents—John Garrigan, at the Dayton federal home, reported that "often I wish I was in the penitentiary [or] that I was hanged or dead"—and undoubted hardships for many of those who left the homes in protest.

Although veterans vigorously defended their entitlement to public compensation for their disabilities, they also tried to deal with misfortune through a revival of their wartime comradeship. In addition to individual efforts to help fellow veterans obtain work, veterans tried to organize for companionship and mutual aid. Most of these groups were short-lived, except for the Grand Army of the Republic, founded in Illinois in 1866. The GAR combined military forms (annual meetings were encampments, misbehavior was adjudicated by courts-martial, and meetings were guarded by sentries, for example) and the secret rituals of fraternal orders like the Masons and the Odd Fellows. As Stuart McConnell points out in his study of the Grand Army, the founders hoped to line up soldier-voters behind Republican candidates and to keep alive the army spirit of mutual aid; veterans themselves also saw meetings as ideal occasions for socializing. Soon after the GAR's founding, local "posts" sprang up around the country, but interest in the organization dwindled by the end of the 1860s.

After a brief period of interest in the war, Americans settled into a decade in which they were more anxious to forget the conflict than to relive it, thus dampening interest in veterans' groups. The GAR hurt its own cause by introducing a system of membership ranks that offended members who believed that wartime ranks were distinction enough among veterans. The order's national membership languished at about thirty thousand through most of the 1870s.

But the Grand Army underwent an extraordinary revival in the 1880s. Civilians rekindled their interest in literature and observances having to do with the Civil War; and the GAR made itself more accessible by dropping some of the more painful Civil War symbolism (a prisoner-of-war blanket, for example, and a firing-squad reenactment) and emphasizing instead a spirit of fraternity among members. Although the GAR had had little to do with passage of the Arrears Act of 1879, the act itself stimulated interest in veterans' groups. Spurred by these developments, membership in the GAR rebounded dramatically, to 60,000 in 1880, 270,000 in 1885, and to a peak in 1890 at more than 400,000 members.

Other veterans' groups arose in the 1880s, but they were more exclusive than the GAR (for example, the Union Veteran Legion limited its membership to veterans who had served for at least two years or been wounded) or were single-issue lobbying groups (such as the Service Pension Association). The composition of GAR posts generally reflected the men in their communities. Some urban posts drew from the business community and charged high dues and "muster fees"; their membership thus consisted largely of professionals and merchants who belonged to—or clerks and bookkeepers who wanted to belong to—the commercial elite. Posts in working-class or rural areas, on the other hand, contained large numbers of manual laborers or farmers, and charged lower dues and fees. Even these posts tended to select local business leaders as officers (for example, post commander or adjutant), and working-class posts seldom took a position on labor issues.

The GAR engaged in a variety of activities. Its meetings, from post gatherings to state and national encampments, were valued chances for socializing. The author Hamlin Garland's father would not dream of missing a post meeting, and at a national encampment "he was like a boy on Circus Day." Charity for needy comrades was also central to the Grand Army. Funds raised through fees and donations bought food, paid the rent, and covered the funeral expenses of destitute veterans and widows, and members provided in-kind benefits such as medical care to comrades in need. GAR men also gave preference to members in hiring or in patronizing businesses, and the organization was instrumental in convincing states to fund veterans' pensions and soldiers' homes.

The Grand Army also served as a disseminator of self-control. Ideal GAR members were, according to a founder, "trained, drilled and disciplined gentlemen," though sometimes this ideal had to be enforced. Drunkenness, that cardinal loss of self-control, was also the most common infraction brought before courts-martial. Members of a court-martial could hand down punishments that included censure and dishonorable discharge. Courts-martial were infrequent, but they demonstrated prominent Union veterans' continuing concern with order and self-control—qualities they believed were lacking in civilian society and must be promoted that much more vigorously among the men who had preserved the Union.

The GAR was, however, noticeably uncomfortable with some of the nation's saviors. Some Northern posts had a few African-American members, but black leadership over white veterans was unthinkable; separate black and white posts were the rule where black veterans were numerous. The South also had GAR posts to serve the substantial population of Union veterans who had moved there after the war. These posts were especially hostile to black veterans, and their virtually all-white membership went unchallenged until the late 1880s. When black veterans tried to organize Southern posts, white Southerners first refused to charter them and then insisted on separate "departments" (administrative units of one or more states) to avoid any chance of African Americans commanding whites. The national leadership rejected this segregation but was unable to enforce its decision; Southern members maintained segregated departments. In the 1890s the attitude of the GAR's leaders was largely the attitude of soldiers during the war—they condemned the grosser forms of racial oppression but were unwilling to make a priority of ending them.

The order's views on women were similar. George Lemon, a Washington pension attorney and unofficial GAR spokesman, published a number of endorsements of women's rights in his weekly newspaper, the *National Tribune*. Lemon condemned wife abuse, called for more egalitarian marriages, and cheered the admission of women to practice as lawyers. But within the GAR, women were expected to be the same faithful supporters they had been during the war—to raise funds, make flags, serve food, and otherwise sustain their men. The Grand Army established a Woman's Relief Corps in 1881 to allow women to perform these duties while remaining safely separate from and subordinate to the main organization.

The GAR's most notorious activity was its pension lobbying. The Arrears Act of 1879, in addition to encouraging a flurry of pension applications, also sorted out the key actors in the emerging pension debate. Lemon and his fellow pension attorneys could be counted on for enthusiastic support of anything that would increase applications. Among politicians, Republicans most consistently cast their lot with veterans: Republicans represented Lincoln's party, and they realized that Democrats' current insistence on governmental cost-cutting could be portrayed as meanness directed at ex-soldiers.

And veterans' leaders, invigorated by the GAR's growth, underwent a change of philosophy. In the organization's early years, leaders had essentially agreed with the basis of pension law—that pensions were compensation for disabilities caused by service to the government, and that veterans' life after the war was a separate existence. In the 1880s, however, leading veterans' spokesmen changed their view—now it was once a soldier, always a soldier. Some veterans' advocates pressed for a pension for all disabled ex-soldiers, whether or not the disability had been incurred in the war; others went even further and demanded a "service" pension, a payment to all ex-soldiers and widows simply for the men's service to their country. A universal service pension could not draw enough congressional support to pass, so pension advocates set their sights on what became known as a "dependent" pension, since disabled veterans depended on someone else for support. In 1887 Congress passed a dependent pension bill, providing for a $12 pension per month for fully disabled Union veterans, and sent it to President Grover Cleveland, a Democrat.

Cleveland, viewing the bill as an administrative nightmare and a raid on the federal treasury, vetoed it. Veterans' advocates already detested the president for having hired a substitute in the war, and when Cleveland tried to return captured Confederate flags later in 1887, leading veterans made a crusade of unseating him at the next election. Republicans and veterans' spokesmen focused special attention on Indiana and New York, "swing states" in contemporary elections. "Corporal" James Tanner, a GAR official and tireless veterans' activist, concentrated on Indiana, where he boasted that he "plastered the state with promises" of pension increases under a Republican administration.

The Republicans nominated former general Benjamin Harrison for president in 1888 and promised pensions "so enlarged and extended as to provide against the possibility that any man who honorably wore the Federal uniform should become the inmate of an almshouse or dependent on private charity." Democrats, on the other hand, promised to govern by "carefully guarding the interests of the taxpayers." Cleveland won the popular vote in the election, but the distribution of the votes, including wins in New York and Indiana, gave Harrison the victory in the electoral college.

Did veterans put their comrade in the White House? It is impossible to know for certain how individuals voted, but we can estimate their behavior with reasonable accuracy. Such an estimate for the crucial state of Indiana can be made from its distribution of veterans, GAR members, and vote totals. At the time of the 1888 election, Indiana had 63,000 veterans, 24,000 of whom were GAR members. As we would expect, an estimate of GAR members' voting shows a considerable Republican majority—virtually all members turned out to vote, and they voted more than two-to-one for Harrison. Indiana veterans who did not belong to the GAR, however, voted quite differently: like noncombatants, non-GAR veterans divided evenly between Cleveland and Harrison. The political activism and soldier-first attitude of the GAR applied primarily to those who joined the order; in their voting behavior, the large number of veterans who did not join were scarcely distinguishable from the nonveteran population.

Veterans' dominance of politics reached its peak under Harrison. Congress revived the dependent pension legislation, modified it to call for a scale of payments from $6 to $12 a month depending on the degree of a veteran's disability, and sent it to the president in 1890; Harrison eagerly signed it. Veterans could now earn a pension if they were disabled for almost any reason (except from "their own vicious habits"), and widows could qualify if their husband had died from any cause. The result was a tidal wave of new applications. More than 650,000 claims were filed in the new law's first year, creating an enormous backlog of paperwork at the Pension Bureau in spite of its efforts to ease the investigation of claims.

Even before the new law had passed, Harrison named Corporal Tanner commissioner of pensions, allegedly telling him to "be liberal with the boys." Tanner's militant promises of "a pension for every old soldier who needs one" drew protests from politicians and newspaper editors and he was forced to resign, but his successor, another GAR official, was similarly generous in approving pension applications. The proportion of applications approved was higher under Harrison than it had been under Cleveland, and there is evidence that approvals under both presidents were aimed at shoring up political support. One study found that new pensions in Ohio during the Harrison administration went primarily to strong Republican areas; another study found a similar Democratic bias in Indiana in the previous Cleveland administration. By the end of Harrison's term more than 70 percent of veterans were on the pension rolls, compared with approximately 20 percent in 1885.

But Republicans had gone beyond the limits of acceptable compensation to veterans. Generosity to ex-soldiers had opponents as well as supporters, and foes became increasingly irate during the Harrison administration. Commissioner Tanner had been denounced as "a loud-mouthed Grand Army stump speaker," and a commentator decried the "indiscriminate and lavish distribution of pensions" under the Dependent Pension Act. Another pension opponent declared that "the ex-Union soldier is coming to stand in the public mind for a helpless and greedy sort of person, who says that he is not able to support himself, and whines that other people ought to do it for him." Public displeasure with the pension explosion offset veterans' loyalty to the Republican party and helped Cleveland regain the White House in 1892. Cleveland immediately moved to crack down on pension approvals: his pension commissioner cut the number of applications approved to about seven hundred a month in his first full year, compared with more than six thousand a month in Harrison's last year.

By this time the influence of veterans in presidential politics was fading. Although Congress would periodically increase pension coverage and payments, Republicans no longer made generosity to veterans the centerpiece of their platforms, and veterans' leaders no longer concentrated their energies on expanding pensions. Indeed, the GAR began to lose members in the 1890s. Although the decline was nothing like the explosive growth of the 1880s, the organization did lose nearly a third of its membership in the 1890s, reflecting a waning interest as well as the dying off of members. The Grand Army had been instrumental in making pensions available to the majority of ex-soldiers, and many saw no further need for the organization; others, however, remained in the order because it offered a way of coping with the passing of their generation.

This passing became an increasing reality for Union veterans in the 1890s. By mid-decade most ex-soldiers were in their fifties, too young to stop working (especially in a country that was just beginning to develop a concept of retirement), but old enough to have a full generation between them and the Civil War. Veterans' children had reached adulthood and most were on their own by the 1890s: 90 percent of men in their mid-fifties had no children under sixteen living with them.

And the nation was changing as ex-soldiers looked on. The United States population was becoming younger and more foreign-born as millions of immigrants came from southern and eastern Europe, and the economy was becoming increasingly dominated by huge, impersonal corporations. The growth of cities and wage employment, whose insecurity many men had tried to escape by enlisting in the 1860s, had continued beyond anyone's expectations: New York City, for example, had nearly tripled in size since 1860, and across the country the number of wage workers in manufacturing had quadrupled. Although interest in Civil War generals and battles continued through the 1890s, many veterans undoubtedly believed that the nation they had saved was becoming dangerously unrecognizable.

As they approached old age in this disturbing society, many Union veterans worried about their legacy. They believed they had made a unique contribution to the nation and had a unique responsibility to preserve their heritage. This meant more than rehashing Civil War battles; it also meant recreating the kind of nation that veterans believed they had saved—a nation characterized by order, discipline, and vigorous patriotism. This was a highly idealized version of antebellum and wartime conditions, but it was a vision that the GAR had long nurtured in its rituals and procedures.

In the 1890s the GAR focused direct attention on the veterans' legacy. The organization began a campaign to instill in schoolchildren the values it saw as essential to reviving a virtuous and orderly society. GAR leaders worked to ensure that history textbooks portrayed the Civil War as a vindication of national unity against the forces of rebellion. They insisted on making the flag a sacred icon, urging schools to use the Pledge of Allegiance and lobbying to make Flag Day a holiday, and GAR officials agitated for military drill for schoolboys. The GAR also applauded the Spanish-American War, portraying this series of one-sided engagements as a fulfillment of the Civil War's patriotic heritage.

At the same time Union veterans were also reconciling with their old adversaries: Blue-Gray battlefield reunions and memorial services had become common events by the turn of the century. Some GAR posts objected to such fraternization as a betrayal of patriotism, but the prevailing view was that, as they had during the war, soldiers on both sides continued to share a bond that could be distinguished from their causes. The *National Tribune* summarized this reasoning when it praised Confederate soldiers for their "manly daring, fortitude, and devotion to an idea (though a wrong one)."

6

Confederate Veterans in the Postwar South

THERE WERE NO grand parades for Confederate soldiers. Their army, and the government that had employed it, ceased to exist at the surrender, and most of them had to make their own way home. When they arrived they found changes that added to the traumas of their army experience.

Although it may seem that no peacetime experience could have the effect that the miseries of army life and the horrors of combat had, we must put the war's psychological impact into perspective. The coarsening of soldiers was real enough, but it also had limits. James McPherson found no significant change during the war in Union or Confederate soldiers' patriotic sentiments. And cultural historian Michael Barton, looking for evidence of a more elemental kind of change in soldiers' diaries, found no trends in Confederates' *identity* during the war. If soldiers had associated themselves with the Confederacy more or less often as the war progressed, or if they had begun to substitute "we" for "I" in personal references, we might conclude that they had indeed become fundamentally different individuals. Yet there was no variation over time in the way they identified themselves; Confederate soldiers came home battle-toughened but not fundamentally altered.

But the society they rejoined was profoundly changing. Part of the change was economic: whites were confronted with a population of freedpeople they would have to employ rather than own, and struggling farmers would have to depend more than ever on cotton and on the merchants who controlled the flow of cash and credit. Part was political: Southerners would have to restructure their governments under the watchful eye of Northern authorities. And perhaps the greatest change of all was the legacy of defeat. White Southerners had long been convinced of their superiority and fiercely protective of their security, but now they were saddled with defeat and uncertainty. In the wake of the Confederate surrender, no one knew what to expect next. Punishment of the war's participants, seizure of land, reprisals by resentful Unionists and former slaves—anything was possible.

Confederate veterans, who were in a position to feel the sting of defeat more painfully than others, reacted in a number of ways. Some preached emigration and tried to start colonies in Latin America and elsewhere. Only a few thousand former Confederates left the country, however, and none of their settlements lasted very long. Other Confederates pulled up stakes for more modest moves, but most were unwilling to leave the South. When federal census-takers first identified Civil War veterans in 1890, only 7 percent of Confederates were living outside the former slave states; in contrast, liberalized land-grant policies for Union veterans encouraged them to move, and nearly 15 percent were living outside what had been the wartime Union. For Confederates, Texas was the one great magnet. Here were vast amounts of land in a former Confederate state; an Alabama woman wrote that her neighbors were "anxious to go to Texas where a great many think they can live without work." By 1890 Texas was home to more Confederate veterans than any other state, despite having been only sixth in population in the wartime Confederacy.

Many veterans, however, returned home intending to stay. In a sample of military-age men in Mississippi, nearly 40 percent of veterans who had survived the war were still in the same county in 1870 as in 1860. This may seem low, but only about 20 percent of noncombatants remained in their prewar county. Veterans may have provided much of what continuity Southern communities possessed.

But reactions to defeat were not confined to decisions about moving. Defeat was an affront to soldiers' manhood, and some Southern veterans took out their anger on civilian society. Veterans played a major role in the violence and lawlessness that erupted across the South soon after the war's end. Former soldiers ransacked Confederate army storehouses, assaulted and robbed civilians, attacked Unionists, and settled old scores with personal enemies. The provisional governor of Texas declared that "human life in Texas is not to day worth as much, so far as law or protection can give value to it, as that of domestic cattle," and in 1866 a Northern observer reported that "Mississippians have been shooting and cutting each other all over the state." Some marauders envisioned themselves as "regulators" who were punishing criminals, and outlaw bands included noncombatants as well as ex-soldiers, but much of the violence in the postwar months consisted of random aggression by defeated veterans with little to lose.

Yet most veterans did not become renegades. A more common Confederate reaction to defeat was a benumbed apathy. Southern men noticed it in themselves: Thomas Harrold of Georgia wrote that "it sometimes appears to me as if my vitality and energy were all gone." Women noticed it: Ella

Thomas, also of Georgia, remarked that her husband, a former cavalry officer, was "cast down, utterly spirit broken," and Kate Stone of Louisiana observed that her recently returned brother "rarely talks at all" and "seems to take little interest in hearing others." And freedpeople noticed it: an ex-slave from Alabama recalled that ex-soldiers were "all lookin' sick. De sperrit dey lef' wid jus' been done whupped outen dem."

This apathy was especially evident in the first postwar elections. In 1865 Southern states rewrote their constitutions to reflect the demise of slavery and the Confederacy, and voters chose state and local officials for postwar governments. Elections before the war had drawn considerable interest, and turnouts of three-quarters or more of white men were common. The elections of 1865, however, attracted fewer than half as many Southern voters as had the elections of 1860. Southern apathy toward politics was widespread, but there is evidence that Confederate veterans were particularly disinterested. The Mississippi town of Kosciusko, for example, held an election for local officials in December 1865 and left behind a list of voters. The town had 98 white men, nearly half of whom were Confederate veterans, but only three of the twelve candidates for office were ex-soldiers. Four in ten nonveterans voted in the election, a turnout that was in line with overall Southern figures, but fewer than three in ten veterans bothered to vote, and only one veteran was elected to office.

Veterans played a more complex role in statewide politics. Historians have noted that most of the men elected in 1865 and 1866 had been political moderates in 1861, and had opposed secession. But many of them were also former Confederate soldiers or government officials who had cast their lot with the South in spite of their views. Among those elected to take seats in Congress, presuming their states were to be readmitted, were ten former Confederate generals and the Confederate vice-president. Were voters thus seeking to continue the Civil War on the legislative front?

Evidence from Mississippi suggests that voters in 1865 looked for leadership rather than simple Confederate patriotism. In races for state representative where voters had a choice between veterans and nonveterans, being an ex-soldier made little difference in a candidate's chances of winning. On the other hand, if the candidate had been a Confederate *officer*, his chances of winning a seat were three times those of other candidates. Having exceptional wealth or a professional occupation, the traditional paths to community leadership, likewise tripled a candidate's chances of being elected. Confederate veterans actually made the contests for the Mississippi House more "democratic" than they had been before the war: a number of veterans of modest means ignored the climate of apathy and entered the races, hoping their service would commend them to the voters. But in this period of confusion and insecurity, voters were more interested in tangible credentials for leadership than in simple patriotism.

The problems of most Confederate veterans were worlds apart from the concerns of winning an election. At least 200,000 Confederate soldiers had been wounded in the war, and thousands of them had endured amputations. Disabled soldiers returned to communities that had few resources to assist them, and the aid that ex-soldiers did receive was sporadic and short-lived. During the war most Southern state governments had supplemented local aid for disabled soldiers and their families, and some states continued public assistance afterward. Arkansas, for example, set aside 10 percent of its revenues for artificial limbs and other aid to veterans and their survivors, and Georgia paid the tuition of veterans attending public colleges. Private charities also distributed food and supplies to needy Southerners, and ex-soldiers and their survivors were among the thousands of whites who received food, clothing, and other aid from the federal Freedman's Bureau. In addition, Louisiana established a soldiers' home in 1866 with a $20,000 appropriation, and the home took in nearly a hundred veterans by 1867. But these efforts would soon come to an end.

Even if they escaped war wounds and postwar poverty, many ex-soldiers encountered domestic troubles. Southern statistics are sketchy for the immediate postwar years, but diaries and letters furnish ample evidence of marital discord, abandonment, and divorce, all of which were undoubtedly aggravated by Confederate defeat and the breakdown of the Southern economy. On the other hand, the war also created a marriage boom that overshadowed the increase in marriages that occurred in the North. Since a much larger proportion of Southerners served in the army, more Southern marriages were postponed during the war, and the killing left proportionally more widows than in the North. The consequences can be seen in Alabama counties that kept good records: marriages per thousand of population increased by nearly 50 percent in the late 1860s compared with the 1860 rate. Among Northern states with usable records, the increase was only about half as great.

The Southern marriage boom indicates that postwar despondency had its limits. In times of widespread stress, young people typically postpone marrying; it is estimated, for example, that 800,000 marriages were put off during the Great Depression of the 1930s. The willingness of Southerners to marry (and to remarry, in the case of war widows) suggests that Southern apathy was largely confined to political matters. Southern men, a large percentage of whom were Confederate veterans, were willing to start a marriage amid the uncertainty of the postwar South even if they saw little point in going to the polls to choose among politicians.

One way in which Southerners could overcome their lethargy was to commemorate the Confederate dead. Memorial Day, as a springtime service for deceased soldiers, originated in the South in 1866, and numerous Southern towns began to build monuments to their fallen soldiers. Most of the monuments built before 1885 were funereal in form—simple obelisks were preferred, occasionally topped by an urn or other funeral symbol—and were located in cemeteries. Though women did much of the fund-raising and supervised the construction of the monuments, local businessmen and professionals usually organized monument societies. Many, if not most, of these men were veterans or the fathers of Confederate soldiers.

Prominent veterans also stepped to the forefront on Memorial Day and at the dedication of monuments, and their speeches were frequently a call to overcome Southern apathy. In a speech delivered in 1869, for example, a Georgian exhorted listeners to "look away from the gloom of political bondage, and fix our vision upon a coming day of triumph" when Southern principles would again prevail. The ceremonies were usually well attended, and their main purpose was the closing of wounds left open by the war.

Politicians were less willing to admit defeat. As we have seen, the representatives Southerners chose had been reluctant Confederates, but they proved equally unwilling to turn their backs on the social order of the Old South. The constitutional conventions of 1865 only grudgingly renounced slavery and secession, and the new state legislatures devoted themselves, in the words of a Republican critic, to "getting things back as near to slavery as possible." The "Black Codes" that were meant to reimpose subservience among African Americans

varied from state to state, but they were based on a common
set of tactics. The codes sought to bind African Americans to
farm labor and to their employers by requiring blacks to sign
labor contracts and discouraging employers from recruiting
each other's workers. The new laws also discouraged blacks
from hopes of equality with whites. Courts could seize black
children, for example, on the pretext of inadequate parental
support and force them into unpaid labor for white employers. The codes also stiffened penalties for theft, a charge for
which conviction was usually automatic for blacks. Convicts
could be whipped or sentenced to virtual enslavement to any
white who paid their fine.

News of the Black Codes provoked a storm of protest from
Northerners who believed the South was flouting the principles vindicated by the war. Worse yet, in the eyes of Radical
Republicans who were the codes' chief critics, was President
Andrew Johnson's endorsement of this defiance. Many mod-
erate Republicans came to share the Radicals' views, and the
party began to use its commanding majority in Congress to
overturn the Southern policies. In 1866, over Johnson's vetoes,
Congress strengthened the Freedman's Bureau and enacted
the nation's first civil rights law, and sent to the states a Fourteenth Amendment that would put guarantees of equal protection and due process of law into the Constitution. In 1867,
again over Johnson's vetoes, Congress required Southern
states (except Tennessee, which had already been readmitted)
to ratify the Fourteenth Amendment and adopt new constitutions guaranteeing the right to vote for black men; federal
military commanders would supervise compliance. By 1870
the ten remaining ex-Confederate states had met these terms
and been readmitted to the Union.

Under the new Southern governments, most of which were
dominated by white and African-American Republicans, aid

to ex-soldiers came to an end. This was not because Republican governments were particularly vindictive toward former Confederates. Relatively few ex-Confederate soldiers, for example, were barred from voting under the newly adopted constitutions. But neither were Republican officials anxious to provide public aid to men and their families who were linked to the recent fight to preserve slavery. As a result, most public assistance for Confederate veterans, such as state aid to destitute ex-soldiers and the Louisiana soldiers' home, was discontinued in the late 1860s; the Freedmen's Bureau had already begun to phase out its relief efforts in 1866.

Yet even before Republican governments came to power, some veterans had begun to put their own stamp on postwar Southern society. We have seen that Southerners, including many veterans, found comfort in laying the Confederacy to rest by commemorating fallen soldiers, but other veterans could not bear so passive an acceptance of defeat. As a result, many ex-soldiers joined, and profoundly influenced the nature of, the Ku Klux Klan.

The Klan was founded in 1866 in south-central Tennessee by six ex-Confederate soldiers, and functioned for a time as a social fraternity. Soon, however, whites in surrounding areas realized that the Klan's secrecy and practical joking could be useful in preserving white supremacy. In 1867 the original founders called interested parties to Nashville to organize an "Empire" of Klan dens under former Confederate general Nathan Bedford Forrest as Grand Wizard. In the next year the Klan adopted a credo, which in addition to affirmations of justice and patriotism pledged Klansmen to help Confederate widows and orphans. In practice the hierarchy had almost no control over local dens, and Klansmen did little to help Confederate survivors, but the importance of the Confederate war experience in the Klan's formation is clear.

The Klan that spread across the South in 1868 grew from several roots. Participating in slave patrols had been a custom (and sometimes an obligation) among white men in the antebellum South. Patrollers typically rode at night, ostensibly to enforce slave curfews, but on occasion, wearing costumes meant to frighten their victims, patrollers harassed slaves for sport. The Klan also drew on the European custom of *charivari*, a raucous festival during which disguised crowds ridiculed and assaulted adulterers, people suspected of fornication, and other wrongdoers. And the Klan clearly grew out of the traditions of frontier justice and the lynch mob.

But no influence on the Klan outweighed that of Confederate military service. Contemporary observers and later historians alike remarked on the sheer number of ex-Confederates in the Klan, especially among its leaders. This was due in part simply to the number of ex-soldiers in Southern communities, but numbers suggest only part of the significance of the Confederate experience. A network of former officers, for example, helped to spread the Klan from place to place. The local gentry who made up most of the Confederate officer corps had met men in the army whom they would not otherwise have known, and on visits and in correspondence they spread knowledge and approval of the Klan.

The war produced other motivations for joining the Klan. After the surrender, Randolph Shotwell returned to his home in western North Carolina. Shotwell knew about wartime boredom, having spent time in a Northern prison, but he nonetheless found the "dull, newsless, lifeless monotony of a village" to be "about unendurable." The Klan, however, offered him something akin to the army experience—companionship, excitement, and another chance to resist what he and his friends saw as Northern oppression, this time in the form of Republican governments. Impelled by these attractions (and, by Shotwell's admission, by liberal doses of liquor), he entered the Klan. Many other veterans undoubtedly joined for similar reasons.

The Klan's early pranks and harassment of African Americans turned into increasingly brutal terrorism against blacks' attempts at self-reliance and against the new Republican governments. Bands of Klansmen rode through Southern towns and countryside, assaulting people they saw as a political or social threat. Klansmen burned homes, churches, and schools, and whipped, tortured, mutilated, and lynched many of their victims. Klansmen's raids were not always secret: they were known to hijack trains in order to corner a victim, and local dens might band together for a major operation. In the largest such raid, an estimated five hundred Klansmen descended on Union, South Carolina, in February 1871. The raiders ordered residents off the streets, seized the jail, and lynched ten black prisoners.

The Enforcement Acts, a series of federal laws passed in 1870 and 1871, finally drove the Klan out of operation. Yet the Klan's terrorism, especially in the deep South, had already undermined Republican governments and contributed to their eventual downfall.

And the Klan never lost its connections to the Civil War. It remained largely a veterans' movement, determined to exorcise the pain of defeat as well as to terrorize its victims. A raid on a Klan den by Arkansas officials, for example, found a Confederate flag on an altar. Klansmen, especially in the group's early days, were fond of declaring to their victims that they were ghosts of the Confederate dead, returned for revenge. In contrast to the farcical militarism of antebellum militiamen, Klansmen aggressively exhibited their military prowess. Klan members staged occasional parades in town squares, complete with precision military drills, and when blacks attempted armed resistance they were often routed by battlefield-style assaults or well-coordinated sieges. Lynchings were sometimes carried out by a Klan firing squad, and Klansmen made a point of forcing the registration of Confederate veterans in places where they were barred from voting. The Klan resembled the army in yet another way. Military leaders are obligated to take the long view—to consider strategic goals and devise tactics to achieve them. Enlisted men, however, have more immediate concerns—above all, survival with the least possible misery. The Ku Klux Klan's leaders likewise had long-term goals of crippling the Republican party in the South and eliminating Northern intervention in Southern politics. As a result, the planters, physicians, newspaper editors, and occasional minister who led the Klan tried to concentrate on political terror. Political activity, to be sure, was broadly defined: running for office as a Republican was sure to bring a visit in places where the Klan was active, but Klan leaders also ordered attacks on anyone who encouraged black self-sufficiency, from teachers to preachers to merchants who were liberal with credit for freedpeople.

Poorer whites took part in these assaults, but they also went on their own raids, intent on punishing social deviants, white and black (although Republican sympathies always increased the chance of such punishment). In these forays Klansmen demolished brothels and whipped suspected prostitutes, adulterers, and wife beaters. On occasion a Klan leader might use this penchant for social regulation to recruit members: a North Carolina legislator and Klan leader promised that members would be able to "protect [their] families from the darkies." But Klan leaders more often denounced unauthorized regulators, insisting they were driving away farm hands and risking federal reprisals. Like army commanders, leading Klansmen thus deplored some of their followers' excesses, but unlike army officers Klan leaders had no punishments to enforce their disapproval. Indeed, the Klan's political successes were likely assisted by common whites' freelance terrorism. Poorer folk may have been willing to sustain the Klan because they were also free to use it for their own ends, in contrast to the army's insistence on restricting soldiers' activities

Federal prosecutions under the Enforcement Acts may have shut down the Klan in the early 1870s, but conservative whites' determination to overthrow Republican state governments remained unshaken. Some of the governments had already fallen: internal Republican divisions had enabled conservative Democrats to regain power in upper South states such as Tennessee, and Klan violence and intimidation of black voters contributed to a Democratic victory in Alabama. Republicans clung to power in several Southern states in the mid-1870s, but conservatives were determined to complete their takeover of the South.

Veterans had fully shaken off their postwar lethargy and were leading the way in reasserting white supremacy. Indeed, apathy about Reconstruction had shifted to the North, where politicians who had once been champions of civil rights for freedpeople were now preoccupied with an economic depression that began in 1873 and with scandals in the administration of President Ulysses S. Grant.

A case in point from Mississippi will illustrate the extent to which Confederate veterans had become reinvigorated. Mississippi's black majority sustained state and local Republican governments until 1875. Then, conservative whites, taking heart from dramatic nationwide gains by the Democrats in the previous year's congressional elections, intensified their campaign to oust the Republicans. To carry out their plan, conservatives would have to mobilize the white vote and ruthlessly intimidate black voters. White mobilization had already begun before 1875 with the formation of local "taxpayers' leagues," groups that called for lower taxes and less public spending while insisting that Republican governments were rife with corruption.

By the summer of 1875 the protests had developed into a political movement, with the coming legislative elections the target. Democratic clubs sprang up around the state, and Confederate veterans were in the forefront of their resurgence. The newspaper in Crystal Springs in south-central Mississippi, for example, published a list of Democratic club members, who comprised nearly three-fourths of the town's taxpayers. Where Confederate veterans had been reluctant even to vote ten years earlier, they were now eager to join the movement to recapture the legislature. Former Confederate soldiers were more than twice as likely as noncombatants to join the Democratic club in Crystal Springs.

Once organized, Confederate veterans and their fellow Democrats gave the 1875 election the air of a military operation. Democratic clubs held parades that featured color guards, cannon, double-file marching, and the "rebel yell." Blacks in Vicksburg complained that white men were "going around the streets at night in soldiers clothes and making the colored people run for their lives." Conservative whites had indeed declared war on African-American and white Republicans. Determined, in the words of a newspaper editor, to "carry the election peaceably if we can, forcibly if we must," heavily armed bands of whites disrupted Republican rallies, assassinated Republican politicians, and warned black men not to vote, no longer bothering with the disguises of Ku Klux Klan days.

On election day Democrats prevented the distribution of Republican ballots, harassed those blacks who did come out to vote, and tampered with the ballot boxes. The result, not surprisingly, was a sweeping Democratic victory and a commanding majority in the Mississippi legislature. Also not surprisingly, Democrats valued wartime leadership in putting men into office. In the Mississippi legislative elections of 1877 (whose records are more complete than those of 1875), Confederate leadership was even more important than it had been a decade earlier. In races contested between veterans and noncombatants, once again Confederate service made little difference by itself, but having been an officer quadrupled a candidate's chances of being elected. Indeed, high Confederate rank became so associated with elective office that the remainder of the century has been identified as the "rule of the brigadiers" across the South.

In 1877, as part of a deal that sorted out the disputed results of the previous year's presidential election, federal troops were withdrawn from Louisiana and South Carolina, and the last Republican governments in the South fell to the Democrats. Southerners thereby completed a remarkable turnabout—the same people who had been unable to mount a large-scale resistance during the war were ultimately successful in doing so afterward.

Despite their dominant role in this resistance, Confederate veterans in the 1870s were affected by the same public amnesia about the war itself that was found in the North. Veterans' return to militarism in their campaign to topple Republican governments, and politicians' campaign references to their wartime service, were not part of any mass movement to relive the war. There were, to be sure, some Confederate organizations in the 1870s: the Association of the Army of Northern Virginia and the Southern Historical Society, the most influential of such groups, devoted themselves to enshrining Confederate heroes and differentiating the South's cause from its defeat. But these were organizations of the Confederate leadership, not the rank and file; only a few thousand Southerners joined during the 1870s. Most veterans preferred to commemorate their fallen comrades in local ceremonies rather than to celebrate the abilities of Virginia generals or contemplate the course of the war.

But just as Union veterans experienced a renewal of group consciousness in the 1880s, so did former Confederate soldiers. The immediate cause of the renewal was different in the South—there was no massive pension crusade to unify Confederate veterans. While the federal government pondered ways to spend its surplus, the Democratic state governments of the South cut back sharply on social spending; aside from a few tax exemptions for veterans, there was little public assistance available to ex-Confederate soldiers.

Instead, the changes in American society that worried Union veterans and helped to cause a public nostalgia for the Civil War also distressed Southerners. People in the South knew about the explosive growth of cities, the enormous increase in foreign immigration, and the expansion of industrial corporations; they realized that the nation's heroes were no longer presidents or military men but corporate lords, such as oil magnate John D. Rockefeller, financier J. Pierpont Morgan, and steel baron Andrew Carnegie, none of whom had fought in the Civil War; and Southerners watched the relationship between owners and workers grow into violent confrontations between increasingly assertive workers and intransigent employers. These developments were concentrated in the North, but the South felt their effects: it had its own vigorous debate about the merits of economic development, and Southern companies had their share of labor disputes. Southerners feared that worse was yet to come as Northern trends penetrated their communities. And in spite of their recapture of state governments, many whites believed that blacks still posed a threat to their control of Southern society.

Americans who were perplexed by these changes tried a number of means to overcome their insecurities. Fraternal orders like the Masons and Odd Fellows, which flourished in the late nineteenth century, fostered common bonds and offered a refuge from the outside world. Putting a stop to disturbing trends was another promising strategy. Rural political movements tried to reverse the concentration of power in the hands of industrialists and financiers. But turning back the clock became especially popular. The Civil War now seemed a time of selflessness and heroism compared to the grasping meanness of the century's closing decades.

Southerners had their own version of these efforts, and Confederate veterans often took the lead. The Patrons of Husbandry, popularly known as the Grange, flourished in the Midwest and South in the 1870s. Begun as fraternal and educational gatherings, Grange meetings brought together farmers who complained about exploitation by railroads, banks, and merchants. Grangers experimented with cooperatives to pool their buying and selling power, and they pushed for state laws to regulate the rates they paid to warehouses and railroads. In the South, Granges were often dominated by Confederate veterans who sought to revive the traditional privilege of white landowners. Two-thirds of the charter members of one central Mississippi Grange branch were Confederate veterans, and a speaker at another branch insisted on "less freedom and more protection to property." The Southern Grange thus became part of the drive to restore white supremacy.

Financial problems with cooperatives and vigorous opposition by businessmen sent the Grange into decline in the late

1870s, and its cause was taken up by the Farmers' Alliance in
the 1880s. The Alliance was more openly political than the
Grange had been—it put up its own candidates for state offices and Congress, and lobbied for federal aid in marketing
crops—and was especially strong in the South. Again Confederates, most of whom were farmers, flocked to the cause, and
they put their stamp on the movement. A Georgia Alliance
leader and Confederate veteran warned that "we are fighting
now against a foe more insidious [than the Union]," and the
Tennessee Alliance described its members as "an army of veterans who are so nobly and determinedly resisting the efforts
of combined capital."

Encouraged by their electoral success—in 1890 six Al-
liance-backed candidates won governors' races, three were
elected to the U.S. Senate, and fifty won seats in the U.S.
House—but frustrated by inaction on legislation to help farmers, agrarian activists formed a national political party. The
Populists, as the new party's adherents called themselves, set
their sights on the 1892 presidential election and reached out
to other workers by endorsing such measures as an eight-hour
day for industry.

The Populists also created a dilemma for Southerners.
Democrats, now firmly in control of Southern politics, had
tolerated and sometimes joined the Farmers' Alliance, but
agrarian activists intent on becoming a competing party were
a serious threat. Democrats relentlessly denounced the new
party, insinuating that Populists were actively seeking African
Americans' support and would eventually subvert white supremacy. Democrats pleaded for white solidarity in defeating
the alleged biracial menace, and their pleas inevitably included an appeal to old soldiers' loyalty.

But loyalties were not so simple for veterans. Many Populist
leaders, moving over from the Farmers' Alliance, were them-

selves Confederate veterans. Nor were veterans willing to abandon the agrarian cause so quickly; moreover, a few Southern states had already restricted blacks' right to vote, thereby easing racist fears of populism. An estimate of voting behavior in Mississippi reveals veterans' divided loyalties as well as their interest in politics. Fewer than one in five nonveterans voted in the 1892 election, and hardly any voted for the Populists; half of all Confederate veterans turned out for the election, however, and about half of those who voted chose Populist candidates (James B. Weaver, the Populist presidential nominee, received about 9 percent of the vote nationwide).

Populism rapidly declined after the 1896 election, but veterans, now mostly in their fifties, had shown they were still in the vanguard of political activism, just as they had been in their twenties when they went to war for another political cause. And some of them had also shown they were willing to reject the party they had helped to revive after the war.

Veterans also participated eagerly in the effort to turn back the clock. In the 1880s Confederate veterans formed groups that were meant to have a broader appeal than did the elite Association of the Army of Northern Virginia and similar organizations. The new groups grew rapidly, and in 1889 they created a new national order, the United Confederate Veterans. Membership figures for the UCV are imprecise, but Gaines Foster has estimated that from one-fourth to one-third of Confederate veterans joined the organization in the 1890s, roughly the same as the proportion of Union veterans in the Grand Army of the Republic at its height. Like the GAR, the UCV was led by local businessmen, but significant numbers of farmers, artisans, and unskilled workers also joined. With this broadening of membership came a broadening of purposes for Confederate veterans.

Confederate monuments, which were originally memorials

to the dead, now became shrines to the common soldier. The UCV and its women's auxiliary, the United Daughters of the Confederacy, took an active role in local monument-building, and they deemphasized funereal designs. New monuments were now as likely to be in a town square as in a cemetery, and most monuments displayed a generic foot soldier rather than a symbol of grief. Instead of mourning the dead soldiers and their cause as did the early monuments, the new memorials admonished the public to honor living as well as deceased veterans and to imitate their example of loyalty and self-sacrifice. The centerpiece of the UCV's broadened appeal was the reunion. Veterans had often held local barbecues and state meetings, but by the 1890s the annual UCV reunion overshadowed all local gatherings. Tens of thousands of former Confederates poured into cities such as Birmingham and Richmond, where they relived the war and recaptured old values. As they had in the army, veterans at a reunion could feel both local identity and membership in a larger movement, and they could reaffirm their willingness to fight for southern womanhood and social stability. UCV camps selected young women to participate in the reunions, honoring them as representatives of women's devotion to the Confederacy (even though the UCV's view of women's role was as sharply limited as the GAR's; the organization vehemently objected to a UDC plan to build a monument depicting an assertive woman, for example). UCV members also relished their role as defenders of social order. Referring to violence between owners and workers in the 1890s, the UCV's commander boasted that he could raise "an army of old soldiers" to put down the troubles, "every man of whom [would] fight to the death to preserve the Union and command respect for the old flag."

At the same time the UCV backed away from some of the combative pro-Southern rhetoric of earlier Confederate groups. These Southern partisans had insisted that secession be viewed solely as a principled act of self-rule and that the Confederacy's defeat be seen purely as the inevitable result of the North's superior numbers. The UCV, for its part, did press for the Southern viewpoint in textbooks and argued for the "War Between the States" as the proper name for the conflict, but the new generation of veterans' leaders was less strident in vindicating the Confederacy than earlier spokesmen had been. Instead the new leaders were more open to reconciliation with their former enemies. Blue-Gray reunions flourished from the 1880s onward, as Union and Confederate veterans got together on battlefields and at Memorial Day celebrations. Although many Southerners remained opposed to reconciliation, the trend continued, aided by the Spanish-American War in 1898, which allowed partisans on both sides to support a common cause.

This upsurge in veterans' activity was accompanied by increased public concern for ex-Confederate soldiers and their survivors. The Democrats' cutbacks in their states' social spending had left little public assistance for veterans until the 1880s. Then, as public interest in the war revived, so did public alarm about reports of veterans in poorhouses and stories of impoverished widows and children. Prodded by veterans' advocates who pointed to such reports and to increasingly generous pensions for Union veterans, Southern state legislators considered providing their own aid to former Confederate soldiers.

State aid had its opponents, including veterans who insisted that public assistance would undermine ex-soldiers' manly self-reliance, but by the early 1890s most of the former Confederate states had resumed their assistance to veterans. One form of aid was the pension: states provided a scale of payments to disabled and destitute veterans and their survivors.

Nine states were paying Confederate pensions by the early 1890s, but their limited willingness and resources for social spending kept pensions modest. Fewer than 10 percent of Confederate veterans and widows received pensions in the early 1890s, and the average payment was $40 a year at a time when more than two-thirds of Union veterans were receiving an average of $160 a year. Later in the decade, Louisiana and Texas became the last ex-Confederate states to enact veterans' pensions.

At about the same time Southern legislators were acting on pensions, they also debated establishing veterans' homes. Again there was opposition—from Alliancemen and Populists in Georgia, who saw soldiers' home advocates as elite urbanites, and from wartime Unionists in East Tennessee—but by 1901 seven former Confederate states had opened homes. Substantial numbers of Confederate veterans came to these homes by the early years of the new century.

The characteristics of those who came to soldiers' homes illustrate the harshness of life for some in the postwar South. In a sample of Tennessee soldiers' home residents, only one-third had suffered a war wound, but 90 percent had previously received some form of public aid (usually food, clothing, or other assistance furnished by county officials). One-third of the men were single, and two-thirds had no family members to help them; 20 percent had been in a poorhouse, and another 20 percent had been unemployed for five years or longer.

Inside the homes, residents found a devotion to discipline similar to that of the Union veterans' homes. Like the Northern homes, Southern institutions boasted of their superiority to poorhouses—soldiers' homes had attractive locations and prided themselves on their generosity to residents—but their officials were also ambivalent about the residents' character. Those who sought shelter in the homes were, after all, heroes of the Southern cause, but administrators were nonetheless suspicious of individuals who could not support themselves. As a result, administrators imposed military rules and work requirements on residents, not only to keep the homes operating smoothly but also, in the words of a Georgia official, to "reform and improve [residents'] behavior and deportment."

Life in Southern homes was punctuated by contests of will between administrators and residents who were convinced that officials were autocratic killjoys. As in the Northern homes, and as in the Civil War armies, the struggles were sometimes furtive, as residents defied rules against drinking, theft, and unauthorized leave, and were at other times open and violent: the Georgia home witnessed a fistfight between the superintendent and a resident, and a resident attacked the superintendent of the Texas home with a cane.

Confederate veterans at the other end of the social scale had a different problem as the nineteenth century neared its end. Ex-soldiers, especially those who had been officers, were used to being at the center of the white community and were accustomed to dominating state and local politics. By the late 1880s, however, they could see their uniquely privileged position slipping away. As old age approached and the postwar generation began to reach maturity, veterans began to worry about their legacy. A South Carolinian wrote that "most of the young men are willing to turn their backs on everything that we were taught to regard as sacred." Building monuments and keeping an eye on textbooks helped, but conventional ways of conveying the war's importance were not always satisfying. "You children simply don't understand," the father of Georgian Mell Barrett would say in frustration when war stories failed to impress his listeners.

Another kind of legacy was more appealing to some veterans. In the years after "Redemption," as Democrats called

their takeover of Southern governments in the 1870s, race relations had remained unsettled. Southern whites quickly established barriers of segregation anywhere the sexes as well as
the races might mix—in hotels, restaurants, parks, and railroad cars. Yet in places where men and women were not likely
to meet, such as country stores, cotton gins, and saloons, there
were few efforts to separate the races. And black men continued to vote in large numbers, even though their actual political influence was minuscule. Redeemer politicians tolerated
black voting and a few Republican candidates, as long as
whites could control the outcome of elections and manipulate
black officeholders. If they felt threatened by black assertive-
ness, whites would resort to the familiar methods of fraud, intimidation of voters, and violence. A Mississippian admitted
in 1890, for example, that "there has not been a full vote and a
fair count in Mississippi since 1875," and a Louisiana observer
noted that "after the polls are closed the election really begins."

Many white Southerners were satisfied with these arrangements. A few states tried legal restrictions on blacks' voting,
such as poll taxes and cumbersome voting procedures, but further efforts to control voting usually met with firm resistance.
"Why agitate and convulse the country when quiet is so desirable and important for the public welfare?" asked Mississippi's governor in 1888, and Louisianians were unwilling to
upset "the existing order of things, with which the people are
satisfied," by toughening voting regulations.

But in Mississippi, which would lead the way in permanently disfranchising African Americans, such reluctance
gave way to a wave of white insecurity by 1890. Republicans
now controlled the White House and Congress, raising fears
of new federal voting-rights laws; whites were worried that
the 1890 census would show a widening black majority in

Mississippi; and, according to historian David Donald, the Confederate generation's fear for its legacy was becoming overwhelming. A former colonel underscored his generation's anxiety about the way it controlled politics: "The old men of the present generation can't afford to die and leave their children with shot guns in their hands, a lie on their mouths and perjury on their souls, in order to defeat the negroes." These men had taken up arms for white supremacy once in the 1860s and again in the mid-1870s, and the time for permanently securing their prize was slipping away. A new governor removed the last obstacle to a constitutional convention, and an election of delegates was ordered for July 1890.

Historians have noted that only 15 percent of Mississippi's eligible voters turned out for the delegate elections and have pointed out that this first "disfranchising convention" was sharply split between the cotton belt and the upcountry, but Confederate veterans were also important in the campaign to change Mississippi's constitution. Estimates of voting behavior suggest deep differences in voter turnout. Very few black men were willing or allowed to vote in an election that would probably lead to their disfranchisement (but those who did vote helped to elect the convention's only Republican). Not many whites voted either: only about one-third bothered to vote for convention delegates. But Confederate veterans, who were 22 percent of the white electorate, were serious about rewriting the constitution—an estimated two-thirds of veterans turned out to vote for convention delegates.

Veterans were equally serious about designing the voting restrictions. Fewer than 40 percent of the Mississippi convention's delegates were ex-Confederate soldiers, but the franchise committee was their preserve. Nearly three-quarters of the committee's members were veterans; committee members were older men and were disproportionately from the cotton belt, but being an ex-soldier was far more likely than age or locale to get a delegate selected to this all-important committee.

The delegates met from August 12 through the end of October and produced a new constitution that was intended to bar most African Americans from voting. A prospective voter would have to negotiate a maze of residency requirements, poll taxes, literacy tests, and other obstacles aimed at disqualifying blacks. These restrictions did eliminate almost all the black vote (and some of the white vote as well), and they impressed political leaders elsewhere.

Indeed, South Carolina followed Mississippi's lead four years later, with similar support from veterans. In the referendum that authorized a constitutional convention, fewer than half of white men voted. An estimated 80 percent of Confederate veterans voted, however, and they favored the convention by two to one. But before other states held constitutional conventions, the struggle between Populists and Democrats had divided veterans' loyalties. Many Populist leaders were unwilling to disqualify poor whites or blacks who were potential supporters, and they denounced proposals for disfranchisement. When Alabama held a referendum in 1901, veterans' loyalties were split between the proconvention Democratic position and the opposition advocated by Populists. Veterans' role was also limited when these later conventions met. Only one-fourth of delegates were Confederate veterans in the conventions held in Alabama and Louisiana, and veterans were less dominant on franchise committees than they had been in Mississippi. All the ex-Confederate states eventually adopted some form of voting restrictions, but by the turn of the century a new generation of political leaders had emerged, one more concerned with taxes and business regulation than with preserving the spirit of Redemption.

The movement to disfranchise black men was nonetheless a remarkable example of public deference to an activist minority. In no Southern state was constitutional disfranchisement a mass movement; voter turnout in convention-related elections duplicated the low participation in Mississippi and South Carolina. But, as in these two states, apparent apathy could mask real interest—Confederate veterans could come out in strength for convention elections, and veterans could dominate the key committee at a convention. It was determination, not sheer numbers, that ensured white supremacy in Southern states, and that determination indicated a generation convinced of its special authority.

This special authority was as evident among constitution-writers as it was among veterans' activists. Although the UCV said little in public about disfranchisement, its leaders sounded remarkably like advocates. The UCV constitution endorsed, for example, a campaign "to instill into our descendants proper veneration for the spirit and glory of their fathers," while the Confederate veteran who headed the Mississippi convention declared that the delegates' goal was "to preserve the morals of this and the coming generation." Other men eventually took over the effort to enshrine white supremacy, but veterans' role in beginning the movement was in itself a notable feat.

Approximately 350,000 Confederate veterans lived to see the end of the nineteenth century. Most of them had remained aloof from the growth of cities, towns, and industry that was changing the South. Younger Southerners had already begun to turn away from farming: at the turn of the century, just over half of Southern whites in their thirties were farmers. Confederate veterans, however, older men who had come primarily from farming areas, resisted change, and nearly two-thirds remained farmers as the century ended. It is common for the elderly to oppose change and relive the past, but it was not just age that impelled veterans to their extraordinary efforts to reverse the clock. In UCV parades and at Memorial Day celebrations, ex-soldiers reminded everyone they were guardians not simply of the past but of an unparalleled experience that remained alive as a warning against tampering with social stability. By initiating the effort to restrict the vote, some veterans went even farther in exercising their special authority: they attempted to prevent future generations from changing a key feature of the social order.

Confederate veterans had fewer tangible signs of special status than did Union veterans—their pensions were a fraction of Union veterans' payments, and a much smaller proportion of ex-Confederates wound up in soldiers' homes—but ex-Confederates had nonetheless made an unmistakable mark on their society.

7

Civil War Veterans in the Twentieth Century

IN THE SPRING of 1910 federal census takers went from door to door to collect information for the thirteenth census of the United States. For only the second time (and the first time that can help modern historians, because detailed information from the 1890 census was destroyed in a fire), the enumerators asked older men if they had served in the Civil War.

By 1910 fewer than one-third of the war's original Union survivors were still alive. Mostly in their late sixties and early seventies, the remaining veterans were a reminder of a different America. Eighty percent were native-born whites, compared with fewer than 60 percent of elderly Northern civilians. According to the author Bruce Catton, who grew up in a Michigan town in the early twentieth century, Civil War veterans were "men set apart" in other ways as well. Catton saw veterans as "the keepers of [their community's] patriotic traditions," because "years ago they had marched thousands of miles to legendary battlefields."

For veterans who wished to sustain this aura of uniqueness, the Grand Army of the Republic remained active in the new century, holding its encampments for comradeship and continuing its work of "patriotic instruction." The GAR was the ideal organization for veterans like the father of the writer Sherwood Anderson. According to his son, Irwin Anderson learned in the years following the war "that he would never be a hero again, that all the rest of his life he would have to build on those days."

Nevertheless, a large number of Union veterans, probably a majority, never joined the GAR. We might assume they considered themselves citizens first and soldiers second, and were willing to consign their wartime experiences to the past. But few of them completely forgot their service. By 1900 the Pension Bureau had made old age (defined as sixty-five) a "disability" for pension purposes; in 1904 the Bureau changed the definition to sixty-two and in 1907 Congress made the ruling into law. Since almost all Union veterans were now older than sixty-two, these changes finally made Civil War "service" pensions a reality.

As a result, previously ineligible ex-soldiers reminded the Pension Bureau of their service and asked for a pension. By 1910 virtually all living Union veterans were on the pension rolls. The average payment was $172 a year, though high rank or multiple disabilities could qualify a former soldier for as much as $1,200 per year. As sociologist Theda Skocpol has pointed out, this was a far more generous pension system than those in Europe at the time, although European pensions were meant for much broader classes of the elderly.

Veterans' pensions were also a higher proportion of typical yearly wages than were the Social Security payments that would begin in the 1930s. Did veterans' pensions serve as an early form of retirement program? Retirement had a different meaning in the early twentieth century than it does today. Some medical experts and business leaders were urging, in the name of efficiency, that employers replace older workers with younger ones, but there was no widely accepted stopping point for a man's working life. Instead, most men expected to withdraw from employment gradually, phasing out physical chores while remaining active as givers of advice. Three-fourths of American men aged sixty to seventy-five reported in 1910 that they still had an occupation.

But the proportion of men who had quit working had risen since 1900, and these nonemployed men were especially likely to be Union veterans. Even when we control for age and material wealth such as ownership of a home, we find that veterans were less likely than nonveterans to be working (this finding applies to white men, since there are few African-American veterans in the census sample). This difference in employment was not simply due to veterans' health problems stemming from the war. In 1890, when fewer than one-third of veterans received pensions, they had been *more* likely to be working than were nonveterans of the same age. Since almost all Union veterans were drawing a pension in 1910, it is likely that a regular income from the federal treasury (plus, in many states, additional state and local veterans' pensions) allowed men to stop working earlier than they would have otherwise.

Veterans' pensions, like the early Social Security payments, were not meant to be a pensioner's sole source of support: an advocate of the 1907 expansion of pensions expected them to be only "a small pittance," enough to keep veterans from "being compelled to go hungry the balance of their few years." Yet the pensions made a difference, allowing a substantial number of veterans to be pioneers in retiring from work, just as the first Social Security payments helped to spur a much larger exodus of older workers from the labor force in the 1930s.

It was widely believed that Civil War pensions also influenced the behavior of women. Attitudes toward women that we have seen throughout this book have followed a pattern. Most Northerners in the nineteenth century revered women who conformed to their assigned roles—care-giver, preserver of home and family, admiring companion—but distrusted women who did not conform—prostitutes, extreme Confederate partisans, and, later, women who would exploit Union veterans and the federal government's generosity. A few pension advocates lavished praise on widows whom they considered virtuous, that is, those who did all they could "to teach lessons of patriotism and pure love of country to their children." At the same time social critics were warning that "there has grown up in the United States a race of widows that is increasing in numbers and degenerating in worth." It was believed that these widows lived with men without marrying, to keep their widow's pension. As a result, conditions that included an income test were eventually added to widows' application requirements, and members of Congress and Pension Bureau officials advocated inquiring into female applicants' character before their pensions were approved.

Social critics and government officials were even more alarmed about another class of women. A pension official insisted that "there is a great abuse of the pension laws by young women, who marry old soldiers for no other reason than to live on the pension money after their husbands are gone." To guard against these "designing women," as they were called, Congress took such steps as disqualifying widows from pensions under the Dependent Pension Act if they had married a veteran after 1890, but there is little evidence that officials' fears were justified.

If "pension marriages" were indeed common, the 1910 census should show a clear difference between veterans' and non-veterans' marital status. Commentators argued that designing women had continued to prey on veterans even after the Dependent Pension Act; if critics were correct, there should have been considerably more married veterans than married civilians in 1910, and veterans' wives should have been younger than wives of civilians. But there are no striking differences: veterans were slightly more likely to be married than were elderly civilians, but veterans' wives tended to be slightly *older* than civilians' wives. Some women undoubtedly did marry elderly veterans for their pensions, but they were the exception and not the rule.

Although the population of Union veterans was dwindling in 1910, soldiers' homes were still growing. The federal homes admitted more than 3,700 new residents in 1900 and maintained a total population of 19,000; by 1910 the population of the homes had reached 20,000, and an additional 12,000 Union veterans were living in state-operated soldiers' homes. The nature of the homes and the ex-soldiers they housed had changed since the early postwar decades. In the early years most residents had been foreign-born and single (foreign born men were more likely to be single than were the native-born), and the majority sought care because of a war wound. By the turn of the century, fewer wives and families were able to care for disabled and impoverished ex-soldiers, and married or widowed native-born veterans came to dominate the homes' population. Now men with diseases (which included, according to official definitions, old age) outnumbered those with wounds. The homes had become old-age refuges: residents, increasingly unable to handle the homes' maintenance, had to be replaced by hired staff, and medical personnel and facilities had to be steadily expanded to deal with the health problems of aging veterans.

But if soldiers' home residents had changed, official ambivalence about them had not. Public officials were so pleased with the spacious grounds and imposing buildings they had provided that they believed the homes could improve public character. Enthusiasts described soldiers' homes as parklike havens of rest and reflection for visitors; the homes would "keep the fire of patriotism burning, that the people may not forget the men who stood by the nation in its hour of peril." Yet the authorities were not as pleased with the men themselves. According to officials of the Ohio federal home, the residents had become more insubordinate with age: "There is less self-restraint among them than among younger men; consequently some of them need constant watching and firm handling."

As usual among authorities concerned with self-control, drinking was the offense that most worried the homes' managers. As it had been when they were soldiers, drinking continued to be among residents' favorite pastimes; their indulgence ranged from an occasional spree in a nearby town to alcoholics' compulsive drinking of smuggled-in liquor. Soldiers' home personnel were among the earliest adherents of the view that alcoholism was a disease, but a remedy was elusive. Seeking in the 1890s to cure alcoholics, officials brought in purveyors of popular remedies, among them Dr. Leslie Keeley's "gold cure," a type of aversion therapy. Seeking to supervise consumption among other drinkers, officials opened beer halls at the federal homes around the turn of the century. The halls appeared to satisfy managers and residents alike and even won the approval of most of the homes' chaplains, but temperance activists were infuriated by the spectacle of government officials selling liquor to former soldiers. Insisting that self-control be maintained even among disabled men in their sixties and seventies, one antiliquor member of Congress demanded that the houses take away residents' alcohol and instead "help them to build up the wasted manhood of their earlier years and live the evening of life temperate, sober, upright, worthy citizens." Congress bowed to this pressure and ordered the beer halls closed in 1907. Residents returned to drinking off the premises and smuggling liquor into the homes, and alcohol-related offenses increased sharply at several homes.

Elderly Union veterans were thus both a privileged and a burdened population. They did have opportunities that were unavailable to their civilian peers. In the new century nearly all ex-Union soldiers could claim a generous pension and many were able to retire, provided they could ignore the condemnation of some social critics. The *New York Times* believed that most ablebodied pensioners were "bummers, deserters, [and] sturdy beggars," and the editors of the magazine *The Nation* declared that "men who would die rather than enter a poorhouse and live at the cost of the community, see no wrong in living at the cost of the taxpayer, believing that, because they donned a uniform forty-nine years ago, they now have an inherent right to aid in their old age."

Former Union soldiers who were impoverished still had an alternative to the poorhouse, but they continued to differ with soldiers' home managers over the nature of a veteran's obligations. Managers saw self-discipline as the least they could expect from residents in exchange for the government's generosity, but many residents saw withholding of their pensions as high-handed, and the policy on drinking, one of an old soldier's few pleasures, as inconsistent. But the homes also offered security and comfort, and as their health grew worse and their options dwindled, veterans continued to seek admission to the homes; only after 1910 did the homes' population begin a continuous decline.

By 1920 fewer than 15 percent of the Civil War's original survivors were still alive, and World War I had added more than 4 million new veterans to occupy the government's attention. The Pension Bureau and the national soldiers' homes were merged into the new Veterans Administration in 1930, and the few survivors of the generation that had preserved the Union and once dominated national politics were now relics of a bygone age.

The Spanish-American War of 1898 was a turning point for many Confederate veterans, and it set the tone for their activities in the twentieth century. The Grand Army of the Republic supported the war, but fighting a foreign enemy was more than simply wise policy to ex-Confederates—this was a chance to prove that Confederate veterans were patriots, not rebels, and to remove the remaining stigma of defeat. Some Confederate veterans were young enough to serve in the war and drew high praise from Southerners, but ex-soldiers' influence extended much further. Young soldiers in the Spanish-American War were fond of using the rebel yell, and a Confederate veteran's son wrote that he and his fellows "owe you of '61 a debt of untold gratitude and admiration for the noble examples & high ideals set for us to follow."

The Spanish-American War's aftermath underscored Confederate veterans' worries about the future. Fighting in Spain's former colonies did not end with the formal armistice of August 1898. Filipino resistance forces fought American control as they had fought the Spanish, and it was not until 1902 that American troops, gunning down women and children and burning villages in response to the rebels' guerrilla warfare, managed to subdue native resistance in the Philippines. American soldiers from the South expressed little sympathy with the Filipinos' desire for self-rule. A few leading Southerners appreciated the parallels between the Filipinos' struggle and the Confederacy's, and a senator from Arkansas refused "to force upon an unwilling people principles and policies against which Lee fought," but many more Southerners insisted that order and stability were the key American interests in the Philippines. The *Atlanta Constitution* demanded that American troops "vindicate the authority of our flag," a senator from the same state insisted that the United States establish a government "capable of maintaining law and order," and a young soldier from Tennessee even wanted to "carry on a war as Sherman did on his march to the sea." The primary lesson of the Civil War that came down to Southerners at the turn of the century was the primacy of order, whether in government, labor relations, or relations between the races.

Former Confederates felt vindicated by the Spanish-American War. Participation in the war "healed many scars," wrote a Southerner, and another believed that "the whole South is to be recognized and rehabilitated." Leading veterans in the North and the South became increasingly conciliatory: in the first decade of the new century the federal government assumed responsibility for Confederate graves in the North and finally returned captured Confederate flags, actions applauded by most Confederate veterans, and in the next decade more than fifty thousand veterans from both sides attended the fiftieth anniversary of the Battle of Gettysburg.

At the same time annual gatherings were losing their focus as public reenactments of the Confederate army experience. As we have seen, United Confederate Veterans' reunions in the 1890s were meant to impress on the public the comradeship and patriotism of Confederate soldiers. After 1900, however, reunions were increasingly dominated by social functions for the elite (one ex-soldier decided that "Reunions of the Confederate veterans as latterly conducted are not for [the rank and file]"), and were increasingly given over to commercial advertising. Whether it was their advancing age, their dwindling numbers, or a combination of causes, veterans in the new century were becoming less jealous of the Confederate tradition they had worked to publicize and pass on to the next generation.

As ex-Confederates grew older they also relied more on pensions. Some states expanded eligibility for pensions (though they still required applicants to affirm their poverty), and more elderly veterans made use of the payments. By 1910 approximately one-fourth of Confederate veterans were drawing a state pension, and the payments, small as they were, appear to have encouraged some to retire. Average pensions in 1910 were still less than $50 per year, but 30 percent of Confederate veterans had stopped working, compared with fewer than 20 percent of elderly Southern noncombatants.

In the next decade most Southern states raised their pension amounts, and Kentucky, Missouri, and Oklahoma began paying pensions. By 1920 the average payment had passed $100, and about half of all Confederate veterans were on the pension rolls. But half had not applied at a time when virtually every Union veteran was drawing a federal pension. Confederate veterans were still more than twice as likely to be living on farms as were ex-Union soldiers; suspicion of government programs ran high in the countryside, and any declaration of poverty stained not only the individual but his kinfolk as well.

The rural aversion to government aid was also evident among veterans who went to Confederate soldiers' homes. The population of soldiers' homes across the South reached its peak at about 2,400 during the decade after 1910. This was less than 10 percent of the population of federal and state homes for Union soldiers, and in a sample of residents just over 40 percent had been farmers, compared with nearly two-thirds of all ex-Confederates.

But if rural Southerners were more reluctant to seek shelter in these homes, the homes themselves followed much the same course as did their Union counterparts. By the decade after 1910, residents were typically in their mid-seventies, and health care for the elderly had become a main goal of the homes. Although the Southern homes were small (six of the fifteen homes had fewer than one hundred residents in 1915, while a typical federal home had more than one thousand), most of them now had their own hospital, with staff physicians, nurses, and modern equipment. Officials boasted of a death rate lower than outside the homes, and there is evidence for their claim: men who passed their seventieth birthday in the Missouri home, for example, could expect to live for thirteen years, compared with nine years among the general population in states that kept uniform death records.

State legislatures were willing to pay for this expensive care, demonstrating the considerable hold Confederate veterans still maintained over their descendants. Louisiana's appropriation to operate its home jumped from $40,000 in 1914 to $65,000 in 1920, for example, and North Carolina's went from $35,000 to $60,000; in Georgia, care for veterans (pensions and the soldiers' home) took up more than 20 percent of the budget in the early twentieth century.

In spite of physical changes in the homes, the climate of discipline and resistance remained. As in Union homes, Southern officials expected elderly residents to be docile, but they were not. In the decade after 1910, officials at the Louisiana home charged a number of residents, most of whom were in their seventies, with a variety of offenses, including drunkenness, fighting, and climbing the institution's fence. Defiance of the rules continued after 1920: the Georgia home expelled a resident for selling liquor in 1926, and the Missouri home dismissed an eighty-year-old resident for insubordination in 1925 and an eighty-six-year-old for fighting in 1932. Most Confederate homes eventually admitted women residents—wives, widows, and occasionally daughters and nieces of veterans—

but the institutions remained predominantly male, with characteristic male contention over the limits of authority and obedience.

Yet the old Confederates were dying off, and most of the homes closed in the 1930s and 1940s. Ex-Confederates' numbers were shrinking everywhere: of approximately 100,000 ex-Confederates in 1920, only about 35,000 were alive in 1930, and perhaps a thousand lived to see the nation's second-costliest war begin in 1941. The ranks of their old adversaries were likewise thinning. There were fewer than 300,000 ex-Union soldiers in 1920, under 100,000 in 1930, and only a few thousand survived in 1940.

The last known Union soldier was Louis Nicholas, who had been a drummer with the Sixth Missouri regiment and who died in 1957. The last known former Confederate soldier was Walter Williams, a forage-master who had served with the Fifth Virginia and who died in 1959. But the last man who had seen some form of Civil War service had, perhaps fittingly, served both sides. Sylvester Magee, born a slave in Covington County, Mississippi, was at first a servant in the Confederate army but ran away to the Union forces, who assigned him to burial details at Vicksburg. Magee died not far from his original home on October 15, 1971.

8

The Civil War Experience in Perspective

WHAT WAS THE meaning of being a Civil War veteran, and how did that meaning differ between Union and Confederate veterans? We have seen marked differences in background and character among the men who joined the two armies. Both sides drew broadly from their populations, but laborers—skilled and unskilled—were especially likely to fight for the Union, and wealthier, slaveholding Southerners were especially likely to join the Confederate army. And while Union soldiers worried about restraining their sentiments and impulses, Confederates tended to express their emotions freely and to lash out at affronts to their honor from friend or foe. There is little in soldiers' writings to indicate that the war fundamentally changed these traits, and traces of them remained long after the war. The GAR's extraordinary concern with self-control and the exceptional fierceness of confrontations in Southern soldiers' homes suggest the depth of character differences between the sections.

Yet warfare is in other ways an equalizer, and we have seen evidence of that as well. A call to arms seeks out and finds common sentiments, even among populations with different motivations for fighting. Mobilizing a popular army exploits loyalty to the community, the desire to conform with peers, the need to keep faith with tradition, and the urge to prove one's masculinity. As a result, young men on both sides led the rush to sign up, and they boasted of their ability to make short work of the other side; in more reflective moments most of them worried about home and community, and soldiers on both sides claimed kinship with the patriots of the American Revolution. Enlisted men on both sides discovered how much they disliked taking orders from men they considered no better than themselves, a dislike that was especially intense among Western and Southern soldiers.

Yankees and Confederates alike developed a profound appreciation for solidarity. Most soldiers considered themselves independent individuals, but the extraordinary conditions of the war had created permanent bonds with other soldiers and barriers against noncombatants. In a veteran's eyes, there were men who knew what it was like to see a friend decapitated by a cannon shell or to march in the mud toward what could be one's own grave, and then there was the rest of the population who would never truly know any of this. Soldiers' bonds had helped to keep the armies together during the war, and they had the capacity to bring veterans together afterward.

But it would take extraordinary circumstances for a widespread revival of these bonds, and here the experience of Union and Confederate veterans diverged. Prominent Union veterans tried to translate wartime comradeship into peacetime organizations, but the GAR and other groups soon withered for lack of a compelling purpose. Southern attempts at organization did little better, but Southerners did find a cause that rekindled the solidarity of the war years. The Ku Klux Klan portrayed itself as the resurrected Confederate army, and post-Klan whites, completing their violent takeover of a

Southern state, employed all the trappings of a military campaign. The call to join old comrades against a perceived enemy made many veterans set aside their individualism and once again become part of a movement.

Union veterans found their cause, and their cause found them, in the 1880s. Eager politicians, a rejuvenated GAR, and the prospect of liberalized pensions all encouraged ex-Union soldiers to renew their old ties and act together. Although many Union veterans drifted away from organized activity afterward, those who remained were effective in ensuring a legacy of patriotic awareness among civilians.

Ex-Confederates' activism continued to follow a different course. They showed their own interest in formal organizations by the end of the 1880s, but this had little to do with pensions. The UCV did advocate expanded pensions and better-funded soldiers' homes, but these issues never approached the political appeal of Union pensions. The South rarely saw the kind of tight two-party competition in which pensions could provide the winning edge, and there was no single government to serve as the focus of Confederate pension lobbying. Confederate veterans played politics for different stakes—the racial functioning of their society.

Their significant role in beginning the movement to disfranchise African Americans was perhaps Confederate veterans' most conspicuous mark on Southern society. Ex-Confederates then turned to efforts that resembled Union veterans' campaigns to keep the war's memory alive and enforce public patriotism. This final parallel between Union and Confederate veterans' activities demonstrates the enduring power of the Civil War over its soldiers. All veterans had intensely personal memories of the war—revolting sights, frightening sounds, wrenching emotions, and countless other recollections—and they wanted people around them to acknowledge their special status. But to ensure this recognition they would have to act, as they had in the war, with their comrades. And so veterans joined secret groups and public organizations, went to the polls, spoke on Memorial Day, wrote to newspapers, and did whatever else they could to ensure they would not be forgotten.

Both sides accomplished some of the same things. Although the scale and nature of these accomplishments differed from North to South, each side made veterans' reunions noteworthy public events, each persuaded public officials to pay pensions and fund soldiers' homes, and each intervened in public education to pass on its version of the war. But Confederate veterans did this and more. Their vital role in subverting Republican governments and later in rewriting state constitutions went considerably beyond the feats of Union veterans. Civil War pensions, which brought Union veterans more attention than any other issue, had no direct connection with the few government pension plans that were enacted in the early twentieth century. Indeed, as Theda Skocpol points out, the main influence of Union pensions was to *delay* adoption of social insurance by public officials who were leery of uncontrolled social spending. Southerners' terrorism and constitutional changes, on the other hand, left a legacy of discrimination and segregation that would last until the civil-rights struggles of the mid-twentieth century.

Why did Confederate veterans have more influence than ex-Union soldiers? The heritage of defeat was certainly important: Confederate veterans' relentless pursuit of white supremacy was partly an atonement for losing the war. And Confederate veterans found themselves in situations where literal or symbolic militancy would produce tangible results. The Klan's activities and the subsequent intimidation of blacks mimicked army maneuvers, and agitators for disfranchisement often characterized their efforts as a paramilitary campaign. A Mississippi newspaper editor and former Confederate officer, for example, called on fellow Democrats in 1888 to "shake off your lethargy and show a little of the spirit of '75," when "the bonfires of the Democratic clans blazed from every hill top [and] the thunder of their campaign guns reverberated through every valley." Militant language and displays of military prowess came naturally to the Civil War generation, and old Confederates made the most of the chances they were given.

Union veterans, for their part, did not forget the martial spirit. Historians have noted in the late nineteenth century a resurgence of militarism that went well beyond the GAR's lobbying. Luminaries who were also Civil War veterans, such as jurist Oliver Wendell Holmes, Jr., and social scientist Francis Amasa Walker, increasingly characterized daily life as combat and expressed contempt for their society's softness and cowardice. But these men were restricted to speechmaking, however bellicose they might become; until the war with Spain, ex-Union soldiers lacked the opportunities that Southerners had to act on their concerns.

In truth, of course, the more than two million survivors of the Civil War had an enormous variety of ways to cope with their memories of the war. Some blotted it out, some vowed never to support another war, others romanticized everything about the conflict, and still others showed the long-term stress disorders that we associate with modern wars. What we have presented here were the most common attitudes and behavior of ex-soldiers.

To most veterans the Civil War was far more than an experience, because most experiences come to an end. Former soldiers believed that this war could not, and should not, end as long as its effects on combatants continued. Historians may not find fundamental character changes in Civil War soldiers, but veterans *believed* that the war had made them different from ordinary Americans, and that civilians did not appreciate the difference. Veterans had seen, as no one else had, the very best and worst that humans could do, and they feared this perception might die with them. Preventing the worst by promoting order and stability seemed to be their only course, and veterans conducted the crusade on a number of fronts—legislative halls, schools, parades, rural villages—with, as we have seen, varying success.

In so doing they set the stage for conservative activism by the veterans of twentieth-century wars. Historian William Pencak points out that the American Legion, which organized in the wake of World War I and took for itself the role of defining "Americanism," used the GAR as a model and established ties with the UCV. There was one legacy that Civil War veterans on both sides could claim equally: the insistence by the citizen-soldiers of each subsequent conflict that this was *their* war. This claim, originating in the deadliest of all American wars, will echo as long as wars produce survivors and memories.

A Note on Sources

Mobilizing the Armies

For a valuable overview of the changing American economy and its implications, see Bruce Laurie, *Artisans into Workers: Labor in Nineteenth-Century America* (New York, 1989). On the prevalence of the self-control ideal in the nineteenth century, see Daniel T. Rodgers, *The Work Ethic in Industrial America, 1850–1920* (Chicago, 1979), and Charles E. Rosenberg, "Sexuality, Class, and Role in 19th-Century America," *American Quarterly* 25 (1973), 131–153. For its institutional forms, see David Rothman, *The Discovery of the Asylum: Social Order and Disorder in the New Republic* (Boston, 1971). Carl N. Degler, *At Odds: Women and the Family in America from the Revolution to the Present* (New York, 1980), discusses child-rearing and self-control; on boyhood and masculinity, see E. Anthony Rotundo, *American Manhood: Transformations in Masculinity from the Revolution to the Modern Era* (New York, 1993). For evidence of nineteenth-century self-restraint, see Daniel Scott Smith and Michael S. Hindus, "Premarital Pregnancy in America, 1640–1971: An Overview and Interpretation," *Journal of Interdisciplinary History* 5 (1975), 537–570. Overviews of turnover in nineteenth-century communities are Donald H. Parkerson, "How Mobile Were Nineteenth-Century Americans?" *Historical Methods* 15 (1982), 99–110, and Richard H. Steckel, "Household Migration and Rural Settlement in the United States, 1850–1860," *Explorations in Economic History* 26 (1989), 190–218.

On war fever against Mexico, see Robert W. Johannsen, *To the Halls of the Montezumas: The Mexican War in the American Imagination* (New York, 1985). Marcus Cunliffe, *Soldiers and Civilians: The Martial Spirit in America, 1775–1865* (Boston, 1968), demonstrates antebellum apathy toward militia duty. The North's various mechanisms to raise troops are covered in James W. Geary, *We Need Men: The Union Draft in the Civil War* (DeKalb, Ill., 1991), and Eugene C. Murdock, *One Million Men: The Civil War Draft in the North* (Madison, Wisc., 1971). A careful study of draft evasion is Peter Levine, "Draft Evasion in the North During the Civil War," *Journal of American History* 67 (1981), 816–834. The decision to recruit African-American troops is explained in Joseph T. Glatthaar, "Black Glory: The African-American Role in Union Victory," in Gabor S. Boritt, ed., *Why the Confederacy Lost* (New York, 1992), 135–162. The decision is also discussed, and numerous documents relating to black troops' experience are presented, in Ira Berlin, et al., eds., *The Black Military Experience,* Series II of *Freedom: A Documentary History of Emancipation* (Cambridge, Mass., 1982). Resistance to the draft is discussed in Phillip Shaw Paludan, *"A People's Contest": The Union and Civil War, 1861–1865* (New York, 1988), and the largest draft riot is examined in Iver Bernstein, *The New York City Draft Riots: Their Significance for American Society and Politics in the Age of the Civil War* (New York, 1990).

Essays on the war's demographic and social dimensions, and comparisons of Union soldiers with noncombatants, are included in the collection edited by Maris Vinovskis, *Toward a Social History of the American Civil War: Exploratory Essays* (New York, 1990). Another comparison of those who joined and those who did not is W. J. Rorabaugh, "Who Fought for the North in the Civil War? Concord, Massachusetts, Enlistments," *Journal of American History* 73 (1986), 695–701. William L. Barton, *Melting Pot Soldiers: The Union's Ethnic Regiments* (Ames, Iowa, 1988), describes recruitment of immigrants, and Kevin J. Weddle, "Ethnic Discrimination in Minnesota Volunteer Regiments During the Civil War," *Civil War History* 35 (1989), 239–259, cites prejudice in appointments and promotions. Charles Brewster's enlistment is examined in David W. Blight, "No Desperate Hero: Manhood and Freedom in a Union Soldier's Experience," in

Catherine Clinton and Nina Silber, eds., *Divided Houses: Gender and the Civil War* (New York, 1992), 55–75.

The events leading up to the outbreak of war, their context, and the course of the war itself are skillfully set out in James M. McPherson, *Battle Cry of Freedom: The Civil War Era* (New York, 1988). William W. Freehling offers intriguing reinterpretations of politics and the war's course in the essays collected in *The Reintegration of American History: Slavery and the Civil War* (New York, 1994), and includes a tour of the South in *The Road to Disunion: Secessionists at Bay, 1776–1854* (New York, 1990).

The issue of class relations in the antebellum South has generated too many studies to list here, but a good introduction and overview is Harry L. Watson, "Conflict and Collaboration: Yeomen, Slaveholders, and Politics in the Antebellum South," *Social History* 11 (1985), 273–298, and among more recent works, Bill Cecil-Fronsman, *Common Whites: Class and Culture in Antebellum North Carolina* (Lexington, Ky., 1992), is a particularly thorough examination. Bertram Wyatt-Brown, "Community, Class, and Snopesian Crime: Local Justice in the Old South," in Orville Vernon Burton and Robert C. McMath, Jr., eds., *Class, Conflict, and Consensus: Antebellum Southern Community Studies* (Westport, Conn., 1982), 173–206, explains the significance of Faulkner's "Barn Burning." Reid Mitchell, "The Creation of Confederate Loyalties," in Robert H. Abzug and Stephen E. Maizlish, eds., *New Perspectives on Race and Slavery in America: Essays in Honor of Kenneth M. Stampp* (Lexington, Ky., 1986), 93–108, and Paul D. Escott and Jeffrey J. Crow, "The Social Order and Violent Disorder: An Analysis of North Carolina in the Revolution and the Civil War," *Journal of Southern History* 52 (1986), 373–402, discuss class relations during the war. Vigilantism is examined in Michael Wayne, "An Old South Morality Play: Reconsidering the Social Underpinnings of the Proslavery Ideology," *Journal of American History* 77 (1990), 838–863: Winthrop D. Jordan, *Tumult and Silence at Second Creek: An Inquiry into a Civil War Slave Conspiracy* (Baton Rouge, 1993); and

Richard Maxwell Brown, *Strain of Violence: Historical Studies of American Violence and Vigilantism* (New York, 1975).

On Southern husbands' expectation of obedience from their wives, see Stephanie McCurry, "The Politics of Yeoman Households in South Carolina," in Clinton and Silber, *Divided Houses,* 22–38, and Joan E. Cashin, *A Family Venture: Men and Women on the Southern Frontier* (New York, 1991). The ties that united Southern communities are the focus of Robert C. Kenzer, *Kinship and Neighborhood in a Southern Community: Orange County, North Carolina, 1849–1881* (Knoxville, Tenn., 1987). On the centrality of honor in Southern male culture, see Bertram Wyatt-Brown, *Southern Honor: Ethics and Behavior in the Old South* (New York, 1982), and Edward L. Ayers, *Vengeance and Justice: Crime and Punishment in the 19th-Century American South* (New York, 1984).

William L. Barney, *The Secessionist Impulse: Alabama and Mississippi in 1860* (Princeton, N.J., 1974), includes a good discussion of the treatment of Unionists. Albert B. Moore, *Conscription and Conflict in the Confederacy* (New York, 1924), remains the only full-length study of the Southern draft. The most extensive comparison of reasons for Union and Confederate soldiers' enlistment is James M. McPherson, *What They Fought For: 1861–1865* (Baton Rouge, 1994). A smaller study of soldiers' letters and diaries is Pete Maslowski, "A Study of Morale in Civil War Soldiers," *Military Affairs* 34 (1970), 122–126. Michael Barton, *Goodmen: The Character of Civil War Soldiers* (University Park, Pa., 1981), carefully applies the techniques of content analysis to soldiers' testimony.

For a comparison of Confederate soldiers and noncombatants see Larry M. Logue, "Who Joined the Confederate Army? Soldiers, Civilians, and Communities in Mississippi," *Journal of Social History* 26 (1993) 611–623; J. William Harris, *Plain Folk and Gentry in a Slave Society: White Liberty and Black Slavery in Augusta's Hinterlands* (Middletown, Conn., 1985), reaches a different conclusion on the background of volunteers but uses more limited evidence on enlistment. Comparisons of Confederate and Union enlistees are Peter Wallenstein, "Which Side Are You On? The Social Origins of White Union Troops from Civil War Tennessee," *Journal of East Tennessee History* 63 (1991), 72–103, and Wayne K. Durrill, *War of Another Kind: A Southern Community in the Great Rebellion* (New York, 1990). Martin Crawford, "Confederate Volunteering and Enlistment in Ashe County, North Carolina, 1861–1862," *Civil War History* 37 (1991), 29–50, discusses the role of the community in raising troops. The Confederate government's attempts to prevent unauthorized travel are described in Kenneth Radley, *Rebel Watchdog: The Confederate States Army Provost Guard* (Baton Rouge, 1989).

SOLDIERS AT WAR

The prevailing American attitude toward death is discussed in Lewis O. Saum, *The Popular Mood of Pre-Civil War America* (Westport, Conn., 1980). The pioneering study of life in the Union army is Bell Irvin Wiley, *The Life of Billy Yank* (Indianapolis, 1952). Most of the more recent studies of Civil War soldiers include men on both sides. Those that devote the most attention to interpretation and analysis are Gerald Linderman, *Embattled Courage: The Experience of Combat in the American Civil War* (New York, 1987), and Reid Mitchell, *Civil War Soldiers: Their Expectations and Their Experiences* (New York, 1988). Other studies that focus more on description include Randall C. Jimerson, *The Private Civil War: Popular Thought During the Sectional Conflict* (Baton Rouge, 1988); Joseph Allan Frank and George A. Reaves, *"Seeing the Elephant": Raw Recruits at the Battle of Shiloh* (Westport, Conn., 1989); and James I. Robertson, Jr., *Soldiers Blue and Gray* (Columbia, S.C., 1988). Studies that concentrate on Union soldiers include Reid Mitchell, *The Vacant Chair: The Northern Soldier Leaves Home* (New York, 1993), and Joseph T. Glatthaar, *The March to the Sea and Beyond: Sherman's Troops in the Savannah and Carolinas Campaigns* (New York, 1986).

A provocative revision of accepted wisdom on Civil War weapons and tactics is Paddy Griffith, *Battle Tactics of the Civil War* (New Haven, Conn., 1989). For studies that assign religion a somewhat greater role in the Union army than does the Linderman analysis, see Gardiner H. Shattuck, Jr., *A Shield and Hiding Place: The Religious Life of the Civil War Armies* (Macon, Ga., 1987), and Gregory J. W. Urwin, "'The Lord Has Not Forsaken Me and I Won't Forsake Him': Religion in Frederick Steele's Union Army, 1863–1864," *Arkansas Historical Quarterly* 52 (1993), 318–340. On Union chaplains, see Richard M. Budd, "Ohio Army Chaplains and the Professionalization of Military Chaplaincy in the Civil War," *Ohio History* 102 (1993), 5–19.

The wartime experience of black soldiers is detailed in Joseph T. Glatthaar, *Forged in Battle: The Civil War Alliance of Black Soldiers and White Officers* (New York, 1990). Civil War medical practice is surveyed in Stewart Brooks, *Civil War Medicine* (Springfield, Ill., 1966), and Paul E. Steiner, *Disease in the Civil War* (Springfield, Ill., 1968); the experience of nurses on both sides is explored in Jane E. Schultz, "The Inhospitable Hospital: Gender and Professionalism in Civil War Medicine," *Signs* 17 (1992), 363–392. Medical care in the Union army is detailed in George W. Adams, *Doctors in Blue: The Medical History of the Union Army in the Civil War* (New York, 1952). An insightful examination of the United States Sanitary Commission appears in George M. Fredrickson, *The Inner Civil War: Northern Intellectuals and the Crisis of the Union* (New York, 1965).

The best study of Union soldiers as prisoners of war is William Marvel, *Andersonville: The Last Depot* (Chapel Hill, 1994). On combat stress, see Eric T. Dean, Jr., "'We Will All Be Lost and Destroyed': Post-Traumatic Stress Disorder and the Civil War," *Civil War History* 37 (1991), 138–153. Judith Lee Hallock, "The Role of the Community in Civil War Desertion," *Civil War History* 29 (1983), 123–134, compares cohesive and unsettled townships. Guerrilla warfare is thoroughly examined in

Michael Fellman, *Inside War: The Guerrilla Conflict in Missouri During the American Civil War* (New York, 1989).

Bell Irvin Wiley also pioneered the study of Confederate soldiers with *The Life of Johnny Reb* (Indianapolis, 1943). On life in specific armies, see Bob Womack, *Call Forth the Mighty Men* (Bessemer, Ala., 1987), and Larry J. Daniel, *Soldiering in the Army of Tennessee: A Portrait of Life in a Confederate Army* (Chapel Hill, 1991). The Celtic influence on Southern tactics is argued in Grady McWhiney and Perry D. Jamieson, *Attack and Die: Civil War Military Tactics and the Southern Heritage* (University, Ala., 1982), and disputed in Richard E. Beringer, et al., *Why the South Lost the Civil War* (Athens, Ga., 1986).

Confederate medical practice is examined in Horace H. Cunningham, *Doctors in Gray: The Confederate Medical Service* (Baton Rouge, 1958). Analyses of Confederates as prisoners are scarce; among the more careful efforts is James I. Robertson, Jr., "The Scourge of Elmira," *Civil War History* 8 (1962), 184–201. Complements to the Fellman study that expand on guerrillas and the Confederacy are Phillip Shaw Paludan, *Victims: A True Story of the Civil War* (Knoxville, Tenn., 1981), and Daniel G. Sutherland, "Guerrillas: The Real War in Arkansas," *Arkansas Historical Quarterly* 52 (1993), 257–285. In addition to the Shattuck study cited above, two articles examine religious enthusiasm among Confederates: Drew Gilpin Faust, "Christian Soldiers: The Meaning of Revivalism in the Confederate Army," *Journal of Southern History* 53 (1987), 63–90, and Samuel J. Watson, "Religion and Combat Motivation in the Confederate Armies," *Journal of Military History* 58 (1994), 29–55.

Analyses of Confederate desertion include Richard Reid, "A Test Case of the 'Crying Evil': Desertion Among North Carolina Troops During the Civil War," *North Carolina Historical Review* 58 (1981), 234–262; Bessie Martin, *Desertion of Alabama Troops from the Confederate Army: A Study in Sectionalism* (New York, 1966); and Victoria Bynum, *Unruly Women: The Politics of Social and Sexual Control in the Old South* (Chapel Hill, N.C., 1992). For two very different views of desertion from specific units, see Kevin C. Ruffner, "Civil War Desertion from a Black Belt Regiment: An Examination of the 44th Virginia Infantry," in Edward L. Ayers and John C. Wills, eds., *The Edge of the South: Life in Nineteenth-Century Virginia* (Charlottesville, Va., 1991), 79–108, and Robert K. Krick, "The Army of Northern Virginia in September of 1862," in Gary W. Gallagher, ed., *Antietam: Essays on the 1862 Maryland Campaign* (Kent, Ohio, 1989), 35–55.

CIVIL WAR VETERANS AND POSTWAR AMERICA

The essential source for understanding the immediate postwar years is Eric Foner, *Reconstruction: America's Unfinished Revolution, 1863–1877* (New York, 1988). A dated but thorough account of soldiers' return is Dixon Wecter, *When Johnny Comes Marching Home* (Boston, 1944). Glatthaar, *Forged in Battle,* includes a discussion of blacks' postwar experience, and Kevin R. Hardwick, "'Your Old Father Abe Lincoln Is Dead and Damned': Black Soldiers and the Memphis Race Riot of 1866," *Journal of Social History* 27 (1993), 109–128, illustrates whites' resentment. Stuart McConnell, *Glorious Contentment: The Grand Army of the Republic, 1865–1900* (Chapel Hill, 1992), analyzes the organizing impulse among Union veterans; Mary R. Dearing, *Veterans in Politics: The Story of the G.A.R.* (Baton Rouge, 1952), and Wallace E. Davies, *Patriotism on Parade: The Story of Veterans' and Hereditary Organizations in America, 1783–1900* (Cambridge, Mass., 1955), trace veterans' political activity.

The best assessment of postwar crime rates is in Eric H. Monkkonen, *Police in Urban America, 1860–1920* (New York, 1981). On drug addiction among Union veterans, see David Courtwright, "Opiate Addiction as a Consequence of the Civil War," *Civil War History* 24 (1978), 101–111. Rhode Island data are from unpublished research by the present author. The standard legislative history of Union pensions is William H. Glasson, *Federal Military Pensions in the United States* (New York, 1918), and the standard account of soldiers' homes is Judith G. Cetina, "A History of Veterans' Homes in the United States: 1811–1930" (Ph.D. dissertation, Case Western Reserve University, 1977). Larry M. Logue, "Union Veterans and Their Government: The Effects of Public Policies on Private Lives," *Journal of Interdisciplinary History* 22 (1992), 411–434, assesses the social effects of pensions and soldiers' homes. On pension applications and party politics, see Heywood T. Sanders, "Paying for the 'Bloody Shirt': The Politics of Civil War Pensions," in Barry S. Rundquist, ed., *Political Benefits: Empirical Studies of American Public Programs* (Lexington, Mass., 1980), 137–159.

Confederate soldiers' attitudes are traced in Michael Barton, "Did the Confederacy Change Southern Soldiers? Some Obvious and Some Unobtrusive Measures," in Harry P. Owens and James J. Cooke, eds., *The Old South in the Crucible of War* (Jackson, Miss., 1983), 65–79. On postwar violence, see Dan T. Carter, *When the War Was Over: The Failure of Self-Reconstruction in the South, 1865–1867* (Baton Rouge, 1985). Gaines M. Foster, *Ghosts of the Confederacy: Defeat, the Lost Cause, and the Emergence of the New South, 1865 to 1913* (New York, 1987), examines veterans' responses to defeat and their organizing tendencies, and Charles Reagan Wilson, *Baptized in Blood: The Religion of the Lost Cause, 1865–1920* (Athens, Ga., 1980), focuses on those who were determined to ennoble the Confederate cause. Mississippi election data are from unpublished research by the present author. For Alabama marriage rates, see Robert A. Gilmour, "The Other Emancipation: Studies in the Society and Economy of Alabama Whites During Reconstruction," (Ph.D. dissertation, Johns Hopkins University, 1972).

The standard history of the Reconstruction-era Ku Klux Klan is Allen W. Trelease, *White Terror: The Ku Klux Klan Conspiracy and Southern Reconstruction* (New York, 1971). On the Klan's attacks and related violence in the period, see George C. Rable, *But There Was No Peace: The Role of Violence in the Politics of Reconstruction* (Athens, Ga., 1984). The Klan's roots are explored in

Gladys-Marie Fry, *Night Riders in Black Folk History* (Knoxville, Tenn., 1975); Bertram Wyatt-Brown, *Honor and Violence in the Old South* (New York, 1986); Charles L. Flynn, Jr., "The Ancient Pedigree of Violent Repression: Georgia's Klan as a Folk Movement," in Walter J. Fraser, Jr., and Winfred B. Moore, Jr., eds., *The Southern Enigma: Essays on Race, Class, and Folk Culture* (Westport, Conn., 1983), 189–198; and William D. Piersen, "Family Secrets: How African-American Culture Shaped the Early Ku Klux Klan," in Winfred B. Moore, Jr., and Joseph F. Tripp, eds., *Looking South: Chapters in the Story of an American Region* (Westport, Conn., 1989), 41–50. Wartime and postwar Southern resistance are contrasted in Kenneth M. Stampp, *The Imperiled Union: Essays on the Background of the Civil War* (New York, 1980).

The epilogue to Linderman, *Embattled Courage,* traces the ebb and flow of late-nineteenth-century interest in the war, and Mark C. Carnes, *Secret Ritual and Manhood in Victorian America* (New Haven, Conn., 1989), examines secret societies. The best and most comprehensive study of the New South, including its agrarian political movements and race relations, is Edward L. Ayers, *The Promise of the New South: Life After Reconstruction* (New York, 1992). As yet there is no detailed study of Confederate pensions; the best place to follow their progress is in the pages of *Confederate Veteran,* a monthly magazine that began publication in 1893. James R. Young, "Confederate Pensions in Georgia, 1886–1929," *Georgia Historical Quarterly* 66 (1982), 47–52, notes the proportion of state budgets consumed by pensions. R. B. Rosenburg, *Living Monuments: Confederate Soldiers' Homes in the New South* (Chapel Hill, 1993), examines the homes and their residents.

An intriguing account of aging Confederates' concern for their legacy is David Herbert Donald, "A Generation of Defeat," in Walter J. Fraser, Jr., and Winfred B. Moore, Jr., eds., *From the Old South to the New: Essays on the Transitional South* (Westport, Conn., 1981), 3–20. The best study of the disfranchising conventions is J. Morgan Kousser, *The Shaping of Southern Politics: Suf-*

frage Restriction and the Establishment of the One-Party South, 1880–1910 (New Haven, Conn., 1974). Data on convention elections in Mississippi and South Carolina are from unpublished research by the author. Theda Skocpol, *Protecting Soldiers and Mothers: The Political Origins of Social Policy in the United States* (Cambridge, Mass., 1992), discusses the nature and consequences of Civil War pensions. William Graebner, *A History of Retirement: The Meaning and Function of an American Institution, 1885–1978* (New Haven, Conn., 1980), and Carole Haber, *Beyond Sixty-Five: The Dilemma of Old Age in America's Past* (New York, 1983), explain changes in the concept of retirement. Data on the Missouri Confederate soldiers' home are from unpublished research by the present author. Information on the last survivors of the war (on both sides) appears in Jay S. Hoar, *The South's Last Boys in Gray* (Bowling Green, Ohio, 1986). Clyde Griffen raises intriguing questions about the war's long-term effects on Northerners' attitudes in "Reconstructing Masculinity from the Evangelical Revival to the Waning of Progressivism: A Synthesis," in Mark C. Carnes and Clyde Griffen, eds., *Meanings for Manhood: Constructions of Masculinity in Victorian America* (Chicago, 1990), 183–204. William Pencak, *For God and Country: The American Legion, 1919–1941* (Boston, 1989), traces the influence of Civil War veterans' groups on the Legion.

Index

A NOTE ON THE AUTHOR

Larry M. Logue teaches American history at Mississippi College in Clinton, Mississippi. He received a B.A. from the University of Pittsburgh and a Ph.D. in American civilization from the University of Pennsylvania, and has written frequently on aspects of American social history. His book *A Sermon in the Desert: Belief and Behavior in Early St. George, Utah,* was awarded the Chipman Prize by the Mormon History Association.